AND

"You're a Temple Knight," she said. "Or at least you were."

"I was Brother Mateo Harnbringer, a Temple Knight of Saint Cunar."

"Was?" said Charlaine. "Brothers don't leave that order by choice."

"Nor did I." He held up his hand to forestall any arguments. "I know what you're thinking, that I'm nothing but a troublemaker, but there's something you need to know."

"I'm listening."

He lowered his voice. "There's a rot inside the Church, one that's eating away at the moral fibre of the place."

"And you know this for a fact?"

"I tried to do something about it, but it cost me my knighthood. Now I am an outcast, doomed to wander the Continent without the blessings of the Church."

"And you chose to speak to us?" said Danica. "If what you say is true, we're forbidden to talk to you. How dare you put our souls in danger!"

Charlaine reached out, placing her hand on her companion's arm. "Calm yourself, Danica. There's no harm in simple talk." She returned her attention to their visitor. "Please, tell us more."

At that precise moment, the door burst open, revealing an armoured man in a green cloak. His eyes wandered the room, while his hand remained on the pommel of his sword.

"Mateo!" he called out. "Where are you, dog!" The dishonoured Cunar ran for the back door, pushing the crowd roughly aside.

"There you are!" yelled the newcomer, drawing his blade. Those near him backed up in fear while Charlaine stood up and moved towards the armed intruder, placing herself in his path.

"By what right do you threaten this man?" she demanded.

"It is none of your concern."

"Ah, but it IS my concern. My order is dedicated to protecting women everywhere, and as you can plainly see, there are women present."

"Stand aside, I say, and let me have at him."

"Put down your sword, man. This is no place for violence. If you wish to speak with this fellow, then do so outside, where the risk to others is minimized."

He glared back. "Who do you think you are?"

"I am Sister Charlaine deShandria, Temple Knight of Saint Agnes."

ALSO BY PAUL J BENNETT

TEMPLE CAPTAIN

POWER ASCENDING: BOOK THREE

PAUL J BENNETT

First Edition: November 2021

ePub ISBN: 978-1-990073-19-9
Mobi ISBN: 978-1-990073-20-5
Smashwords ISBN: 978-1-990073-21-2
Print ISBN: 978-1-990073-22-9

DEDICATION

To my wife, Carol, who gave me wings to let my imagination fly.

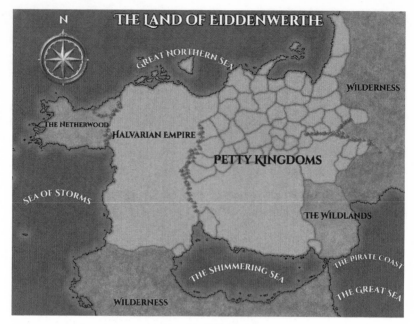

Map of the Eiddenwerthe

Map of Petty Kingdoms

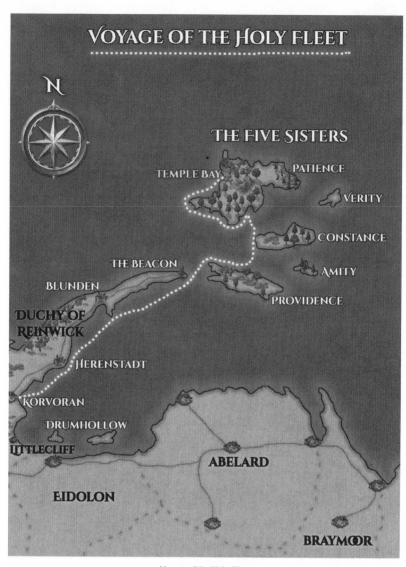

Voyage of the Holy Fleet

CAST OF CHARACTERS - TEMPLE CAPTAIN

MEMBERS OF THE CHURCH IN REICHENDORF/THE ANTONINE

Anton Schulinger - Primus, head of the Church

Arnold - Lay brother of Saint Mathew

Avalyn - Lay mother of Saint Agnes

Brigida - Temple Knight of Saint Agnes, serves Commander Hjordis

Bryson - Temple Knight of Saint Ansgar

Collette Fontaine - Newly promoted Temple Captain of Saint Agnes

Dimas - Temple Captain of Saint Cunar

Ebert - Temple Knight of Saint Mathew

Eustace - Temple Knight of Saint Cunar

Hjordis - Temple Commander of Saint Agnes

Hywel - Holy Father in charge of the Mathewite mission in Reichendorf

Isabeau - Newly promoted Temple Captain of Saint Agnes

Jamarian - Temple Commander of Saint Mathew

Julianne Rydel - Matriarch of the Order of Saint Agnes

Kaylene Gantzmann - Grand Mistress, Temple Knights of Saint Agnes

Lara - Temple Knight of Saint Agnes, serves Commander Hjordis

Leamund - Temple Captain of Saint Cunar, naval architect

Loretta - Temple Knight of Saint Agnes

Meteo Harnbringer - Ex-Temple Knight of Saint Cunar

Nicola - Temple Captain of Saint Agnes, aide to the Grand Mistress

Selena - Temple Knight of Saint Agnes

Septimus - Temple Knight of Saint Cunar

Stramond - Temple Commander of Saint Cunar

Thorley - Temple Knight of Saint Mathew, archivist

Zander - Temple Captain of Saint Ansgar

TEMPLE KNIGHTS OF KORVORAN

Adriana - Temple Knight of Saint Agnes

Anya - Temple Knight of Saint Agnes, assigned to *Valiant*

Damora - Temple Knight of Saint Agnes

Felicity - Temple Knight of Saint Agnes

Goya - Temple Knight of Saint Agnes

Grazynia - Temple Knight of Saint Agnes, assigned to *Valiant*

Josephine - Temple Knight of Saint Agnes

Klavel - Temple Knight of Saint Mathew
Laurel - Temple Knight of Saint Agnes, assigned to *Valiant*
Leona - Temple Knight of Saint Agnes
Leonov - Temple Knight of Saint Mathew, Hails from Ruzhina
Marlena - Temple Knight of Saint Agnes
Nadia - Temple Knight of Saint Agnes, assigned to *Valiant*
Salvatore - Temple Commander of Saint Mathew
Vivian - Temple Knight of Saint Agnes, assigned to *Valiant*
Waleed - Temple Captain of Saint Cunar, Kurathian by birth
Winifred (Deceased) - Previous Temple Captain of Saint Agnes
Zivka - Temple Knight of Saint Agnes, assigned to *Valiant*

People In Korvoran

Aleksy - Lay brother of Saint Mathew
Ansel Dulworth - Merchant Captain of the *Barlowe*
Asborn Henrickson - First Mate of the *Lydia*
Augustus Conwyn - Governor of Thansalay
Azreth - Halvarian Necromancer
Barbek Stoutarm - Dwarven smith in Korvoran
Brendan - Member of the crew of the *Lydia/Valiant*
Draclin Winfyre - Halvarian Ambassador to the Court of Reinwick
Edgerton - Captain of the *Monarch*
Elena - Poor woman
Eloise Rundak - Farmer
Elsbeth Fel - Sacred Mother of Akosia
Enid - Servant in service to the Duke of Reinwick
Exius (Deceased) - Fire Mage
Fernando Brondecker - Son of the Duke of Reinwick
Gernik - Dwarf apprentice to the Dwarven smith Barbek Stoutarm
Gilford (Deceased) - Member of the crew of the *Lydia/Valiant*
Hergran Longrit - Captain of the *Millicent*
Jean - Poor woman
Kurlan Stratmeyer - Baron of Blunden
Larissa Stormwind - Water Mage at the Court of Reinwick
Len - Husband to Jean
Lyle Handley - Captain of the *Lydia*
Marwen - Soldier in service to the Duke of Reinwick
Miranda - Poor woman
Rascalian - Bard
Rayden - Holy Father of the Order of Saint Mathew

Rovantis - Halvarian Fire Mage
Taggert - Captain of the *Sea Wolf*
Theodora Brondecker - Duchess of Reinwick
Wilfhelm Brondecker - Duke of Reinwick

OTHER PEOPLE

Aeldred - First King of Therengia
Akosia - Goddess of Water
Argano - King of Ilea
Aurelia (Deceased) - Temple Knight of Saint Agnes, served in Ilea
Charlaine deShandria - Temple Captain of Saint Agnes, served in Ilea
Claudia - Holy Mother of Saint Agnes, serves in Rizela
Cordelia - Temple Knight of Saint Agnes, served in Ilea
Cyric - Temple Knight of Saint Mathew, investigator
Danica Meer - Temple Knight of Saint Agnes
Dedrick - Fisherman from the village of Littlecliff
Deiter Heinrich - Duke of Erlingen
Delmont - Lay brother of Saint Mathew, at the Battle of Erlingen
Erika - Temple Knight of Saint Agnes, served in Ilea
Erskine - Temple Commander of Saint Cunar, at the Battle of Erlingen
Erkson Tane - Smith in Reichendorf
Francesca Gratuli - Baroness of Rizela
Frederik Altenburg - Baron of Altenburg
Galrath - Knight of Erlingen
Giselle - Temple Captain of Saint Agnes, served in Ilea
Gwalinor - Sea Elf and Life Mage
Helena (Deceased) - Temple Knight of Saint Agnes, served in Ilea
Ludwig Altenburg - Son of Baron of Verfeld
Luther - Fisherman from the village of Littlecliff
Marius - Father General of Saint Cunar, Admiral Holy Fleet in Corassus
Marcy - Associate of Brother Mateo in Reichendorf
Nina - Temple Captain of Saint Agnes, served in Ilea
Otto - King of Hadenfeld, cousin to Ludwig
Radwell - Commoner in Torburg
Rolf Wilkerson - Commoner in Torburg
Rordan - King of Abelard
Rupert - Fisherman from the village of Littlecliff
Sarin - Kurathian Admiral, victor of the Battle of Grey Cliffs
Sartellian - Last name given to Fire Mages trained in Korascajan
Sebastien - Marlena's brother

Severn - Commoner in Torburg
Spirit (Spirit of the Sea) - Danica's horse
Stormcloud - Charlaine's horse
Stormwind - Last name given to Water Mages trained at the Volstrum
Tavio deLuna - Self-proclaimed King of Calabria
Teresa - Temple Knight of Saint Agnes, served in Ilea

PLACES
PETTY KINGDOMS
Abelard - Kingdom on the Northern Coast
Andover - Kingdom on the Northern Coast, birthplace of Danica
Ardosa - Kingdom known as the heart of the Petty Kingdoms
Braymoor - Kingdom on the Northern Coast
Carlingen - Kingdom on the Northern Coast, Saint Agnes training site
Corassus - City State on the Southern Coast, home to the Holy Fleet
Ebenstadt - City State on the eastern reaches
Eidolon - Kingdom on the Northern Coast
Erlingen - Duchy, south of Andover
Galoran - Kingdom north of the Antonine
Grislagen - Kingdom southwest of Hadenfeld
Hadenfeld - Central Kingdom, birthplace of Charlaine
Holstead - Duchy on the eastern reaches
Ilea - Kingdom on the Southern Coast
Novarsk - Kingdom on the eastern reaches
Regensbach - Petty Kingdom where the Antonine is located
Reinwick - Duchy, northern Petty Kingdom
Ruzhina - Kingdom on the Northeastern Coast
Ulrichen - Kingdom southeast of Erlingen

CITIES/TOWNS
Blunden - City of the Duchy of Reinwick
Chermingen - City in the Duchy of Erlingen
Draybourne - Capital city of the Duchy of Holstead
Galmund - City in the Duchy of Erlingen
Gossenveldt - City of the Duchy of Reinwick
Harlingen - Capital city of the Kingdom of Hadenfeld
Herenstadt - City of the Duchy of Reinwick
Karslev - Capital city of Kingdom of Ruzhina
Korvoran - Capital city of the Duchy of Reinwick
Littlecliff - Fishing village in Andover, birthplace of Danica
Malburg - City in Kingdom of Hadenfeld

Reichendorf - Capital city of the Kingdom of Regensbach
Rizela - Port city in Ilea
The Antonine - The Holy City, within the city of Reichendorf
Torburg - Capital city of the Duchy of Erlingen
Wintervale - Town in Kingdom of Andover

OTHER PLACES

Alantra - Capital of Calabria
Amity - Smallest of the Five Sisters Islands
Calabria - Kingdom, occupied by Halvaria
Constance - One of the Five Sisters Islands
Cunara - Training facility in Calabria used by the Halvarians
Drumhollow - Island off the shore of the Kingdom of Eidolon
Dun Galdrim - Dwarven stronghold fell to the Halvarians fifty years ago
Eiddenwerthe - The world in which everything exists
Fair Wanderer - Inn in Torburg
Grand Sanctum - Oldest building in the Antonine
Great Northern Sea - North of the Petty Kingdoms
Grey Cliffs - On the Eastern Coast of the Southern Continent
Halvaria - Large empire west of the Petty Kingdoms
Korascajan - Magical Academy for Fire Mages
Kouras - Kurathian Island
Kurathia - Series of Southern Island ruled by princes
Patience - Largest of the Five Sisters Islands
Providence - One of the Five Sisters Islands
Scattered Isles - Series of Islands north of Halvaria
Shimmering Sea - South of the Petty Kingdoms
Temple Bay - On the Island of Patience
Thalemia - Ancient kingdom on the shores of the Shimmering Sea
Thansalay - Province of Halvaria
The Anchor - Tavern in Korvoran
The Beacon - Tower built by the rulers of Reinwick
The Five Sisters - A series of five islands, northeast of Reinwick
The Oarsman - Tavern in Korvoran
Therengia(Old Kingdom) -Destroyed roughly 400 years ago
Urichen - Large, untamed wilderness that is sparsely populated
Verity - Easternmost of the Five Sisters Islands
Volstrum - Magical Academy for Water Mages

BATTLES

Battle of Alantra (1096 SR) - Between Ilea/Holy Fleet and Halvaria

Battle of Erlingen (1093 SR) - Between Andover and Duchy of Erlingen
Battle of Grey Cliffs (Unknown)- Between Kurathians and the Sea Elves
Battle of Krosnicht (1090 SR)Civil war in Kingdom of Abelard
Battle of Temple Bay (1097 SR)Between Halvaria and Northern Fleet
Campaigns of Aeldred (Ancient History)- Military Campaign of the first
Therengian King
Hidden Crusade (Unknown)- Between Cunar Temple Knights and the
High Elves

THE CHURCH

Council of Peers - Ruling council of the Church of the Saints
Order of Saint Agnes - Protector of women
Order of Saint Ansgar - Internal investigators of the Church
Order of Saint Augustine - Guardians of the Holy Relics
Order of Saint Cunar - Primary warriors of the Church
Order of Saint Mathew - Protectors of the poor and sick
Order of Saint Ragnar - Dedicated to eradicating Death Magic
Temple Knight - Holy Warrior of the Church
The Primus - Ultimate Church authority elected by Council of Peers

SHIPS

Triumphant - Flagship of Holy Fleet in Corassus

THE NORTHERN HOLY FLEET

Barlowe - Merchant ship, part of the Church expedition to Patience
Millicent - Merchant ship, part of the Church expedition to Patience
Monarch - Merchant ship, part of the Church expedition to Patience
Peri - Merchant ship, part of the Church expedition to Patience
Rose - Merchant ship, part of the Church expedition to Patience
Valiant (Lydia) - Flagship of the Northern Fleet
Vigilant (Sea Wolf) - Warship of the Order of Saint Agnes

THE HALVARIAN FLEET

Annihilator - Double-masted warship
Devastator - Double-masted warship
Invincible - Double-masted warship
Ravager - Double-masted warship
Terror - Double-masted warship
Vengeance - Double-masted warship
Warrior - Double-masted warship
Water Drake - Single-masted warship

THINGS

Crossed Swords - Mercenary company
Moonfish - Fish that glows slightly, found in the Great Northern Sea
Phoenix Ring - Rings used by smith's guild for secure correspondence
Shadowbark - Heavy dark-coloured wood

1

REGENSBACH

Summer 1097 SR*
(*Saints Reckoning)

The rain came down in sheets, flattening the grass and soaking the two riders. Undeterred, they pressed on, determined to reach their destination by nightfall.

"By the Saints," called out Danica. "Have you ever seen weather like this?"

In answer, her dark-haired companion risked a glance skyward. "This is nothing compared to what the fleet faced after Alantra."

"You think so?"

"Yes," said Charlaine, "but we shouldn't need to bear it much longer. That inn is around here somewhere." A distant flash lit the sky, then, a few moments later, the expected rumble followed.

"They say storms like this are an omen of big change."

Charlaine laughed. "We're going to the Antonine to see the head of our order. How much bigger can it get?"

"I see some light over there," yelled Danica. "That must be it."

They angled their mounts southward, and soon, the grey shadow of a large country inn came into view. They trotted past the gates and into the cobbled courtyard, their hoofbeats echoing off the brick walls.

Charlaine dismounted first, passing the reins to a stable boy, who stood there gaping at her scarlet tabard with the three white waves that marked her as a Temple Knight of Saint Agnes.

"Take our horses to the stables," she said. "We'll check in on them later." Danica followed suit, her waterlogged boots squishing as she walked.

The interior of the place was warm and inviting, chasing off the chill of the rain. Those packed inside huddled in small groups, talking and drinking ale. A stout individual with a protruding belly and a red face rushed forward to greet them.

"Can I help you, Sisters?"

"Have you a room available?" asked Charlaine.

"Of course. If you'd like to have a seat, I'll have someone prepare it." He leaned to his side, peering around her to take in her raven-haired companion. "Is it only for the two of you, or will any others be joining you?"

"Just us two." She turned to Danica. "Come on. Let's take a seat, shall we?"

They made their way through the crowd to find a free table by the fireplace. Charlaine threw her wet cloak over the back of the chair and sat with an audible sigh.

"I can't wait to get some sleep. I'm exhausted."

"So am I," said Danica, "but we've work to do before we rest."

"We do?"

"Yes. We need to dry off our armour. You, of all people, should know that."

"Let's hope I'll have the energy once I've eaten."

A young woman appeared at their table. "Good evening, Sisters. Are you on your way to the Antonine?"

"We are," said Charlaine. "Do you know if it's much farther?"

"No, not far at all. If you left first thing in the morning, you'd be there long before noon."

Danica smiled. "I expect you get a lot of us Temple Knights in here."

"Not as many as you might expect. Did you travel far?"

"I'll say. We came from Ilea."

The girl frowned. "I don't know where that is."

"It's on the southern coast," said Charlaine. "About as far away as you can go and still be within the Petty Kingdoms. We've been on the road for months."

"When did you leave?"

"Late last winter, if you can believe it."

"You must be here on important business to travel so far."

Charlaine smiled. "We go where we're ordered. Can we get something to drink, perhaps a couple of ales?"

"Of course," replied the girl. "Anything to eat?"

"What have you got?"

"There's the mutton pie?"

Charlaine turned to Danica. "What do you think?"

"I don't know. The last time you had that, it gave you terrible indigestion."

"Just some bread and cheese, then."

The girl ran off without another word.

"Well, that was rude," said Danica.

"Nonsense," said Charlaine. "She's just busy."

Danica stared down at her hands. "Don't look now, but it appears we've garnered some attention." Her eyes flitted over to the side.

A tall man approached, dressed in nondescript clothing, yet he carried himself like a warrior. His scarred countenance lent credence to the idea he was, in fact, a seasoned fighter, prompting Charlaine to turn and face him.

"Can I help you?"

"I don't think I've seen you around these parts," he replied.

"That's because we've only just arrived."

"Have you been to the Antonine before?"

"What makes you so sure that's where we're heading?" asked Danica.

"Where else would two sister knights be going around here?"

"We could be on patrol."

"Just the two of you?" he said. "Don't be daft. Temple Knights travel in groups of six."

Charlaine scrutinized the man in more detail. His boots were sturdy, his tunic worn but serviceable. Everything about him screamed danger, yet something in his eyes gave his face a hint of honesty.

"You're a Temple Knight," she said. "Or at least you were."

He grinned, revealing a not unpleasant smile. "That I was. I was known as Brother Mateo Harnbringer, of the Temple Knights of Saint Cunar."

"Was?" said Charlaine. "Brothers don't leave that order by choice."

"Nor did I." He held up his hand to forestall any arguments. "I know what you're thinking, that I'm nothing but a troublemaker, but there's something you need to know."

"I'm listening."

He lowered his voice. "There's a rot inside the Church, one that's eating away at the moral fibre of the place."

"And you know this for a fact?"

"I tried to do something about it, but it cost me my knighthood. Now I am an outcast, doomed to wander the Continent without the blessings of the Church."

"And you chose to speak to us?" said Danica. "If what you say is true, we're forbidden to talk to you. How dare you put our souls in danger!"

Charlaine reached out, placing her hand on her companion's arm. "Calm yourself, Danica. There's no harm in simple talk." She returned her attention to their visitor. "Please, tell us more."

At the precise moment he was about to explain, the door burst open, revealing an armoured man in a green cloak. His eyes wandered the room, while his hand remained on the pommel of his sword.

"Mateo!" he called out. "Where are you, dog!" The dishonoured Cunar ran for the back door, pushing the crowd roughly aside.

"There you are!" yelled the newcomer, drawing his blade. Those near him backed up in fear while Charlaine stood up and moved towards the armed intruder, placing herself in his path.

"By what right do you threaten this man?" she demanded.

"It is none of your concern."

"Ah, but it IS my concern. My order is dedicated to protecting women everywhere, and as you can plainly see, there are women present."

"Stand aside, I say, and let me have at him."

"Put down your sword, man. This is no place for violence. If you wish to speak with this fellow, then do so outside, where the risk to others is minimized."

He glared back. "Who do you think you are?"

"I am Sister Charlaine deShandria," she replied, "Temple Knight of Saint Agnes. And you?"

"Brother Eustace, Temple Knight of Saint Cunar. That makes me the senior order. Now, stand aside, I say!"

The room fell silent as everyone watched the drama unfold. Danica appeared at her companion's right, her hands resting on her weapon.

"Is he giving you trouble?" she asked.

Charlaine locked eyes with Brother Eustace. "What say you, Brother? Is there to be trouble this day?"

There was the briefest hint of defiance in his eyes, and she fully expected him to launch into an attack. But then he stepped back, raising his arms to indicate he had scabbarded his sword.

"It appears he has made his escape," the Cunar said. "I shall leave this establishment, but I promise you I will report your actions to your superiors."

"See that you do," said Charlaine.

They stared at each other until Brother Eustace finally looked away before turning and leaving abruptly.

"What was that all about?" asked Danica.

"I'm not exactly sure, but I imagine it has something to do with Brother Mateo."

The inn quickly returned to its previous noise level while they headed back to their table to find two ales waiting for them. Danica sat down and reached out for her tankard.

"Well," she said, "I don't know about you, but I'm content to leave all this behind us."

Charlaine lifted her ale but didn't drink. Instead, her eyes had a faraway look.

"What are you thinking?" asked the raven-haired knight.

"That this bears investigating," replied Charlaine.

"You can't be serious? The man's an exile!"

"I understand that, but tell me, why would an exile try to warn us?"

"Perhaps he's simply mad?"

"No," said Charlaine. "He seemed to have his wits about him."

"And?"

"And what?"

"Come now," said Danica. "I know you too well. I can tell when that mind of yours is thinking."

"I'm curious as to why Brother Eustace was here. Brother Mateo is an exile, by his own admission, yet here is another knight of the same order that cast him aside, actively seeking him out."

"Yes," said Danica, "and it definitely didn't look like he wanted to chat. What do you make of that?"

"Clearly, he intended to silence the man permanently. The real question is why?"

"I imagine it has something to do with the reason he was dismissed from the order."

The server returned, setting down a plate of bread and cheese. "Anything else?" she asked.

"No," said Danica. "That will do for now. Thank you."

"Hold on a moment," added Charlaine. "The man who was here earlier, do you know him?"

"The man you faced down?" asked the girl. "No. Why?"

"How about the other fellow? The one who came to our table?"

"I think I've seen him once or twice, but he never sets foot inside."

"Why do you think that is?" asked Danica.

"Maybe he wants to avoid people?"

Danica turned to Charlaine. "Makes sense, I suppose. Fellow knights are forbidden to talk to him."

"I'm not convinced that's it," said Charlaine. "When was the first time you saw him? Do you remember?"

The girl looked decidedly uncomfortable. "I don't know, three weeks ago? Maybe a little longer?"

"That's all, thanks. You may return to your duties."

The girl scampered off as fast as she could.

"Well," observed Danica. "That was certainly strange."

"It was, wasn't it? I think the timing of great interest, don't you?"

"In what way?"

"Word was sent ahead that we were coming. It might merely be a coincidence, but I can't help but feel he was specifically searching for us."

"Why would you say that?"

"Judging from the looks of this place," said Charlaine, "I'd say it isn't a common gathering place for Temple Knights. It also lies on the road to the southwest, and we know from our own travels, there's not much in that direction except the open road."

"How would he know we were even coming?"

"I'm sure word of our exploits in Ilea preceded us—it's not as if it's a secret. The real question is, why us?"

"He was trying to warn us," Danica said. "Do you think that has something to do with it?"

"Likely."

Danica snapped her fingers. "I know why. I bet it has to do with the victory. You're a hero with a reputation for being honest. If you remember, he warned about something eating away at the... how did he put it?"

"The moral fibre of the place?"

"Yes," said Danica. "What do you suppose that means?"

"I don't know, but I intend to find out."

"All right, I'm in. What's our first step?"

"Well, to begin with," said Charlaine, "we need to report to whoever commands the local garrison of our order. That is, after all, our duty."

"I thought we were supposed to meet the Primus?"

"And we likely will, but our first responsibility is to report to the senior member of our order."

"Wouldn't that mean the Grand Mistress?"

"It would," said Charlaine.

"That's intimidating."

"Not at all. She's still a fellow sister, regardless of rank."

"Easy for you to say. You're used to mingling with the rich and powerful."

"Why would you say that?"

"You presented your plan to the Baroness of Rizela, not to mention dealing with the Admiral of the Holy Fleet."

"I might remind you I wasn't the only one there. Correct me if I'm wrong, but as I recall it, you were there at my side on both those occasions."

"Oh yes," said Danica. "I suppose I was. Still, the Mistress of the Order? I don't think I've ever met someone that important in my life. Do we tell her anything about Brother Mateo?"

"I'm not sure that would be wise at this point. And let's be honest, what has he really told us? All we have are some cryptic words of warning."

"True, but surely you're not suggesting we simply ignore them?"

"Not at all," said Charlaine. "Once we get settled in, I'd like to see what we can dig up about Brother Mateo. That might give us some idea of what's going on around here."

"And if it doesn't?"

"Then we'll dig deeper, but we'll need to be careful. If he's right about this, we may have a hard time telling friend from foe."

"And if he's wrong, we're just being overly cautious?"

Charlaine chuckled. "Better safe than sorry."

The next morning found them approaching Reichendorf, one of the larger cities of the Petty Kingdoms, its massive walls dominated by still larger towers. Even Danica, who'd seen the great fortress of Corassus, was impressed.

Despite its intimidating nature, their entry was unremarkable. Being peacetime, the gatehouse guards paid little attention to the comings and goings of its citizens. Apparently, a pair of Temple Knights was a common enough sight in these parts.

Several times through the narrow streets, they were forced to slow their progress as the press of people became worse. Danica fidgeted in the saddle.

"At this rate, we won't reach the Antonine till well after dark."

"It's not as if we're in a hurry," said Charlaine. "You should relax and try to enjoy the scenery."

"Scenery? What's there to see? The only thing in sight is all the people crowding the streets."

They turned down a side alley in an attempt to avoid the traffic. Charlaine's head snapped around as the sound of a hammer striking steel rang out.

"Do you hear what I hear?" she asked.

"If you mean the sounds of a smithy, yes. Let me guess, you'd like to investigate?"

"Of course." They rode on, the sounds growing louder. Finally, they spotted the hammer and anvil, the universal sign of the smith. Charlaine dismounted, tying off Stormcloud's reins to a post.

"Coming?" she asked her raven-haired companion.

"Do I have to?" groaned Danica. "It's not as if I haven't seen a smithy before. Anyway, why are you so interested? You have your own."

"Correction, I HAD my own. There's no guarantee our next posting will let me continue my work."

"And so we must investigate all the smiths in Reichendorf?"

"Not all of them," said Charlaine, "but I want to get the lay of the land and find out if the guild has a presence here."

"Why?"

"Call it common courtesy if you like, but the tradition is for a smith to announce their arrival to the guild upon reaching a new city."

"You didn't feel that urge in all the other cities we passed through on the way here."

"True, but then again, we never stayed for more than a single night. This time, however, we'll likely be here for weeks."

"Well, when you put it that way," said Danica, "we'd better mind our manners and say hello." She climbed down out of her saddle and tied off Spirit. Her task complete, she stepped up to the door and opened it, sweeping her other hand in a grand gesture. "After you."

"Why, thank you," said Charlaine, exaggerating her manner as well.

Outside, the sound of hammering was loud enough to echo down the street, but it was downright deafening here, inside the building. Three forges blasted away, flooding the room with oppressive heat.

"By the Saints," said Danica. "I can hardly breathe. How do they stand it?"

"You get used to it," noted Charlaine.

"Can I help you?" called out a voice.

A bald, thick-set individual moved closer, extending his hand. "I'm Erkson Tane."

Charlaine shook his hand, briefly pressing her own thumb between his thumb and forefinger—the secret handshake of the smith's guild across the Petty Kingdoms. If this fellow was a member, he failed to respond in kind.

"Are you looking for armour or weapons?" the man asked.

"No, we're just here to have a look around. Tell me, do you do commissions for the Temple Knights?"

"Not unless they pay upfront."

"Why is that?"

"Why do you think?" replied Tane. "They're notoriously slow at paying their tab."

"And do the other smiths feel the same way?"

"I don't know. You should ask them."

"Might I enquire as to where I could find them?"

"You can enquire, but it'll do you no good."

"Why is that?"

The man's face contorted into a look of disgust. "I'm not in the habit of sending business to my rivals. Now, if you're not interested in commissioning a work, you'll need to leave. I'm a busy man."

"My apologies," said Charlaine. "I didn't mean to intrude."

The man stomped off as the Temple Knights stepped outside.

"He didn't look too happy with us," noted Danica. "And what was all that business about not settling tabs?"

"I have no idea," replied Charlaine, "but it sounds like someone isn't doing their job. Either that or the Church is short on funds."

"We'd best get on our way to the Antonine unless you want to find another smith?"

"No, not until I find out more about what's going on here."

"You think there's more to this, don't you?"

"Of course," said Charlaine. "Don't you? First, we receive this mystic warning from Brother Mateo, and then we learn the smiths don't trust the Church to make payment. I've never heard of such a thing."

"Your father was a master swordsmith. Did he ever deal with the Church?"

"He did."

"And?"

"They were always most accommodating when it came to payment. Something is going on here that gives me an uneasy feeling. You?"

Danica shrugged. "I don't know. Maybe we're overreacting? The Church is a giant bureaucracy. Perhaps that accounts for the late payment?"

"From Temple Knights? What kind of precedent does that set?"

"I suppose you'll just have to take it up with the Grand Mistress."

Charlaine laughed. "I'll just wander up to her and say, 'Pardon me, Your Grace, but are you having trouble paying your bills?'. I can think of no easier way to find myself back in the middle of nowhere."

"Hey, now," said Danica. "If it hadn't been for your first posting, we never would have met."

"That's true, and I wouldn't change that for anything."

2

THE ANTONINE

Summer 1097 SR

Located in the heart of Reichendorf, the Antonine was a city unto itself, surrounded by fortified stone walls the colour of dull steel. A single massive gate was guarded by Temple Knights of Saint Cunar, resplendent in their grey-and-white tabards overtop their gleaming plate armour.

Unlike the guards of Reichendorf, these sentinels took great interest in the approach of the two sister knights as they halted before the gate, waiting as one of the Cunars drew closer.

"Your names?" he demanded.

"I am Sister Charlaine deShandria, and this is Sister Danica Meer. We've been ordered here by our superiors."

"Have you any proof of this?"

"I do, in the form of written orders. Would you like to see them?"

He nodded, waiting as she fished through her satchel and then handed the document to him. The guard scanned the contents before eyeing them suspiciously.

"It says here you were summoned by the Primus himself."

"That is correct," said Charlaine. "We've recently come from Ilea, where we fought alongside the Holy Fleet."

"The fleet put out to sea?"

"It did, and won a great victory over the Halvarians."

"Praise to the Saints," replied the guard. He turned to his companion, who stood nearer to the closed gate. "All right, you can let them in."

"Tell me," said Charlaine, "is the gate always closed?"

"It is now and has been for the last three weeks. We've had some trouble with the locals, you see. Nothing we can't handle, but there's a desire to avoid further bloodshed, hence the precautions."

The gate began opening, the chains clanking as the winch turned.

"You've come a long way," the guard added. "I expect you're eager to make your commandery."

"Indeed."

He turned to face the gate. "Once the doors open, you're going to ride straight through and take the first road on your right. That'll take you past the Mathewite commandery and through the gardens. Once you see the fountain, you'll need to turn left. Your commandery is just a few hundred paces beyond."

"Thank you," said Charlaine.

The squealing chains halted. "You can ride through now. May the Saints watch over you."

"And you."

They urged their horses forward through the gatehouse. The doors protested once more as the great mechanism closed behind them. Danica waited until they were well out of earshot before speaking.

"Did he say what I thought he said?" she asked.

"You mean about the bloodshed? I'm afraid so."

"What in the name of the Saints could explain that?"

"I don't know," said Charlaine, "but the farther into the Antonine we go, the more uncomfortable I'm becoming."

They rode past a group of Cunars practicing their melee skills, then turned to the right. The commandery of the Temple Knights of Saint Mathew watched over them as they continued on their path.

"Quite the building," noted Danica. "I wonder if our own is as ornate?"

"It won't be long before your question is answered."

"Strange, isn't it?"

"What is?"

"You'd think the Order of Saint Mathew would have a less decorative exterior. They take a vow of poverty, don't they?"

"You know they do," said Charlaine, "but that's an individual vow, not the order as a whole. You're right, though. It is a little unexpected."

The fresh scent of flowers drifted towards them, eliciting a smile of appreciation.

"That must be the gardens," noted Charlaine.

"They're beautiful."

"Yes, and well looked after. Someone has gone to great trouble to maintain them."

"They're immense," said Danica. "I wonder how far back they go?"

"We can find out later. I don't know about you, but I'm sore from being in the saddle."

"Me too, and hungry as well. I hope we haven't missed mealtime."

The road formed a circle around a fountain in the middle of their route.

"This must be our turn," said Charlaine. Off to the left they went, past a large green field where a number of sister knights trotted back and forth.

"Looks like riding practice," said Danica. "Some things never change."

"I must admit, it seems strange to see such training on an individual level. Captain Giselle always had us practice in groups."

"Not everyone is as dedicated as her."

"No, I guess not," said Charlaine. "I only hope our next assignment gives us someone who knows her business."

"I'm sure it will," said Danica. "They wouldn't bring us all the way here just to send us back to the middle of nowhere, would they? I was hoping to go to one of the big cities in the north."

"That's where you're from, isn't it?"

"More or less. I'm actually from Andover, but there are lots of other Petty Kingdoms that border the Great Northern Sea. What about you? Have any preferences over where you'd like to go?"

Charlaine smiled. "I'm content to serve wherever needed. If that happens to be in the north, then so be it."

"Maybe the Primus would be open to suggestions?"

"He's not the one who determines our assignments. That's the duty of the Grand Mistress."

"I suppose that means we need to get on her good side."

"Why? Were you thinking of arguing with her?"

"No, of course not," said Danica. She was about to say more, when she noticed her companion's look of mischief. "Ha ha. Very funny."

"In all seriousness," continued Charlaine, "our new assignments were probably decided on months ago."

"That makes sense. I only wish I knew what they were. We don't even know if we're going to the same place. What if they break us up?"

"Then we'll deal with it. You and I will always be great friends, Danica, regardless of any distance that may separate us." She could sense her comrade's mood darkening. "In any event, you're likely worrying over nothing. We made a great team at Alantra. Surely the Church wouldn't want to break that up?"

The raven-haired knight forced a smile. "No, I suppose not."

"Oh look," said Charlaine. "There's the commandery."

Before them stood an immense structure, with huge columns lining its front.

"Saint's alive," said Danica. "I never expected it to be so enormous."

"They say there are five entire companies stationed here." Charlaine pointed to their right. "Look over there. You can see the entrance to the stables."

"We should probably head in that direction, don't you think?"

"I suppose we should," agreed Charlaine.

They trotted off the road and across the grass. Other riders took note of their presence but made no move to intercept or welcome them. Soon, they entered the massive stables, a large room occupying fully a third of the commandery.

An older sister noted their entrance and walked over to them. "New arrivals?"

"Yes," said Charlaine. "We've just come in from Ilea."

"Stable your mounts in the back two stalls on the left. You can visit them as often as you like during your stay, but my people will be responsible for looking after their care and feeding. Any questions?"

"I do have one," said Charlaine. "Who should we report to?"

"That would be the watch commander. Once you see to your horses, there's a door nearby leading into the commandery. Just beyond that is the duty office. You'll find her there."

Charlaine was about to thank her, but the woman turned unexpectedly, yelling at one of her stable hands.

"Looks like it's this way," said Danica.

Finding the stalls was easy enough, and then a stable hand came to take over the job of brushing down and feeding the horses, freeing up the two Temple Knights.

The watch commander proved to be a sour-faced individual, who appeared to be put out by having to deal with two new arrivals. All attempts to engage her in conversation failed, but at least she did her duty and assigned Charlaine and Danica rooms on the upper floor. Then came the time-consuming process of actually finding them.

"This place is an absolute maze," complained Danica.

"Oh, come now. It's no worse than the Temple of Saint Agnes in Rizela. That place had a terrible layout."

They rounded a corner, almost colliding with another sister knight.

"I'm sorry," said Danica. "I didn't see you there."

"The fault was entirely mine," replied the sister. "I'm afraid I wasn't watching where I was going. I'm Sister Selena. You?"

"I'm Danica, and this is Charlaine. We just arrived from Ilea."

"Ilea? Why does that sound familiar? Wasn't there a big sea battle down there recently?"

"Yes," said Charlaine, "the Battle of Alantra. We were there."

"You must tell me about it sometime. Are you here for long?"

"I'm not sure. We were summoned by the Primus. Other than that, we know very little."

"Well, if he summoned you, you'll be here awhile yet. Nothing ever moves quickly in the Antonine."

"Are you stationed here?" asked Danica.

"No, they sent me here for training. I was told I'm in line for a captaincy, and you know what that means."

"Leadership classes," said Charlaine. "Have they started yet?"

"Not for another few days, I'm afraid. They're waiting on the arrival of some others. Still, it gives me time to enjoy the inner city."

"Inner city?" asked Danica.

"Yes. That's what they call the Antonine."

"I suppose it makes sense. It is inside Reichendorf."

"I should let you get to your rooms. I'll see you around?"

"By all means," said Charlaine.

Sister Selena continued down the hallway, leaving them alone.

"There's my room"—Danica pointed—"and yours is across the hall." She stepped forward, opening the door to reveal a single room with a bed, table, and a small basin. "This reminds me of the cells back in Rizela. Do you remember?"

"Of course, how could I not? It's definitely a far cry from our shared accommodation back at the outpost."

"What shall we do now?"

"I don't know about you, but I'd love a good wash."

"Excellent idea." Danica disappeared into her room but left the door open. Her voice soon drifted out to the hall. "I have a pitcher of water, you?"

"The same. Give me a hand to get out of this armour, then I'll return the favour."

They stepped into the dining hall to be met by dozens of voices echoing off the walls. It was a two-storey affair, with high windows that let in a reasonable amount of light. Along the front stood a long table with iron pots full of stew and plates with bread and cheese. A trio of sister knights stood by to lend whatever assistance was necessary but simply ended up looking bored. Charlaine and Danica picked up some platters and made their way down the line.

"This stew smells delicious," said Danica, helping herself to a wooden bowl into which she ladled some food, then laughed as her stomach gurgled.

"You must be hungry," said Charlaine.

"What can I say? This certainly beats Sister Helena's porridge." She fell silent, a tear rolling down her cheek.

"She died doing what she loved," Charlaine reminded her.

Danica nodded, unable to speak as she wiped her eyes, then set down the bowl. "I know. It's just hard to believe she's no longer with us. It's the same with the others. I keep thinking they're going to walk through a door someday, and we'll all laugh about things."

Charlaine placed her hand on her comrade's shoulder. "I know, but we must cherish the happy memories we have, not dwell on the sadness." She stared into Danica's eyes, seeing them settle once more into determination.

"You're right, of course. Look at me, blubbering away like a complete idiot."

"It's not idiocy to mourn family. They will always be here with us, in our hearts. Now, pick up your food, and let's get a seat before everything gets cold, shall we?"

Just as Charlaine dipped her spoon into the stew, a shadow fell across her bowl. Looking up, a middle-aged woman stood, staring down at her."

"Are you Sister Charlaine?" the newcomer asked.

"I am," she replied. "And you?"

"Temple Captain Nicola. I was sent to fetch you."

"Now?"

The captain grinned. "Unless you'd like to explain to the Grand Mistress why she had to wait?"

Charlaine cast a quick glance at her bowl. "No, of course not." She pushed it towards Danica. "Here, you have it." She stood, straightening her cassock. "Lead on, Captain."

The Grand Mistress was housed on the top floor, her windows to the west, as was the tradition. It was said that this was to face the Holy City of Herani, but here in the middle of the Continent, that was more to the south than west. Still, tradition was tradition.

Outside her office stood two sisters of the order, their armour gleaming, their tabards clean and crisp. Charlaine wondered if they had ever seen battle, then chided herself for her churlish thoughts. Members of the order were sisters, regardless of whether or not they had fought in service to their Saint.

Captain Nicola knocked on the door, then opened it slightly, peering within. "Sister Charlaine is here, Your Grace."

"Bring her in," came the reply.

With a wave of her hand, the captain bid Charlaine to enter before taking up a position by the door, closing it behind her but remaining to witness the exchange.

"Sister Charlaine," began the Grand Mistress. "So good of you to come."

Charlaine was unsure of how to respond. After all, it wasn't as if she could refuse the summons.

"You wished to see me, Your Grace?"

"I've read several accounts of your experiences down in Ilea, and I'm impressed. Captain Giselle talks highly of you, as does Holy Mother Claudia. There's even a letter here from Father General Marius singing your praises. I must admit this is the first time I've received correspondence from an admiral."

"I only did what was necessary," said Charlaine.

"You did much more than that. In the short time you were in Ilea, you demonstrated great leadership. It only seems fitting I make you a Temple Captain."

"Temple Captain? Are you sure? I've only had the one assignment so far."

"You earned it," said the Grand Mistress. "We need more sisters like you, Charlaine. You and your kind are the future of our order."

"I am humbled."

"As well you should be, considering your vows. The official ceremony won't be until the end of the week, but from this moment hence, you will carry out the duties and responsibilities of your new rank. Have you any questions?"

"Might I ask if Sister Danica will be given a similar reward for her service?"

The Grand Mistress's eyes flicked to Captain Nicola for the briefest moment before returning to Charlaine. "It's admirable you should show such concern for a fellow sister. There is no position of captain available to her at this time. However, there's another option I've been considering. Tell me, would you consent to have her under your command?"

"Of course," said Charlaine. "I would be honoured."

"Good, then it's settled." The Grand Mistress dipped her quill and began writing. Charlaine waited for an explanation, but none was forthcoming. The silence dragged on, and then the Grand Mistress passed the note to Captain Nicola. Her gaze returned once more to her newest captain.

"I shall be sending you north... eventually, but in the meantime, you must complete your training as a captain. There's a leadership course beginning shortly. Both you and Sister Danica are to attend."

"Yes, Your Grace."

"I'll have more news for you concerning your next assignment at the conclusion of your training. Now, you've taken up too much of my time already. You'd best be on your way."

Charlaine bowed. "Of course, Your Grace."

She turned, leaving the room with a feeling of euphoria.

Captain Nicola entered the hallway after her, closing the door quietly. "Congratulations, Captain."

Charlaine grinned. "I don't know what to say."

"The usual response is 'thank you', but failing that, a simple handshake is sufficient." Nicola held out her hand.

Charlaine shook it. "Thank you. I certainly didn't expect this. After all, I've only been a knight for a couple of years."

"I have a feeling this won't be the last we see of you. Keep up the good work, and may the blessings of Saint Agnes go with you."

"And with you."

Charlaine returned to the dining hall, where Danica was finishing up her meal.

"How did it go?" asked the raven-haired knight.

"She promoted me to captain."

"Congratulations! Any word on a new assignment?"

"Some vague mention of the north, but other than that, no. Oh, and you're going with me."

Danica smiled. "That's excellent news indeed. If we had some decent wine, I'd suggest we toast it."

"Wait. There's one other thing."

"Yes? Go on, I'm listening."

"You and I are both to take those leadership classes."

Danica frowned.

"Something wrong?" asked Charlaine

"I'm not so good in a learning environment."

"Don't be absurd. You learned a lot just by being in Ilea."

"That was different. There, I was amongst fellow sisters. I don't have difficulty learning day to day, but put me under the tutelage of a teacher, and I'm lost."

"How would you even know that? Ever been tutored before?"

"No, I'm merely a simple country girl, raised by the sea."

"So what you're saying is you're intimidated by the thought of being told what to do?"

"I suppose so."

"That," said Charlaine, "is just plain silly. You spent all your time down south following orders. If that isn't the very definition of being told what to do, I don't know what is."

"You're right. Sorry, I just feel so out of place here."

"So do I, Danica, so do I."

3

ASSESSMENT

Summer 1097 SR

An early morning knock on her door drew Charlaine's attention. Before she could get up, a sour-faced Temple Knight with her hair pulled back in a severe bun, barged into the room.

"Are you Sister Charlaine?" she demanded.

The woman's unwelcome interruption irritated her. "I am Captain Charlaine deShandria. And you are?"

"Sister Loretta. You're to come with me."

"To what end?"

"As you are aware, you were chosen to participate in leadership training."

"And that starts today?"

"Only the assessment," said Loretta. "I must judge your current capacity to handle various tasks and then decide what training is necessary to compensate for your weaknesses."

"And do all candidates go through this procedure?"

"They do. Now, have you finished your interrogation, or do you have more questions?"

Charlaine stood. "Will I need my armour and weapons?"

"Of course. What do you expect? That you'll be working with lay sisters?"

"Then I shall need some time to dress appropriately."

"Make it quick," said Sister Loretta. "I haven't all day. I still need to find someone named Sister Danica."

"She's right across the hall. Shall I fetch her?"

"I'm more than capable of doing that myself. Now get into your armour."

Charlaine felt her resolve stiffen. "Captain."

"Pardon?"

"You will address me as, Captain. That is my rank."

"Duly noted… Captain. Now, if it's not too much trouble to ask, would you please begin getting into your armour?"

Charlaine smiled. "Of course."

Loretta turned, crossing the narrow hallway to rap on Danica's door. As Charlaine pulled on her gambeson, there was some back and forth between the two women, but the voices were muffled. Her head poked out only to hear the exchange escalate.

"Well," Danica was saying, "who pissed in your porridge?"

"How dare you speak thus to me! I am your superior."

"No, you're not! You're just a knight, like me. Don't you dare claim otherwise!"

Charlaine stepped into the hallway. "Is there a problem here?"

"This woman is disrespecting my authority," claimed Loretta.

"And what authority is that? Are you not a Temple Knight, like her?"

"Yes, but—"

"There are no buts, Sister. Either you are a Temple Knight or not. Unless, of course, they've seen fit to promote you to captain?" She watched as the woman's face reddened. "Come now, you might have had a rough morning, but that doesn't excuse your lack of manners."

"The fact still remains that Sister Danica is proving to be obstinate."

"You're the one who was obstinate," countered Danica. "What with your 'Get dressed immediately', and 'Hurry up, woman'. You'd think there was a war on or something."

Charlaine looked at each in turn, recognizing the frustration behind their eyes. "I believe we'd be better served if we all took a deep breath. Danica, come and help me armour up, then I shall return the favour." She looked at Sister Loretta. "To where shall we report?"

"The north field. Horses are waiting."

"We don't bring our own?"

"Part of the evaluation is determining your skill at riding," the knight snapped. "We can hardly do that with an unknown horse." Loretta paused a moment, taking a breath. "Sorry. As you surmised, it's been a rough morning."

"Then let us hope it gets better. Sister Danica and I will be there directly."

"Very well, Captain." Sister Loretta turned and left, her footsteps echoing down the hall.

Charlaine looked at her companion. "What's got into you?"

Danica's face reddened. "Sorry. She woke me from a fitful sleep, and then she was all over me, barking out orders."

"You could've handled it better."

"You're right. I should have, but she reminded me so much of Sister Erika before she mellowed out."

"You mean when she bossed you around?"

"Exactly. I know I shouldn't let it bother me, but I just felt the need to strike back."

"It's only natural, considering your background. You were treated terribly before you joined the order, and that part of you still resides within your heart. Those scars will never heal, but you can learn to live with them."

"And I'll do my best to do so. I promise."

Charlaine stared into her eyes, observing her honesty. "Very well. Now, help me get into this armour, or we'll be late for this evaluation."

"Evaluation?"

"Yes, didn't you hear Sister Loretta?"

"Sort of," said Danica. "But all she told me was to hurry up and get out of bed. What's this about an evaluation?"

"She's going to assess our abilities and then recommend what we need training in."

"Are you telling me I just argued with the very person who has to determine our weaknesses?"

"I'm afraid so."

Danica's shoulders slumped. "Great! What else can go wrong today?"

Charlaine laughed. "Look at it this way; it can only get better!"

The northern field was several acres in size, an area of green filled with riders in armour trotting back and forth. Charlaine watched them perform precise manoeuvres for a bit, then turned towards them, coming to a halt before Sister Loretta.

The sister turned toward her assembled charges. "As you can see, it takes skill and discipline to perform these types of tactics. Now, we know the sisters here are more than capable of carrying out orders. The real question is if any of you are up to the task?" She looked around at her students, meeting their gazes. "Who wants to go first?"

"I shall," said Charlaine.

The leader of the riders dismounted, walking the mount over and handing the reins to her. Charlaine placed her hand on the horse's neck. The beast was a little skittish, most likely excited by its previous movements.

"Well, what are you waiting for?" called out Sister Loretta.

"What manoeuvres would you like me to lead?"

"Move the sisters down to the end of the field in column, then deploy into a double line and advance. Keep the lines straight before breaking into a charge at the midpoint."

"I should like a moment or two to get used to this horse."

Sister Loretta was taken aback. "You what?"

Charlaine mounted. "Only a fool would take an unknown horse into battle. If one is to seek combat, they must be familiar with their mount. After all, their very life may depend on it. I shall just be a moment."

She turned her mount around, trotting it across the width of the field. Charlaine was an accomplished rider due to her Calabrian upbringing, but something about this horse bothered her. She dismounted, then checked the straps, finding the girth to be too tight. This would result in the horse being uncomfortable, especially at the gallop, as it would be unable to breathe properly. Looking at the leather straps, she could easily see the most commonly used buckles and made the adjustment. Likely this had been done on purpose, to give the students some trouble. It saddened her to think the horse must pay the price for such a trick.

She remounted, then trotted back across the field, feeling the horse falling into a comfortable gait. Upon returning, she took up a position to the right of the formation.

"Column of march," she called out. The sister knights fell into pairs, a common formation on the roads of the Petty Kingdoms, for such pathways were generally narrow. In rare cases, they would ride four abreast, but only across fields where no obstacles stood in their way. Such a formation was also, of necessity, loose, allowing those following to speed up or slow down with little chance of colliding with their colleagues.

As they approached the end of the field, she wheeled them, waiting for the tail end to make the turn before ordering them into a double line. Once the movement was completed, she ordered the advance. Under battlefield conditions, a depth of four knights was preferred, but given the limited numbers here, she thought two more efficient.

They began at a slow pace, increasing gradually until they were halfway down the length of the field. She withdrew her sword, holding it aloft before sweeping it down, the signal to begin the charge.

Many thought of the charge as a mad rush to engage the enemy, but Captain Giselle had driven home the need to maintain discipline in the ranks. Thus, they did not go full out, which would have caused the faster horses to meet the enemy first. Instead, they maintained a coordinated advance as they thundered past Sister Loretta, who watched in stony silence.

Having completed their manoeuvres, Charlaine slowed her knights, adjusting their ranks before pivoting into a column once again to return to their starting point.

She halted them and dismounted, passing the reins off to one of the waiting knights. Removing her helmet, she then advanced to stand before Sister Loretta.

"Impressive," the woman said. "I assume you've done this type of thing before?"

"My last captain insisted we all learn the basics."

"She obviously had some experience. What was her name?"

"Giselle."

The effect was immediate but far from what Charlaine expected. Instead of recognition, she saw only loathing.

"You should be careful," Loretta warned. "Such advice could lead to heavy casualties."

"Quite the reverse, actually. Captain Giselle's training is what allowed us to defeat the Halvarians."

The sister stepped closer, lowering her voice. "You're loyal, that's understandable, but I wouldn't go about invoking her name if I were you. Many in the order are dismayed by her actions in Erlingen."

"It was a battle," said Charlaine, "and the actions of her knights proved crucial to victory."

"Be that as it may, she alone survived."

"Only due to the assistance of a Mathewite."

They stared at each other.

"You have the makings of a great leader, Charlaine. See that you don't ruin it with your politics."

"Politics?"

"Yes," said Loretta. "Like any large organization, the sisterhood consists of many individuals with sometimes varying opinions."

"I'm well aware."

"But you're a captain now. It's plain to see you're well qualified for the position, yet there's more than ability at play here. If you want to advance any further in the order, you'd better learn to tread the fine line between perseverance and insolence."

"I only seek to serve my Saint."

"Well said, but it's not your Saint who forms the hierarchy of our order; it's people, and that means decisions you may not agree with."

"Understood," said Charlaine, "and I thank you for the guidance. I shall take it under advisement."

Sister Loretta turned to the rest of the students. "Sister Charlaine has set a high standard. Let's see if everyone else can do as well."

The exercise continued with each taking their turn. Charlaine's anxiety built as Danica waited for her turn, but it ended up she'd fretted for nothing. Giselle's training allowed the young knight to sail through the ordeal without any trouble at all.

When the last student finished, it was well past noon, and everyone was dismissed for their midday meal. The dining hall was busy, but she and Danica were soon seated, digging into thick slabs of beef.

"This," said Danica, through half a mouthful of food, "is some of the best meat I've ever eaten."

Charlaine watched her dig in. "It seems training gives you an appetite."

"Mind if I join you?" They looked up to see Sister Selena.

"By all means," replied Charlaine. She waited for the woman to sit before continuing. "I couldn't help but notice you're having some difficulty this morning."

"I'll say. My last assignment gave me next to nothing in the form of command experience. If I hadn't been watching the others, I never would have known what to do."

"Well, that's what the assessment is all about—finding your weaknesses and building upon them."

"True," said Danica, "but I'm relieved it's finally over. It wasn't half as bad as I thought it was going to be."

"It's not over," warned Selena. "In fact, it's barely begun."

"What's that supposed to mean?"

"They'll be testing us for days."

Danica's mouth fell open. "Days?"

"Oh yes. Didn't they tell you?"

"They most certainly did not!"

"This afternoon, they'll be evaluating our prowess with weapons."

"That doesn't sound too bad."

"Agreed," said Charlaine. "We've had more than ample training with them."

"Those are the easy parts," said Selena. "Then we must be assessed on all manner of things."

"Such as?"

"History of the order, standing orders, teachings of Saint Agnes, not to mention all the administration that goes with being a captain."

Danica looked intrigued. "What do you mean, administration?"

"Well, you'll need to be able to handle the finances of your command, set duty rosters, post sentinels, and so on."

"That sounds complicated."

"Not so much," said Charlaine. "I used to help my father with the finances back when I was a smith." She paused a moment. "Well, that's not entirely true—it was my mother. My father never really had a head for them."

"Tell me," said Selena, "is there anything you can't do?"

"Lots. For one thing, I'm at a complete loss when it comes to ships. Oh, I can fight on them, but as to sails and the wind? That's a whole different matter."

"Luckily for you, none of that will be on our assessments."

"How about you, Selena?" asked Danica. "What was your last assignment like?"

"I was stationed in Harlingen."

"That's the capital of Hadenfeld," said Charlaine. "I was born in Malburg. Do you know it?"

"I've heard of it but never actually been there. I did once meet King Otto though."

"What did you make of him?"

"A jolly, old fellow," replied Selena, "but getting on in years. As a consequence, he can sometimes be a little out of it."

"You mean not in his right mind?"

"Precisely. I'm told he suffers from bouts of melancholia, but I never witnessed it myself. You say you were born in Malburg; was your family merchants, then?"

"My father was a smith, as was I, although I suppose that's more of a trade."

"You were a smith?"

"Yes," said Charlaine. "Why? Is that so hard to believe?"

"Not particularly, but it is rare. You do have a foreign look to you, however."

"My ancestry is Calabrian."

"Ah, well, that would explain it," said Selena. "Your people are much more accepting of such things." She paused briefly. "I mean no offence, merely that—"

"I know what you meant," said Charlaine, "and you may rest assured I take no offence. As to my heritage, I've been called a foreigner more times than I care to admit. And to my being a smith, it was quite common for women to take up a trade back in Calabria."

"It's a pity the Continent isn't more like that," said Danica, "then there would be less work for our order."

"I'm not sure I follow," said Selena.

"Our prime responsibility is to protect women, right? There would be less need if they were in more positions of authority."

"Nonsense. There are plenty of noblewomen."

"True, but few who have any real power. How many of the Petty Kingdoms are ruled by a female?"

"She has you there," added Charlaine. "Not that there's much we can do about it. Our job is not to play politics but to ensure the safety of our charges."

"An interesting argument," noted Selena, "but we are Temple Knights. Our actual duty is to protect the places of worship. Looking after women is the job of the lay sisters."

"How can you be so callous?" said Danica. "Have you never known a woman in need?"

"Can't say I have nor do I wish to. It would only interfere with my duty to the order. You'd do well to remember that yourself." She smiled. "You're still young, Danica, and full of passion, a trait that serves you well, but as you age, I think you'll begin to see the wisdom in following the rules. I assume you want to one day be a captain?"

"What has that to do with anything?"

"It's quite simple, really. Advancement in the order involves doing what you're told and not asking too many questions. Do that, and nothing can stop you."

Danica frowned. "If we followed the rules, we never would have defeated the Halvarian fleet!"

"Come now, fighting aboard a ship is different, but I'd hardly call that breaking the rules."

"You don't understand. We weren't just shipboard troops; Charlaine here helped plan the whole thing."

Selena's eyes swivelled to Charlaine. "Is this true?"

"Many were involved. I would be remiss if I didn't mention the contribution of my fellow sisters, especially Danica, but I'm afraid it's not something I'm at liberty to discuss."

"What does that mean?"

Charlaine smiled. "As you so eloquently put it, our job is not to play politics, yet the higher in rank we progress, the more it begins to affect us."

"Now you're just being cryptic."

"Suffice it to say, we're all here to become better leaders. That means leading troops, certainly, but there are other duties we must face with equal devotion."

"Such as?" asked Selena.

"Being at court."

"That's the job of a knight commander," said Selena.

"True, but in smaller detachments, a captain would have that responsibility. Earlier, you asked if there was anything I couldn't do."

"Yes, and you said something about ships."

"I've been on ships, and while I don't claim to know much about them, they don't hold any fear for me. The idea of going to court, however, is something I would gladly avoid."

"You surprise me," said Selena. "I would have thought you a natural in such circumstances. You come across as someone who is calm and collected, and you're amiable enough to carry on a conversation."

"On a battlefield, definitely, but in a palace, surrounded by nobles? That's a whole different thing."

"You'll do great," said Danica. "After all, you managed to behave with the baroness."

"Baroness?" said Selena. "Now that sounds like an interesting story. You must tell me more."

Charlaine opened her mouth to speak, but as luck would have it, Sister Loretta appeared, ringing a bell to call the knights back to work. They all rose, their meals left unfinished.

"Looks like it'll need to wait till another time," said Charlaine.

4

PROMOTION

Summer 1097 SR

The assessments continued over the next two days. With weapon skills out of the way, the focus shifted to administrative capabilities. This involved the ability to read and write as well as organizational skills.

Added into the mix was learning how to interview a prospective new sister—an important part of recruitment and the only way to ensure their order continued to grow. They also needed to learn bookkeeping to safeguard the financial health of their commands. This particular skill came easily to Danica, who had a mind for details. Charlaine, on the other hand, struggled. She'd helped her mother with the smithy's accounts for years, but the finances of a temple command were far more complex than anything she had ever expected.

Adding to the pressure was the announcement of a formal dinner at the end of the week following the weekly knights' assembly. On such occasions, all the orders would gather at the great courtyard before the Council of Peers, where promotions were handed out, punishments dealt with, and important announcements made.

Charlaine was informed she would receive official recognition of her new rank of captain. That alone didn't bother her, but the need to make a speech at the formal dinner afterwards wore on her.

"Just be yourself," said Danica.

They sat in Charlaine's room, ostensibly to go over the day's assessment, but they were spending more time letting off steam than anything else.

"I'm not one for speeches," Charlaine admitted.

"You've spoken in front of nobles before, not to mention commanding patrols."

"That's different. I have to stand up before the entire order. That's a far cry from half a dozen friends."

"It wasn't friends you spoke to at the baroness's estate. At least not initially."

"Captain Giselle was there for support."

"And I'm here now," said Danica.

Charlaine reached out, taking her hand. "Yes, you are, and I'm extremely grateful for that. I suppose the problem isn't so much that I have to speak, but I have nothing to say. When we were in Rizela, I had a plan to present, but here? What in the name of Saint Agnes could I speak of?"

"Talk about Ilea."

"I can't. It's too painful. Like you, all those deaths still haunt me."

"Then talk about the sisterhood: about Cordelia, Teresa, and the others. What if you spoke of Sister Giselle and how she influenced you?"

"I'm not sure that would be wise," said Charlaine. "Her name doesn't appear to carry much weight here."

"You could always discuss politics."

Charlaine's face grew serious. "Politics. That word comes up a lot around here."

"What makes you say that?"

"Sister Loretta advised me to avoid politics, and then Selena more or less suggested the same thing."

"And?"

"Doesn't that strike you as odd? We're supposed to be preparing to visit the courts of the Continent. You'd think politics is exactly the kind of thing we should be involved in."

"There's a difference between understanding such things and actively participating."

"Is there?" said Charlaine. "Our order is sworn to protect women. Our very existence makes a political statement."

"Do you believe this has something to do with Brother Mateo's warning?"

"I'm not sure, but I'm starting to feel like there are two completely different ideologies going on here, both struggling for dominance."

Danica frowned. "Would you care to explain that to a mere sister knight?"

"When I met the Grand Mistress, she appeared to appreciate the efforts of Giselle. Everyone else, however, seems to dismiss her. It's almost as if..."

"As if what?"

"Giselle showed the entire Continent we could be taken seriously as a force on the battlefield. I think that ruffled a few feathers."

"You did the same thing in the south."

"We both did," said Charlaine, "and I think there's some resentment because of that."

"Resentment? But we saved Ilea!"

"You remember Captain Nina?"

"How could I forget? The only thing she was ever passionate about was getting a promotion." Danica's eyes opened wide in understanding. "I get it now. She wanted to follow the rules and advance in the order, just like Selena said."

"What do you think would have happened had the raiders come with her in charge?"

"I can't say for certain, although doubtlessly, it wouldn't have ended well."

"Giselle encouraged us to think for ourselves. If it hadn't been for her, we never would have rebuilt the smithy."

"Or set up the watchtowers," added Danica. "And Nina would never have encouraged you to take your plan to the baroness."

"Precisely, but change comes at a price."

"Yes, and it makes people uncomfortable. I suppose that means some folks here aren't going to like us."

"Come now," said Charlaine. "Don't be glum; everyone likes you."

"Erika didn't."

"Not at first, but you eventually won her over. We'll just need to do the same thing here."

"And have you a plan for doing this?"

"Not yet, but I'm working on it."

"There's more, isn't there?" said Danica. "I can tell from that look you get."

"What look?"

"The one where you stare off into the middle of nowhere. I can almost hear your mind thinking."

Charlaine laughed. "I must pay more attention to my manner. You're right though. There is more to this. The two ideologies are one thing, but add in the warning of Brother Mateo, and it takes on a darker meaning. I believe the rot he spoke about might threaten the very existence of the orders, or at least he thought it did."

"Yes, but what is the rot, precisely?"

"Of that, I have no idea, but without further information, there's no way of knowing."

"Well, I, for one, have an idea," said Danica. "Would you like to hear it?"

"By all means."

"I discovered they keep an archive here in the Antonine. A history of all the orders."

"And?" pressed Charlaine.

"I thought it might be interesting to learn more about our order. Not only the basics, we all know those—I mean the details. Maybe we could find something that might explain this behaviour?"

"Which behaviour? The desire to blindly follow the rules or to use one's initiative?"

"Either... or both. Look," said Danica, "I know there's a good chance we'll find nothing, but at least it's a start. This whole assessment thing will be over soon enough, and then we should have a few days before our actual training begins. It's the perfect opportunity."

"You're right, but we'll need to give some thought as to where to start. After all, the order is over a thousand years old. We can't possibly read everything. I would suggest we start with the events surrounding Giselle's battle, especially the aftermath. That will likely give us some idea about what people thought of it at the time."

"How will that help?"

"Her actions were instrumental in winning the battle, yet someone painted her in a bad light. We need to find where it all started."

The end of the week finally arrived, and with it, a conclusion to the constant testing just in time to prepare for the evening's ceremonies. As a fighting order, the Temple Knights of Saint Agnes wore a tabard that fell to their knees, but a longer surcoat was used for occasions like this. It presented an impressive sight but took some getting used to. It wasn't hard to walk in, but the question was what to do with the excess material while mounted? Luckily, such thoughts were unnecessary when they realized the entire knight's assembly would occur on foot.

The sisters gathered informally in front of the commandery later that morning. This allowed the senior members of the order to ensure all assembled understood the coming proceedings and allowed for time to adjust any ill-fitting surcoats. Soon after, they adjourned to the dining hall for their midday meal to find it consisted of only bread and water.

"Are they to starve us now?" said Danica.

"It's symbolic," explained Selena. "It's meant to represent the purity and sacrifice of our order."

"So we have to sacrifice our meat?"

"Have you no knowledge of our traditions?"

"It must be a local tradition," said Charlaine. "It's not practiced outside of the Antonine."

"Maybe," said Selena, "but you're here now, and that means you have to observe it."

Danica's belly growled. "It's not me you must convince—it's my stomach."

"You'll survive. Besides, you need to leave room for later."

"Oh yes, the formal dinner. I'd forgotten about that." Danica turned to Charlaine. "Did you decide what you're going to talk about?"

"Yes. I'm going with your suggestion to speak of the sisterhood."

"That's probably the safest course of action."

"Safe?" said Selena. "What's that supposed to mean?"

"Merely that she doesn't want to offend anyone."

"Who would you offend? You know the dinner is only for our own order, don't you?"

"Yes, but that's still a lot of sisters," countered Charlaine. "I've never talked to that many people in my life, plus the Grand Mistress herself will be present. That makes it even worse."

"That's not all," said Selena. "Maybe I shouldn't be telling you this, but there's a rumour the Matriarch of Saint Agnes will attend."

"Is that normal?"

"Very much so from what I've been told."

"Don't look now," said Danica, "but it seems our meal is over. Everyone is heading back outside."

"Come along, then," said Charlaine. "We don't want to be late."

The Temple Knights of Saint Agnes assigned to the Antonine formed five full companies. In a separate company led by Sister Loretta, the visitors, including Charlaine and Danica, followed their fellow knights as they marched out of the commandery and up the grand avenue leading to the Council of Peers. Here, they joined their brother orders, falling into line facing the building whose front consisted of a great set of stone steps. A platform protruded from above these, accessible only from the top, an arrangement designed to allow the Primus to address the faithful.

Charlaine had never seen anything like it. Even the great temple in Rizela paled in comparison to the structure before them.

The sisters remained in place as a small group of Ragnarites took up the position beside them, looking immaculate in their green-and-white tabards. Danica, tired of waiting, began to shuffle her feet, complaining under her breath about the delay.

A murmur spread throughout the crowd before a hush fell over all when a solitary figure, dressed in white and gold, took to the balcony. With a mantle of grey hair below a bald pate, it looked as if he wore a crown. But there was no denying he captured everyone's attention, for this was the Primus—the leader of the entire Church.

"Brothers and sisters," he began, his voice strong and steady. "We stand here today to honour those who serve the Saints."

As he spoke, the grand masters of the six orders came out of the building, descending to take positions by their respective Temple Knights. The Primus kept talking, but Charlaine struggled to hear the words as the wind carried away his voice.

He mentioned something about promotions, and then suddenly Sister Loretta told her to step forward. Charlaine moved from the ranks, marching towards Captain Nicola, who stood just in front of the Grand Mistress. Two other sister knights soon joined her, standing side by side. Captain Nicola waited as the other orders performed a similar action, then turned precisely and bowed.

"Grand Mistress," she said. "The candidates are present and accounted for."

The Grand Mistress stepped closer, looking each sister in the eyes, a hint of a smile creasing her lips. "It is with great happiness I bestow upon each of you the rank of Temple Captain. Sister Charlaine, step forward and kneel."

Charlaine did as she was bid, her head bowed. Two other sister knights appeared at her side and grasped her surcoat, pulling it over her head to remove it.

"Agnes has seen fit to give you the courage and wisdom to serve this august order. Let our blessed Saint watch over you and keep you safe." Two more shadows loomed over her, and then they placed a new surcoat over her shoulders.

"Arise, Charlaine deShandria, Temple Captain of Saint Agnes."

She stood, her eyes meeting those of the Grand Mistress.

"Be well," the woman said in a low voice, "but be careful and guard your tongue." Then she raised her voice once more. "Return to your sisters," she commanded before turning to the next candidate.

Charlaine wheeled around, marching to resume her original position in the company. It was only when she halted beside Danica that she took the time to examine her new surcoat.

The Temple Knights of Saint Agnes wore a scarlet surcoat emblazoned with three waves. However, instead of the white stitching she was used to, her new surcoat was embellished with silver thread. Charlaine smiled. Only the ceremonial coat was so marked, for sister knights wore no symbols in battle save for that of their order. Thus, the marking of rank would only be seen at court or on occasions such as this.

"Looks good on you," whispered Danica.

Charlaine couldn't help but smile. "Thank you."

In their absence, someone had gone to great lengths to rearrange the dining hall. The Grand Mistress and the senior members of the order would sit at one end of the hall while lines of tables ran the length of the room, allowing each sister to view the head table merely by turning to the side. Charlaine was guided to her chair by a lay sister.

"Your seat is here," her host announced before leaving the new captain to her own devices.

Charlaine took in those around her. Across from her sat the other two new captains, Collette and Isabeau, chatting away like they'd known each other for years. Someone squeezed past her, then took a seat to her right, only to be revealed as Danica.

"I believe this is reserved seating," Charlaine whispered.

"I know, but the lay sister told me this was where I should sit."

"It appears someone's looking out for me after all."

Danica looked up and down the line of tables. "Oh look, we're up here with all the captains."

Charlaine chuckled. "Don't let it go to your head."

Captain Collette looked across at her. "Say, you're Sister Charlaine, aren't you? Sorry, I mean Captain Charlaine?"

"Yes, I am, and this is Sister Danica."

"I hear you made quite an impression on the Grand Mistress."

"I don't know about that."

"She's being modest," said Danica. "It's one of her weaknesses."

"I wouldn't say weakness," commented Isabeau. "Rather, I would say it's a strength. After all, Saint Agnes says humility is next to saintliness."

"She said no such thing," declared Collette.

"Well, perhaps I'm paraphrasing."

"You two know each other?" asked Charlaine.

"Yes, we served together back in Reinwick."

"Isn't that on the coast?"

"Indeed, just north of Andover. It's a duchy."

"Andover?" Charlaine turned to Danica. "That's your home, isn't it?"

"Not anymore," replied the young knight, "but yes, I was born there. Actually, it has two coasts: one to the east and a smaller one to the west."

"And which one did you live on?"

"The east. It has better fishing, or so I'm told."

The room fell silent. They all looked up to see the Grand Mistress entering, followed by her regional commanders. Everybody stood as they took their seats, then at a nod from Captain Nicola, they sat back down.

Sister Kaylene Gantzmann had held the post of Grand Mistress for more than twenty years. Now, in her declining years, there was talk of her relinquishing the position, making way for younger blood, but Charlaine had her doubts. In their brief meeting, the Grand Mistress projected the impression her health was still intact. The thought that such talk was politically motivated annoyed Charlaine.

The Grand Mistress stood, drawing all eyes towards her.

"Fellow sisters," she began, lifting a goblet of wine, "I begin this evening's festivities with a toast." She waited as each sister raised their cups. "To Primus Anton Schulinger—may he enjoy the best of health."

She took a sip, the knights following her example.

"The Order of Saint Agnes has a long and hallowed history, one which has brought the teachings of our blessed Saint to all corners of the Continent. A large reason for this was the tireless efforts of the Matriarch of Saint Agnes herself, Mother Julianne Rydel. May her leadership be strong and glorious."

Again a sip, and then she set the cup down, waiting for the room to settle into silence once more.

"Mother Julianne couldn't be with us this evening but sends her best wishes and congratulations to those elevated in rank this day. Now, I know the last thing you want to hear is me rambling on about the glory days of the order, so I think it only right I turn over the pulpit to our new captains, don't you?"

The crowd cheered, the noise nearly shaking the very roof off the hall. She waited for it to die down before continuing. "Our first speaker this evening will be Sister Charlaine deShandria, who came to our order late in life, giving up the life of a master smith to take up her Holy vows. In her first assignment to Ilea, she proved instrumental in fighting off raiders. She also contributed greatly to the defeat of Halvaria in the great sea battle known as the Battle of Alantra." There was a pause as a murmur spread throughout the room. There'd been rumours of Charlaine's accomplishments, but few had given them much credit. Now, however, with the Grand Mistress confirming things, it took on a whole new life. She smiled for a moment before she raised her hands to hush the voices.

"Now, let's hear from Sister Charlaine herself, shall we?"

She sat, letting the applause grow.

Charlaine looked at Danica. "Here goes nothing."

"You'll be fine. Just be yourself."

Charlaine stood, receiving applause for her actions. She should have felt happy at the recognition but couldn't shrug off a feeling of... unease? Her eyes roamed around the room, looking at the crowd. Hundreds of sister knights were here, each staring back at her. Some looked enthralled, others bored, but the ones she noticed the most were those with malice in their eyes. What was it she was seeing? Jealously, perhaps? Or something more sinister?

"Sisters," she began, waiting as all fell silent once more. "I am but a humble smith, a woman who joined the order late in life. I was an only child, yet in the brief time I have served Saint Agnes, I've come to think of my fellow sisters as my family." She paused, overcome with emotion. The audience appeared to be hanging on her every word. She closed her eyes to fight her panic. Things only got worse as the silence lingered. Opening her eyes, she looked at Danica, who simply nodded. There was her strength.

"I won't bore you with the details about my exploits, but I do wish to acknowledge the fact that I didn't act alone. If not for the bravery and courage of my fellow sisters, we would not have been victorious. Some of those same sisters gave their lives in service to our blessed Saint, so I honour their contributions today with a toast." She held up her cup. "To Sister Helena, the first to fall. She lies in the crypt of the fallen in Rizela where all such heroes go."

They all took a drink, but Charlaine remained standing. "And to Sister Aurelia, who now lies at the bottom of the Shimmering Sea. Gone, but never forgotten."

A great sadness built within her, choking her words in her throat. She looked once more to Danica, but the raven-haired knight had tears streaming down her face.

Charlaine's gaze shifted to the head table to see indifference. The sight angered her, so much so, she threw caution to the wind. "Last but not least, I must thank Captain Giselle. Without her encouragement and training, I would have been woefully unprepared to meet the enemy." She drained her cup before sitting back down.

Around the room, only a few joined her toast. Others simply glared at her as if she had slapped their faces. Is this what the order had come to?

THE ARCHIVES

Summer 1097 SR

T he temple records were housed in the Council of Peers, the very same
building where the Primus had addressed them. Danica entered
through the front doors to be quickly met by a Temple Knight of Saint
Augustine.

"Sister," the man said. "What can I do for you today?"

"I'm looking for the archives," replied Danica. "I understand they're
located somewhere within."

"They are, but access to this building is limited to those in authority.
Have you permission from your superior?"

"Captain Charlaine sent me," she replied, thinking on her feet.

He stared at her a moment, likely trying to decide if she told the truth,
but then he simply nodded. "The building is large, and we can't have you
wandering around and getting lost. If you wait here, I'll see if I can't find
someone to take you there."

"Thank you," said Danica.

The Augustine wandered over to his companion, sending the fellow
deeper into the labyrinthine structure. A short while later, a lay brother
wearing the brown cassock of Saint Mathew appeared. He paused,
exchanging words with the guard before wandering over to where Danica
waited.

"I assume you're the one looking for the archives?"

"I am. I'm Sister Danica."

"Greetings, I'm Brother Thorley. I have the honour of being one of the archivists here. If you'll follow me, I'll show you the way."

He led her through a doorway and then along a long hall that ran the length of the place. Towards its end, he opened a door that revealed a wide set of stairs heading down into an area with much lower ceilings and narrower halls. Brother Thorley took a moment to light a lantern that hung on the wall just past the stairwell.

"The archives are down here," he said, "though it would help if I knew what you were looking for. Our collection is substantial and occupies a large portion of this floor."

"I seek information about the Battle of Erlingen," said Danica. "Have you heard of it?"

"I've heard of the place, but there've been several battles there over the years. Are you referring to the most recent one, back in ninety-five?"

"No, this one would've been earlier, perhaps ninety-two or three?"

"Oh yes, I know it well. There's a very nice account by one of my brethren, a Brother Cyric."

"I recognize that name," said Danica. "His testimony was presented at Captain Giselle's trial."

The lay brother's eyebrows rose, but he said nothing. Instead, he simply motioned with his free hand for her to follow, leading her through a doorway into an immense room with columns set every ten feet or so, arching up to support the low ceiling.

"We've done our best to organize these records by date, but it is a never-ending battle. Add to that the carelessness with which visitors treat them, and you can understand how difficult the task becomes."

"Carelessness?"

"Yes," said Thorley. "Many request a record and then fail to return it to its proper location. Not that we have many visitors down here, you understand. Usually, it's the higher-ups who come here, seeking some clarification on a subject."

Bookshelves divided the room, although, in truth, no tomes were present. Instead, scrolls and folded papers occupied the space, many held in small wooden trays.

Brother Thorley picked his way through several of these, quickly peering at one or two papers before continuing on. At last, his searching came to a halt, and he placed his lantern down. Reaching out, he grasped a scroll case and unscrewed the end, out of which he retrieved an illuminated manuscript. This he rolled out to show her.

"Here it is." He passed it to Danica. "An account of the battle."

Danica took the document, sitting on the floor to allow the light to play over it. The writing was in a sure, steady hand, but what drew her eyes were the illustrations. "Are all the documents down here so decorative?"

"Not at all, but Brother Cyric likes to be precise, thus the illustrations. Is this what you're looking for?"

"I don't know yet. I'll need to read it. Is this the only account of the battle?"

"No, there are three others. I'll see if I can find them for you, shall I?"

"If you would be so kind."

She began reading through the account while Brother Thorley searched through the records.

The battle was a fairly straightforward melee, with opposing armies lining up to face each other on a relatively flat field. Once the fighting started, however, it became a bloody affair, with each side inflicting tremendous losses on the other. Of particular note was a clash between two mages, one wielding the power of fire, the other of air.

It was then that she found the reference to Giselle. Of how she had heroically stood with her fallen sisters, fighting to the very end, only to be carried to safety by Brother Cyric. He heaped high praise upon her actions, but details concerning her rescue were scarce. In frustration, Danica tossed the scroll to the floor, an action that didn't go unnoticed.

"Is there a problem?" asked Brother Thorley.

"This account fails to reveal the details I need."

The lay brother smiled knowingly. "Likely because Brother Cyric was being too modest. I have another account here, if you're interested, told by a lay brother named Brother Delmont. He affirms Cyric defeated the Fire Mage, then carried your sister knight to safety."

"I assume you read this before?"

"I have. Rarely do we come across an account like this, especially from my order."

"Meaning?"

"It is both detailed and enthralling, a far cry from the dry reports we so often see from my brethren." He passed her the account, allowing her time to read it through. "Is that more suited to your needs?"

Danica passed it back. "Not quite. I understand what happened there..."

"But?"

She smiled. "But it doesn't tell the entire story. Both of these accounts remark on the decisive part the sisters played in the battle. Yet neither explains why Sister Giselle is scorned."

"Could it be due to the loss of her command?"

"I thought of that," said Danica, "but other leaders lost troops. Why does her reputation suffer, while others go unscathed? I hoped to find the first record that spoke negatively of her, to see where this problem originated."

"Ah, I might be able to help you with that, but it shall require us to move further back into the archives."

"Why is that?"

"It was likely seen as a disciplinary matter. Anything of that nature is kept in a separate area, in case it's needed for a tribunal."

He took a moment to return the original document to the scroll case before picking up the lantern once more. "Come along. Let's see if we can get to the bottom of this mystery, shall we?"

Danica trailed along behind him. "How long have you worked here?"

"Years, but don't ask me the exact number. My memory's not that good anymore. I started here after my induction into the order. Before that, I was a scholar in service to a wealthy noble, if you can believe it. After he died, I lost my sponsor."

"And so you became a lay brother?"

"It was either that or starve. Don't get me wrong, I was always a devout worshipper, but I never, in my wildest dreams, thought I'd end up taking Holy vows, at least not as a child."

"Life has a way of taking us in unexpected directions," noted Danica.

"So it does," Brother Thorley agreed. "Ah, here we are." He pointed to some overstuffed shelves. "Somewhere in amongst all that paper is the answer you seek." He glanced around, locating an unlit lantern and bringing it closer. "Give me a moment to get this lit for you, and then I'll leave you in peace."

Danica stared at the great pile of papers. This was going to take a while.

It was well past noon before she found what she was looking for. After the battle, a Temple Knight of Saint Cunar, a commander, no less, had taken umbrage with the fact Giselle had not died with her fellow sister knights. His report to his own regional superior detailed in no uncertain terms of how she had disgraced the honour of the order. It was written by someone named Brother Erskine, and if the date were to be believed, it had been penned only a week after the events took place.

Soon she located other missives of a similar nature, all dated after Erskine's letter. Determined to find out more about this individual, she sought out Brother Thorley. He, in turn, directed her to yet another section of the archives where they kept the records of individual knights.

She finally found what she was looking for by dinner and left the building seeking Charlaine.

. . .

Charlaine, for her part, was busy all day long with the responsibilities of being the duty officer. This mainly involved checking doors to ensure they were locked and inspecting rooms to make sure no illicit goods were found inside. It wasn't the most exciting responsibility, yet it had to be done, else the order would descend into chaos, or so the commander had informed her.

It was, in truth, hard to take the duties seriously. Her breaking point came when she was forced to discipline a sister for having an extra blanket in her room—apparently, a gross violation of the rules.

Charlaine returned to her assigned office to avoid any further confrontations and began reading through the duty logbook. Here, the officer of the day would make a note of any irregularities, the purpose being to inform their superiors of what transpired on a day-to-day basis.

The last few days had been fairly mundane, but as she skimmed over the older notes, she found her own name mentioned. The date coincided with her arrival, and that would have been the end of it had Charlaine not been curious. With little else to keep her busy, she went further back in time to find an entry indicating the person on duty was to inform Temple Commander Hjordis should Charlaine arrive.

She stared at the logbook, trying to make sense of the entry. Was it simply informing the duty officer of her imminent arrival or something more sinister? Had she not met Brother Mateo on the way into town, she might have dismissed the idea as trivial. Now she wondered if the opposite might be true. Try as she might, she could see no reason for such strange behaviour, so she put it aside for the time being, contenting herself with finishing her shift, which ended at dinnertime.

She attempted to occupy her mind with other thoughts, trying to guess where her next assignment would take her. Still, her thoughts kept drifting back to Brother Mateo's words. Finally relenting, she went even further back in the logbook, looking for any similar warnings concerning other people.

Another skim through soon confirmed there was no sign of any others, forcing her to consider the ramifications. Someone was watching for her— the real question was who? She resolved to discover who this Commander Hjordis was and what her interest was in Charlaine's arrival.

Her replacement finally appeared in the form of Sister Collette, bringing an end to such thoughts. She passed over the book, informed her fellow sister that nothing of note had occurred during her shift, then made for the dining hall, intent on getting some food into her belly.

She was halfway down the hallway when she noticed a pair of knights heading in the opposite direction. As they drew closer, however, they moved to intercept her.

"Sister Charlaine," greeted the larger of the two.

"That's me. What can I do for you?"

The sisters halted, one standing before her, the other shifting to cut off any retreat. "We just wanted to have a word with you."

"Then speak."

"It's come to the attention of some that you're poking your nose in where it's not welcome."

"What's that supposed to mean?" asked Charlaine.

"That little stunt you pulled could get you into a lot of trouble."

"What stunt is that?"

The taller sister sneered. "You're a captain now. You should sit back and learn to enjoy the privileges of rank rather than stirring up a hornet's nest."

"And what hornet's nest would that be?"

"I believe you know as well as I."

"And if I choose not to?"

"This is simply a warning. Step out of line again, and the consequences will be dire."

"Is that a threat?"

The woman smiled. "You may take that any way you like."

"Who sent you?" asked Charlaine. "Was it Commander Hjordis?"

She saw the twitch, confirming her suspicions. "Look, I don't want any trouble. I promise from now on I'll behave in a manner more suitable to a Temple Captain. Will that suit your purposes?"

The knight stepped aside, a smile tugging at the corners of her mouth. "Of course. We're not your enemy—all we want is for the order to prosper."

"As do I," said Charlaine.

They parted, letting her continue to the dining hall, where she quickly spotted Danica amongst the others. She gathered some food and took a seat opposite her comrade.

"I wondered when you were going to show up," said Danica. "I have some interesting news."

"So do I," said Charlaine, lowering her voice. "A couple of our sister knights just threatened me.

"Threatened? Why?"

"They appear to have taken offence at me speaking about Giselle. Talked of me following the rules and behaving myself."

"They don't know you very well, do they?"

"No, I can't say that they do."

"What are you going to do about it?"

"Do?" said Charlaine. "There's not much I can do. Wait, there was one more thing. I discovered someone was watching for my arrival, a commander by the name of Hjordis, although for what purpose I cannot say."

"Maybe this Hjordis simply serves the Primus and wanted to know when you arrived?"

"If that were true, then why threaten me? Why not simply tell me?"

"You make a compelling case. Unfortunately, I have no answer for you. I did, however, manage to track down the man responsible for starting this whole 'Giselle is a bad example' thing."

"And it was?"

"A Temple Commander named Erskine, a Cunar, if you can believe it. Though why he had an interest in Giselle is anyone's guess."

"I think it's time we took this to the Grand Mistress."

"Take what?" asked Danica. "It's not as if we have any actual proof of a conspiracy."

"True, and she may dismiss it out of hand, but we can't just leave it. Too much is at stake."

"So what is it that we do have?"

"A pair of names," said Charlaine. "One Cunar, the other Saint Agnes. Let's hope she can make a connection between them."

"And if she's in on this conspiracy?"

"Then it makes no difference what we do."

"I suppose that's true. When do we want to go see her?"

"We'll speak to Captain Nicola first thing in the morning and see when she can fit us in."

"And in the meantime?"

"Simple," said Charlaine. "We eat our dinner."

The office of the Grand Mistress was, as usual, guarded by a pair of Temple Knights. Thankfully, Captain Nicola was within hailing distance, leading to them being ushered into the aide's office.

"I'm afraid the Grand Mistress is quite busy," the captain said. "Is there something I can help you with?"

"This is for her ears alone," replied Charlaine. "It concerns a matter I'm sure she would find of immense interest."

"Has this something to do with Captain Giselle?"

Taken aback, Charlaine stared, open-mouthed. "How did you know?"

"Come now, it doesn't take a genius. We all heard your toast at dinner, not to mention the response, or should I say the lack thereof?"

"There's more."

"Go on," insisted Nicola.

"On our way to the Antonine, a former Temple Knight of Saint Cunar accosted us, warning us something was rotting the order from the inside."

"I hardly think the rantings of an excommunicate are something to consider reliable."

"And ordinarily, I'd agree," continued Charlaine, "but subsequent events support his supposition."

"In what way?"

"Several times I've been warned to not play politics and to mind my business and toe the line. Then just yesterday, I was approached by two sister knights and threatened."

Captain Nicola knitted her brows. "Can you identify those knights?"

"Possibly, but I doubt it would do any good. There were no witnesses." She noted the captain's response. "This doesn't surprise you. What is it you're not telling us?"

In answer, Sister Nicola rose. "Wait here," she commanded. "I'll be back shortly." She stepped from the room, leaving Charlaine and Danica the sole occupants.

"What do you make of that?" asked the raven-headed knight.

"I'm not sure."

"You don't suppose we put our foot in it, do you? What if she comes back with guards?"

"She won't."

"How can you be so sure?"

"There are guards just outside. If she'd wanted us arrested, all she needed to do was call out."

The door opened, revealing Captain Nicola. "Come with me," she said.

She led them to the door of the Grand Mistress, waiting as the guards opened it. Inside they went, the captain once more taking up her familiar position.

"Ah," said the Grand Mistress. "It seems we meet again, Captain Charlaine. I assume this is Sister Danica?"

"Yes, Your Grace."

"Come, take a seat. We have much to discuss."

6

THE GRAND MISTRESS

Summer 1097 SR

"What do you know of the history of our order?" asked the grand mistress.

"It was originally formed to protect Saint Agnes," replied Charlaine, "although she wasn't referred to as a saint until after her death. In essence, they were nothing more than bodyguards, but they eventually became guardians of our places of worship."

"That is the story that most are familiar with, but the order has been evolving ever since its founding. As you yourself experienced, we no longer simply guard temples. Our knights actively patrol regions, keeping women safe and safeguarding their lives and property. Of course, not every kingdom allows women to own land, and we must abide by the local laws, but we have become much more than a simple temple guard."

"I'm not sure where this is going," said Charlaine.

"There are some who are jealous of our successes and wish to see our role in the Continent diminished."

"You mean the Halvarians?"

"Doubtless they would wish us ill, but no, I was referring to others. The Petty Kingdoms are well named, for they'll fight amongst themselves in the blink of an eye. Many of them resent the power and influence of the Church, even as they rely on it to hold the threat of Halvaria at bay."

"And so they seek to weaken us?"

The grand mistress nodded. "So I believe. It's not that they openly oppose us, but their words carry great weight, and so constant has their condemnation been that now such doubt has carried to the order itself." She leaned forward, looking Charlaine directly in the eyes. "There are those within our ranks who feel our role should become less... how shall I put it —militaristic."

"Are you saying they want to disband the Temple Knights?"

"Not disband so much as reduce our influence. They would see us return to the ways of our ancestors, confining ourselves to guarding temples."

"I assume you don't agree?"

"No, I don't. We're trained warriors, just as much as the other orders. True, we rarely march to battle, but our sisters are as effective as any knight on the Continent when we do. If anything, I would say we need to encourage our members to take a more active role in events."

"More active?"

"I want the order to seek representation at all the courts of the Petty Kingdoms. Perhaps, if we can influence rulers, we can help keep them from falling back to the age-old habits that caused this near-constant strife with their neighbours."

"Then why not issue orders to that effect?" said Charlaine.

"That's easier said than done. I might be the Grand Mistress of the Temple Knights, but issuing orders and having them followed is only possible with the support of my commanders. I'm afraid many of those take exception to my ideas."

"Then replace them. You have the power."

"And do what? Lose half the order? No, we must win them over to my point of view."

"Our point of view," corrected Charlaine. She glanced quickly at Danica, who merely nodded. "We both feel the same as you."

The grand mistress sat back. "I hoped you'd say that. In many ways, you represent the future of the order, the two of you. You possess compassion and skill, yet you're not swayed by the opinions of others. These are the very qualities we need right now."

"And here I thought we were just stubborn," said Danica.

"Obstinacy has its uses as well, but you must take care, as you've already discovered. There are those who will work to discredit you. When you praised Giselle, you made yourself a target. Now, they will seek to damage your reputation in any way they can. I can protect you to a certain extent, but even I can be toppled."

"Surely not?" said Charlaine. "You are the grand mistress. That's a lifetime appointment, isn't it?"

"I serve at the whim of the Matriarch of Saint Agnes. Were she to order me to step down, I would have little choice but to obey."

"And you believe she would do that?"

"Though it saddens me to say so, I believe it to be inevitable. There is already mounting pressure on her from the other orders, particularly the Cunars."

"The Cunars?"

"Yes. They see our increased battle readiness as a threat to their supremacy as the leaders of the Holy Army. It wasn't always thus. Half a century ago, our order commanded the Holy Fleet in Corassus. It was, in some ways, the height of our success, but then we received a new matriarch, one who was not as dedicated to our success. Control of the fleet fell to the Cunars and the rest, as they say, is now history."

"Until Giselle came along," added Charlaine.

"Yes, her example lit a fire within the order. It showed how we can make a difference in the politics of the Petty Kingdoms. Your actions in Ilea added to that reputation, although somehow you managed to share that glory with the Holy Fleet. That was a very shrewd move."

"It was hardly intentional. I did what I thought was necessary—we all did."

"And that shall not go unrewarded. When last we met, I told you I'd be sending you north. You won't be leaving right away, of course. You still need to complete your training, but I've decided to send you to the Duchy of Reinwick. Korvoran, its capital, to be exact. There you shall take command of the local garrison of sister knights." Her gaze swivelled to Danica. "As to your fate, I have something a little more challenging in mind."

"Care to explain?" said Danica.

"You are to speak of this to no one, but I am entrusting you with the task of raising a northern fleet. You'll only start with a single vessel, and you'll report to Captain Charlaine. It will be your responsibility to acquire a ship, equip it, man it, and carry out regular patrols off the coast."

"And the entire crew is to be comprised of Temple Knights?"

"Eventually, but to begin with, I suspect you'll need to hire locals to operate the vessel. You shall, however, have a contingent of sister knights to act as shipboard warriors. The number will depend on what size ship you select. I shall provide you sufficient funds for the task, but until such time as you actually sail, it needs to be kept as quiet as possible."

"Might I ask why all the secrecy?"

"The Temple Knights of Saint Cunar will insist they should take command of any military assets."

"And when they do?" asked Danica.

"The ship and its crew are to be the sole responsibility of the Temple Knights of Saint Agnes. I will brook no interference from any of the other orders. Do I make myself clear?"

"Yes, Your Grace."

The grand mistress returned her gaze to Charlaine. "As for you, I should point out that as captain, you will be the ranking member of our order in the region. As such, I fully expect you to exert your influence at the duke's court."

"To what end, Your Grace?"

"The Duchy of Reinwick is dominated by a war-mongering child. I would see this behaviour tempered, and I think you're just the person to do it."

"Me, deal with nobility?"

"You're already skilled in dealing with those in authority. After all, you dealt with the Baroness of Rizela and the Admiral of the Holy Fleet, not to mention the self-proclaimed King of Calabria."

"She has you there," said Danica.

"I'll concede the point, but those encounters were far from formal occasions."

"Fear not. You will not be sent unprepared." The grand mistress lifted a document from her desk. "I have here your leadership assessment. It seems you're more than qualified in military matters but show a weakness for social etiquette. We shall take matters in hand to ensure that we rectify that shortcoming." Her eyes swivelled to Danica. "As for you, I believe a few lessons in fleet organization are in order. You won't be just commanding a ship, you'll be laying the groundwork for an entire fleet."

"When do we leave, Your Grace?" asked Charlaine.

"Not for some weeks yet. Your lessons will begin as soon as I can arrange them. Once you complete those to my satisfaction, you'll head out. In the meantime, you must keep these plans to yourself, understood?"

"Yes, Your Grace," they echoed in unison.

"Good. Now, is there anything else you wanted to talk to me about?"

"I made a discovery," Danica offered.

"Go on."

"I was researching the Battle of Erlingen, the one in which Sister Giselle fought."

"To what end?"

"We were trying to discover where the negative opinion of her started."

"And what did you discover?"

"The first mention of her in a bad light is from someone named Brother Erskine, a Temple Commander of Saint Cunar."

"That's no surprise there," noted the grand mistress. "The Cunars want all the glory for themselves. What was the gist of the complaint?"

"That Giselle should have died with her command."

"That's ridiculous," said Charlaine.

"I would agree," added the grand mistress, "and a complete waste of a valued knight, but you know how stubborn our brethren can be when it comes to such things."

"So what do we do about it?" asked Danica.

"There's nothing you CAN do other than put it behind you."

"And the threats against us?"

"You must deal with them as best you can. I won't tell you these assignments will be easy, but they are necessary to move forward as an order. I know this puts a lot of pressure on you two, but I'm hoping your example will inspire others to see the value in the Temple Knights of Saint Agnes."

"We will do all we can, Your Grace," said Charlaine.

"Good, that's all I ask. Now, you'd best go and get some rest. Once your training begins, you'll have little time for anything else."

They both rose, bowing deeply. Captain Nicola led them back into the hallway.

"Well," said Danica. "That was certainly unexpected."

"Has she no one else she can trust?" asked Charlaine.

"Very few," replied the captain. "Which makes your secrecy of utmost importance. If word got out of your new assignments, there would be a lot of disgruntled people."

"I'm not sure what you mean," said the young knight.

"I do," said Charlaine. "The grand mistress would be accused of playing favourites. Hardly the type of thing the matriarch would approve of."

"If you have any questions in the future," said Captain Nicola, "run them by me, and I'll see they're passed on. That way, we can avoid any gossip."

"Is it really that bad?"

The captain nodded. "I'm afraid so. It wasn't always this way, but we've seen a constant erosion of our privileges as an order in the last few years. If you're both successful, we'll halt that, possibly even reverse it."

"And if we fail?" asked Charlaine.

"Then the order as we know it may cease to exist."

That evening found Charlaine looking over the Book of Saint Agnes, searching for anything that might help their cause, but there was little there in terms of the Saint's desire to form a temple order. Danica, on the other hand, pulled out a handful of crudely drawn maps.

"What have you got there?" asked Charlaine.

"I made a rough copy of some of the maps in the archives. I thought they might prove useful to us."

"I suppose it'll help us find the place."

"It's more than that," said Danica. "There's quite a complex political landscape in that part of the Continent."

"In what way?"

"Below Reinwick lies Andover—they've been rivals for years. They both want to dominate sea trade."

"And where is Erlingen?" asked Charlaine.

"South of Andover. We'll likely pass through it on the way north. They recently repelled an invasion attempt by Andover."

"When was this?"

"Two years ago. It failed due to the Duke of Erlingen's army capturing the King of Andover."

"And then what? Did the duke then invade Andover?"

"No, he was intent on demanding tribute. The entire area's been on the brink of war ever since. It would only take a small spark to ignite the entire region."

"The Duke of Reinwick must be the key," said Charlaine. "That's why the grand mistress put such an emphasis on him. What did she call him?"

Danica chuckled. "A war-mongering child."

"Is that accurate?"

"In what way?"

"Is he an actual child?"

"Most definitely not. He has children of his own. I suspect she was referring more to his behaviour. How are you with children?"

"I have little experience with them if truth be told. Still, I was a child once myself, so at least I have some idea what to expect."

"I don't envy you. It's going to be a difficult job."

"What about yours?" said Charlaine. "You will be the founding mother of an entire fleet. A person can't face much more pressure than that."

Danica shrugged. "Actually, I find the entire prospect quite exciting. I'm looking forward to getting on with it. I already have some ideas."

"Like what?"

"Well, for one thing, I wouldn't have them use oared galleys; they'd flounder in the Northern Sea."

"Then what would you propose, cogs?"

"No, they're too slow, although I suppose we might eventually need some for cargo purposes, ferrying supplies and whatnot. I'm thinking we'd need smaller, faster vessels, ones capable of making much better speed in the capricious winds of the north."

"You HAVE been giving this a lot of thought. How many of my knights are you going to steal?"

"Half a dozen, I should think, at least in the beginning."

"Then choosing those six will be our first priority once we arrive."

Sister Selena suddenly appeared at the door, and Charlaine wondered how much she overheard.

"Have you heard?" asked the newcomer. "They've assigned everyone's training."

"We'd best go take a look," said Danica.

The trio headed down the hall to where a group of sister knights gathered around a notice board.

"I'm to report to the practice field," said Selena. "Looks like more riding practice for me."

"I'm to report to the Temple of Saint Agnes," said Charlaine, "and seek out someone named Mother Avalyn."

"I know her," remarked another knight. "She's a lay mother rather than a knight. I'm guessing you need to learn the rules of court?"

"How did you know?"

The woman grinned. "This isn't my first time training here."

Charlaine searched for Danica's name. "It says here you're to report to the Cunar commandery."

The hallway drew quiet, all eyes turning on the raven-haired knight.

"Are you sure?" Danica replied.

"Absolutely. You're to seek out someone named Brother Leamund."

"Why in the Saint's name would they send her there?" asked Selena.

"I have no idea," replied Danica, "but I don't suppose I'm going to find out why by standing around here."

"You should be careful," warned Selena, lowering her voice. "The Temple Knights of Saint Cunar are not to be trusted."

"Why in the Continent would you say that?"

"They took the Holy Fleet from us. Now they want the rest."

"Surely you're exaggerating?" said Danica. "I mean, what else could they take?"

"Our reputation, for one."

"You're not suggesting they would do anything untoward, are you?"

"Like assaulting someone?" said Selena. "No, of course not, but they'll twist you to their way of thinking."

"Which is?"

"Women don't belong in fighting orders."

"Come now," said Danica. "I know they don't all believe that. Charlaine and I even worked with the Admiral of the Holy Fleet. He was a Cunar and showed us nothing but respect. He didn't hold anything against us for being part of the order."

"Suit yourself," said Selena, "but don't say I didn't warn you."

"Ignore her," said Charlaine. "These are official orders. Even a Cunar wouldn't use official regulations for personal gain."

"Why would one even want to see you?" asked Selena. "It's not as if you're the one who saved Ilea."

"But she did," said Charlaine. "If it hadn't been for Danica, we never would have made it back to the fleet. You shouldn't be so quick to dismiss her achievements."

"Come now, we both know you're the golden one here."

"What are you implying?"

"We all heard how you single-handedly saved Ilea and defeated the Halvarians."

"I'm not sure who you've been talking to, but nothing could be further from the truth. We all played an important part, Danica included."

"Even so, you're the sole one to earn a promotion, and after only a single assignment. If that doesn't smack of favouritism, I don't know what does."

"Do not confuse favouritism with ability," said Danica. "If you'd seen Charlaine in the thick of battle, you'd understand."

By this point, everyone had turned to witness the exchange. It was getting decidedly uncomfortable, especially with them both outnumbered so severely. The arrival of Sister Loretta quickly put an end to such thoughts.

"What's going on here?"

"Nothing," remarked Selena.

"It doesn't look like nothing. You, Sister Charlaine, what's happening here?"

"We were just discussing our new training assignments."

Loretta gave them all a withering glare. "Get back to your rooms. The hallway is no place for socializing."

They all hesitated, and for a moment, Charlaine wondered if the situation might not turn even worse.

"That's an order," bellowed Sister Loretta. "And if I see any of you loitering around here in future, I shall take your names to the grand mistress."

The sisters all fled, eager to be out from under the watchful eye of their instructor.

7

TRAINING

Summer 1097 SR

"This," said Mother Avalyn, "is the dining hall."

Charlaine looked around the room, noting its finery. A long table was set with a variety of cutlery, not to mention an assortment of plates, bowls, and cups, which boggled the mind.

"As you see," Avalyn continued, "there is seating for numerous individuals, but before we get to all that, we need to familiarize you with the basics of eating."

"I'm a grown woman," said Charlaine. "I already know how to eat."

"There's more to eating than simply stuffing food in your mouth. Take this, for example. Which knife would you use to begin your meal?"

Charlaine examined the place setting but could see no sign of where to begin. "The one on the outside?" she guessed.

A smile broke out on Mother Avalyn's face. "That's very good. There's hope for you yet! Now sit, and I shall go over the proper etiquette that such an honour demands.

The knight took her seat, then waited as the Holy Mother moved to the head of the table. "Much of what you learn here will be equally as applicable in court as it is within the order. As you know…"

Her voice droned on, and Charlaine struggled to keep up. It wasn't that she didn't want to learn how to conduct herself appropriately, but the ornate setting only seemed to remind her of Ludwig. She tried to get him out of her head, but his smiling face kept intruding. No, she reminded herself, that was all settled years ago. He was a baron's son, and she a simple swordsmith. Under pressure from his father, she'd been forced to leave Hadenfeld, joining the Order of Saint Agnes and eventually becoming a Temple Knight. Suddenly she became aware her host had fallen silent, and she looked up to see Mother Avalyn staring at her expectantly.

"Pardon?" asked Charlaine.

"Pay attention, girl. This is important."

Charlaine fought hard not to laugh. She was twenty-seven, hardly a girl anymore, but this whole situation struck her as funny.

"Am I amusing you?"

"No, of course not. Sorry, Mother."

"Now then, where was I? Oh yes, which implement do you use for soup?"

"The spoon?"

"Yes, but which one?"

Charlaine stared down at the table. There were three such spoons: which one to pick?

"The one on the outside?" she guessed again.

"Yes, precisely."

Relief washed over her.

"Now, what do you do when your host puts down his utensils?"

"You stop eating?"

"Is that a question," asked Mother Avalyn, "or a definitive answer?"

"An answer."

"You surprise me. I didn't think you'd been paying attention."

"I mean no disrespect, Mother, but I come from a humble background. Such things don't come easy to me."

Her mentor stopped. "You intrigue me. Tell me more."

"I was a smith by trade."

"You made nails?"

"No," said Charlaine. "Weapons and armour. I was even a member of a guild."

"A master smith! How interesting. What made you decide to give up the trade?"

"I had to leave the city under less-than-ideal circumstances."

"A child out of wedlock?" asked the Holy Mother.

"No, nothing like that. I developed a close friendship with a noble's son."

"I assume his father objected?"

"He did."

Mother Avalyn nodded her head sagely. "I've run across tales like this before. Tell me, was the parting amicable? Other than the father, I mean."

"It was. Mind you, it's all over now that I'm a Temple Knight. I would never allow anything to get in the way of my vows."

"You are a Sister of Saint Agnes, Charlaine, and as such, you are free to leave the order at any time. Surely they explained that to you when you joined?"

"They did, but the situation was untenable. The baron is a relative of the king."

"The king? My, you have expensive tastes."

Charlaine blushed. "Could we please return to the lesson?"

"I think it best we talk more first. I see in you someone with great potential, yet something is holding you back. I think it's this noble's son."

"I'm not sure I understand."

"You were rejected by a baron. Deep inside you sits resentment at the way he treated you. Until you can get over that, you shall have a hard time adjusting to the rigours of court."

"Who said anything about going to court?"

Mother Avalyn wore a patronizing smile. "My dear, do you really believe I don't know why you're here? I have known your grand mistress for years. Why, we even come from the same city."

"You knew her before she joined the order?"

"I did. Mind you, back then, she was just plain old Kaylene Ganztmann. We ran off together to join the Church, so in many ways, our story is not unlike yours."

"And did you join because of a lost love?"

"No. War came to Braymoor in the form of an invasion. Both our families were wiped out."

"I'm sorry."

"Why should you be? It wasn't as if you were there to prevent it."

"Might I ask how old you were?"

"Just old enough to become lay sisters. Kaylene didn't switch to a Temple Knight until some years later."

"And now she's the grand mistress."

"She is," said Mother Avalyn. "She is a remarkable woman and my oldest friend. A friend, I might add, who asked me to pay particular attention to your education. She must think a lot of you."

"I live to serve."

The lay mother barked out a laugh. "As do we all, but you would be better served to find a new expression. The lords of the Petty Kingdoms have little love for it."

"Why is that?"

"They view Temple Knights as a necessary evil, as they help stave off the inroads of Halvaria. At the same time, we represent a devotion to discipline and duty they see as excessive, maybe even fanatical."

"But we are not unthinking brutes."

"That does not alter their perception of us. Your grand mistress informs me you're going to Reinwick. Is that true?"

"I cannot say."

"I admire your loyalty, but it's wasted on me, for I know the truth of the matter. Now, what do you know of Duke Brondecker?"

"He's said to be annoying. I believe the word was childish."

The Holy Mother nodded. "An accurate description from what I've been told. He is also said to possess an enormous ego, one that his advisers encourage on a daily basis."

"I'm not sure I follow?"

"Once you get on his good side, it's rather a simple matter to remain there."

"And how do I that?"

"Flattery, mostly, but manners will help. It's common for senior members of the Church to be invited to a ruler's palace from time to time. The order's garrison in Korvoran is a single company consisting of fifty knights, at least in theory. As you know, these numbers can fluctuate quite a bit over time, but that's neither here nor there. What all of this means is that you, as a captain, will be the ranking member of our order, giving you access to these meetings."

"And that's it?"

"No, not in the least. You'll also need to hold your own against our fellow orders, the Cunars and Mathewites, both of which have been there for some time. That means you must work twice as hard to get noticed. It also means they might throw their seniority around a bit."

"You mean try to order me about?"

"I doubt they would be that blunt, but they might talk over you at court to put you in your place."

"I shall bear that in mind."

"All of that I can prepare you for. Saints know, I spent my fair share of time at court." She sat back, adopting a far-off look.

"Something wrong?" asked Charlaine.

"Wrong? No, I was just struck by an idea. Maybe you would find learning all of this easier with a different approach."

"Different, how?"

"I have friends in Reichendorf, wealthy friends who spend a great deal of time with nobility. I shall see if I can't arrange an invitation for us to a nice dinner or two. I think the experience would be good for you."

"I don't know what to say."

"How about thank you?"

"A most heartfelt thank you," said Charlaine.

Danica halted, her eyes settling on the immense building before her. The Cunar commandery was a massive structure with thickened walls and towers at the corners. Everything about it looked martial, with little thought to artistry, yet at the same time, it held a charm all its own. This was a warrior's fortress, of that there could be no doubt, for it represented centuries of warfare and a past steeped in conflict.

"Are you lost, Sister?"

She turned to see a Temple Knight of Saint Cunar, the sash proclaiming him a captain.

"I was told to report here," she answered.

He looked as though his eyes would pop out. "You are mistaken. Women are not allowed within the commandery."

"In spite of that, my orders say otherwise." She held out the note.

The Cunar moved closer, his head dropping to examine the paper. "This must be a mistake." He swept his gaze around the area, quickly spotting a knight wearing a lighter shade of grey.

"Commander Stramond!" he called out.

The individual turned, making for their position.

"What is it?" he demanded, his tone revealing his annoyance.

"This woman says she is to report to the commandery, sir."

"What of it?"

"She is a woman, sir. It is forbidden."

Commander Stramond looked at Danica with a critical eye. "I see no woman, merely a fellow Temple Knight. The restriction does not apply."

The knight stared at his superior, his mouth agape. He clearly wished to protest, but the commander spoke first, his words directed at Danica. "Who are you here to see?"

"Someone named Brother Leamund."

"That would be Captain Leamund to you," he replied. "Come, I'll show you the way." He set off at a quick pace, forcing her to catch up. "Never mind Captain Dimas," he said. "He's more used to dealing with new recruits."

"Is it true, what he said?"

"You mean about women? It is. Our warriors take a vow of celibacy, and in order to ensure that, the commandery is off limits to those of the opposite sex."

"So I'm really not allowed inside?"

"You are a Temple Knight of Saint Agnes and, as such, are considered a warrior rather than a woman."

"I'm not sure how I feel about that."

The commander grunted. "Take it as a compliment."

They entered the building, passing a pair of guards who gave her dirty looks, but the presence of her guide stopped them from taking any action. A grand set of stairs led upward, and Commander Stramond took them two at a time. The man must have been in his fifties yet appeared full of energy.

Danica struggled for breath as they reached the top, but her guide was relentless. Down the hall they went, past several checkpoints, each manned by brother knights.

Finally, he halted by a doorway, turning to one of the guards. "Is Captain Leamund about?"

"Yes, sir. He's inside."

The commander pushed open the door and stepped inside. "Come along," he said. "I haven't got all day."

They entered to find tables filled with models of ships scattered around the large room, while in the centre sat an oversized table, upon which were heaped all manner of papers: drawings, by the look of them.

An old man looked up from his work there. "Stramond? What are you doing here?"

"You have a visitor. Sister...?"

"Danica. I was sent over from the Commandery of Saint Agnes?"

"You were?" He looked up, trying to sort out something. "Oh, that's right. You spent time with the Holy Fleet, if I recall."

"Yes," she replied. "I was at the Battle of Alantra."

"Good, good. Come in. We have much to discuss."

"I assume I can leave you here?" asked Commander Stramond.

"Yes, by all means," said Danica. "And thank you, Commander. You've been most helpful."

The commander turned around abruptly and left, closing the door behind him.

Danica took in her surroundings, her eyes drawn to a ship model. "This is the *Triumphant*, isn't it?"

"It is, or at least it's the original design. Changes were made later in its construction, but for the most part, it's the same."

"Do you collect models like this?"

"Collect? No, I make them. I'm the one who designed the *Triumphant* and its sister ships."

"You're a ship designer?"

"Well," said Brother Leamund, "I prefer the term 'naval architect', but it's really the same thing."

"Fascinating." She moved to another model, this one even larger. "What's this?"

"An abandoned project. The common thought was that the more banks of oars, the better, but there comes a point where one sees diminishing returns. The cost alone would be astronomical, and the fact of the matter is the Church can no longer afford such luxuries."

She wandered over to the table, peering down at the drawings. "What have you here?"

He smiled. "I was told your grand mistress was looking at building a fleet." Her eyes swept the room as if worried someone might overhear. "Don't worry," he soothed. "No one else knows of this."

"Wasn't it meant to be a secret?"

"Yes, but your superiors thought it best to seek my advice on the matter. It is to be a cold-sea fleet, yes?"

"A cold sea?"

"Yes, in the north?"

"That's correct," she said. "It will initially be based out of Reinwick."

The old man nodded his head. "The north presents its own challenges from a ship design point of view. The water is cold, hence the name, but more importantly, the seas are rougher. Quite unsuitable for using galleys. Have you any familiarity with the north?"

"I was raised in a fishing village in Andover. We lived on the East Coast, astride the Great Northern Sea."

"Then you have likely seen it at its worst. The ships there are often clinker-built—that's when the planks are overlapping."

"My parents' fishing boat used that technique. It allows the hull to twist with the waves."

He nodded. "An interesting way to explain it, but essentially correct. What's of more concern is the nature of sea warfare. On the Shimmering Sea, ships ram and board, a tactic you saw at Alantra. However, the seas are rougher in the north, making such tactics much more difficult to accomplish. Have you given much thought to such things?"

"I have, in fact. I thought to train my knights how to use crossbows and hopefully mount a ballista on the ship, deck space permitting."

"A ballista might prove difficult. With the rough seas, you'll need to forgo oars which means more sails, and more sails means more rope, thus impeding the use of such a weapon."

"Have you an alternative solution?" she asked.

"I believe I do. It would see your people armed with grappling hooks. If you bring the enemy vessel alongside, you can board it. There are not many warriors who could repel a determined attack by Temple Knights."

"You make it sound easy."

"Easy, no, but effective," he said. "It would also require a fast ship. Otherwise, you'll never be able to get alongside."

"Yes, but close enough to use a grappling hook? Wouldn't that result in a collision?"

"That is one of the dangers. Are you familiar with arbalests?"

"The Dwarves use them, don't they?" said Danica. "Aren't they just very large crossbows?"

"They are. They could be mounted on the railing of your ship and used to send a grappling line across to the enemy. You could then attach the other end to a windlass and haul it closer."

"How heavy are they?"

"I'm glad you asked." He shuffled through some pictures. "I have here somewhere a sketch I made. Ah, here it is."

The drawing showed a double-handed cranequin used to reload the weapon. "We tried using some of these amongst the auxiliaries of our order, but reloading it in the field proved too time-consuming. On a ship, however, with the weapon mounted, the process would be much easier."

"And how many of these would you recommend?"

"That largely depends on the size of the ship. I would say, at a minimum, to mount one per side, forward of the mainsail. That would allow you to use them in a pursuit situation."

"Are these difficult to make?"

"Any maker of crossbows should be able to follow my instructions. I thought I might make up a pair of them and ship them to you, care of the Korvoran Commandery."

"That would be very much appreciated," said Danica. "Thank you."

"Now," said Brother Leamund, "let's talk sailing, shall we? Do you know what makes a fast ship?"

"A small waterline and a narrow beam?"

"Actually, you'd want a longer hull, generally resulting in a longer waterline, but you're correct about the width."

"So I'm looking for a long, thin boat?"

"More or less," he said. "It has to handle well, and that has more to do with the sails."

"I thought we might use a lateen rig," said Danica.

"Very good. It will slow you a little when the wind is behind you, but the triangular sail will enable you to sail almost directly into the wind if need be. Of course, such sails are rare in the north. I assume you observed them down in Ilea?"

"I did, and I was most intrigued by their handling."

"As you should be," said Brother Leamund. "Now, it's on to provisioning, I think."

They talked long into the afternoon.

8

SISTERS

Summer 1097 SR

D anica collapsed on her bed. The day had been a full one, spent poring
over ancient accounts of sea battles. Most were dull, but at least she
was beginning to understand how the Holy Fleet had evolved over the
years.

"Busy day?" said Charlaine.

"I never knew just how many battles the fleet had seen. You'd think we
were in a state of constant war."

"In effect, we are. The Holy Fleet has been trying to limit Halvarian
expansion for years."

"Well," said Danica, "we don't need to worry about that anymore. At least
not for quite some time. The Battle of Alantra destroyed any hope of
Halvarian dominance on the Shimmering Sea."

"Halvaria also has a coast on the Great Northern Sea. They say their
fleet harbours in amongst the Scattered Isles. They might not have troubled
the northern kingdoms just yet, but it's only a matter of time before they try
to assert their control there as well. I suppose that puts a lot of pressure on
you."

"You needn't remind me. I'm fully aware. It's why I'm working so hard to
absorb all the information I can. How long has it been now, a month?"

"Only three weeks," said Charlaine, "but it seems like ages since I saw
you at mealtimes."

"It can't be helped. There's so much to learn. How have the classes been going for you? Have you managed to embarrass yourself yet?"

Charlaine laughed. "It's not so bad once you get used to it. The nobles around here are polite enough, and if I use the wrong knife, they're more than willing to forgive the breach of manners."

"Do you believe you're ready to face the Duke of Reinwick?"

"Only time will tell, but I'm optimistic. How about you? Think you're prepared to take command of a fleet?"

Danica grimaced. "Let's start with a single ship, shall we?"

"And how are you to acquire one? Will you have one built?"

"I have the funds, but I thought it might be a better idea to purchase an existing one."

"Why is that?"

"Well, for one thing, I have no sense of what the shipyards are like in Korvoran, nor do I know what their skill level is. Purchasing an existing ship will allow me to research its history, find out what kind of a sailer it is, and how it handles the bad weather. There's a lot of that in the north."

"What?" asked Charlaine. "Bad weather?"

"Yes, storms can crop up with little warning. A person could sail out of the harbour on a cloudless morning and run into rain by noon. Of course, it's not the rain that's the problem so much as the waves. I suppose I'll need to find sisters who aren't susceptible."

"Susceptible to what?"

"Being seasick."

"And how do you do that?"

"Simple," said Danica. "Take them out on a ship."

"I sense a lot of sailing in our future."

"Well, sailing for me, but you'll be far too busy befriending the duke, not to mention running the commandery, or did you forget you're to become the new head of it?"

"Trust me," said Charlaine. "I haven't forgotten anything."

Footsteps approached, not the footfall of sandalled feet but those of boots. Moments later, a trio of sister knights appeared in the doorway.

"Sister Danica Meer?"

"Yes?"

"By order of Commander Hjordis, you are hereby placed under arrest. Surrender your weapons and come with us."

"What's the charge?" demanded Charlaine.

"That's none of your concern, Sister. I suggest you stay out of it."

Charlaine found her temper rising. "That's captain to you, and Sister Danica is under my command. I have a right to know, as does she."

"Then you'll need to take that up with the commander."

"What's your name?"

"Sister Lara." The woman peered into the room. "Come, Sister Danica. Let's not make a spectacle of this."

"I haven't done anything wrong!" insisted the raven-haired knight.

"That's for the order to determine." Lara swivelled her gaze to Charlaine. "And as for you, Captain"—she almost sneered out the word—"if you know what's good for you, you'll keep your nose out of it."

"Is that a threat?"

"Not at all," replied Sister Lara, "merely a suggestion." She turned to her companions. "Sisters, arrest the prisoner."

They moved into the room, taking up positions on either side of the bed.

"Are you coming along peacefully," asked Sister Lara, "or are you going to make this difficult?"

"I won't fight you," said Danica, "but by the Saints, I won't turn my sword over to you."

"I'll take care of your weapons and armour," said Charlaine.

Danica stood, allowing them to seize her, twisting her arms behind her back, and binding them with rope.

"Is that entirely necessary?" asked Charlaine.

"This is standard treatment for a criminal."

"You haven't even told me what I'm charged with!" shouted Danica.

"Breaking your Holy vows," said Lara. "Now, out with you."

The guards pulled her roughly out of the room, then made a big show of pushing her down the hallway, cursing as they went.

Charlaine watched, helpless to intervene with the arrest. "I shall find out who's responsible for this," she called out. "I promise you."

Captain Nicola stared back. "And you say it was under the orders of Commander Hjordis?"

"Indeed," said Charlaine. "I should have mentioned it sooner, but there was a note in the duty officer's log to inform her of my arrival at the Antonine."

"What's the charge?"

"Breaking her vows."

"That could mean any number of things," said the captain. "It sounds like it's more of a fishing expedition."

"Why do you say that?"

"They'll arrest her now and worry about finding evidence later."

"Can they do that?"

"Technically, no, but Commander Hjordis is in charge of overall discipline, which gives her a great amount of leeway when it comes to interpreting things."

"But surely the grand mistress can intervene?"

"I can certainly bring it to her attention, but I wouldn't expect too much to happen until we know the exact charges."

"And when will that happen?"

"I'm not sure," admitted Nicola. "Typically, they're announced within a day of the arrest. However, these are not normal times, not by any stretch of the imagination."

"I assume the commander opposes the grand mistress's ideas?"

"That would be an accurate appraisal."

Charlaine shifted in her seat. "Could this be some sort of power play?"

"To have the grand mistress removed? Quite possibly. If word got to the matriarch about all of this, it could well lead to her removal."

"So what do we do?"

"What can we do other than wait? We must bide our time. Only then will we see what they're really after."

"Am I allowed to visit Danica?"

"I can arrange it. Fortunately, we still hold on to the principle that a person is innocent until such time as their guilt is proven. That doesn't, however, guarantee she won't be mistreated. Guards have been known to take out their frustrations on those they consider to be beneath them."

"But we're all sisters…"

"I know that, and you know that, but that's a far cry from it being a common practice. Saints know we do our best to practice what we preach, but beneath all the fancy words, we're still just people, each with our own weaknesses."

"Weaknesses," said Charlaine, mulling over the word. "I think that's the key to this."

"How?"

"Everyone has weaknesses. We just need to find those of Commander Hjordis."

"I might remind you that a commander outranks us both. I shan't tell you what you can or can't do, but I will advise you to be careful."

"Understood."

"Good," said Captain Nicola. "In the meantime, I shall take what we know to the grand mistress. For your part, you should visit Danica and ensure she's all right."

"And if she's not?"

"You're still a captain; exert your right of command. Bear in mind you can't order her release, but there's much that can be done to ensure she's not mistreated."

If truth be told, the dungeon of the commandery was not much different from the sisters' cells, save for the iron bars that made up the doors.

Charlaine found the area easily enough, then submitted to the search that divested her of her weapons. She was eventually let into the cell where Danica sat shivering, her breath visible in the chilly air.

"How are you holding up?" asked Charlaine.

"Not too badly, all things considered."

"Meaning?"

"I've one or two bruises from the ordeal but otherwise intact."

"Have they revealed the nature of the charges? Breaking vows is awfully vague."

"They're accusing me of having lain with a man."

"What man?"

"A Cunar."

"They can't be serious?"

"I'm afraid they are," said Danica.

"But you didn't lay with a man, did you?"

"No, of course not. You know my background. Do you believe I'd ever let one touch me?"

"No, and I can't say I blame you, but they must have gotten the idea from somewhere? Can't you just tell them the truth?"

"What? That I was secretly plotting with a naval architect to develop a northern fleet? That would end the career of the grand mistress."

"You have a good point, but we can't let you rot away in here, especially when you're innocent."

"I've suffered worse," Danica replied, "though I'd kill for a decent blanket."

"Now, that," replied Charlaine, "is something I can deal with." She walked to the door, calling over the guard. "You there. Sister Lara, isn't it? Fetch a blanket, and make sure it's a decent one. That's an order."

The sister knight grumbled but soon made her way into the hallway to carry out her new orders.

"What do you know of Commander Hjordis?" said Charlaine.

"You mentioned her some time ago. Other than that, I know nothing about her. Why?"

"She's the one who ordered you arrested. I'm told she's in charge of maintaining discipline."

"I wonder if she knows Brother Erskine?"

Now it was Charlaine's turn to be surprised. "The Cunar from Erlingen? Why would you think that?"

"It can't be coincidence, can it? I find out about Erskine, and suddenly I'm under arrest?"

"That was some weeks ago."

"Then how do you explain my predicament? Nothing else has been out of the ordinary."

"You make a compelling case. Do you think she found out about our orders?"

"How does that explain my arrest?"

"She might try to force a confession out of you?"

"For breaking vows I didn't break?"

"No," said Charlaine, her voice lowering. "I mean, Hjordis wants you to confess that you're on a special assignment for the grand mistress."

"To what end?"

"To discredit her. She's hanging on by a thread, Danica. She as good as told us that. A matter like this could easily sway opinion against her."

"And do what, cause the order to rise up?"

"No, but it might persuade the matriarch to take action and remove her from her office."

"You really believe she'd do that?"

"I think these are desperate times," said Charlaine, "and desperate times lead to desperate measures."

Sister Lara returned, bearing a blanket. Charlaine took it, examining it to make sure it wasn't threadbare before she carefully unfolded it and placed it around Danica's shoulders. "Here, this ought to help. I only wish I could do more. Should I seek out Captain Leamund? He could speak on your behalf?"

"And tell them what? That we're working together? That would reveal everything."

"I can't let you take the blame for something you didn't do."

"It seems you'll have little choice. We've been through much, you and I, but right now, you need to watch your own back, particularly since I'm not able to."

Charlaine felt her anger rising. This entire situation made her want to scream, but Danica reached out, taking her hand.

"It will be all right," the younger knight soothed. "You must have faith. Agnes will not let me suffer."

"You're right, of course." Charlaine rose, nodding at the guard to let her out. She stepped outside the cell, waiting as the door was locked once more.

"Take care of her," she said to the guard, "and make sure she is treated with respect, or I shall hold you personally accountable."

"Yes, Captain. You have my word."

Charlaine returned to her room but found the solitude overwhelming. She sought out the dining hall, hoping to find someone, anyone, to talk over her problems with. Instead, all the sisters shunned her to the point that the room became unbearable. Determined to get some fresh air and clear her head, she went outside and wandered for some time, her mind in turmoil, only to end up standing before the great structure that housed the archives.

It brought to mind Danica's visit there, and so she headed inside, although with no immediate objective in mind. As a captain, she was ignored by the guards posted within, but Brother Thorley happened to be wandering the halls as she entered.

"Can I help you?" he called out.

"My name is Sister Charlaine."

"You're a friend of Sister Danica's, aren't you?"

"Yes, how did you know?"

"She mentioned you on her last visit. She is well, I hope?"

"I'm afraid not. She's been arrested."

"My goodness. Whatever for?"

Charlaine stepped closer, lowering her voice. "She's been accused of... how shall I put this"—the brother of Saint Mathew simply stared back, unsure of how to answer—"laying with a man," she finished.

"By the Saints," he replied. "Who made such an accusation?"

"Commander Hjordis."

He nodded his head in understanding.

"I assume you're familiar with her?" Charlaine asked.

"Oh yes," he said. "She's not the kind of person you would want to be on the bad side of. Is that what brought you here?"

"Yes and no. I didn't come here consciously, but I'd be lying if I didn't admit Hjordis was on my mind."

"Perhaps it's the Saints who guided you here?"

"At this moment, I'd be willing to admit to almost anything."

"There may be something you can do."

Charlaine sobered, all other thoughts driven from her mind. "What are you suggesting?"

Brother Thorley looked around as if to make sure no one was within earshot. "'They say Hjordis is an ambitious woman, and she desires the position of grand mistress for herself.'"

"That would explain her actions, but there's little I can do about it."

"There's an old saying:'He who prepares for war is seldom called upon to fight'."

"I fail to see how that applies here."

"Would you consider going into battle ill-equipped?"

"No, of course not."

"Then arm yourself."

"Are you suggesting I fight?"

"No, not with your sword, with knowledge. Knowing your enemy is as important as facing them."

"Are you saying Commander Hjordis has a weakness?"

"I wouldn't know, but if I were to take you below to the archives, you would have access to her records. You might find something helpful there."

"It's worth a try," said Charlaine. "Lead on."

Thorley led the way, taking time to snag a couple of lanterns. Charlaine had never visited such an immense collection of written works, but under the Mathewite's guidance, she quickly located the section she needed.

"I'm afraid there are other duties that require my attention, so I'll leave you to it. I will check on you later, however, as I wouldn't want you to get lost down here."

"Thank you, Brother. You've been most helpful." She began searching through the shelves, desperate to learn anything that might prove of value.

The lantern was burning low, her patience wearing thin, but she was determined not to give up. She'd found sporadic information about Commander Hjordis but little that could be of use. The woman joined the order in the distant Duchy of Holstead and had been sent to Corassus for her initial training. There was no record of any battle experience, but she had gained the reputation as an efficient administrator early on. Her superiors talked in glowing terms of her organizational ability, but for some reason, stopped short of recommending promotion. As a result, it took over twenty years for Hjordis to reach the rank of captain. After that, however, her progress was more rapid. She made commander a scant three years later, and two years after that was named head of discipline for the order, a position she'd held for the last five years.

She shook her head. There was more to this than the records might indicate. To her mind, being an efficient administrator was not the prerequisite for such a position, leaving her to wonder how Hjordis achieved some recognition. An idea started to take hold. It began as a nagging suspicion that all was not as it was being presented. Charlaine started digging through Hjordis's background in more detail, finding out about the people she had worked with.

By the time Brother Thorley returned, she was struggling to keep her eyes open.

"Find anything of use?" he asked.

She yawned, then turned to face him. "I did, although I can't see how it will help Danica."

"Would you care to elucidate?"

"I gleaned very little by reading of her career, but when I looked into those she served with, I found evidence of something more disturbing. It seems the commander left a trail of destruction and chaos in her wake."

"Truly?"

"Yes. If these records are to be believed, she's either been extremely lucky in her postings or has managed to manipulate events to her advantage. Every detachment she's been assigned to has been rife with disobedience and unruliness. I suspect she used her position to sow distrust and unrest, placing herself as the only candidate worthy of promotion."

"Are you suggesting she lied? If that could be proven, she would be guilty of disobeying her vows."

"Yes," said Charlaine. "It would, wouldn't it?"

9

COMMANDER HJORDIS

Summer 1097 SR

C harlaine returned to the Agnes commandery, intent on dinner. As she
approached the dining hall, a pair of sister knights intercepted her.
"You're to come with us," they announced.

"To what end?" she replied.

"To see Commander Hjordis."

"And if I refuse?"

"I wouldn't advise that. In any case, it's in your best interest to meet with
her. Who knows, maybe all your troubles could be made to vanish?"

"Very well," said Charlaine. "Take me to her."

They led the way, and soon the small party was in the upper halls of the
commandery. A double door loomed large, guarded by two more sister
knights. Upon the trio's arrival, they swung them open, revealing a richly
decorated interior where Commander Hjordis sat behind her desk, her eyes
watching like a hawk.

"Leave Sister Charlaine here," she commanded. "The rest of you can wait
outside."

"Are you arresting me?" asked Charlaine.

"Not at all, but considering your recent activities, I thought it best we
have a little chat. Surely you don't mind?"

"I wasn't given a choice."

"I'm afraid my guards are a mite overzealous. They should have made it clear this was an invitation. Come, sit. There's no need to be formal here."

Charlaine took a seat, her gaze sweeping the room. "You have done quite well for yourself," she said.

The commander followed her gaze, a brief smile on display. "I admit it's been an interesting career." Her eyes returned to her visitor. "I suppose I could say the same for you. I hear you've been busy in the south."

"You know full well I have. Is that what this is all about? My accomplishments in Ilea?"

"Not at all."

"Then what?"

"I am far more interested in what you're up to here."

"I'm undergoing training," said Charlaine.

"So I heard." Hjordis glanced down at some notes. "It says here you've been learning how to behave at court. I assume that means the grand mistress has seen fit to send you to a duchy of some sort."

"What makes you say that?"

"It's quite simple, really. You're a captain, and within our order, you would command a single company, exactly the number we would expect in such places. Of course, there are exceptions, but by and large, only the duchies are small enough to warrant such a force. Now, had you been a commander, I would expect a larger kingdom would benefit from your experience."

"And this bothers you?"

"Believe it or not, I hold no malice towards you. The truth is, within the order, I'm responsible for maintaining discipline and doling out punishment when it's deemed suitable. I see no infractions on your part."

"But?" pressed Charlaine.

Commander Hjordis smirked, making her look like a viper, readying to strike. "You should be careful in your associations, Charlaine. They can lead you astray. I'd hate to see a promising career cut short by poor judgement."

"You mean Sister Danica?"

"That name has crossed my desk."

"What is it you want?"

"Want? Why, the same thing as you, Sister. I want the order to flourish. I'm surprised you need to ask."

"Then why bring me here?"

"You've only been a Temple Knight for a little over two years, and you already made captain. Keep up the good work, and you may make commander by the age of thirty. Quite an accomplishment by any standard."

"I live to serve my Saint," said Charlaine.

"As do I, but like any organization, our order is ruled by people, people who can make all-too-human mistakes."

"Such as?"

"Well, I shan't get into particulars, but suffice it to say,our reputation of late has been under considerable strain, at least in the eyes of the other orders."

"And you wish to put an end to such things?"

The commander smiled. "I merely wish to better define our responsibilities. You are to be commended on your recent actions, but you need guidance, guidance I can offer."

"And why would you do that?"

"I don't know. Perhaps I see a little of myself in you. You are a rarity, Charlaine, a natural leader with the power to do great things, but you lack clarity."

"In what way?"

"Our order is at a turning point. Step one way, and we become a dominant military force, step the other, and we fade into obscurity."

"You sound like the grand mistress," retorted Charlaine.

"I shall take that as a compliment. Now, do I have your attention?"

"Most assuredly."

"Good, then consider this. Our grand mistress is timid, not in itself a bad trait, but we find ourselves at a point where decisive action is called for."

"How so?"

"The Cunars are calling for an end to the order's duties, outside of our traditional role of protecting temples, I mean. They feel that they are best qualified to lead the Holy Army or the fleet, for that matter."

"They already command the fleet."

"Do they?" The commander smiled. "It appears there are rumours to the contrary. You know, fifty years ago, it was we who crewed the fleet at Corassus."

"And?"

"And it's quite possible we could do so again."

"What has that to do with me?"

"Do I need to spell it out for you?"

"It seems you do," said Charlaine, "for I haven't a clue what you're suggesting."

"I know the mission the grand mistress is sending you on."

"If you already know, then why am I here?"

"Because I need you to say it. Admit to me what she plots, and I can use it to see that our order prospers."

"You mean that YOU prosper. That's what this is all about, isn't it? Personal power? You want to be the new grand mistress."

"I do," admitted Hjordis, "and you're going to help me."

"What makes you think that?"

"Because I have your friend locked up in irons, awaiting trial."

"What are you suggesting?"

"I have a lot of leeway in the manner in which I carry out my duties. It wouldn't be too hard to convince me to release Sister Danica, should you prove more amenable to my offer."

"So that's it? I help you get rid of the grand mistress, and you release Danica?"

The commander nodded. "I see you grasp the situation quite admirably."

"I am only one person. What makes you think that my testimony would cause the downfall of the grand mistress?"

"Come now, don't play the fool with me. You know as well as I that she hangs on by a thread. One more scandal and the matriarch is sure to dismiss her."

"Allowing you to assume the position?"

"Who better than someone with a dedicated interest in the future of our order?"

Charlaine's mind was in turmoil. At face value, it appeared she had little choice but to go along with this plan, but something didn't seem right.

"Come now," cajoled Commander Hjordis. "You barely know the grand mistress. Surely you realize the advantage to being loyal to her replacement?" She leaned forward. "You could be a commander in just a few years. Who knows, maybe one day, you'll even take over as grand mistress. After all, I can't live forever."

"This is an incredible offer, far more significant than I expected to confront today."

"Then take some time and think it over, but not too much, mind you, else you might miss your chance."

"When do you want an answer by?"

"This time tomorrow."

"So soon?"

"There are wheels in motion," the commander replied. "Wheels that will stop for no one. And quite honestly, you have little choice if you value your friend's future."

Charlaine stood. "Very well. I shall pray for guidance and then give you my answer."

"Excellent."

. . .

She made her way to the dungeons, her soul heavy. Charlaine had always thought of the Church as a place of holiness and sisterly bonds. Now it felt like her family was being torn apart. The thought sickened her.

Danica lay in her cell, sleeping on the cold floor, her form wrapped in the blanket. At first, Charlaine took her for unconscious, but as the cell door opened, so, too, did her comrade's eyes.

"You're back," said Danica, noting her serious look. "What's wrong?"

Charlaine moved closer, crouching before her. "I just came from Commander Hjordis."

"And?"

"I can get you out of here, and all the charges against you dropped."

"But?"

"What makes you think there's a but?" said Charlaine.

"Your manner, for one. We've known each other for some time now. I can tell when you're struggling with something. Tell me what it is."

"She wants me to reveal our orders from the grand mistress. If I agree to do that, she'll let you go."

"No!" insisted Danica. "You can't."

"I must, don't you see? It's the only way this ends well for you. If I don't take this offer, you'll be banished from the order, denied even the right to receive the blessings of the Saints."

"Listen," said Danica. "If you give in to her now, you'll never be rid of her. She'll hold the threat of punishing me over your head for the rest of your life. Is that what you want, a life of servitude?"

"It's a price I'm willing to pay, if I must. I can't see you punished for my actions."

"And what of the order? I assume she'll use the information to oust the grand mistress?"

Charlaine nodded, too upset to speak.

"And then, I suppose, she'll take the position for herself?"

"Very likely," muttered Charlaine.

"Then you definitely can't give in. The entire future of our order depends on it."

"Does it, though? We don't make policy for the Temple Knights. What difference, then, who commands us?"

"It makes a great deal of difference," said Danica. "What is it that Hjordis craves?"

"That's easy—power."

"And if your treatment is any indication, this is a common tactic of hers, yes?"

"Undoubtedly."

"Then she won't stop with the position of grand mistress."

"What are you inferring?"

"What's to stop her from becoming matriarch?"

"She is a Temple Knight, for one," said Charlaine, "not a lay sister."

"Do you believe that will stop her? She has a lust for power and a will to do anything to achieve her ends. That's a dangerous combination."

"Then what do you suggest I do? Refuse her and see you banished?"

"I have gone through much in my few years," said Danica, "and I will treasure our friendship till my dying day, but I could not live with myself knowing you were coerced into this because of me. If I am to be banished, then so be it. Better that than to compromise your morals."

"I hear your words, but I can see no other way out of this. Hjordis is ruthless. She's destroyed many a career with her actions."

"All the more reason to make a stand now. People like her must be stopped. What would Saint Agnes expect of you were she alive to bear witness to such things?"

Charlaine felt a calmness settle over her. "You're right. I'm getting too wrapped up in this. There has to be a way to stop her once and for all."

"That's the Charlaine I know. Now, go seek out the answers you need to put an end to all this… all this… I'm not even sure what to call it."

"Scheming?"

"It's as good a name as any."

Charlaine rose, her mind made up. "I shall, and I promise you I won't give in to the temptation."

"Good," said Danica. "That's all I can ask."

Charlaine returned late to her room. The meeting with Hjordis and the subsequent visit to Danica had taken up most of the evening, leaving her spent, not to mention hungry. She tried to sleep, but her stomach had other ideas. Thus, she found herself wandering down to the dining hall where she came across Sister Selena, reading through the Book of Agnes by candlelight.

"I'm not disturbing you, am I?" asked Charlaine.

"Not at all. I was just studying. I find the words of Saint Agnes soothing to the soul. What brings you down here at this time of night?"

"I hoped to find something to eat."

"You're too late for that. The kitchen closed some time ago—it's locked up tight."

Charlaine slumped into a chair. "That's disappointing."

"You could always try the Grand Sanctum. I hear their kitchen never closes."

"The Grand Sanctum?"

"Yes, it's like a commandery but used by lay brothers and sisters of all the orders. Mind you, they won't have much in the way of meat, but I would think bread would be easy enough to find."

"How do I get there?"

"Go through the stables," said Selena, "then head across the training field. You'll see it on the far side; it's the building with the domed roof."

"And I'm allowed entry?"

"I don't see why not. We take turns guarding the place."

"We take turns? How does that work?"

"Each day, a different order is responsible for standing watch."

"Even the Ragnarites?"

"Yes, even them. It's likely the only place outside of the Council of Peers that you'll see them, but they have the same responsibilities as us in that regard."

"And who guards tonight?"

"I have no idea. You'll have to see for yourself."

Charlaine rose. "Thank you, Selena. Hopefully, one day, I can return the favour."

"How about tonight?"

"Tonight? What did you have in mind?"

Selena laughed. "Only that you bring me back something to eat. A little bit of cheese would be nice."

"I'll see what I can do."

The Grand Sanctum, the oldest building in the Antonine, was constructed of ancient stone. As the original meeting hall of the Council of Peers, it was where they elected the first Primus, Antony, after whom they named the Antonine.

As the orders grew, so too did their demands for space, resulting in a newer, larger building dedicated to the upper echelons of Church power. The Grand Sanctum thus came to house the immense bureaucracy that enabled the very same Church to function—a bureaucracy that never slept, necessitating a more flexible kitchen schedule.

As Charlaine drew closer to her destination, she spied some blue-clad guards making their rounds. The Temple Knights of Saint Ansgar had a presence in most of the larger Church fortresses and cities, but this was the first that she had seen of them. Their order held the responsibility of investigating internal matters, including corruption or malfeasance. Suddenly she realized that perhaps therein lay the answer to her problems.

"Excuse me," she called out.

The guards halted, turning their attention towards her. The one with the lantern held it aloft, illuminating her face. "Can we help you, Sister?"

"Yes," said Charlaine. "I need to report a member of my order."

"Might I ask what it concerns?"

"I believe she may have broken her vows."

"That type of thing is usually handled by your superiors."

"But that's just it. She is a superior."

"I'm afraid there's little we can do about that."

"What if she broke Church law?"

"Now you're just looking for an excuse."

"Give her a chance," suggested the other guard. "There may be merit to her claims."

"Go on, then," said the lantern holder. "Let's hear the specifics."

"I've come to believe that a sister of my order has falsified reports and taken action to discredit others, despite their innocence."

"Oh yes? Have you any proof?"

"I'm afraid at the moment I have only my own word as a Temple Captain."

"And you are?"

"Temple Captain Charlaine deShandria."

"Wait," said the second guard. "Aren't you the one who stopped the Halvarians?"

"I was one of them, yes, but many others contributed to our victory."

"Still, your name carries some weight." He turned to his companion. "Should we send her to see Captain Zander?"

"About what? A simple accusation? If we did that, we'd have no end of things to investigate."

"True, but consider the source. Sister Charlaine isn't your average Temple Knight."

"And so that means we are to afford her special privilege? That's not how it's supposed to work."

"It's not our job to decide when and where to look into things like this. The captain makes those decisions."

The lantern holder let out a sigh. "Very well, if we must." He turned his attention to Charlaine. "Are you familiar with the location of our commandery?"

"I can't say that I am."

"How about the Cunar commandery?"

"Yes, I've seen it from afar."

"Our building lies east of it, across from their practice field. When you go inside, you'll see a large set of stairs. Take those to the second floor and then turn to the right. Captain Zander will be at the end of the corridor."

"Is he your senior officer?"

"No, but he is the prime investigator in the Antonine. That makes him the person you need to see."

"And will he take action?"

"I can't say for certain. That largely depends on what you say to him. I can tell you, however, that it better be something important, or you may find it coming back to haunt you."

"For instance?"

"A lot of the complaints we receive are merely the result of disgruntled subordinates. Our job is to investigate wrongdoing, not serve as arbitrators in differences of opinion."

"Understood."

"Good. Now, you must excuse us. We need to get back to our assigned duties."

"Of course," said Charlaine. "Sorry for the interruption."

Her first instinct was to seek out this Captain Zander as quickly as possible, but then reason took hold as she realized it was well past midnight. She turned, ready to return to bed, only to have her stomach growl. It seemed her appetite had other ideas.

10

CAPTAIN ZANDER

Summer 1097 SR

A fter a fretful sleep, Charlaine had made her way to the Ansgarite building. Now, as she ascended the steps, she wondered if she was doing the right thing. In her heart, she knew it was her duty to report Commander Hjordis, an action that Danica would prefer. Despite this, she worried she had placed her friend in danger, a problem she couldn't simply ignore.

She reached the top floor and entered the corridor, seeking the captain's office. She soon found it, along with three other Temple Knights sitting on chairs in the hallway, awaiting an audience.

Charlaine took a seat beside a Mathewite who looked pale and sickly. Even as she did so, he sniffled, causing her to momentarily regret her choice of seats. She thought of moving, but then the brother decided to engage her in conversation.

"I hear the captain is a hard man to deal with."

"Deal with?" said Charlaine.

"Yes. They say he can be extremely brusque."

"I imagine we would all be that way if we had to contend with complaints all day long."

The brother sniffed again, then dabbed his nose with a kerchief. "I suppose I hadn't considered that. Still, it behooves us to behave civilly, don't you think?"

Charlaine looked him in the eye. "I would prefer to judge a person on their merits rather than petty gossip, wouldn't you?"

The man wore a petulant look as though he were a young child who had just been chastised. He turned away, dabbing his nose once more, just as the office door opened, revealing a Temple Knight of Saint Ansgar.

"Next," he said.

A lay brother wearing the pristine white surcoat of the Order of Saint Augustine stood. "That's me."

"The captain will see you now." The Ansgarite held the door open as the fellow entered, then cast his eyes over those in the hall and frowned. Moments later, he closed it, leaving the hallway once more in silence.

Charlaine waited, feeling her nerve waver. She caught herself tapping her foot and forced herself to relax, closing her eyes and taking a couple of deep breaths. The morning wore on, and her back ached from sitting so long. As a Temple Knight, she was used to being active and found the endless waiting to be tedious. She glanced at the others. Beyond the Mathewite sat a Cunar Temple Knight, although he had chosen to wear a simple cassock in lieu of his armour. It made her wonder what would bring such a man here this day.

The door finally opened again, and the Augustine exited, looking none too pleased with the result. The captain's aide swept the hall yet again, his eyes resting on the Cunar. "Not you again, Brother Septimus?"

"I'm afraid so, Brother Bryson. It seems there is no end of problems here in the Antonine."

Bryson let out an audible sigh. "Very well, step inside, but be quick about it. We haven't all day."

The door closed, and the Mathewite found his tongue once more. "I don't believe I introduced myself. I'm Brother Ebert."

"Sister Charlaine," she replied.

"I know that name. Weren't you the one who served with the fleet?"

"I did, yes."

"And what brings you here this day?"

"I'm afraid that's something I can't divulge to those outside my order."

Ebert tapped his nose. "I understand." Moments later, he sneezed, spewing forth a cloud of mist. Luckily, he'd turned at the moment he let loose, avoiding covering her in his nasal discharge.

"You should see a healer," she suggested.

He wiped his nose. "It's merely a cold, a consequence of having to live in a damp, cool cell. Tell me, are your quarters as bad as ours?"

"I'm unfamiliar with your order's sleeping arrangements, but I found my room at the commandery to be reasonably pleasant."

Ebert grunted. "I should have known."

"Why?"

"It's our commander. He has the gout, so he feels that if he must suffer, so must we. That's why I'm here today."

"To complain about your room?"

"Of course? How else shall I seek restitution?"

"Captain Zander is an investigator for the Order of Saint Ansgar, not the officer in charge of billeting."

Brother Ebert wore a pained expression. "Don't tell me what he can and can't do. I'll have you know I'm aide to the chief administrator to the order."

"Then why not take your complaint to him? Surely he would be better placed to do something about it?"

"I…" His voice trailed off. She waited patiently, then the man stood. "You're right," he said, having made up his mind. "I shall go and see him directly." He headed back towards the stairs, walking with purpose.

Just then, the door opened, and voices drifted out into the hallway.

"I'm sorry we couldn't be of any help," Brother Bryson was saying. "It might be in your best interest to request a transfer. I hear Corassus needs more Temple Knights?"

"A fine idea," replied Brother Septimus, "and one which I shall embrace with enthusiasm." He stepped from the room, pausing to turn to his host. "Thank you, Brother Bryson, you've been most helpful." His conversation complete, he made his way down the hallway, ignoring Charlaine's presence.

"I wish all such issues could be dealt with so easily," remarked Brother Bryson. His eyes met hers. "You're next."

Charlaine stood, taking a moment to straighten her cassock before following the Ansgarite. The office of Captain Zander was sparse of furniture, save for a simple table with a chair on either side and a small journal he kept open before him.

"Come, sit," he said. He waited until she was comfortable before beginning with a question. "Who are you?"

"Sister Charlaine deShandria, Temple Captain of Saint Agnes."

"And what can I do for you today?"

"I am here because I have nowhere else to turn."

"That sounds serious. Would you care to explain?"

"Upon my arrival in the Antonine, I was warned of a rot within the Church. Not too specific, I grant you, but enough to put me on the alert. It soon became apparent to me there are two competing ideologies at work within my order."

"Ah, the politics of the Church. I'm afraid that's been a problem for generations, not just for your order but for all of us. Still, people are allowed to have differing opinions on matters. It's all part of being Human."

"There's more," said Charlaine.

"Go on."

"I travelled here with a fellow sister, Danica Meer. She is now under arrest and held within the dungeons of the commandery."

"On what charge?"

"Breaking her vows, but there's more to the story."

"Then, pray continue, and I shall try to avoid interrupting other than to clarify matters."

"We both met with the grand mistress of the order. She ordered us to undertake a mission of great importance, but it was to remain secret."

She took a breath, calming her nerves. "Part of the preparation for this involved Sister Danica seeking help from the Temple Knights of Saint Cunar, necessitating a visit to their commandery. This visit was later used against her, insinuating that she'd broken her vow of chastity."

"And did she? Break her vow, I mean. I only ask to be completely clear."

"She categorically denies it."

"And you trust her word?"

"Implicitly. She and I have been through a lot in the last two years. I have no reason to believe she would even consider such a thing."

"Then I shall take your word for it. Who lodged the complaint?"

"Commander Hjordis. She's in charge of discipline within the order." She saw him purse his lips. "I'm guessing you're familiar with her?"

"I am, as a matter of fact. This isn't the first time her name has been brought to our attention. Still, from what you told me, it's her job to ensure your fellow sisters follow the rules."

"I'm afraid there's more. She called me to her office for a meeting..." Charlaine hesitated.

"And?" prompted Captain Zander.

"She told me she would drop the charges against Danica if I revealed the grand mistress's plan."

"And what did you say?"

"I was hesitant to accept, so she gave me till later today for my answer."

"And you came here instead?"

"I did," said Charlaine, "but I visited Danica first. I was ready to give in to the commander's demands, but Danica warned me that if I did, I'd never be rid of Hjordis's iron grip."

"She's absolutely right. Clearly, Sister Danica has a good head on her shoulders. People like Hjordis will stop at nothing to advance their cause, whatever it might be."

"So you'll look into it?"

"Possibly, but I have a few more questions first. Are you familiar with the power struggle going on within the orders?"

"You mean ours is not the only one so afflicted?"

"That's exactly what I mean. For years, we've seen a sickness developing within the Church. It started as whispers of discontent, but within a decade, people grew bolder. Now, it seems, many question the role of the Church, particularly the temple orders."

"Are you saying they want to reduce our numbers?"

"Some do, while others, a small minority at this time, are calling on them to disband entirely."

"From whence came these ideas?"

"I wish I knew," said Captain Zander. "Every time we get close to finding an answer, someone dies, sealing their lips forever."

"People have actually died?"

"Oh yes. It's a deadly game someone's playing."

"And you believe this might be connected to my troubles?"

"I think it a distinct possibility. I mentioned earlier that her name was known to us. As it happens, it's in connection with one of these deaths."

"Then why haven't you taken her into custody?"

"I would love to," said the captain, "but we Ansgarites have limits as to what we can do. Without some kind of proof, I'm powerless to do much of anything."

"So, I wasted my time in coming here," said Charlaine.

"Not entirely. It might be possible Commander Hjordis's plot will be her undoing, but it will require your help, as well as that of Sister Danica."

"What do I need to do?"

"Go and meet with Commander Hjordis. Tell her you agree to her offer."

"I can't do that! What about the grand mistress's plans?"

"Don't worry, we won't tell her the truth. Let her believe it's something else."

"Like what?"

He thought things over for a moment. "You have battle experience, don't you?"

"I do," she replied. "So does Danica, but I fail to see what that has to do with anything."

"What if you told her the intention was to raise a special company of sister knights? Unless, of course, that's what she actually envisions?"

"No, that was never part of the grand mistress's plan."

"Do you think you can convince the commander of it?"

"I could, but that would constitute a lie, and my oath prevents me from doing so."

The captain dismissed the idea with a wave of his hand. "It was just a thought."

"What kind of proof would it take to bring her to justice?"

"A written confession would be ideal, but I doubt we'd get that lucky."

"What if we convinced one of her subordinates to confess?"

He leaned forward. "That's an excellent idea. It's not as if she could have gotten this far without help."

"So that's it, then. All I need to do is gain the confidence of one of her people and convince the woman to reveal all. No pressure there!"

"You make it sound far worse than it has to be," said Captain Zander. "If you can get the names of the people loyal to her, we can begin exerting pressure."

"Pressure? You mean torture?"

"Saints, no. What do you think we are, Halvarians? No, we would simply bring them in for questioning and use the power of persuasion to convince them of the error of their ways. There's nothing quite like a reformed sinner when it comes to confessions."

"All right," said Charlaine. "I'll see what I can do."

"Good. Now, be careful how you go about this. You don't want to put them on alert. Too many questions, and they'll begin to doubt your loyalty."

"And if the commander begins to suspect my loyalties?"

"We'll do our best to keep you safe, if that's what you mean. In the meantime, we'll keep a watchful eye on her and see who she talks to. That might give us an idea of how far out she's spread her net."

"And what happens when she wants to know the plans of the grand mistress?"

"I'm still curious as to why."

"That's easy," said Charlaine. "She'll use it to spread lies about the grand mistress, discrediting her in the eyes of the matriarch."

"I suppose she covets the position herself?"

"She admitted it quite openly."

"Not, in itself, something nefarious. However, the manner of achieving these aims leaves much to be desired."

"What of the other orders? You mentioned whispers?"

"Yes, there's a growing desire within the Cunars to take over all military operations."

"Yes, Commander Hjordis spoke of it. Is there support amongst the Council of Peers for such a decision?"

"Not at present, but that could easily change. The patriarchs who oppose the motion are old and in ill health. Should they be replaced with younger, more active members of their respective orders, I fear the outcome will no longer be in doubt."

"So you disapprove of such a move?"

"I will, of course, abide by the decisions of the Council of Peers, but I think it a bad idea to put that kind of power into the hands of any single order. They say that power corrupts, and I can think of no greater power than leading all the armies and fleets of the Church. Of greater concern would be the chance that it would be used to enforce a theocracy over all the Petty Kingdoms."

"I doubt the Continent would stand for that."

"Have you seen what happens when the Church declares a crusade? Warriors from all over gather to fight in the name of the Saints."

"Yes, but that doesn't mean they would place their homes under Church control."

"But some would, likely resulting in war engulfing the entire land. If that happened, I have no doubt that Halvaria would rush at the chance to take advantage of the chaos."

"Halvaria?" said Charlaine. "Could they be behind all of this?"

"It would certainly serve their interests, although I have no proof either way. We've always done our best to prevent the Halvarian Heresy from growing within the order, but there's only so much we can do."

"The Halvarian Heresy? What's that?"

"The Empire of Halvaria worships their ruler as a god. This is in direct opposition to our beliefs, not to mention the beliefs of those who worship the old religion."

"At the same time, does the Church not preach peace and harmony with our neighbours?"

"You know our teachings well, but in this case, we are talking about beliefs that are in direct conflict with each other. How can a man be a god?"

"Or a Saint?" asked Charlaine. "Be careful of what you ask. You might find it coming back to bite your hand."

"Not so," said Captain Zander. "We worship the Saints as people. Their actions and words inspire us, but they were mortal men and women, working for the betterment of all."

"And the Halvarian leader?"

"The emperor is a man, make no mistake, yet their entire religion is based around him and his ancestors. They claim divine blood infuses their veins, giving them godlike powers."

"Have we any proof of these power?"

"None whatsoever. There's always the possibility that he might be a mage of some sort, but information about him is sparse, making it hard to tell the difference between myth and reality."

He paused, gathering his thoughts. "Of course, all of this could simply be a well-practiced play, presented for our benefit. Likely, he's just a king with an overpowering ego. Saints know we have enough of those in the Petty Kingdoms. Look at me, waxing poetic about Halvaria. You fought them in Alantra. What was your impression of them?"

"My first impression was they're barbaric, and subsequent events did nothing to convince me otherwise."

"Barbaric—an interesting turn of phrase. Might I ask what it was that gave you that impression?"

"They force the conquered into their armies, keeping them under control by the use of brutal measures, and that's not all. At the Battle of Alantra, they hung my fellow sisters from the masts to instill fear in us."

"And did it work?"

"No, it only made us fight all the more ferociously."

He nodded sagely. "They are, I believe, the greatest threat to the existence of the Church and the Petty Kingdoms."

"You believe war to be inevitable?"

"I do," said Captain Zander, "but there's little we can do about it at the moment. Sadly, our organization is at a crossroads. If we make the right decisions, we shall grow and prosper, but if we err, it will be the end of us all."

"And here I thought it was just one bad commander."

"Well, Commander Hjordis is definitely that, but she is also, I fear, a symptom rather than the cause of our dilemma. However, we must do what we can, when we can, and if that means stopping the likes of her, then so be it. Give me some time to discover what can be done."

"And in the meantime?"

"Play along with her, if you can. I understand you vowed not to lie, but could you mitigate the situation by telling a half-truth?"

"Do you have a suggestion of how to do that?"

"Without knowing what your orders were, I cannot say for certain, but what if you gave the wrong impression by being selective about what you reveal?"

"Though it does not come naturally to me, I shall see what I can do."

"That is all we can ask of you."

11

AN AGREEMENT

Summer 1097 SR

C harlaine stood before the door, eyeing the guards. "I'm here to meet with the commander," she said.

A guard stood aside, allowing her entry. Inside sat Commander Hjordis, flipping through pages of a thick book, her eyes quickly scanning their contents. She looked up at the sound of the door opening.

"Sister Charlaine, this is a delightful surprise. What brings you here today?"

Her voice was pleasant enough, yet Charlaine couldn't help but feel the tension in the room. Undoubtedly, the commander was not used to waiting on others. The irritation of such an action showed on her face.

"I have considered your offer," Charlaine announced.

"Have you, now? And what conclusion did you come to? Are you to join those of us who wish to see the order prosper, or have you seen fit to throw away your friend's life?"

"I have given it much thought, Commander, and concluded it would better serve my interests by working with you rather than against you."

Commander Hjordis smiled. "You surprise me. I'd expected more resistance. Your reputation paints you as a person dedicated to the teachings of Saint Agnes. It couldn't have been easy to set that aside to further your career."

"The two are not incompatible. You yourself stated you had only the best interests of the order in mind. Surely that's what Saint Agnes would have wished of any of us?"

"Keep that up, and you'll go far. It's not everyone who can justify their actions by the most holy of books. Now, just to be clear, you will tell me what you know of the grand mistress's plans in exchange for Sister Danica's release?"

"I will," said Charlaine. "But before I begin, I'm interested in knowing your plans for the future of the Temple Knights."

The commander sat back, obviously pleased with the turn of events. "As I said before, I want to see the order prosper and grow. For too long, we've lived in the shadow of our Cunar brothers. It's time we took matters into our own hands."

"Meaning?"

"We need to increase our presence in the major cities of the Continent."

"That would be expensive," said Charlaine. "How do you intend we pay for it?"

"I would pressure the Matriarch of Saint Agnes to institute a system of tithes for our worshippers."

"Many of those worshippers are poor. How could they afford such an expense?"

"People have a way of finding the coins when they need it, and, let's face it, we're their protectors. It is only fitting that they pay for that service."

"So you are saying we charge them in exchange for keeping them safe?"

"Precisely," said Hjordis. "It will allow us to fill our coffers and give meaning to the order."

"How does that separate us from common mercenaries?"

"We are Holy Warriors, Charlaine, not brigands. We shall be providing an essential service."

"Have you considered the political ramifications of this?"

"We are the Church. We will brook no complaints."

"It's not the Church that will object, but the nobles of the Petty Kingdoms. They will see the tithes as an effort to rob them of taxes."

"I'd thought," said the commander, "that you were in agreement with my beliefs. Am I now to consider that you changed your mind?"

"Not at all. I am merely concerned that without proper preparation, the outcome from such a plan could well prove impossible to handle. I do think, however, that with a little more care, such designs could be tempered to be more palatable to our worshippers."

Commander Hjordis stared back, although whether she was upset or impressed was difficult to tell.

"I hope I have not given offence," continued Charlaine.

"Offence? No, but you have given me pause. I would be interested in hearing more about the matter, but I fear I have little time for such things at present. Now, as to the plans of the grand mistress, what can you tell me?"

"If truth be told, not much. She was light on details."

"How light?"

"I am to be sent north, but as to what I'm to do there, is anyone's guess."

"And Sister Danica?"

"She is to be placed under my command. She proved valuable during the campaign in Calabria, and it's thought her presence in the north might prove beneficial. She's from that region, you see."

"Which region? You talked of the north but indicated no actual destination."

"I'm sorry," said Charlaine. "Did I not mention we're to go to the Duchy of Reinwick?"

"You most certainly did not," said Commander Hjordis. "However, you have now corrected that error." She fell silent, staring at her visitor.

"Is something wrong, Commander?"

"I'm trying to reason out why the grand mistress decided to send you north. Reinwick is, by all accounts, a most dull and uninteresting place, yet she chooses to send one of our most accomplished knights there."

"Perhaps she thought it a reward for past service?"

"You aren't from the north, are you?"

"No," said Charlaine. "I was born and raised in Hadenfeld."

"Then why, I wonder, did she see fit to assign you to Reinwick? Have you relatives there?"

"None that I'm aware of."

"And she said nothing of your true purpose in going there?"

"I believe she intended to give me the details once my training was complete."

The commander appeared mollified. "Pity. It would've been nice to know now instead of having to wait. Still, she will eventually reveal the details of your assignment, and then we shall know what it is she's up to. Meanwhile, you must bide your time and complete your training. I shall expect you to keep me informed of any developments regarding your assignment."

"Of course," said Charlaine. "Now, have I your permission to release Sister Danica?"

"You do." The commander turned to the door. "Sister Brigida?"

The door opened, revealing a seasoned Temple Knight. "You called, Commander?"

"Sister Danica is to be released. Please escort Sister Charlaine here down to the cells so that she may bear witness."

"Yes, Commander."

Hjordis returned her attention to Charlaine but stood there silently, likely trying to gauge the new captain's dedication to the cause. "I am releasing Sister Danica as part of our deal," she finally said. "Cross me, and you shall regret it for the rest of your life."

Charlaine nodded. "Understood." She rose, following Sister Brigida from the room.

They made their way to the cells where they held Sister Danica. Though still chilly, Charlaine was pleased to see that extra blankets had been made available.

"You've done well, Sister Lara," she said, looking at the guard. "You are a credit to the order."

In response, the woman simply nodded, then moved to unlock the cell door.

"What's going on?" asked Danica.

"You're being released," announced Sister Brigida. "By order of Commander Hjordis."

The raven-haired knight looked at Charlaine. "What did you do?"

"What my conscience dictated. Were the roles reversed, you would likely do the same."

"And here I thought you knew me!" spat out Danica. "You have compromised your very principles, Charlaine, and now I must bear the shame for that."

"No, that is a burden I alone bear."

"Touching," said Sister Brigida, "but could you continue this discussion out of earshot of the rest of us? I have no interest in listening to it, nor do I suspect, does Sister Lara here."

"In that case," said Charlaine, "we shall take our leave of you." She looked at Danica. "We have much to discuss, you and I, but this is neither the time nor the place." Charlaine led her comrade from the building, then out across the practice field.

"How could you?" said Danica.

"Your life was in danger."

"My life is not yours to save."

Charlaine whirled on her companion. "You're wrong, Danica. I could do nothing to save Helena or Aurelia, for that matter. It's my actions that resulted in you being arrested in the first place, don't you see? That alone makes you my responsibility."

"Then perhaps it would be better if I were to stand on my own two feet."

"Meaning what?"

"I cannot go where you tread, Charlaine. You've lost sight of your faith."

"My faith is as strong as ever."

"Is it?" said Danica. "Your actions would indicate otherwise."

"What's that supposed to mean?"

"Where is the Charlaine I knew in Ilea? The one who fought at Alantra? That woman would never have compromised her morals."

"Who says I've compromised anything?"

"Is that the best you can come up with?" demanded Danica. "You're working for Hjordis now, the very person who the grand mistress warned us about, yet you seem to be fine with that."

"That is none of your concern."

"Isn't it? Your actions have placed an immense burden on my soul, one that will haunt me for the remainder of my days."

"What was I supposed to do? Let you rot in a cell?"

"I was willing to endure that because I knew it ensured the purity of your soul. We are both servants of Saint Agnes, Charlaine, but somewhere in all this, you have lost your way." Danica stormed off in a huff.

"Come back here," called out Charlaine.

"Why? We have nothing to talk about." Even though her voice grew distant, Charlaine could still feel the sting of her words. She wanted to tell Danica everything, but the Antonine was full of ears, and even here, on the practice field, the risk of being overheard was too great. She would just need to bide her time and hope an opportunity presented itself.

The afternoon dragged on miserably as she was forced to endure yet another social gathering, offering polite conversation to wealthy patrons, while inside, she was devastated. Danica had been a big part of Charlaine's life for the last few years. So much so, she looked upon her as an actual sister rather than just as a Temple Knight. Yet no matter how she tried to calm herself, the sting of her friend's rebuke would not subside.

That evening at mealtime, she searched for her comrade, but Danica was nowhere to be found. Charlaine sat eating in the dining hall, wondering what she could do about the situation, when Sister Selena appeared.

"Mind if I join you?"

"By all means," said Charlaine, "but I feel I must warn you, I'm not much of a conversationalist today."

Selena laughed. "I suppose that means it's up to me to do most of the talking." She placed her bowl on the table, then took a sip of her wine, declining to sit until she'd drained the cup dry. "My, but that's fearful stuff."

"If you don't like the taste, then why drink it?"

"It's not as if they have anything better to offer. How's the training going?"

"Oh, you know, the usual."

"Seriously?" said Sister Selena. "You get to go to all those grand social events, and that's all you can say? I'd be as happy as a badger in a beehive if I were you."

"Trust me," said Charlaine. "It's not nearly as interesting as it sounds. You're forced to make polite conversation about all manner of things. Yet you're not supposed to make any remarks about the politics of the region."

"Why is that?"

"I suppose our superiors are worried it may be taken as a statement on the Church's position on things. We are supposed to be neutral."

"After all the Cunars have done?"

"Why?" asked Charlaine. "What have they been up to?"

"I've heard they throw their weight around court all the time. Typically, that involves offering their military opinion on things even when they're not asked."

"And they don't get censured for that?"

"Not in the least," said Sister Selena. "In fact, their order encourages it. They have the largest standing army on the Continent, and they want everyone to know it."

"Yes," said Charlaine, "but it's scattered throughout the Petty Kingdoms. It's not as if it's all in one place."

"You know that, and I know that. Saints alive, even the Cunars know it, but it's all about the perception. In their minds, telling that same story over and over only makes their legend grow. And let's face it, it's that legend that keeps Halvaria at bay."

"Does it, though? Their presence definitely didn't stop the raids in Ilea."

"I suppose that's true," said Sister Selena, "but we're not the ones pressing the case that we helped defeat the empire. Our brother Cunars are under no oath to remain humble. I'm not a gambler by nature, but I would be willing to bet most of the Petty Kingdoms believe the victory at Alantra was only possible due to the presence of the Holy Fleet, and we all know who commands that!"

"But that's just it," said Charlaine. "It WAS due to the Holy Fleet."

"Maybe, but they weren't the only ones there! I understand that as

Sisters of Saint Agnes, we promise to be humble, but what about Rizela? It was their fleet that initially engaged the Halvarians, wasn't it?"

"It was," said Charlaine.

"So there you have it. You could make the argument that without the fleet of Rizela, the Holy Fleet couldn't have been victorious."

"Your argument has merit, but the truth is Ilea is a long way from here, and without someone to represent them, the story isn't likely to change."

"I know," said Sister Selena, "but a girl can still hope, can't she?"

Charlaine laughed. "I don't know if hope is the right word. You know the old saying, you can lead a horse to water, but you can't make it drink. Though maybe, in this instance, I should say you can lead a Cunar to the temple, but you can't make him humble."

"Well, at least the Mathewites follow their vows."

"And the other orders, I would imagine, but I doubt they take a vow of humility."

"I would agree," said Sister Selena, "although I must admit to knowing very little of them. Have you ever met a Ragnarite?"

"I have," said Charlaine. "Two of them, in fact, and in both cases, I found them to be quite polite. Still, I have little idea what their actual vows entail."

"I sense a longer story."

"And at any other time, I might oblige you with one, but I'm afraid my heart just isn't in it at the moment."

"Has that something to do with Sister Danica?"

"Yes. How did you know?"

"A lucky guess," said Sister Selena. "You haven't had a falling out, have you?"

"I prefer to think of it as a difference of opinion."

"And that takes precedence over your friendship?"

"So it would seem," said Charlaine. "I know it's only temporary, but I really do miss her."

"Then you should go and tell her."

"I tried, but she just stormed off."

"I had a similar thing that happened to me years ago. My younger sister and I had a misunderstanding that ruined our relationship."

"What happened?"

"We had a difference of opinion about the man she wanted to marry. I knew him to be a spendthrift, despite not having any funds. I was convinced he wanted to marry my sister for the dowry."

"The dowry? Your family must have been well off."

"Oh, we were," said Sister Selena.

"And were you the eldest?"

"I had an older brother, but as for girls, it was only my sister and me. Making matters worse was the fact I refused to marry anyone."

"How is that an issue?"

"It's tradition that the eldest marries first, but I wasn't ready to settle down. In the end, I joined the order."

"And what happened to your sister?" asked Charlaine. "Did she marry the fellow?"

"She did, although what became of them is anyone's guess."

"I'm not sure I see how this is similar to my predicament."

"Well," said Selena. "I lost my sister because I was stubborn and refused to budge. Would I do it again? No, but then again, we don't get the chance to go back in time and correct our mistakes."

"And you think I'm in the wrong?" asked Charlaine.

"No, but I think you do, and unless I miss my guess, you're going to do something about it."

"Like what? Danica won't listen to me."

"Get out of the Antonine and take Danica with you. Once you're away from all this"—she waved her hand around—"I think cooler heads will prevail."

"And where would we go?"

"Into Reichendorf," said Sister Selena. "It's not as if it's very far. All you need to do is pass through the Antonine's gates, and you're there."

"And if Danica refuses?"

Selena smiled. "You're a Temple Captain now, Charlaine. Make it an order if you must."

"Any specifics on what we should visit?"

"That depends. What are your interests?"

"I'm quite fond of smithies," said Charlaine.

Sister Selena wrinkled her nose. "Really?"

"Yes, I used to be a smith. Why? You don't think that's a good idea?"

"I'm not saying it's bad, just that almost anything else would be better."

"Like what?"

"I don't know, but you could start by getting a meal. After all, you've both been eating here since your arrival. It'll do you good to sit amongst normal people for a change."

"Are you saying Temple Knights aren't normal?"

Sister Selena laughed. "I know they're not. We live in an insulated world, Sister, and that tends to give us a narrow view of things, but you know what? There's a whole wide world out there just waiting to be seen."

"You're right," said Charlaine. "I'll take your advice and get Danica out of the Antonine. Then we'll have it out, one way or the other."

12

THE CITY

Summer 1097 SR

"Why do I have to go?" argued Danica.

Charlaine stared down at her friend lying in bed. "Because I ordered you to. Now, get dressed and clean yourself up. There's work to be done."

Charlaine crossed to her own room, hearing quite clearly the curses sent her way by her recalcitrant fellow knight.

Danica finally appeared in the doorway, although her scowl hadn't faded. "Where are we going?"

"Into Reichendorf, if you must know."

"And are we to visit the stables first?"

"No," said Charlaine. "I believe we'll walk instead. It's not far."

"And then what?"

"You'll just have to wait and see. Now come along, or it'll be well past noon before we reach the gate."

They set out in their cassocks, decrying the armour of their order, but still wearing their swords. The day was the warmest they'd seen since their arrival, and by the time they reached the Reichendorf gate, they were sweating profusely. The pair of Cunar guards stationed there paid them little attention, other than to remind them the gates closed at dusk.

They walked in silence, something Charlaine found uncomfortable. Once they cleared the gate, she could hold her tongue no longer.

"There's something I need to tell you," she said.

"If this is another lecture," warned Danica, "then you needn't bother."

Charlaine halted, but when her companion kept walking, she reached out, grabbing her by the bicep and causing her to turn to face her. "I must talk to you about Commander Hjordis."

"Go on." Danica's teeth clenched.

"It's not what you think. After the commander made me the offer, I went to visit the Temple Knights of Saint Ansgar."

"You did?"

"Yes, and they advised me to play along with her plan."

"So you lied to her?"

Charlaine smiled. "Not lied so much as omitted telling the entire story."

"But why go along with her at all?"

"To buy time. Captain Zander needs to look into things."

"Captain Zander?"

"Yes. He's an investigator for the order."

They continued on their way for some time.

"I... don't know what to say," Danica finally admitted. "I thought you'd sold your soul to an evil witch."

"I'd hardly call Commander Hjordis a witch."

Danica smiled. "You know what I mean."

"I do, and I apologize for not saying something sooner, but I couldn't risk her people finding out."

"Her people? Does she have that much influence?"

"I believe she does, and that's not all."

"What else is there?"

"Others are involved. And when I say others, I mean other orders."

"What makes you think that?"

"They arrested you for consorting with men," said Charlaine, "and that has to have something to do with you going to the Cunar commandery."

"Why would you say that?"

"Where else have you been, other than our lodgings? They couldn't possibly be so dim as to suggest you snuck men into our own commandery?"

"I must admit that makes sense," said Danica. "But why?"

"She wants to be grand mistress—she told me so herself. The very fact that she offered your release as a condition of my cooperation confirms she has few lines she's not willing to cross. That makes her an exceedingly dangerous adversary."

"Still, how do you know the Cunars are working with her?"

"I believe one of them alerted her to your presence at their commandery.

Tell me, who did you interact with while there, other than your tutor, of course?"

"A man by the name of Commander Stramond, but he was most helpful. He even led me to the naval architect's workshop."

"And no one else talked to you?"

"There was one fellow. A captain named Dimas, but Stramond put him in his place."

"So either one of those might have informed Hjordis?"

"I suppose," said Danica. "Come to think of it, Dimas was incensed by my presence. Do you think he might be the one in league with her?"

"It's hard to say," said Charlaine. "The bonds of rank run deep in the Cunars. I can't imagine a lowly captain passing information on to one of our order, can you?"

"But isn't that precisely what the commander wanted of you?"

"Yes, that's true. In any event, the individual doesn't matter so much as the fact your presence was discovered and reported."

"So what do we do now? Do I go on acting as though I'm mad at you?"

"I hadn't thought that far ahead. I was more worried about you being mad at me. Tell me, and be honest about it, did you really believe I'd give up so easily?"

"Well," said Danica, "let's just say that if this whole Temple Knight thing doesn't work out for you, you could probably find a job as a storyteller. The better question is whether or not Commander Hjordis believed you."

"That's beyond my control," said Charlaine, "but it's definitely something we should keep in mind for any future interactions with her."

They reached a crossroads and turned north, walking down a major thoroughfare, past throngs of people going about their business. Charlaine paused at a fruit stall, selecting a pear and tossing the vendor a coin.

"Hungry?" asked Danica as they continued on.

"Not particularly," replied Charlaine, "but I suspect someone's following us, and I wanted to see what they'd do?"

"And?"

In answer, Charlaine turned slightly, looking at a store window before quickly glancing behind them.

"Still there," she said.

"What do you want to do?"

"For now, nothing, but keep alert. I shouldn't like to get taken by surprise."

"Where to now?"

"Hungry?"

"Not particularly," said Danica. "How about you?"

"I can wait."

"You know, there's a Mathewite mission somewhere around here. It might be an idea to pay them a visit; maybe get some idea of where they stand regarding Commander Hjordis."

"I'm not sure how we'd go about doing that," Charlaine retorted. "I don't imagine we can just stroll up to them and say 'Good morning, Brother. Can I ask you if you're plotting with a Temple Commander of Saint Agnes?' I can't see that as ending well, can you?"

"No, I suppose not. Still, we could look around, couldn't we?"

"It certainly wouldn't do any harm, and who knows, we might learn a thing or two that concerns our present circumstances. Have you any idea where this mission of theirs is?"

"No, but I'm sure we could find out easy enough." Danica caught the eye of a passerby. "Excuse me, could you tell us where to find the mission of Saint Mathew?"

"Certainly, Sister," the man replied. "It's but a short walk from here." He pointed down the street. "Two blocks down," he continued, "and then turn to your left. It's a large red-stone building that'll be on the north side of the street. You can't miss it."

"Thank you," said Danica. She turned to her companion. "I don't suppose it gets any easier than that."

The mission of Saint Mathew was not a place of worship; it was where the order could carry out its sworn oath to care for the sick and poor.

The building was constructed of a deep-red stone cut into large bricks, giving it a unique appearance. As Charlaine and Danica stood in front trying to decide their next move, a portly fellow with a thick, unruly mop of hair exited. In stark contrast to this was his neatly trimmed beard—a common affectation amongst members of the Order of Saint Mathew.

"Good day, Sisters," he said in greeting.

"Good day, Father," replied Charlaine.

"How did you know I was a Holy Father?"

"Your cassock."

"But I could have been a simple lay brother?"

"Not so," said Charlaine. She pointed to the white axe emblazoned on his chest, augmented by a yellow outline. "You have the yellow thread that denotes your position."

He gazed down at his chest and let out a loud guffaw. "By the Saints, you're very observant. I daresay most would fail to note the distinction. I'm Father Hywel, and you are?"

"Temple Captain Charlaine and Sister Danica."

"Please to meet you, Sisters. May I ask what brings you to the mission this day?"

"Curiosity more than anything," said Charlaine. "I couldn't help but notice you have no guards. Do the Temple Knights of Saint Mathew not protect you?"

He smiled. "There is little need of it at the mission. The people hereabouts respect what we do for them and allow us to work in peace."

"Have you no criminals in Reichendorf?" asked Danica.

"There are many who resort to crime to support themselves," said Father Hywel, "but they all agree our work here is important. Thus, we are allowed to continue our duties without incident."

"And so they go unpunished?"

"It may surprise you to know some of those very criminals donate funds to help us continue our good work."

Danica was shocked. "Surely not? They're criminals. How can you take their coins?"

"How can we not? Were we to leave it to the wealthier merchants, we would all surely starve. What matter the source of funds if it does the Saint's will?"

"That's an interesting way of paying for all of this," said Charlaine. "Might we have a look inside?"

"Of course, by all means. Shall I give you a tour?" He stepped inside, urging them to follow. "This is an ancient structure dating back centuries. Some say it was built by the Old Kingdom, but no one really knows for sure. In any case, it was built well, likely to house warriors."

"Did you say Old Kingdom?" asked Danica.

"Yes, although you might be familiar with the more common name, Therengia."

"Yes," said Charlaine. "I've been reading about them as part of my training. I didn't know they were in these parts, though."

"Oh yes. Some say this was the very heart of their realm."

"I wonder if that's why the Church built the Antonine here?" said Danica.

"Why would you think that?" asked Charlaine.

"Well," continued the younger knight. "Once Therengia was defeated, the Petty Kingdoms drove their people to the ends of the Continent?"

"I'm not sure I see the connection?"

"If this was their home, building atop it would prevent its re-emergence, wouldn't it?"

"There is a certain logic to that," noted Charlaine, "but it would only make sense if it was their capital."

"What about the Campaigns of Aeldred?" said Danica.

"The what?" said Father Hywel.

"It's a book we're studying back in the Antonine," explained Charlaine. "It details King Aeldred's campaign against Thalemia. It's required reading for all captains of our order."

"You read the works of a heathen?"

"The book is a second-hand account, written by members of the Church, but based on historical records available to them." Danica turned to Charlaine. "How do you suppose they got those records?"

"All right, I'll admit your argument makes sense, but that's a far cry from accepting it as fact."

"Well," said Father Hywel. "Interesting as such conjecture is, it matters little in the long run. We, on the other hand, have much to keep us busy here at the mission."

"Yes, of course," said Charlaine. "Please continue, Father. Sorry for the interruption."

The front door led directly into a large room where a series of long tables and benches resided.

"This is where we feed the masses," the Holy Father explained.

"How long has the mission been here?" asked Danica.

"It was established some four hundred years ago, give or take a decade or two. We have few records of that time, but it appears the first contingents of our order took up residence here even as the Antonine was under construction."

"The Antonine is only four hundred years old? I thought it was older?"

"How could it be?" said Charlaine. "You yourself speculated it was built on the ruins of the Therengian capital."

"Oh yes," said Danica. "I hadn't thought of that." Her eyes lit up.

"I know that look," said Charlaine. "You've just realized something."

"I did. As you know, I visited the Church archives when we were seeking information about Giselle."

"And?"

"The archives are immense. I didn't think much about it at the time, but there must be far more than four hundred years of records in that place."

"Possibly," noted Father Hywel, "but the members of the Church would have brought their own records with them, wouldn't they?"

"Perhaps," said Charlaine, "but records would mean a lot of paper, and paper is heavy. Far more reasonable to assume they travelled relatively lightly."

"You know more about Church history than I do," said Danica. "Where was the head of the Church before the Antonine was built?"

"If memory serves, I believe Corassus, but the fortress there didn't have enough space to house everyone."

"Partially correct," said Father Hywel. "Prior to the establishment of the Antonine, the Church administration was scattered throughout the Petty Kingdoms. Each region fell under the jurisdiction of the local Church officials. Unfortunately, that led to several disagreements over doctrine, so it was thought a central structure more desirable."

"Interesting," noted Danica, "but I'm still of the opinion there are ancient records in those archives, even some that might date back to the Therengians."

"As a note of caution," said the Holy Father, "we try to use the expression 'Old Kingdom' rather than Therengian."

"Why is that?"

"Mostly superstition. You must remember, from an outsider's point of view, Therengia was the enemy. Even today, many rulers of the Petty Kingdoms have nightmares about its re-emergence."

"I'll keep that in mind," promised Danica.

Father Hywel led them into the kitchens. Here, three large ovens took up most of the outside wall.

"This is all new construction since we moved in," he explained. "Before that, there was only a small fireplace in the back."

"How many do you feed daily?" asked Charlaine.

"It's been estimated we serve over two hundred meals a day, not including our own people. Many who use our services cannot find work, and without any income, cannot find lodging. As a result, we house those we can." He led them through a doorway and down a hall to another large room. "This is one of our dormitories, which houses the men. We have another similar-sized room for women, along with half a dozen smaller rooms for housing families."

"And they live here permanently?"

"No," said Hywel. "They are provided shelter for the night on a first-come, first-served basis, although many find themselves returning night after night. It pains me to say it, but our mission here only scratches the surface of the problem."

"Is this a problem in all the Petty Kingdoms?" asked Charlaine.

"So I am led to believe. Of course, some rulers are more generous in terms of donations, but by and large, there's little interest amongst the affluent to share their bounty with the destitute."

"Can nothing be done to sway them?"

"That is the magic question," said Father Hywel. "Solve that, and the Continent would be a happier place."

He led them back to the entrance. "There is more to the building, but I must respect the privacy of our lay brothers."

"I would expect no less," said Charlaine. "Thank you, Father Hywel. You've been most gracious. I will soon be travelling north to my new command, but I promise you I shall do all I can to help the local Mathewite mission."

"That is most kind of you. Farewell, Sisters, and may Saint Agnes watch over you."

Charlaine and Danica made their way down the street.

"That was illuminating," said Danica.

"It definitely was. I never realized so many people were in need. It makes our own problems seem less important by contrast."

"Less important, yes, but still in need of being addressed. What do we do about Commander Hjordis?"

"Well, for a start, we can deal with the person who's been following us."

Danica's eyes wandered the crowd. "They're still here?"

"She is," replied Charlaine, "and I believe it's time we confronted her."

"What are you suggesting?" asked Danica.

"You should storm off in a huff, then come up from behind them."

"What does she look like?"

"Short with blonde hair tied up in a bun, wearing a pale green dress with a dirty white apron."

"Strange garb for a sister, isn't it?"

"I don't think she's a member of the order," said Charlaine.

"Then who is she?"

"That's what we'll endeavour to find out." She halted, then took a step back, shouting, "If that's what you think, then it's time I took my leave of you!"

"I've had enough of this nonsense," yelled Danica in reply, then turned, quickly disappearing into the crowd.

Charlaine continued up the street, slowing to allow her comrade to get into position. After going half a block, she halted, pretending to peer into a workshop where a carpenter plied his trade. Out of the corner of her eye, she noticed Danica move into position, then confront the individual. Charlaine rushed over, her hand on the hilt of her sword.

"Who are you?" demanded Danica.

The woman's eyes darted around with the look of a cornered animal. "I meant no harm," she said.

"Who are you," asked Charlaine, "and why are you following us?"

"My name's Marcy," the woman replied, then lowered her voice. "I'm here on behalf of Brother Mateo."

"Mateo?" said Danica. "Isn't that the exiled Cunar?"

"Yes," said Charlaine. "What's he want?"

"To talk to you," the woman replied. "Nothing more."

"Then take us to him."

"He's an exile," warned Danica.

"Yes," said Charlaine, "but we've already talked to him once, so doing so a second time is hardly any worse." She turned her attention back to Marcy. "Is he close?"

"He is but two blocks away."

"Then lead on, and I promise you no harm shall befall either of you."

13

BROTHER MATEO

Summer 1097 SR

Marcy led them along a back street, turning down a winding pathway that emerged into a courtyard, where several decrepit doors marked the dwellings of poor folk. She went to one of these, knocking before entering the structure.

Inside, the building wasn't much better than the door, what with the filthy, peeling wattle-and-daub walls. Several small rooms branched off the entranceway, but Marcy continued, passing through the far door into a narrow alleyway where Brother Mateo waited.

"Thank you for agreeing to see me," the man said. "I know you take a great risk in doing so."

"The last time we met," said Charlaine, "you hinted at a rot inside the Church, but you were short on details."

"I apologize for that, but if you recall, we were rudely interrupted before I could say any more."

"And now, it seems, that's no longer the case."

"True." He paused, gathering his thoughts. "I was a Temple Knight of Saint Cunar before my exile, and like many of my brethren, one of my duties was guarding the commandery. On one particular day, I stood outside the office of Temple Commander Stramond, along with a fellow knight. Just to be clear, we were outside his office, but the argument emanating from within was impossible to ignore."

"What was this disagreement about?"

"Stramond was furious with someone for leaving him exposed. I didn't grasp its significance at the time, but later, I learned he was under intense scrutiny by the grand master of our order. In any case, it's the other occupant of the room who surprised me—Commander Hjordis."

"Wouldn't you have seen her arrive?" asked Danica.

"When I took up my guard duties, the meeting was already underway. At first, I only knew it was a woman's voice. It wasn't until she left that I saw who it was."

"Is there anything else you can reveal about their discussion?"

"The subject of the conversation shifted to the grand master. Commander Stramond had been having some issues with him of late, resulting in the scrutiny."

"What you speak of is only hearsay," said Charlaine.

"There's more," said Mateo. "Two days later, we received word the grand master was dead. Admittedly, he was old but was an active man, often leading weapon practice himself."

"Do we know the cause of death?"

"They said his heart gave out, but I suspect he was murdered."

"What would lead you to that conclusion?" asked Charlaine.

"The manner in which his death was handled. Very few people had access to the body once his death was announced, and even the Mathewites were denied access to it."

"The Mathewites?"

"Yes," said Mateo. "It's common practice for a member of the Order of Saint Mathew to examine the deceased to discover the cause of death. It's their calling—looking after the sick and dying."

"Were there any physicians present?"

"None at all."

"Who announced the death?"

"Commander Stramond."

"Strange," said Danica. "Did Stramond try to claim the position of grand master for himself?"

"No," said Brother Mateo. "Then again, only the Patriarch of Saint Cunar can make that decision."

"Suspicious, maybe, but not exactly a bloody dagger, if you understand my meaning. We'll need a lot more if you expect anything to be done about it."

"There's more, but I had to break confidence to learn it."

"Go on," urged Charlaine.

"Someone else was involved, a senior member of the Augustines."

"The Order of Saint Augustine looks after Holy relics," said Danica. "I hardly see how they would be involved."

"He was here the day the grand master died."

"That could simply be a coincidence," said Charlaine.

"True, but Commander Stramond lied about it."

"When?"

"After the grand master's death, all the Cunar commanders gathered to choose an interim grand master. I was present at that meeting, serving as a guard. There were twelve of them, all told, and each related the events from their own point of view. Commander Stramond never mentioned his meeting with the Augustine, although there was no apparent reason not to. Surely that indicates something untoward was going on?"

"Did he push to be made interim grand master?"

"No, not at all. In fact, when it was offered, he categorically refused."

"Are you suggesting he's responsible for the death?" asked Danica.

"Not in the sense that he did the actual killing, no, but I have no doubt he was involved in its planning."

"And this Augustine, do you know who he is?"

"No," said Brother Mateo, "but I'd recognize him if I saw his face again."

"I'm not sure that's helpful," said Charlaine. "You're an exile. The mere act of talking with you is grounds for us to be arrested, and bringing word second-hand isn't going to convince anyone. They'll only accuse us of making it up."

"What if I was to testify? I could take my case to the Ansgarites?"

"That would mean entering the Antonine where you'd be arrested on sight."

"I'd be willing to do so if it unmasks this plot. The scheming of Commander Stramond led to my expulsion from the order. I'm sure of it."

"Why do you say that?"

"I was one of two Temple Knights who saw the Augustine enter the night of the grand master's death. Care to guess what happened to my brother knight?"

"Let me guess," said Charlaine. "He was exiled?"

"Worse, he was killed—stabbed while wandering the markets of Reichendorf. Two days later, I was arrested and charged with breaking my vows."

"Which vows?"

"I was accused of leaving my post. It was all a lie, of course, but what could I do? Witnesses were lined up against me to give false testimony. Commander Stramond suggested the sentence of exile."

"So there are a lot more involved other than Stramond?"

"Most assuredly, although how much they knew about the details is debatable."

"It's clear Commander Stramond has surrounded himself with allies," said Charlaine. "At the very least, something's definitely going on."

"Not necessarily," said Danica. "After all, you hand-picked your team when we went to Calabria. I would imagine many leaders collect followers as they advance in rank. You could even make the argument we're in the same boat."

"I see your point, but there's a big difference between collecting followers and having them lie for you."

"Assuming Brother Mateo is telling the truth. How do we know he's not just a disgruntled ex-Temple Knight, trying to get even with the man who exiled him?"

Charlaine turned to Mateo. "What do you say to that, Brother?"

"I understand your concern, and were it within my power, I would give you the proof you need. You've been at the Antonine for a while now. You tell me everything's normal, and I'll cease making these accusations."

"You convinced me," said Danica. "The only question now is how do we get him to give evidence?"

"I shall surrender myself at the gate," said Brother Mateo, "but you, in turn, must get me an audience with an Ansgarite investigator."

"We shall do our best," said Danica.

"We'll do more than that," added Charlaine. "We must. The moral fabric of the Church is on the line."

They began the trip back to the gates of the Antonine. Brother Mateo remained sombre, which was no surprise since the man was about to surrender himself into custody. If things went badly for him, he could face execution.

The first sign of trouble was when they turned onto a street to find it devoid of townsfolk. In their place were four women, each armed and armoured—two occupied the middle of the road, while the others stood slightly off on each side, threatening their flanks. Though they wore no cassocks, there could be no doubt they were Sisters of Saint Agnes, for what woman but a Temple Knight could afford to wear plate armour?

"Stand aside," said Charlaine. "We have no quarrel with you."

"I'm afraid I can't do that," came the reply.

Charlaine recognized the voice, that of Sister Lara, who had been Danica's jailer. Her hand shifted to the hilt of her weapon. "You have no authority here."

"I have a sword," replied Lara. "That is authority enough."

Danica drew her blade, followed a moment later by her comrade. Unarmed as he was, Brother Mateo could do little but move to the rear and watch the situation unfold.

The enemy moved first, rushing in to carry the fight to the trio. Charlaine, quick to block, countered with a thrust, but the armour of her opponent made such a move ineffective. To her side, Danica, suffering a similar fate, was forced to back up, a minor cut on her arm evidence of the uneven duel.

Charlaine blocked another blow, then used her forearm to push her opponent back, knocking him from his feet. The knight fell to the ground, but another soon took her place, driving Charlaine back with a flurry of blows.

Danica, meanwhile, fought two opponents. She blocked a swing with her sword, but its impact forced her to the side, directly into her comrade. One of their assailants used the momentary confusion to rush past, and then Brother Mateo cried out in pain.

Charlaine stabbed out again, scraping her blade along a vambrace. Her foe, inexperienced in battle, panicked, backing up to avoid injury instead of letting her armour absorb the blow. Charlaine used the opportunity to wheel around, only to see Brother Mateo on the ground, a knight standing over him, pulling her sword from his stomach.

Charlaine's sword reached out, attempting to strike his assassin, but it was too late. Their task complete, the women began withdrawing, keeping their fronts to Charlaine and Danica, lest they pursue.

"Leave them," called out Charlaine. She knelt by Brother Mateo. The Cunar clutched his stomach, the blood flowing freely between his fingers. He looked up, his face pale, and tried to speak, but nothing came out. His hands twitched before he lay still.

Charlaine placed her fingers over his eyes, closing them before she risked a quick glance down the street. Their attackers were out of sight, likely using the side streets or alleys to avoid pursuit. The fight had been bloody and quick, but the sound had carried. Even now, they heard a hue and cry coming from the nearest gate.

A shadow loomed over her, and she looked up to see Danica. "Is he dead?" the younger knight asked.

"He is—murdered by those sister knights."

"A terrible fate for an honourable man."

"Honourable?" said Charlaine. "I might remind you he was an exile. We are yet to determine the truth of his allegations."

"Still, it's a most painful way to die."

"Agreed, and likely intended to be so."

"Whatever do you mean?"

"He was unarmed," said Charlaine, "and unarmoured, while our assailants wore full plate armour. It would've been easy enough to kill him with a stab through the heart. Instead, they chose to punish him with a painful death."

"What do we do now?"

Charlaine looked down the street. Temple Knights of Saint Cunar, no doubt drawn by the sounds of conflict, approached as townsfolk began emerging from their places of safety.

"Drop your weapons," came a command.

Charlaine stood, her weapon lowered.

The Cunar captain, unimpressed with this show of defiance, called out again. "I said, drop your weapons! Do it now, or I shall give the order to cut you down where you stand."

"Do it," said Charlaine, looking at her companion. "There's little sense in fighting an unwinnable conflict." Her sword dropped to the street.

Danica did likewise, and then the guards moved closer, their leader standing over the body. "This is the exile, Mateo Harnbringer." His eyes swivelled to Charlaine and Danica, then back to his men. "Arrest them," he said.

"On what charge?" said Danica.

"Consorting with an exile."

Their arms were seized and pulled behind their backs, cords tied around their wrists while another individual retrieved their weapons.

"Who are you?" asked the Cunar captain.

"Temple Captain Charlaine, and this is Sister Danica, Temple Knight of Saint Agnes."

The man grunted, then watched as his men completed their task.

"This is not what you think," continued Charlaine.

"Silence," ordered the Cunar leader. "It's not your place to argue the matter here, nor is it mine. The truth shall come out at the tribunal."

"Tribunal?"

"Yes. You've been found in flagrant disregard of Church law. It is now up to those of higher rank to determine your fate. Since you are a Temple Captain, your case will be dealt with first." His eyes turned towards Danica. "Your fate, however, will primarily rest with that of your superior here."

"And what fate would that be?" asked Charlaine.

"At the very least, exile, but I would be lying if I said that was the only potential outcome."

"What could be worse than that?"

"In such cases, execution cannot be ruled out." He paused a moment, meeting her gaze. "I know your reputation, Sister, but I've heard much these last few weeks. I wish you well, but you've made enemies here at the Antonine. For now, however, we must get you back to the inner city where your tribunal can be arranged."

Charlaine examined their surroundings. The Temple Knights of Saint Cunar had been the ones to take them into custody. Thus, they were being held in the cells beneath the Cunar commandery. That could change at any moment, but at least for now, they were together.

The room was nothing more than a rectangle, with bars at one end separating it from the room beyond. On the far side was a single door, along with a hook on which hung a lantern, the only light source.

"What do we do now?" asked Danica.

"There's little we can do," Charlaine replied. "Our only option is to wait."

"I fell asleep. How long have we been here?"

"With no windows, it's hard to say, but I'd guess it must be late afternoon by now. Why? Somewhere else you need to be?"

Danica chuckled. "Not until classes resume. Then again, this isn't too bad."

"Not bad? How can you say that?"

"Hey now, at least a giant lizard didn't bite my leg!"

"True enough," agreed Charlaine, "yet the end result could be worse."

"Couldn't you appeal to Commander Hjordis? You did tell her you'd help."

"She's the one who sent the sisters after Brother Mateo. I doubt she's in a mood to do us any favours."

"Then how about the grand mistress?"

"We can't risk it. She's already on a precipitous ledge; something like this could easily be her undoing. Better, I think, to leave her out of it completely."

"Even at the cost of our lives?"

"You were willing to give your life at the Battle of Alantra," said Charlaine. "Can you do any less now?"

"Yes, but at least at Alantra, we would have gone down fighting. All this standing around only leads to madness."

The door opened, admitting a man clothed in the grey cassock of a Temple Knight of Saint Cunar. Danica watched as he lifted the lantern from its place of rest, bringing it closer.

"Brother Leamund?"

"You know this fellow?" asked Charlaine.

"I'll say. He's the naval architect I've been learning from."

"Greetings," bid Brother Leamund. "I'm sorry our meeting has to be under these circumstances, but I thought it best you be made aware of what's happening."

"We're listening," said Danica.

"Your case has been remanded to the Temple Knights of Saint Agnes, but the charge of consorting with an exile is of interest to all the orders. As a result, the tribunal shall consist of commanders from the three principle orders: our own, the Agneses, and, of course, the Mathewites."

"Any idea of which individuals will comprise this tribunal?"

"I'm afraid that's the bad news," said the Cunar, "at least from what I understand of your predicament. Commander Hjordis will be in charge, but then again, she is the one responsible for the enforcement of discipline within your order. Assisting her is Commander Stramond, whom I believe you know."

"And the Mathewite?"

"Commander Jamarian. He's only just arrived from a place called Draybourne."

"Never heard of it," said Danica.

"It lies far to the east, in the Duchy of Holstead."

"I don't know whether that's good news or bad."

"For us? I would suspect good," said Charlaine. "It sounds like the outer fringes of the Petty Kingdoms, an area likely far removed from the politics of the Antonine."

"Politics?" said Brother Leamund. "Is there something I should know?"

"There is a struggle within our order," explained Danica.

"What kind of struggle?"

"Let's just say there are those who wish to further their own ends."

"Ah," the Cunar replied. "I've seen the same thing in our own order. It's a common problem, I'm told, keeping the spirit of the Saints alive without corrupting men with power... or women, for that matter."

"Is there any word on when this tribunal will sit?"

"Oh yes. Tomorrow."

"So soon?"

He nodded. "Word of the exile's demise has spread, along with the fact you were in his company. I'm afraid the upper echelons of the Church will be eager to put such matters to rest before discontent grows."

"Discontent?"

"I fear your reputation precedes you. Word of what you two did in Ilea is on everyone's lips, and people aren't happy with how you're being treated."

"And how did that happen?" asked Charlaine.

He smiled. "I might have mentioned it once or twice."

14

TRIBUNAL

Summer 1097 SR

They were led into a large chamber where the adjudicators sat at a table set up at the far end. The rest of the room was lined with chairs for those wishing to witness the tribunal. Today, the place was packed, forcing many to stand.

Their guards paused at the door, waiting for the arrival of the prisoners to be acknowledged. Sister Lara stood by, watching people take their seats.

"I forgive you," whispered Charlaine.

Sister Lara stared back, a look of shock on her face. "For what?" she replied.

"I know you only did the bidding of Commander Hjordis."

"She is a rising star within the Church. She may even make grand mistress one day."

"Be careful," warned Charlaine. "Those whose light shines brightest often burn anyone who's close by."

A small gong announced the adjudicators were ready to begin.

"Bring in the prisoners," ordered Commander Hjordis.

Charlaine and Danica were led to a pair of seats that sat empty.

"This tribunal has been called to administer disciplinary punishment on Temple Captain Charlaine deShandria and Sister Danica Meer."

"I must object," came a woman's voice.

All eyes turned to the source of the objection.

Commander Hjordis sneered. "And you are?"

"Temple Captain Collette Fontaine," the woman replied.

"And what is the basis of your objection?"

"Under article forty-three of the Church's charter, this tribunal is to determine guilt or innocence of those charged, not issue punishment. That's the sole prerogative of the grand mistress."

"I am well aware," replied Commander Hjordis, "but matters of discipline are my responsibility. Thus, it falls to me to decide what measures to take."

"It does, Commander, but only after a finding of guilt. In cases such as this, the accused must be given a chance to defend themselves or at least have someone speak on their behalf."

"And are you volunteering to do such?"

"I am," announced Captain Fontaine.

Commander Hjordis let out an audible sigh. "Very well, it shall be so noted. Someone find her a seat so we may continue with this tribunal."

Charlaine had only witnessed one tribunal in her brief career, that of Captain Giselle, and even then, she missed most of it. This one started with a long and tedious explanation of the events leading up to Brother Mateo's expulsion from the Temple Knights of Saint Cunar. The evidence given made it sound like a straightforward case but tempered with Mateo's own version of events, Charlaine could easily see how power and influence had eliminated any chance of mounting a viable defence.

By noon, after half a dozen witnesses had each sworn to Mateo's guilt, she started to wonder why such evidence was being brought up in the first place. Brother Mateo was an exile. That fact was not in doubt, yet the tribunal took extraordinary steps to paint him as a vile and disgusting traitor. To Charlaine's mind, they could only be doing so to sway the audience. Then she remembered the words of Brother Leamund.

Looking around the room, she noted the presence of many temple sisters and wondered who amongst them was sympathetic to her cause. The thought brought to mind her warning to Sister Lara. Was she herself the one who was burning brightly? Were those around her about to be scorched? A terrible burden settled over her shoulders, the weight of it oppressive. Her eyes swivelled towards Danica, but the young knight's attention was focused on the adjudicators.

The tribunal adjourned for a break. While those in charge gathered in private to discuss a matter of Church law, Sister Collette appeared beside them.

"I hope I'm not interfering?" she asked.

"Not at all," replied Charlaine. "Although I can't help but wonder why you're doing this?"

"Do you remember your vows?"

"Of course. To which one, in particular, are you referring?"

Sister Collette closed her eyes, the better to recall. "Do you swear to keep your word and never lie? To show mercy to enemies of the Church and be kind, brave, and generous to others?"

"Are you saying you're doing this to be generous?"

"No." She lowered her voice. "I'm saying there are those here who are enemies of the Church."

"They ARE the Church," implored Danica.

"That doesn't mean they represent the ideals of Saint Agnes."

"Does that mean you're going to be generous to them?"

"All right," said Sister Collette. "I admit it wasn't the best of examples, but it's still clear there's something strange happening here. I served on a tribunal back in Korvoran, and it was nothing like this. It's supposed to function as a court, with evidence presented from both sides, but it seems like all this panel wants to do is convict you. Hardly what I'd call fair."

"And so you thought to come here and defend us?"

"Not at all. I only came to witness the whole thing, but that opening statement just twisted my braids."

Danica laughed at the strange turn of phrase but sobered when she saw the expression on Collette's face.

"Look," continued Captain Fontaine, "it's clear they're going to do everything in their power to convict you. If I'm to help you, you must tell me all you know, no matter how insignificant you feel it is."

Charlaine's eyes drifted over the crowd. "This is not, I think, the best venue in which to discuss these matters."

"Then I shall arrange some privacy. Give me a moment, and I'll see what I can do." She left them, consulting with the guards at the door.

"Do you believe she can help?" asked Danica.

"At the very least, she can get word to those who can."

"Yes, but will that be enough?"

"Only time will tell," admitted Charlaine.

The tribunal resumed later the same day. Having found a place in private to inform Sister Collette of all they knew, Charlaine and Danica once again took their seats.

The guard who arrested them was the next witness. His testimony lacked any embellishment or opinion, simply stating the facts, with few questions regarding the events of the day. The adjudicators briefly whispered to each other as he returned to his seat, then Commander Hjordis rang the small gong, silencing all within.

"The case against Sisters Charlaine and Danica rests. It is now time for them to present their defence against these charges."

Sister Collette rose, taking a moment to prepare her thoughts before speaking. "I call on Commander Stramond to testify."

The room exploded into chatter. Stramond, who sat as an adjudicator, stared back, dumbfounded by the request.

"You cannot," said Commander Hjordis. "He sits in judgement."

"I have the right to call any witness I wish, do I not?"

"She is right," answered Commander Jamarian. The Mathewite turned to his fellow adjudicators. "Church law is clear on this. Determining the truth is more important than the minutiae of procedure."

"Very well," said Hjordis. "I shall allow it."

Commander Stramond rose, looking decidedly unhappy. He moved out in front of the table, taking the seat placed there for witnesses.

"Commander," began Sister Collette, "would you please state your position within the Temple Knights of Saint Cunar?"

"I am a Temple Commander," the man responded, "responsible for overseeing the training of knights of our order."

"You train Cunar knights here at the Antonine?"

"No. We have several commanderies dedicated to training, spread throughout the Continent. My job is to make sure each location follows the procedures and methods detailed by those in charge."

"So you're essentially an administrator?"

The commander's face reddened. "Do you mock me? I carry out important, nay, essential work for the order. You, as a mere captain, and a new one at that, couldn't possibly understand the intricacies of what I do."

"My apologies, Commander. I merely sought to clarify. Do you carry out this training yourself?"

"No, I do not. That is the responsibility of the lower-ranking members of the order. Look here. This has nothing to do with the charges against the defendants. Get on with it, or I shall have you removed from the room."

"How do you know Commander Hjordis?"

"I beg your pardon?"

"It's a simple enough question," insisted Sister Collette.

"With all due respect," added Jamarian, "answer the question."

"We have worked together on occasion," said Stramond.

"Can you be more specific?" pressed Collette.

"What has this to do with anything?"

"With the tribunal's permission, I will get to that in a moment. Please answer the question."

"If you must know, I met the commander about two years ago. She sought out my advice on a disciplinary matter."

"And has she ever visited you at the Cunar commandery?"

"I fail to see what that has to do with the matter at hand."

"I would agree," said Commander Hjordis. "You were granted permission to ask questions of Commander Stramond, but such questions need to be pertinent to the facts of the case."

"Understood," said Sister Collette. "I shall get straight to the point." She looked the Cunar commander directly in the eyes. "Did you report Sister Danica for spending time in the Cunar commandery?"

"Of course I did," the man replied. "How else was I to put an end to her incessant enquiries!"

"What's this now?" asked Commander Jamarian.

"It is nothing," replied Commander Hjordis. "It merely relates to a previous disciplinary matter."

"Yet it also involved Sister Danica?" asked Jamarian. "I think that makes it pertinent, don't you?"

"Not at all."

The Mathewite straightened his back. "I'm afraid I must insist." His eyes fell on the accused. "Sister Danica, what was the nature of this disciplinary matter?"

"I was charged with breaking my vow of celibacy."

"And did you? Break your vow, I mean."

"No, I had legitimate business at the commandery. In fact, Commander Stramond escorted me into the building."

"And yet he reported you?"

"So it would seem," replied Danica.

"And what happened to these charges?"

"Dismissed, or at least I assume they were."

"What do you mean by that?"

"I was released from my imprisonment after Temple Captain Charlaine agreed to Commander Hjordis's terms."

"By the Saints," said the Mathewite. "This gets more complicated by the moment." He directed his gaze towards Charlaine. "What, pray tell, were the commander's terms?"

"She wished me to reveal the plans of the grand mistress," said Charlaine.

"That," said Hjordis, "has no bearing on the matter currently before the tribunal."

"I believe it does," said Commander Jamarian. "In fact, it puts a whole new light on this entire assembly. So much so I must insist Commander Stramond be removed as adjudicator."

A woman's voice sang out from the back of the room. "Commander Hjordis should be removed as well."

Jamarian squinted. "What was that? Come forward and state your case."

Sister Lara moved to stand before the adjudicators, blatantly ignoring Commander Stramond, still sitting in the witness chair.

"I am Sister Lara, Temple Knight of Saint Agnes. I have come to unburden my soul."

"This is hardly the place for such things," warned Commander Hjordis.

"Pray continue," said Jamarian. "I would hear your words."

"Commander Hjordis sent me to kill the exile."

"Go on."

"We followed the two sisters on the off chance they would reveal his location."

"But we didn't even know we'd see him," burst out Danica.

"You've been followed for some time," said Sister Lara, "ever since you arrived, in fact. The commander warned us you'd be trouble."

"And why was this exile of particular interest?" asked the Mathewite.

"Because of what he knew."

"Which was?"

"That someone murdered the former Grand Master of Saint Cunar."

The entire room broke into an uproar. Commander Hjordis rang the gong in a desperate attempt to quiet everyone.

"This is an outlandish accusation!" she shouted. "The fact still remains these sisters were in the company of a known exile!"

A deep voice penetrated the crowd. "This charade has gone on long enough." A man, wearing a simple brown cassock devoid of any indication of this order, pushed his way to the front of the room.

"My name is Zander, Temple Captain of Saint Ansgar." All within fell silent once more. "Commander Stramond," he continued, "you are under arrest, pending a full investigation."

Stramond rose to his feet, his face red as he pointed at Commander Hjordis. "It was her idea," he spat out. "All to protect her precious career!"

"This tribunal is dismissed," ordered Commander Jamarian.

"You don't have the authority," countered Hjordis.

"I believe I do. I might be new to the Antonine, but I've been a commander far longer than you. And, unlike your own limited knowledge, I am fully conversant with my rights and privileges regarding tribunals." He looked at the guards. "Arrest Commander Hjordis."

The guards stared back. The situation was a difficult one, for their own commander had been placed under the guardianship of the Ansgarite. Now a Temple Knight of Saint Mathew ordered them about.

"Do it," snarled Captain Zander.

They made their way to the table, drawing swords. For a moment, Charlaine wondered whether the guards were about to declare their loyalty to Hjordis, but then they turned their weapons towards her.

"Come with us, Commander," barked out the senior guard. "You're under arrest."

Commander Jamarian rose, coming around the table to stand before Charlaine and Danica. "It's clear there's much more going on here than would first appear. In consideration of your past service, I believe it best the charges against you be rescinded. You are free to go, but I shall need written statements from both of you before you leave the Antonine."

"Thank you, Commander," said Charlaine.

"No, thank YOU. Had you not come here, none of this would have come to light."

"I was ordered here. It's not as if I had any choice in the matter."

"Still," said the Mathewite, "the results are the same. Perhaps Saint Agnes sent you?"

Charlaine bowed her head. "I go where I'm needed."

"What will happen to Commander Hjordis?" asked Danica.

"Her actions far exceeded her authority. I expect your grand mistress will turn over the investigation to the Temple Knights of Saint Ansgar. That is, after all, why the order exists. In the meantime, she will be held in seclusion to avoid any co-conspirators attempting to aid in her escape."

"You think that likely?"

"I think it an advisable precaution under the circumstances, don't you? She did order the execution of someone."

Captain Zander crossed the room, joining the small group. "It seems we owe you a debt of gratitude, Sister Charlaine," he said. "I don't know what you said to Sister Lara, but it's broken their silence. Three more sisters came forward ready to testify against their former commander."

"I forgave her," said Charlaine.

"That's it? Simple forgiveness?"

"I can't speak to her motives in coming forward, but perhaps she had a change of heart. It's one thing to follow a leader you admire, quite another to commit murder in her name."

"Well," said Captain Zander, "much as I'd like to stay and chat, there are a lot of interviews to see to. Good luck, Captain Charlaine. You too, Sister Danica. May you always have the blessings of the Saints."

"He's correct," added Commander Jamarian. "There's plenty of work to do to sort out this mess. I wish you well, and remember to leave me those statements."

"I'll make sure of it," replied Charlaine.

The guards hauled away Stramond and Hjordis, and then a small group of sister knights, Lara amongst them, left under guard. Those who had come to witness the tribunal now wandered out, although the noise level had risen considerably. Tales of what happened here would eventually be carried to the four corners of the Petty Kingdoms, but for today it was more about trying to make sense of the sudden reversal of fortunes.

The room was almost empty before Charlaine and Danica made their way to the exit, only to notice Temple Captain Nicola waiting for them.

"The grand mistress wants to speak with you," she stated.

"That's it?" said Danica. "No congratulations, or thank-you's?"

"Very well," said Nicola. "Congratulations. The grand mistress wants to see you."

"Lead on," said Charlaine. "It's not as if we have any other pressing business."

Grand Mistress Kaylene Gantzmann sat behind her desk, her fingers steepled before her.

"I think you've spent enough time in the Antonine. I'm sending you to Reinwick. You'll leave first thing tomorrow."

"What about our training?" asked Danica.

"You learned enough. I'll send some books with you, but there's little more that can benefit you here." She handed over a scroll case to Charlaine. "In that, you'll find your orders to assume command of the commandery in Korvoran. Unfortunately, the last captain died of an illness, so they've been under the temporary supervision of one of the sister knights. I tell you this because there may be some resentment at your appointment."

She took up another scroll, passing it to Danica. "This authorizes you to draw the Church funds necessary to purchase and equip a ship. It is overly broad in nature, so I'm putting my faith in you not to overspend. In addition, at the commissioning of said ship, you are granted the rank of Temple Captain."

Danica smiled. "Thank you, Grand Mistress. You honour me."

"In other circumstances, I would promote you before you left, but the presence of two such captains in Korvoran would raise too many suspicions, especially amongst our Cunar brethren. Speaking of which, you are to say nothing to them of our plans. Is that clear?"

They both nodded. "Might I ask something?" said Danica.

"By all means."

"Where, precisely, do I acquire these funds? Ships can't be purchased with promises. They need coins."

"Financial arrangements have been made through the Temple Knights of Saint Mathew."

"They have?"

The grand mistress smiled. "It's a commonly held secret their order specializes in the transfer of funds, an arrangement that has benefited both our orders for decades. They help transfer coins, and in exchange, we pay them a small percentage." She searched through some papers on her desk. "That reminds me; there's something else. Ah, here it is. A list of individuals you can trust." She passed the note to Danica. "I wouldn't bother opening it until you get there, and bear in mind the list is several months old, so some of them may no longer be in Reinwick. Have you any questions?"

"Might I enquire as to how long this assignment will last?" asked Charlaine.

"As long as is needed. Typically, that would be anywhere from five to ten years, but that largely depends on events in the north."

"Are you talking of specific events?"

"It has come to our attention the Halvarians are spending considerable funds to make certain, how can I put this... diplomatic advancements. In actual fact, we believe they may be trying to destabilize the region, much as they attempted to do in Ilea. That's why I want you there. Of course, I don't expect them to use the same tactics, but still, be on the lookout. Oh, and I'm told there's a Halvarian ambassador at the duke's court, so be careful. Now, Captain Nicola will see you are given funds for the trip. I look forward to seeing your reports, both of you."

"You want us to report directly to you?" asked Charlaine. "Should we not be under the jurisdiction of the regional mistress?"

"Ordinarily, yes, but this is a special case. Feel free to send your more mundane reports her way, though. I'd hate for her to feel left out."

"Where is the regional mistress stationed?"

"In the Kingdom of Eidolon, but they'll have all that information at your destination. Now, get out of here, both of you, before I'm forced to promote you again." She laughed at her jest. "Seriously, though, be careful. We don't yet know the full reach of Commander Hjordis."

15

ON THE WAY

Summer/Autumn 1097 SR

Charlaine halted Stormcloud, then turned to look back at Reichendorf. Danica pulled her own horse up alongside, following her friend's gaze.

"Do you think we'll ever return?" the younger knight asked.

"I'd like to believe we might. Hopefully, by that time, all the scheming and plotting will be done. I've had enough of it to last a lifetime."

"Still, here we are, on our way to a court full of Halvarians."

"Well," said Charlaine, "only one Halvarian. Let's not get carried away."

"So tell me, is Hadenfeld on the way?"

"Nowhere close, but we'll be passing through Andover. We could make a little side trip and visit your old home if you like? You could show everyone how well you've done within the order."

"That would be nice, but let's wait until I've got a ship to command. I'll need to sail up and down the coast anyway, and the village has a nice anchorage."

"It has no harbour?"

"No, why? Does that surprise you?"

"I thought it had lots of ships?"

"Those are fishing boats," said Danica. "They pull them up onto the beach."

"Then what's an anchorage?"

"A safe area for ships to anchor. In other words, the waters are deep enough not to run aground, and it has some protection from the sea."

Charlaine laughed. "Now, you're pulling my leg. Why would a ship need protection from the sea?"

"The Northern Sea is nothing like what we saw in the south."

"In what way?"

"For one thing, the waves can get massive. A good anchorage will provide some shelter from that, often in the form of an outcropping of land or, as you mentioned, a bay or harbour."

Charlaine smiled. "It's a good thing they made you the ship captain, not me."

"Speaking of which, have you any idea how to get to Reinwick?"

"I have a map, although it's not the easiest thing to read. The plan is to travel through a succession of Petty Kingdoms, heading mainly north."

"Mainly north?"

"Well, north with a nudge to the west. I suppose we should get going if we want to reach a roadside inn by nightfall."

"Then lead on," said Danica. "After all, you're the one who knows the way."

They urged their horses forward, quickly settling into a comfortable pace.

"I am curious about one thing," continued Danica. "How am I to arrange everything when I'm only a Temple Knight?"

"I'm not sure what you mean," replied Charlaine. "You have funds at your disposal, don't you?"

"Yes, but how do I explain my absence from the commandery? The other sisters will no doubt be curious as to why I'm spending so much time in the city."

"I've given that some thought, and I believe I've come up with a solution."

"Which is?"

"I'll make you my adjutant. Then, whenever you need to leave, you can say you're on assignment for me. It also means you'll have access to a desk, which you'll probably need if you're going to sort out all the finances of buying and crewing a boat."

"You mean a ship," corrected Danica. "But you're right. There's so much to consider, of which the first step will be to spend some actual time at sea."

"How do you intend to do that?"

"It's easy enough. I have yet to see a captain who wasn't willing to take an extra coin or two to allow passengers."

"Can't you just hire a shipbuilder?"

"To build what?"

"A ship, of course."

"Yes, but what type? And what about its rig?"

"Wait," said Charlaine. "Now you've lost me."

"It means the sails, yardarms, masts: everything that's required to operate the ship. The Shimmering Sea is a calm body of water, ideal for galleys of various sizes, but the Northern Sea is something else. I need to come to grips with what makes the most sense given the treacherous waters. I also must assess the role the ship will assume. Will we be pursuing pirates or fighting warships? And who are our potential enemies?"

"That's easy—Halvaria."

"And have you any idea what type of ships they use in the north?"

"No, I don't, but I'm starting to realize how complicated this is. Did the grand mistress offer any ideas on the matter?"

"I'm afraid not, but luckily, the naval architect did."

"Brother Leamund?"

"Yes, although I suppose we should refer to him as Temple Captain Leamund."

"Only for official purposes," noted Charlaine. "Our order is much less formal than our Cunar brethren. Speaking of which, I was surprised to see he wasn't a higher rank. I would have thought a man with his responsibilities would be given the rank of Temple Commander."

"They offered, but he refused. According to him, a promotion would require so much more of his time, and he was unwilling to give up his studies."

"So what was his advice concerning the northern fleet?"

"That we start with a small ship, one with good sailing characteristics. It wouldn't carry much of a fighting complement but would provide much-needed experience about sailing in these waters without overwhelming us."

"Sound advice. Anything else?"

"Yes," said Danica. "After much discussion, we came to the conclusion it might be worthwhile to hire a vessel, at least in the beginning. That way, it would come with a crew who knew their business."

"How many people does it take to sail a ship?"

"That depends on a great many things. Generally speaking, they don't use oared vessels in the north, which means the men are primarily used to sail. A typical small merchant could easily get away with only a dozen or so, based on a single sail. That's assuming four to be on duty at all times, with extras to take shifts or help out when necessary. Naturally, a warship would need more in case we got into a fight."

"And how does one fight without oars? At Alantra, there was a lot of ramming, but most of the battle was warrior to warrior. I can't imagine that's easy in rough seas."

"Yes, that's yet one more thing I need to consider."

"I don't envy you your task," said Charlaine.

Danica laughed. "What about you? You have to take over an entire company of Temple Knights. Tell me that isn't intimidating."

"As a smith, I had to deal with customers all the time."

"Yes, but fifty of them? And all at once?"

"There might be fifty of them, but they're still disciplined knights. I doubt they'll be much trouble. To be honest, I'm more concerned with the reception I'll get at court. Apparently, I'm expected to spend time at the duke's estate."

"Oh, I see how it works," said Danica, adopting a nasal voice. "Now you're a Temple Captain. You get to spend all your time amongst the elite members of the ruling class."

"Trust me, I'd much prefer to confine my efforts to the commandery, but duty calls, and I must obey."

"Well, at least we have the trip to look forward to. Just think, weeks of travel with no superiors to deal with. Tell you what, I'll race you to the next hill!" She galloped off.

Charlaine laughed, urging Stormcloud into a gallop. "Do you really believe you can outrun a Calabrian?"

The road led them north, through Galoran, where the terrain grew rougher, slowing their progress. For a week, they struggled until they turned westward into the flatter lands of Ardosa, often called the heart of the Petty Kingdoms. This small kingdom was renowned for its fine wines, which they exported to all the great courts of the Continent.

The journey through the fair and prosperous countryside was pleasant, but summer was nearing its end, bringing cooler weather. Before they knew it, they were riding north through Ulrichen, a wild, untamed land with few roads and even fewer cities. It was a curious thing to see such wilderness here in the middle of the Continent, but they had little time to appreciate the beauty of it.

Before long, they crossed into Erlingen at a place called Galmund, and the signs of civilization became more pronounced. The roads here were a marked improvement over those of Ulrichen, and they made good time. Five days later, as they arrived in Torburg, capital of the duchy, a heavy rain moved in, flooding the land and putting an end to thoughts of travel for a few days.

Thus, they found themselves temporarily stranded in an inn called the Fair Wanderer, a cozy, little place in the heart of the city frequented by local merchants who also sought shelter from the vicious weather.

Charlaine and Danica stabled their horses, then made their way inside, where the innkeeper soon had them settled into a room. They dropped off their armour and changed into their cassocks before heading downstairs for a meal.

The common room was bursting with so much noise, Charlaine had to yell for Danica to hear her. She pointed. "Over this way. I can see a table."

The patrons moved aside, respecting their Church attire, and they finally took their seats.

"I've never seen a place so crowded," said Danica.

"I'm not surprised, considering the weather. It was often like this back in Malburg. We had a saying back then: 'When the weather comes, it's time to wet your whistle'."

"I don't understand."

"You know, your lips that you whistle with?" Danica looked confused. "Never mind."

A serving girl appeared at their table. "What can I get for you, Sisters?"

"Two tankards of ale, if you please," said Charlaine, "and maybe something to eat?"

"There's some pottage left if you're interested?"

"That will do fine. Two bowls, please."

The server ran off, eager to gather the food.

"This is so different from the dining hall," noted Danica.

"Did you not have places like this back home?"

"There was a tavern, but much smaller than this. Then again, it was only a small village." She was about to say more when a trio of men sitting at the next table laughed loudly.

"And then, he says, 'I ain't got the foggiest!' I tell you, it was the funniest thing I ever heard."

Again the laughter.

"Well," said Danica, "someone's having a good time."

One of the men, a tall, lanky individual with a patchy beard, noted their presence. "Excuse me, Sisters. I didn't mean to disturb you."

"You didn't," said Charlaine. "Tell me, are you local to these parts?"

"I am. You, on the other hand, are not from around here, else I would have recognized you."

"We're on our way north, in fact."

He turned to his companions with a smug look. "See? I told you."

"Do you have sister knights here?"

"We do. They often help out at the tournament field, especially the grand melee."

"That sounds interesting," noted Danica. "What's that?"

The man stared at her with a blank expression on his face. "You mean to tell me you've never heard of a tourney?"

"I'm from a small village."

"It must be small, indeed, to have never held a tournament. We hold several a year here in Torburg. So many, in fact, that His Grace, Duke Heinrich, has a permanent section of the city marked off for it, and a good thing too."

"Why do you say that?" asked Charlaine, her interest piqued.

"Why, if it hadn't been for the tourney, we never would have defeated the invasion from Andover."

"Yes, I'd heard of that. Quite the victory, I'm told."

He leaned closer, lowering his voice. "So everyone says, but if the truth be known, the victory was largely due to the actions of one man—Sir Galrath of Paledon."

His blond-haired companion sneered. "That's not what I've been told."

The tall fellow turned towards his companion. "What's that supposed to mean? Who else could capture the King of Andover?"

"It was that foreign mercenary—what was his name?"

"Ludwig something," added the third man, a heavy-set individual.

Danica looked over at Charlaine. "You knew a Ludwig, didn't you?"

"Yes," she replied. "Ludwig Altenburg, but that couldn't possibly be him. Hadenfeld is hundreds of miles away."

"That's him!" shouted the large fellow. "He was working for the Crossed Swords."

"What's that?" asked Charlaine. "An order of knighthood?"

"No, common mercenaries, if you can believe it. Mind you, they no longer exist on account of the casualties they suffered in the fight."

Charlaine caught her breath. "Do you mean to say he died?"

"Oh no, not Lucky Ludwig. He was the hero of the day, but then he left with a couple of his friends. They say he went home, wherever that is."

"You must tell us more."

"I'd love to," the man responded, "but I'm afraid it's a long tale, and I lack the drink to give the story its proper due."

"A situation easily remedied," said Charlaine. She caught sight of the serving girl. "A round for this table, if you please?" she said, pointing at their new friends.

"Thank you," he said, wiping his hand on his shirt, then extending it. "My name's Rolf, Rolf Wilkerson. And this is Radwell and Severn." He indicated his companions.

"I'm Charlaine deShandria, Temple Captain, and this is Sister Danica."

His eyes widened. "Temple Knights? You surprise me. I'd noticed the cassocks, but I took you for lay sisters."

"Wearing swords?"

He leaned forward, noting her scabbard. "To be honest, I hadn't noticed them."

The girl reappeared, a tray full of drinks. "The food will be along shortly," she said.

They all waited as she distributed the tankards, then disappeared back into the crowd.

"So you were saying?" prompted Charlaine.

"Oh yes, Lucky Ludwig. They say he was in service to one of the barons, but I don't recall which one. In any event, he and those mercenaries found themselves in the thick of the fighting up at Chermingen. They were in this old ruin in the middle of the battlefield, they say, and then, during the attack, they sortied out, pretending to be Andover's men. They got so close to the king, they were able to capture him."

"Bah," said Radwell. "Sir Galrath did that. You're just taking one person's story and handing all the glory to another."

The two fell to bickering.

"It seems your Ludwig has become somewhat of a folk hero," said Danica.

"I know he was unhappy with his father. What I don't understand is how he came to be here, so far from home. Then again, I don't suppose it matters. He's not my Ludwig anymore. I need to put such things behind me."

"Yet I sense you still care about him."

"And I probably always will, but he is part of my past now. I must look to the future."

"Still, you must admit it's a strange coincidence. Perhaps Saint Agnes has something in mind for you two?"

Charlaine gave her a withering glare but then couldn't hold it, breaking into a chuckle instead. "I've given up trying to understand such things."

"No, you haven't," accused her companion. "Part of you will always believe Saint Agnes looks out for you."

"I suppose that's true."

A bowl of pottage was placed before Charlaine, the smell making her mouth water. "This looks quite delicious. Thank you."

"You're welcome, Sister," came the girl's response.

. . .

After three days of a near-constant downpour, the rain finally ceased. Everyone said such weather was not unusual for this part of the Continent. Still, Charlaine questioned if the delay was the Saints giving her time to come to grips with her past. She had to admit, the news of Ludwig was unsettling at first, but then she began to wonder if she wasn't being tested.

On the first cloudless day, they headed north once again, leaving her past behind them. Several days later, they passed through Chermingen and then into Andover. The general mood of the populous changed considerably in this new realm, for they had suffered a humiliating defeat at the hands of their rival, Erlingen.

As visible foreigners, Charlaine and Danica were greeted with suspicion and distrust despite their obvious affiliation with the Church. Close to the border, the roads were well travelled and easy to navigate, thanks to the system of mile markers instituted by the current ruler. As they moved farther north, however, the signs became less frequent, and they heard rumours of the massive ransom the king here had been forced to pay to gain his freedom.

The biggest surprise lay at the border, where the Duke of Reinwick's warriors questioned them but clearly had no intention of delaying members of the Church, particularly a pair of Temple Knights. They were sent on their way with directions to Korvoran and a wish for their safe travels.

The trees had turned by now, displaying a riot of red and yellow leaves that fell from high to lay thick upon the road, almost as if a colourful carpet had been laid out for them, welcoming them to their new home.

The sea came into view, a magnificent vista stretching out as far as the eye could see. The Shimmering Sea had sparkled with light, but the water here in the north was dark and dangerous. Even from the safety of the coast, Charlaine noticed the heavy waves farther out.

"Ah," said Danica. "It feels like home." A stiff, cold breeze blew in, causing her to shiver. "Yes, now I'm miserable and cold, exactly like I used to be as a child."

16

KORVORAN

Autumn 1097 SR

The Duchy of Reinwick was, in essence, a large spit of land thrusting out into the Great Northern Sea. The sparsely populated western shore consisted mainly of thick oak forests that helped absorb the chilly winds blowing in over the water. Only one town graced this shore, the village of Gossenveldt, and it had no actual port to speak of, merely a collection of fishing vessels that were pulled up onto the shore at night.

The eastern side of the country, the primary inhabited region, was where most of the land trade travelled up the great road that connected the larger cities of Blunden, Herenstadt, and the capital, Korvoran. Of course, the main form of trade in Reinwick and its economic lifeblood came from the sea. Merchants from all over the northern Petty Kingdoms came to trade their goods. Even Halvarian ships occasionally made anchor here.

The road led Charlaine and Danica through the southern gates of the capital city, paralleling the coast. The weather here was considerably cooler than that which had graced the shores of the Shimmering Sea, and Charlaine was glad of a thick cloak to keep her warm.

The city was tightly packed, with little space between the buildings. Even the streets were narrow, making the entire place feel cramped and crowded.

They had gone all of three blocks when the docks came into view—one moment, a warehouse stood before them, the next, a sea of masts stretched out across the horizon. Originally, Korvoran had been built around a shallow bay, but over the years, they added a pair of jetties that snaked out into the sea, like two enfolding arms, leaving only a narrow channel through which to enter. Charlaine was reminded of Rizela, but whereas that southern city had great towers to protect it, here there was naught but a small tower atop which sat a navigational fire.

"Glorious, isn't it," said Danica.

"It looks so crowded," noted Charlaine. "It's almost as if there are too many ships and not enough space."

"That's because you're used to the south, where ships can anchor along the shore. Here the waves are unforgiving. Anyone who wants their ship to remain safe will bring it inside the harbour. The fees alone likely make the city quite prosperous."

"Fees?"

"Oh yes. They levy a charge against each ship to enter the harbour."

"And how do they do that? With galleys, like they have down south?"

Danica laughed. "No, that wouldn't be practical. They have a harbourmaster, whose job is to track the comings and goings of ships."

"And how do they decide how much to charge?"

"That's simple. It's based on tonnage."

"I'm not sure I understand."

"It's a calculation," replied Danica. "Based on the capacity of the boat to carry cargo. Naturally, local ships pay much smaller fees."

"I suppose that's going to impact your operating costs once you find a ship."

"That's where you come in."

"Me?" said Charlaine. "I don't control those types of things."

"True, but I'm hoping you can get us an exemption from the duke. After all, we'll be patrolling the waters off the coast and helping to keep the trade lanes free of brigands."

"I'll see what I can do," said Charlaine, "but I'm not making any promises." Their horses slowed as they drew closer to the docks where merchants, packed in closely, eagerly waited to get first crack at the wares being unloaded.

Charlaine looked around, trying to make sense of all the activity. "How do they keep track of all this?"

"They don't. This is what we call organized chaos. You can always tell the more valuable cargo. It'll have the longest lineup of merchants waiting for it."

"And you learned all this from a fishing village?"

"Saints, no," replied Danica. "I learned everything from Brother Leamund."

Charlaine shook her head. "I'm glad it's you and not me who has to see this thing through. This is all so overwhelming."

"Truly? I find it quite exhilarating."

"So do you see any ships here you like?"

Danica swept her gaze over the multitude of vessels in the bay. "A number, but I doubt their captains would be willing to part with them."

"Why not?"

"A good ship will make a tidy profit for its crew. Why would they consider selling?"

"A notion I hadn't considered. Does that mean you'll need to settle for a less successful merchant?"

"I suppose it does, but let's not worry about that yet, shall we? We still need to find the commandery and get you settled in as its new captain."

"It won't be long now," said Charlaine. "I was told it's only two blocks north of the main docks."

Danica glanced up the street, but a covered wagon blocked her view. "This is going to take forever. I think we made better time getting to the city than we did navigating the last two blocks. At this rate, we'd be better off to walk."

"Then let's do so." Charlaine dismounted, attaching a lead to Storm-cloud's bridle before navigating through the crowd as best she could. It wasn't much faster, but it at least gave them a break after spending much of the day in the saddle.

Finally, after leaving the docks, the commandery came into view—an immense, two-storied stone building, topped with a wooden roof. Distinctive scarlet banners hanging on either side of the main entrance marked it as belonging to the Order of Saint Agnes. As they drew closer, the large, double door opened, disgorging a pair of Temple Knights.

"Greetings," called out Danica. "This is Temple Captain Charlaine deShandria, the new captain of this commandery, and I am Sister Danica."

"Good day to you," replied one of them. "I'm Sister Marlena, and this is Sister Damora."

As they stood there waiting, Charlaine noted they looked similar in age to Danica. She let them fidget for a bit before ending their discomfort.

"Is it not the custom to let the new captain enter the premises?" she asked.

Both sisters blushed profusely. "Sorry," said Sister Marlena. "I'll see to it at once." She ran back to the doors and began pushing one aside, allowing them access.

"The stables are straight ahead," she called out. "On the opposite side of the courtyard."

"Where are the sentinels?"

The young sister knight stared back, suddenly turning pale. "You mean guards? I suppose that would be us."

"You suppose?"

"I mean, yes, Captain. We are assigned gate duty for the day."

"And why is that?"

"I beg your pardon?"

"It's a simple question," responded Charlaine. "Why are you two guarding the gate?"

"We have the least seniority," Sister Marlena replied.

"Who's in charge here?"

"Sister Josephine."

"Then go and fetch her, and do so quickly. I should like to speak to her once we see to our horses."

"Yes, Captain." Sister Marlena ran off with a terrified look. Her companion, meanwhile, closed the gate behind them.

"What do you make of that?" asked Charlaine.

"It's not the most promising of signs," replied Danica.

"That's putting it mildly. It seems I'm going to have my work cut out for me here."

Danica smiled. "I'd love to help, but there's a ship I need to see to."

"Don't think you're getting off that easily. I'll need your help here first, or did you forget you need a crew?"

"You present a compelling argument."

They led their mounts into the stable, only to be greeted by a pungent odour. Charlaine wrinkled her nose. "This stable needs a good mucking out."

"Agreed," said Danica, "and I gather the horses need some exercising."

"Why would you say that?"

"Those saddles are covered in a fine layer of dust. Someone's not been doing their job. How long ago did they lose their captain?"

"Several months, at least," said Charlaine. "The grand mistress received notice of the previous captain's death before we left the Antonine. I was told a senior sister would be in charge, and there might be some resentment."

"That must be Sister Josephine. Do we know anything about her?"

"No, nothing. In fact, we know nothing about any of the sisters here."

"The previous captain must have kept some records?"

"I'm sure she did, but it's going to take me a while to get through them, especially considering the size of the garrison."

"Which is?" asked Danica.

"It's a full company, or at least it was at last report. That means fifty mounted knights and assorted extras, likely no more than a dozen."

"So sixty souls, then?"

"I would assume so," said Charlaine.

Sister Marlena entered the stables as they brushed down their mounts.

"Sister Josephine is here," she announced.

Charlaine looked up in surprise. "Where? I don't see her."

"She's waiting outside."

Danica rolled her eyes before giving Charlaine a look of amusement.

"Then tell her to come in here. Immediately," Charlaine added.

The young woman ran off, and then muted words drifted their way.

"This ought to be interesting," said Danica.

Charlaine was about to open her mouth, but Sister Josephine chose that exact moment to make her appearance.

"Captain Charlaine? My name is Sister Josephine. Welcome to Korvoran. Sorry about the mix-up. We weren't expecting you."

"You've been without a captain for some time now. Did you not think they would send a replacement?"

Sister Josephine stared back. She was older, likely three or four years Charlaine's senior, but lacked the look of an experienced Temple Knight.

"Have you any orders for us?" Josephine finally asked.

"Yes. Gather everyone, and assemble them in the courtyard."

"There are some who are out guarding the Temple of Saint Agnes. Shall I recall them?"

"No, I'll speak with them later. Oh, and one more thing; I want to see them all armoured and armed. Is that clear?"

The woman stared back, her face aghast at the very notion. "Everyone?"

"This is a fighting order, is it not?"

"Of course, Sister."

"That's Captain."

"Yes, Captain. Sorry. I shall see to it at once."

"Good, and send Sister Marlena back in here. I have need of her."

"Yes, Captain." Sister Josephine fled the stables—there was no other term for it.

"Well," said Danica. "That was certainly interesting."

"Listen, until you get your ship, you're going to need to billet with the other knights."

"I expected no less. What of it?"

"I shouldn't want them to take out their frustrations on you."

Danica laughed. "I'm no longer that shy sister knight you met when you first came to Ilea. I can take care of myself. In any case, it will let me get to know the sisters a bit better and figure out what's going on here."

"You wanted to see me, Captain?"

Charlaine turned. "Yes, Sister Marlena. I need you to show us to my new office."

"Both of you?"

"Yes. Sister Danica will be acting as my adjutant."

"Of course. If you'll follow me, I'll show you the way."

She led them across the courtyard and into the building. Similar to many commanderies, it was built around a hollow square with the lower level dedicated to the barracks, stables, and kitchens, while the upper floor housed the senior sisters and offices.

A corridor ran through the entire building, creating a circuit of sorts, discounting the stables. On each side of the lower level were various barracks rooms interspersed with armouries to make it easier for knights to quickly prepare for battle.

As they walked, several sister knights exited their rooms, intent on dressing in their armour. Many of them halted at the sight of their new captain, but Charlaine quickly ordered them to continue. After passing a few such rooms, they came upon a large set of wooden doors.

"What's this?" asked Danica.

"The doors are for repelling intruders," noted Sister Marlena.

"Then why are they closed?"

"In order to keep the noise down."

"What noise?" asked Charlaine.

"Some of the sisters can be quite boisterous at times."

"Tell me, how many sisters are in each room?"

"Four on average, although some are singles."

"But they all eat in one dining hall, yes?"

"Of course," replied Marlena.

"And what time is dinner served?"

"It varies."

Charlaine was taken aback. "How can it vary? Surely the meals are organized?"

"You must speak to Sister Josephine about that."

They passed through the doors and then went up a set of stairs. The upper floor had a similar design, with heavy wooden doors dividing the building into defensive zones. Up here, however, the doors remained open.

"Your office is just down here," said Sister Marlena, continuing farther down the corridor before finally halting at an ornate door and pushing it open.

Charlaine stepped through into a room almost as big as their dining hall back in Ilea. Like other orders, the captain's office faced west, following the tradition set many years ago to honour the Holy city of Herani, said to be the birthplace of Humanity. However, the truth was that foreign land was more to the southwest. To avoid complex calculations, the Church had simply decreed the habit of a west-facing window be continued, so all full commanderies now followed the same model.

The afternoon sun flooded in through the windows, while the stone floor had several red carpets thrown down to keep the coldness of the rock at bay. In the centre of the room, a stack of books and papers sat on a round table. Large bookshelves ran the length of each wall, the southernmost one interrupted by a single door.

"That leads to your quarters," said Sister Marlena. "It has a second door that opens into the hallway."

Charlaine poked her head through the door for a peek. The captain's quarters also had a western-facing window with thick curtains hung on either side. The room's furnishings were typical of all sleeping chambers for Temple Knights, although a bit larger than those of the rank and file. Of particular interest, however, was the alcove containing an armour stand.

"Very nice," she commented.

"Of course, you'll need an aide to assist you in getting into your armour."

"Why would I need an aide?"

"I can only speak of the previous captain's arrangements."

"How long have you been here, Marlena?"

"This is my first assignment. I only joined the order two years ago and spent almost half of that in training."

"Did you train in Erlingen?"

"No, in Carlingen. Why do you ask?"

"Simple curiosity. Sister Danica trained in Corassus. It would be interesting to sit down sometime and compare experiences."

A knock on the door drew their attention. Sister Damora took a step in, looking very nervous.

"The company is assembled," she announced.

"Good, return to the courtyard, and I'll be along shortly."

"Yes, Captain."

"You too, Sister Marlena."

The duo scuttled from the room.

"Where do you want me?" asked Danica.

"Once we get down there, fall in just behind me. When I move forward to inspect the troops, I shall want you by my side."

"You're going to inspect them?"

"Of course. While I do, I'll need you to take names."

"They're bound to be a complete mess if this commandery is any example. How am I to keep all the names straight?"

"That's just it," said Charlaine. "You don't really need to. Just go along with what I say and nod your head knowingly. I'll take care of the rest. Now, do you remember the way back to the courtyard?"

"Certainly. Shall I lead, or will you?"

They entered the courtyard to see the entire company before them. As their feet hit the cobblestones, someone, presumably Sister Josephine, called them to order, and those assembled went quiet.

Charlaine was surprised when, out of the corner of her eye, she spotted a knight leaning to one side. She shifted her gaze to the woman who was propping herself up with a crutch, one leg missing below the knee. Immediately, she changed directions, heading directly for the injured warrior.

"What's your name, Sister?" she asked.

"Sister Leona."

"You are excused from the assembly, Leona."

"I am a sister knight," the woman replied, bristling.

"So you are, and I appreciate your dedication, but there's no need to demonstrate your dedication here." Charlaine scanned the remaining sister knights. "Sister Damora," she called out. "Fetch a chair for Sister Leona." She turned to Danica. "Have her seated right over there, within earshot."

"Yes, Captain," said Danica.

"Your armour does you credit, Sister Leona. I presume the loss of your limb was a consequence of battle?"

"It was, Captain. My last assignment was in Erlingen. I was there when the chapter was destroyed in battle."

"You were with Captain Giselle?"

"Yes, although not in the battle itself."

"I'm afraid you'll need to explain that one to me. I thought her entire command was destroyed?"

"And so it would have been had the enemy not raided our camp a couple of nights before the battle. I was wounded and thus unable to fight that fateful day."

"I served under Captain Giselle in Ilea," said Charlaine. "She became a mentor to me."

"Then I wish you well," said Sister Leona, but then lowered her voice. "I fear you have your work cut out for you here."

"We shall talk later," Charlaine whispered back, then returned her voice to normal. "Go and wait over there, Sister, then take a seat once your fellow sister returns with a chair."

"Yes, Captain."

Charlaine walked to the front of the formation, then stood facing them but said nothing. Once Sister Leona's chair was set up and Danica returned to her, she began her speech.

"I am Captain Charlaine deShandria, the new leader of this commandery. It is my job to make sure each and every one of you are equipped and prepared to carry out the duties of Temple Knights. Over the next few days, my adjutant, Sister Danica, and I, will be inspecting every aspect of this place to ensure it meets the requirements of our order. Today, however, I am beginning with you. I will talk with each of you and examine your weapons and armour. My intention is not to punish, but to determine when and where improvements can be made."

She paused, considering her next words carefully. "Let me be clear on this, though. First and foremost, we are a fighting order. I expect every one of you to be capable of handling yourselves in a melee should the need arise. As a consequence, weapons practice will commence first thing tomorrow morning. I shall examine the duty roster and make some adjustments, so be prepared for changes." She turned to Danica and nodded before making her way towards the first sister knight.

"What's your name?" she asked.

"Sister Goya."

"Where are you from, Goya?"

"Ebenstadt."

"Never heard of it."

"It's far to the east," the woman replied, "past the Kingdom of Novarsk."

"How long have you served?"

"Eight years, Captain."

"Seen any battle?"

"No." She looked down, her face reddening.

"That's nothing to be ashamed of," said Charlaine. "We should all hope for peace." She began making her way down the line of Temple Knights, speaking to each in turn.

17

THE LEADERS

Autumn 1097 SR

D anica popped her head in the door. "Sister Leona's here to see you."

"Good, good," said Charlaine. "Send her in."

The injured sister knight entered the room, looking somewhat concerned.

"You asked for me, Captain?"

"I did. Please take a seat. This is not a disciplinary meeting, merely a friendly chat."

Leona visibly relaxed. "Sorry, I feared you wished to dismiss me from the order."

"No, not at all. You're still a valuable member of my command. I thought we might put some thought as to how you might best be employed. Can you read and write?"

"I can."

"Have you considered an administrative position?"

"I've never been offered one."

"That surprises me," said Charlaine. "What did the previous captain have you do?"

"Very little, if truth be told. I've been relegated to kitchen duty for months on end."

Charlaine saw the look of disgust. "I assume that's not something you enjoyed?"

"Not at all."

"Are you any good with numbers?"

"I was married to a merchant before I joined the order. I reckon I can keep track of expenses, if that's what you mean."

"That's precisely what I mean. Over the next few days, I'll be going over the finances of this commandery. I should very much like you to be present. Your official title would be…" Her words trailed off as she looked at Danica. "I haven't a clue what we would call her, do you?"

"Treasurer?"

Charlaine smiled. "Perfect. Treasurer, it is, then. Now, as to your leg, has anyone tried to find a Life Mage?"

"For what?" asked Sister Leona. "My wounds healed long ago."

"Yes, but I'm told those with sufficient knowledge can do so much more. I shall make a note to ask at court. Maybe the duke has someone available. In the meantime, I'd like to get you down to the Mathewites. I assume they have a mission somewhere in town?"

"They do."

"Good. Hopefully, they can arrange for a more suitable crutch for you, one that might be a little easier on your arms. We'll need to find you an office to use and, of course, a table and nice, comfortable chair."

"There's no shortage of rooms," said Danica, "but we may be in want of some furniture."

"We'll make a list of our requirements and then pare it down once we find out what our funds are like. Did we finish the new duty roster?"

"Yes, and it's been passed along. That reminds me. Weapons practice should be commencing shortly. Did you wish to lead it yourself?"

Charlaine looked up, meeting her companion's gaze. "No, I think I'll let you do that."

"Me? What makes you think I'm any good in a fight?"

"I've seen you fight plenty of times. Have them pair off but limit their space. Better yet, force them to use daggers. That's right up your alley."

"You want them to simulate a knife fight?"

"Yes, why not? It'll tell us who can adapt to new situations."

"Fair enough," said Danica. "I'll go put on my armour and get down there."

"Good, and keep a close watch on everyone. You're going to need to pick out a dozen or so eventually."

Danica smiled. "That's right, I am. Very well, Captain. I shall be off."

"What's she picking people out for?" asked Sister Leona.

Charlaine's mouth fell open, but she quickly recovered. "Just some special training I have in mind. Any other questions?"

"As a matter of fact, yes. I wondered how Captain Giselle was doing?"

"Quite well, the last time I saw her. If you don't mind me asking, how long did you serve under her?"

"Four years," said Leona. "There was talk of a tribunal after the battle, but that was set aside when the Duke of Erlingen intervened on her behalf."

"I thought there might have been. Unfortunately, the loss of her company cost her dearly, leading her to be assigned to a remote outpost."

"And that's where you met her?"

"Yes," said Charlaine. "She was, in truth, my second captain. Good thing, too, or I might still be languishing in the middle of nowhere. Giselle believed in being prepared for battle at all times, something I mean to emulate."

Sister Leona nodded her head. "That sounds like the Captain Giselle I knew. I only hope her career will recover. It must be a terrible burden, bearing the loss of so many under her command."

"It is," replied Charlaine, "and that's why we have to do all we can to ensure we never suffer such a loss again."

"You've lost friends as well, haven't you? I can see it in your eyes."

"I have, down in Ilea. Several of my sister knights were lost battling the Halvarians, but we must do what we can to limit their expansion."

"They have a small delegation here."

"So I heard," said Charlaine. "Do you know anything about them?"

"Only rumours, but I'd rather not repeat them."

"Well, if you do learn anything that might be of use to us, feel free to come and see me."

Danica poked her head back in. "Sister Grazynia is here to see you," announced Danica.

"I thought you were off to get ready for training."

"I was, but then I ran into Grazynia."

"What does she want?"

"She bears a message from the Temple of Saint Mathew."

Charlaine turned her attention back to the sister in front of her. "It seems I'm to be busy today. If you'll excuse me, Sister Leona. I have other business to attend to."

"Of course." The woman stood, making her way from the room.

"Send her in, and for Saint's sake, Danica, go and get ready for that training."

Sister Grazynia, one of the taller knights of the order, entered the office, wayward strands of her blonde hair escaping its ponytail.

"Well?" prompted Charlaine.

"Here it is, Captain." The knight handed over a folded paper.

Charlaine examined the seal, confirming its origin before flipping it over and noting it was addressed to the acting commander of the Temple Knights of Saint Agnes. She broke the seal, unfolding it to discover an invitation from Commander Salvatore to attend a dinner at the Duke of Reinwick's estate. The Mathewite was the senior Church representative in all of Reinwick and left no doubt that refusal was not an option. In fact, it was more of a command than an invitation, but his unmistakable gift for words made it seem less threatening.

"Are they waiting for a response?" Charlaine asked.

"They are," replied Sister Grazynia. "There's a brother knight waiting downstairs."

"You didn't see fit to bring him up?"

"Men are not permitted in the commandery."

"Temple Knights are excluded from that restriction," said Charlaine.

"Since when?"

"It has always been so. If rules like that were rigidly enforced, we would never be able to cooperate with the other orders, nor they with us."

"But what of the Book of Agnes?"

"What of it?"

"It forbids members of the order to associate with men."

Charlaine sat back. "Have you actually read the Book of Agnes, Sister Grazynia? Because I have, and I can assure you, there's no such decree. Agnes had a close working relationship with Mathew, a tradition we continue with to this day. In future, should a Temple Knight arrive with a message, he is to be escorted to my office. You can pass that on to the other sisters."

"And your reply, Captain?"

"Please inform our brother knight I shall be pleased to accept the invitation."

Sister Grazynia bowed her head before she exited the room.

Charlaine's invitation suggested they travel to the duke's estate together, so she rode over to the Mathewite commandery. Knowing temple doctrine dictated the wearing of ceremonial tabards for occasions like this, she went fully armoured, save for helmet and shield, only to find Commander Salvatore waiting in his cassock.

"I'm sorry, Your Grace," she said. "I was only following protocol."

"I wouldn't worry if I were you. I'm sure Captain Waleed will be dressed much as you." He lowered his voice. "He has a penchant for being dramatic."

"Captain Waleed?"

"Yes, the head of the Cunar detachment in these parts. Quite an interesting fellow once you get to know him. He was once a Kurathian mercenary, although he gave up that life many years ago."

"How long has he commanded here?"

"Oh, must be three years now, maybe four. I'm afraid I'm not very good with dates." His eyes wandered down to her horse. "That's a fine steed you have there. Is it a Calabrian?"

"It is," replied Charlaine. "This is Stormcloud, a gift from the King of Ilea."

"And what, pray tell, did you do to earn his favour?"

"I, and my fellow sisters, assisted in destroying the Halvarian fleet."

The commander's eyes shot up. "Indeed? You must tell me all about it, although not at this precise moment. Such things are best left to when we are in the duke's company. He revels in such tales."

"Do you have a large detachment here in Korvoran?"

"Not here, but I oversee the commanderies in the surrounding kingdoms as well. Of course, we protect our lay brothers at the mission here. You'll have to come and visit it sometime."

"I should love to," replied Charlaine.

A call drew their attention, and they both turned to see a Temple Knight of Saint Cunar riding towards them.

"Ah," said the commander. "It appears Captain Waleed has finally deigned to put in an appearance." He raised his voice. "Good of you to join us, Captain. I was starting to think you got lost. Allow me to introduce Captain Charlaine."

"Charlaine deShandria?" the Cunar replied.

"You've heard of her?"

"Of course, who hasn't? She made a name for herself down in Ilea. Even managed to work with the Holy Fleet, or so I'm told." His eyes moved to take in Charlaine. "You surprise me. I hadn't expected a Calabrian."

"I was actually born in Hadenfeld, but my parents are both from Alantra."

"Ah," said Waleed. "That explains it. I was born in Kouras."

"Is the Church popular down there?"

"Yes, although it's said many of the princes pay only lip service to it, preferring to worship the old Gods in secret. As for myself, I've always been a believer, as were most of my mercenary companions. Still, that was many years ago, far more than I'd care to admit, if truth be told. What of you, have you served the order long?"

"About three years," she replied. "I joined back in ninety-four."

"Three years, and you're already a captain? Well, there's no holding you back!"

She laughed. "Much of the credit must go to my last captain, Giselle."

"I know that name," said the commander. "She was at the Battle of Erlingen, wasn't she?"

"She was."

"And she set a fine example for all of us," added Captain Waleed. "Now, much as I'd like to chat, perhaps we should get underway? I shouldn't like to keep the duke waiting. You?"

"By all means," agreed the Mathewite. "Let us be off."

Commander Salvatore, or Father Salvatore, as he liked to be called, served as host as they rode through the city, pointing out noteworthy landmarks and places of interest.

Eventually, they arrived at their destination—a magnificent estate with a circular road set in front. Well-dressed groomsmen waited to take their horses, while another servant led them inside to meet Lord Wilfhelm. Introductions were made, and then the entire group was ushered into a large dining hall, where servants led each guest to their assigned seats.

"Will the duchess be joining us?" asked Father Salvatore.

"Shortly," said the duke. "She's consulting with one of the court mages at present."

"I trust nothing is amiss?"

"No, it's of a more trivial matter." Wilfhelm's penetrating gaze fell on Charlaine. "Sister Charlaine, what brings you to Korvoran?"

"I've been appointed to the command of our detachment here."

"Have you, indeed? Fascinating, and you, only a captain. A rare honour, wouldn't you say, Salvatore?"

"Indeed, Your Grace, but I might remind you the last person to occupy that position was also a captain."

Duke Brondecker suddenly rose to his feet, surprising the others, who scrambled to do likewise. "Ah, there she is. My lovely wife, and it appears she has brought a guest."

The duchess entered the room wearing a red velvet dress, the front turned back to reveal a gold skirt beneath.

"I thought Larissa might join us for dinner," she said.

"Of course," replied the duke. "We have ample room. Come. Let's find her a seat, shall we?"

The servants scurried around, finding an extra chair. Larissa Stormwind was of a similar age to Charlaine but paler of skin and with light brown hair rather than the dark shade more common to the region. Her plain, blue dress with white highlights and severe lines stood in stark contrast to the fine clothes and smile of the duchess.

"Good afternoon," she said, finally taking her seat. "I am honoured to be in such distinguished company."

"And so you should be," said Father Salvatore. "For this is none other than Sister Charlaine deShandria, one of our more distinguished colleagues."

"And to what do you ascribe your distinction?" asked Larissa.

"I am but a humble servant of the Church," replied Charlaine.

"She's being far too modest," the commander added.

"We shouldn't overwhelm her," said Captain Waleed. "After all, we took oaths of humility, did we not?"

Father Salvatore, suitably chastised, mumbled for a bit, then continued. "You're right, Brother Waleed. You must think me churlish."

"Not at all, Father, merely excited by the prospect of fresh brains to pick." He looked at Charlaine. "I'm afraid not much happens here, so he's always on the hunt for new and interesting conversations."

"Ha," said Lord Wilfhelm. "A man after my own heart." A bowl of soup was placed before him, distracting him from his thoughts. Without any preamble, he began shovelling it into his mouth.

"It appears the time to eat is nigh," noted the commander, who then followed the duke's example.

By early evening, they still sat at the table, albeit now stuffed with food. Duke Brondecker talked at length, particularly about the state of his duchy, although it was of litte interest to Charlaine. In fact, the more he spoke, the less he seemed to reveal, leaving her to wonder whether he was very clever or just exceedingly dull. The conversation, however, soon turned to the temple orders.

"I understand," said Lord Wilfhelm, looking at Charlaine, "that your command is larger than the Cunars."

"Is it? I had no idea."

"How many sister knights do you have?" asked Captain Waleed.

"Fifty. Well, I suppose fifty-two, now that Danica and I are here."

"Danica?"

"My adjutant. She made the trip with me from the Antonine. We served together in Ilea."

"In any case, that's more than we have. The Cunars number only forty."

"I have even less," noted Father Salvatore. "Then again, our duties here are somewhat limited."

"He's being modest," said Captain Waleed. "He might be smaller in numbers, but he has seniority over both of us."

"Because of his rank?" asked Charlaine.

"No, because his order was the first to build here."

"That," added the duke, "is because my ancestor was a devout follower of Saint Mathew who invited the order to come to Korvoran. They've been here ever since."

"And the other orders?" asked Charlaine.

"The Cunars came along about twenty years ago, and we hoped their presence might dissuade our neighbours to the south from considering military action against us. As to your own order, my mother invited you some fifteen years ago, shortly before her passing. She was always a firm supporter of your cause, you see, and I couldn't very well refuse her request."

"Might I ask how long you've ruled Reinwick, Your Grace?"

"I became duke at the ripe old age of fifteen. In those days, I wasn't considered of age, so the first year of my reign was under the control of my mother, bless her soul. And to put things into perspective, I am now fifty-three."

"Is the border with Andover an ongoing concern?"

"It is. In fact, you might say it's of great concern to us. They've always been an economic rival, but they've been actively cutting off our land trade of late. Luckily for us, we have a large fleet of merchant vessels."

"Yes," said Charlaine. "I believe I saw many of them down at the docks. If I may be so bold to ask, have you a navy?"

"Although there are many ships flying my flag, I would hardly call them a navy. They are mostly used to enforce the dockyard fees and dissuade pirates, though in that regard, they are often lacking."

"And are pirates common hereabouts?"

Duke Brondecker looked at Larissa Stormwind. "Efforts have been made to reduce their effectiveness, but I'm afraid to little effect. They say they lurk amongst the waters of the Five Sisters."

"Five Sisters?" asked Charlaine.

"A series of islands," noted Father Salvatore, "at the most northeastern tip of Reinwick. Theoretically, they belong to Reinwick, but there are no towns or villages upon them."

"Why is that?" asked Charlaine.

"They are inhospitable," noted Lord Wilfhelm, "and the weather around them is atrocious. Many ships have been lost in those waters over the years, to the point that merchant ships now avoid the area at all costs."

"Sounds like the perfect place for pirates to hide out."

"Only if they want to wreck their ships. Know anything of sailing?"

"Not much," Charlaine admitted. "What little I've gleaned is from my time with the Holy Fleet."

"Ah well," said the duke. "I wouldn't wish to disparage the Holy Fleet, but this is the Great Northern Sea, not the calm waters of the south. I daresay you'd have a hard time sailing one of those oared vessels up here."

"Do your ships ever patrol the coast?"

"They do, but only as far north as Blunden. We also can't go too far south, or we'll enter Andover's territory, or worse, that of Eidolon."

"Why would you say worse?"

"The King of Eidolon is difficult at the best of times. Should any ship enter his waters, he claims he will seize it, and that's not a claim I wish to test, so we instruct the merchants to avoid it whenever possible."

"A wise precaution."

"Finally," said Wilfhelm, glaring at Larissa Stormwind, "someone who agrees with me."

"What of your West Coast?" asked Charlaine.

Duke Brondecker shook his head. "No pirates there—nothing to raid."

"There is Gossenveldt," noted Captain Waleed.

"Yes, but that's only a fishing village. Hardly worth the time it would take to land a boat."

"These pirates," said Charlaine, "any idea whence they came?"

"I wish I did. Oh, I have my suspicions, but nothing I can prove. Why do you ask? Looking to chase them down, are you? I'm afraid that would be difficult, for there's no Holy Fleet in these parts."

"Nor is there ever likely to be," added Captain Waleed. "The cost would be too great, although it's an interesting idea to consider."

18

THE SEA WOLF

Autumn 1097 SR

D anica pushed past the fish stalls and fishing boats to the bigger vessels, ranging from large, two-masted cogs to old-fashioned knarrs. Most were merchants, with wide beams and decks crammed with barrels and sacks, but a few of the smaller ones looked, to her eyes, like they might make nimble sailers.

She made her way onto the jetty, where even more ships were moored. One, in particular, caught her attention: a massive cog with three sails, possibly the largest she had ever seen. Men swarmed the deck, lifting crates and barrels from its hold as dozens of others carried sacks ashore across their shoulders.

A shout drew her attention. Men pointed towards a black, two-masted ship, flying a red flag bearing crossed swords, that had just passed the end of the jetty and was closing in fast.

Danica paused, her eyes fixed on the ship's advance. Clearly, the crew knew how to handle it. As it drew closer, she saw a bearded man standing on its foredeck. The ship started turning, and then he gesticulated wildly, sending a streak of flame towards the tightly packed ships moored at the docks.

Moments later, as smoke billowed forth, everyone ashore broke into a panic. She searched for the duke's ships, but they were at the far end of the bay. Even had they been ready, it's doubtful they would have been able to intervene, for the nimble raider continued until it was facing back out to sea. By this time, the sails had been dropped, and she watched in fascination as the ship kept moving, defying the wind that came in from the sea.

Movement on the deck revealed the presence of a woman with blonde hair holding her hands up, obviously in the midst of some type of spell, although Danica had no idea what it might be. The water churned up against the side of the ship, propelling it forward, and then, at last, she understood. This was a Water Mage.

Smoke drifted into Danica's eyes, temporarily blinding her. She wiped them, desperate to learn as much about the raider as possible. Then a group of men bumped her out of the way as they carried buckets of water in a vain effort to put out the fires. Danica tore her gaze from the strange ship to take in the chaos in the harbour once more.

The Fire Mage's spell had done its work, setting two ships ablaze. So tightly packed were the vessels, however, that others were now in danger of catching fire. Crews scrambled to put some distance between their own ships and those that were burning. In their rush, they collided with others. The entire situation became a jumbled mess of hooked yardarms and tangled ropes.

Someone handed her a leather bucket. "Get water," he yelled, ignoring for the moment the cassock marking her as a Temple Knight. She joined the others who gathered water and soon saw a problem, for each individual filled a bucket, then rushed to fight the fire.

"Form a line," Danica called out, "and pass the water to the next person."

It took a while for people to understand until she took the initiative, ordering people around, desperate to do what she could to help. More joined in, so many, in fact, they quickly had more people than buckets. Danica passed off her own and made her way to the head of the line, where the fires raged.

The initial two ships burned fiercely, the heat driving people back. Above her, the yardarms were ablaze, the fires making their way along the ropes that held them in place. It was clear the ships were lost, but maybe those alongside might still be saved.

She looked to her right, where sat a small merchant vessel. Burning canvas had landed on the deck, and the crew rushed around trying to put it out. Danica jumped aboard.

"Cut those lines," she ordered, "and get this ship out of here." She grabbed a crewman by the arm. "Where's your captain?"

"Ashore," the man replied.

"Get an axe and cut us loose. I'll man the tiller."

"We haven't any sail set."

Danica looked up at the single mast. The sail was still furled, but its proximity to the burning ships made the very idea of setting sail all but impossible.

"Have you oars?" she asked.

"Aye, four, but they won't help in this tight space."

"Break them out," Danica ordered. "We'll use them to push off from that." She pointed at the burning ship.

She gathered up a coil of rope sitting nearby before moving towards the stern. The ship faced the jetty, its rear end jutting out into the bay. She climbed the steps onto the raised aft deck and spotted a nearby rowboat. Someone, most likely an agent of the harbourmaster, was trying to untangle the mess of ships seeking to escape the fire.

A yell caught their attention, and she hefted the rope. A nod from the rowboat was all she needed. It took but a moment to tie off one end on the railing, and then she dropped the other over the stern of the ship. The tiny boat came closer, and someone grabbed the rope, then the rowers dug in with all the strength they could muster.

Danica glanced forward, noticing a few of the crew had untied two oars and were now using them to push against their burning neighbour. Down by the water, the rope went taut, and then the Temple Knight felt the ship begin to move. A wave of heat washed over them, and she looked up to see a burning rope fall to the deck.

"Cut the rigging!" she yelled. The men grabbed axes or drew knives, ready to saw away at the ropes, but someone had the wherewithal to slosh a bucket of water across the deck, extinguishing the flames.

Ever so slowly, the ship pulled away until it was well clear of the burning ships. Danica, breathing a sigh of relief, leaned over the aft railing, signifying everything was good. The rope was released, and she hauled it aboard. Right as she was finished piling it in a loop, a crewman appeared.

"Where to now, Sister?"

"Have you a full crew aboard?"

"No," the man replied, "but more than enough to move the ship, if that's your wish."

"What's the name of this ship?" she asked.

"The *Lydia*."

She scanned the area, her eyes finally settling on a spare dock on the other side of the bay. "We'll take the *Lydia* over there for now. Any idea where your captain might be found?"

"Aye, at the Oarsman. It's a tavern down by the shipyard."

"Good," said Danica. "Once we dock, we'll send for him. I'm sure he's sick with worry right now."

"I'd suggest we use the oars. There are too many ships floating loose to trust the sails."

"Very good." She suddenly became aware she had somehow assumed command of the ship. "I'm sorry, I should have introduced myself. I'm Sister Danica, Temple Knight of Saint Agnes."

The man bowed his head slightly. "Asborn Henrickson, first mate."

"Sorry for taking over. Had I realized who you were—"

"There's no need to apologize, Sister. You've done far more than I could. Without your steady hand, the *Lydia* would surely have been destroyed."

"I did what I thought was best."

"I assume this isn't your first time aboard a ship?"

"Why do you say that?" asked the Temple Knight.

"You know your way around a deck."

"I was raised in a fishing village not too far from here."

"Aye, but those are small vessels, nothing like the *Lydia*."

"True, but I also served with the Holy Fleet."

"Now, that's something I'd like to see," said Asborn. "Though I hear there are no Church vessels on the Great Northern Sea."

"Not yet, anyway."

The *Lydia* slowly made its way towards its new berth. "The ship that attacked," said Danica, "do you know it?"

"Well, I know OF it. That's the *Sea Wolf*. It's been striking terror into honest sea traders for years."

"Has no one sought to put an end to it?"

"And how would they do that?" asked Asborn. "There's no ship capable of catching it. And even if you could, how would you handle those mages? You saw how effective that fire was on our ships."

Danica looked back at the mayhem the raider had caused. One of the first targets had burned to the waterline and sunk, the second sure to follow. All around them, the fight to contain the flames continued, but it was obvious at least three other vessels were in jeopardy.

"'Ware the dock!" came the warning.

The crew began using reverse strokes to slow their approach, and then the hull of the *Lydia* scraped along the dock. Two men, rope in hand, jumped ship to tie it off, but Danica's eyes were on the well-dressed fellow who had made an appearance on the dock.

"Who in the name of the Saints gave you permission to take my ship!" he shouted. He jumped onto the deck and strode straight for Danica, but the sight of her scarlet cassock stopped him short.

"I'm Sister Danica," she announced. "I sought only to spare the *Lydia* from the flames. Now she is safe, I shall gladly return it to your capable hands."

"I... thank you, Sister Danica," he said. "Pardon me, where are my manners? My name is Captain Lyle Handley."

"You have a fine ship, Captain, and an excellent crew. They are the ones who deserve your praise."

"The *Lydia* represents a substantial investment. You must at least let me reward you somehow."

"My vows prevent me from accepting any reward other than your gratitude." She thought about it for a moment, then changed her mind. "On the other hand, maybe there is something you can do for me?"

"Anything."

"The next time you sail, I should very much like to be aboard."

"We are a merchant vessel," said Captain Handley. "We sail all along the northern coast of the Petty Kingdoms."

"Then what about a trip to the nearest town on your route? I would like to see how this ship handles."

"I believe I can do better than that," he replied. "Once we replace the damaged rigging, we'll take her out for a brief trip to make sure everything is shipshape. Would you like to accompany us?"

"Very much so," said Danica.

"Then I'll send word to your temple when our repairs are complete."

"It is not the temple you should contact. Rather, it's the commandery."

"I shall do as you ask."

"Thank you," said Danica. "Now, if you will excuse me, I should let you get back to your ship."

She stepped ashore, looking landward to get her bearings before she began walking, mulling over what she had just witnessed.

The *Sea Wolf* had made a daring raid, but to what end? They plundered nothing, merely damaged a few ships. Was that, then, their purpose? Or was it to instill fear in the traders? She knew most vessels in the north traded along the same routes, sheltering at safe anchorages on the way. Surely it would be less work to simply waylay ships out at sea? The *Sea Wolf* definitely had the manoeuvrability for it. Perhaps, she reasoned, this was but one small part of a carefully calculated plan. But for the life of her, she couldn't figure out the reasoning behind it.

She arrived at the commandery to find her captain in her office.

"Is that smoke I smell?" asked Charlaine.

"There was a fire down at the docks," replied Danica.

"The docks?"

"Yes, a seaborne raider caused it."

"I presume they managed to defeat this menace?"

"Not at all. The ship merely turned around and sailed back out to sea, leaving chaos in its wake."

"I'm no expert on sailing," said Charlaine, "but that must have taken some fine seamanship."

"Actually, they employed mages."

"What type of mages?"

"At least one Fire Mage and a Water Mage. There may have been others, but as far as I could tell, there were just the two of them."

"This is troubling news."

"There's more."

"Go on," urged Charlaine.

"The raider is known to them—a ship called the *Sea Wolf*. I'm told it normally stays well out to sea, but something gave them the courage to become bolder."

"Did they inflict much damage?"

"They did. Two ships were already destroyed when I left, with another two or three likely to succumb to the fire. A major victory, by my reckoning."

"I shall have to take this to the duke. He won't be pleased."

"I think I should accompany you. I can offer a first-hand appraisal of the situation."

"An excellent idea," said Charlaine, standing. "We'll go right now. With any luck, we'll get there before any official report."

"Is there an advantage to that?"

"Well, if nothing else, it will serve to remind him we are an active company of Temple Knights."

They retrieved their horses, riding through the gate at a fast pace.

"You say this ship was called the *Sea Wolf*?" asked Charlaine.

"Yes, and it seems to have a rather nasty reputation for piracy."

"Piracy I can understand, but a raid just to damage ships? That's more an act of war."

"That's what I was thinking," said Danica. "But it flies a red flag, a typical mark of a pirate."

"Why does red signify a pirate?"

"It's an old tradition dating back to the first mercenary companies. Red was meant to symbolize resistance or rebellion to their leadership."

"So pirates are mercenaries?" asked Charlaine.

"No, but if you give it some thought, they do represent a form of rebellion against the established order."

"So they serve themselves?"

"They do. Then again, pirates need some way of selling off all their stolen goods, which means someone in the Petty Kingdoms must be helping them."

"It would, wouldn't it? You just gave me an idea."

"Which is?" asked Danica.

"I think this ship, the *Sea Wolf*, is trying to foment trouble amongst the northern realms."

"Who would want to do that?"

"Who do you think?" asked Charlaine.

"Surely you're not suggesting it's Halvaria?"

"Why wouldn't it be? War in the north would only serve to divide the Petty Kingdoms. You and I both know how tenuous the peace is hereabouts. It wouldn't take much at all to destroy what little goodwill is left."

"But we have no proof, and without that, what can we do?"

"We can get this ship of yours ready to sail."

"I don't have a ship yet," said Danica.

"Then we must make finding one a priority."

Duke Brondecker's estate came into view. Word of the raid had plainly been received, for several warriors milled near the entrance, eager for news. Charlaine looked for someone of import, but the duke's men bore no symbol of authority she could recognize. Someone inside must have observed their scarlet cassocks, for a servant soon sought them out.

"If you'll come with me," he said. "The duchess wishes to speak with you."

He led them around the back, where they entered using a servants' door. Through the labyrinthine corridors they went, finally emerging into a small, carpeted chamber.

"Ah, there you are," said the duchess. "There is much to discuss between us three."

The knights both bowed. "You honour us, Your Grace," said Charlaine, "but it is your husband who is in charge of the defences of Korvoran, is it not?"

"It is," the woman agreed, "yet as the day's events illustrated, he is not up to the task."

"What is it you would have us do?"

"I am no fool, Captain. I made enquiries and learned all about your exploits in the south. I am here to make you a proposition, one that will, I believe, prove beneficial to us both."

"You have our attention," said Charlaine.

"Good. Tell me, what do you know of this marauder?"

"Sister Danica saw it with her own eyes." Charlaine looked at her companion.

"Yes," the younger knight agreed. "I was told it was the *Sea Wolf*, a known raider."

"It was, indeed. That ship has been harassing our trade for months and is said to be the fastest ship afloat."

"I doubt that," said Danica.

"Would you care to explain?"

"I saw little physical evidence of a superior design. It's a fast ship, I'll grant you that, but I did note the presence of what I believe to be a Water Mage. That's what gives the ship the advantage."

"So it can be caught?"

"Any ship can be brought down. All it requires is the resources."

The duchess smiled. "And if the resources were to be made available?"

"What are you suggesting?"

"I've invested a lot of my wealth in ships over the years and have no wish to see my investments end in disaster. I propose to build a ship capable of chasing down and destroying this *Sea Wolf*, once and for all."

"And how does that concern us?" asked Charlaine.

"Because I am suggesting the Church crew this ship."

"Surely the Cunars would be more suitable?"

"I am a loyal devotee of Saint Agnes," said the duchess. "And besides, I don't trust men not to make a mess of it. You two have experience at sea, do you not?"

"We do," said Danica, "but we are not allowed to place ourselves under any command but the Church."

"But you can assist others from time to time?"

"Of course."

"Good, then I shall see fit to build this ship and then donate it to your order. Will that suffice?"

"Yes, Your Grace," said Charlaine. She looked at Danica before returning her gaze to the duchess. "The truth is we came to Korvoran for that very purpose."

"You did?"

"Yes," added Danica. "I've been empowered to purchase and equip a vessel in the name of the Temple Knights of Saint Agnes. Naturally, the Church had no idea the *Sea Wolf* had become a problem, but it seems our aims are in agreement."

"And had you a specific idea as to how to accomplish this objective?"

"My orders give me a lot of leeway, Your Grace, but foremost amongst them is the need for secrecy."

"Good, then we shall endeavour to keep it that way."

"This ship you're building," said Danica. "Might I ask its design?"

"There is no ship under construction, at least not yet anyway. I only came up with the idea this very afternoon, stirred on, no doubt, by news of this raid. I should be happy to consult with you on it, especially considering it will become Church property. I propose I finance the construction, leaving your role secret for the moment. Upon its launch, you will assume control of it, and I shall transfer its ownership to the order."

"Might I ask why?" said Charlaine. "Could you not launch it under the flag of Reinwick?"

The duchess frowned. "I thought of that, but a Reinwick ship of war couldn't sail into waters belonging to other sovereign nations without raising some… concerns. The Church, however, is free to sail wherever it may, unrestricted by any kingdom's borders."

"A clever plan, Your Grace."

"Yes, it is, isn't it? I will make arrangements for Sister Danica to visit the shipbuilder as soon as possible. In the meantime, you should give some thought as to the best way to track down and eliminate this menace. I'll send word once I've conferred with my shipbuilding associates."

"We look forward to hearing from you," said Charlaine.

19

THE SHIP

Autumn 1097 SR

C harlaine stood on the foredeck, taking in the view. The sky was not so much blue as a grey smudge across the horizon over the large, open body of water. Unlike the Shimmering Sea, the wind here was bitter, necessitating heavy cloaks to ward off the chill. Danica joined her, a broad smile upon her face.

"You're enjoying this far too much," said Charlaine.

"It's true, I am. What do you make of the *Lydia?*"

"I'm no expert on ships, but the deck isn't pitching much, so I assume she's a handy sailer."

"That she is, although I can't help but feel that square sail of hers will prove troublesome."

"In what way?"

"A square sail gives you a good speed as long as the wind is behind you, but on occasion, you must sail into the wind, or as near to it as you can get. It's called close-hauling."

Charlaine smiled. "I sense you're about to tell me how that can be accomplished."

"I am—by the use of a triangular sail. They call it a lateen rig."

"Oh yes, I remember now. You told me about it down in Ilea. But wouldn't you need to reconfigure the mast?"

"Not so much the mast as the rigging. Some of these ropes must be moved around, but I believe it's possible."

"Look at you, thinking all about ship design. Brother Leamund would be proud."

"We used them on the fishing boats back home. Those ships were much smaller, but the principle is the same."

"You must give some thought to fighting tactics. This area is not conducive to the type of fighting we used on the Shimmering Sea. I doubt ramming would be very useful with these waves."

"Likely not," said Danica, "but boarding is still the best option. The trick is to bring the other ship alongside and hold it in place rather than ram it. I was thinking we could rig a ballista and have it fire a large grappling hook. The idea would be to penetrate the enemy's hull or maybe grab the railing and then winch it towards us like the *Triumphant* did at Alantra."

"What of the mages?"

"That's an entirely different matter."

"I'd suggest crossbows," said Charlaine. "They proved their worth at Alantra."

"The bigger issue is having a Fire Mage set fire to the ship."

"How do you counter that?"

"I'm still working on it. You don't suppose there's a Water Mage in Korvoran we could hire?"

"What about Larissa Stormwind?"

"Who?"

"Larissa Stormwind," repeated Charlaine. "I met her at the duke's estate. I believe she's a court mage. The duchess knows her quite well."

"Do you think she'd be willing to accompany us?"

"Let's not get ahead of ourselves. We've yet to acquire a ship."

The deck tilted slightly as the *Lydia* turned, then the ship slowed as the sail went limp.

"We're luffing," said Danica, then noted Charlaine's look of confusion. "We're turning into the wind, so the sail can no longer catch it. The ship will almost stop before the sail begins picking up again as we cross the path of the wind. It's a dangerous manoeuvre to do if you're in the middle of a fight. If you don't time it just right, you can end up dead in the water."

"Would a triangular sail counter that weakness?"

"To a certain extent, yes, but it would need to be mounted fore and aft, not side to side like our current sail."

"You evidently enjoyed your time in the Antonine. Not thinking of becoming a naval architect yourself, are you?"

"No. I much prefer to be on the deck of a ship than designing one, but I must admit to a fascination for the art of shipbuilding."

The turn complete, the sail billowed out, catching the wind once more, and the ship lurched forward. It wasn't so much that you could feel the speed, but the sound of the water against the bow picked up considerably.

"I could stay here all day," said Danica.

"I wish I could, but I have work to do."

Captain Handley joined them. "Well? What do you think?"

"She's a fine sailer," said Danica. "You had me worried for a moment when we made that turn, but she seems to handle well."

"So she does," he agreed. "Do you like her?"

"I do, although I wonder about the sail. Do you believe she could take a triangular one, rigged fore and aft?"

In response, he looked up at the yardarms. "I reckon so, with a bit of work. We'd need to change up some of the rigging, else it'll interfere, and sew up a new sail, of course. Why? Thinking of offering to buy the *Lydia*, are you?"

"I didn't realize it was for sale?"

"Anything's for sale if the price is right."

"What of your crew?"

"What of them? You'd need a crew who's familiar with the ship, wouldn't you?"

"Yes, but it would become Church property. Surely you're not suggesting they would take up Holy vows?"

"No, of course not, but you'd need to train up a crew of your own, and that requires experienced hands."

"You have me intrigued," said Danica.

"Well, think it over for a few days. I have no plans to sail in the next few weeks, so I'll be around."

"Why is that?"

"I'm getting old," said Captain Handley. "And the truth is, I'd like to settle down here in Korvoran and spend some time with my wife while I still can. The funds from the sale of the *Lydia* would be more than enough to let me do so quite comfortably."

"Surely there are others who would be willing to purchase her?"

"There are, but you earned that right when you saved her from the flames. Had you not done so, I would have been ruined, and any hope of settling down in my old age would have vanished."

Danica turned towards Charlaine. "What do you think?"

"I think it's a good idea. It could serve as a training ship while the other is under construction. Not to mention allowing you to get to know these waters. I assume that's the expression?"

"It is." The younger knight returned her gaze to the captain. "What do you say you and I sit down after we return and work out some details?"

Captain Handley smiled. "I would be happy to. Now, you must excuse me. I have a ship to run." He wandered down the deck, humming to himself.

"You made someone happy," noted Charlaine.

"It's funny the way things work out. When we first came here, I worried I wouldn't be able to find a ship. Now, we quite possibly have two."

"Don't get carried away. You haven't even chosen a design yet, and construction will take months."

"Yes, but now I can experiment with the *Lydia* before I make choices for the *Vigilant*."

"*Vigilant?*"

"I decided that's what we're going to call the other ship."

"And this one?"

"We'll stick with what she's called for now, but once it's turned over to the order, I thought we might rename it to *Valiant*."

"*Valiant* and *Vigilant*," said Charlaine. "I like it, but I hope you're not going to name all the ships starting with a V. I think you'll run out of names fairly quickly."

"Oh, I don't know," said Danica. "I can think of quite a few. *Vanguard, Voracious, Victorious, Valorous, Vanquisher, Venturous...* I could go on."

"Please don't," said Charlaine.

They returned to port, sailing in between the other traders to finally tie up on the quay. Charlaine left Danica to her negotiations, electing to return to the commandery to take care of some much-needed administration. Upon arrival, however, she found only a solitary Temple Knight guarding the entrance.

"Sister Marlena," she said. "Where is the other sentinel?"

"I have none," the young woman replied.

"I specifically detailed two sister knights to guard each entrance. Don't try to tell me otherwise. Who is scheduled to accompany you?"

"Sister Josephine."

"And where is she?"

"I don't know, Captain."

"When you assumed your role as guard, were there not two others from whom you took over?"

"There were, most assuredly."

"Yet no one raised a concern?"

"No, Captain."

"Why not?" asked Charlaine.

"I beg your pardon?"

"This was a breach of discipline. Why was it not reported?"

"It's never reported. It's just not our way."

Now it was Charlaine's turn to be surprised. "Says who?"

"Sister Josephine."

"Sister Josephine is not in charge."

"Begging your pardon, Captain, but she is, at least when you're not around."

"I would have thought Sister Leona the senior knight."

"And under normal circumstances, she would be, but on her deathbed, Captain Winifred named Josephine as successor."

"It seems I have another issue to deal with."

"Pardon?"

"It's nothing that need concern you, Sister Marlena. Resume your duties. I shall have another sister knight join you directly."

Charlaine entered the commandery, her eyes falling on one of her knights. "Sister Grazynia, put on your armour. You're to stand sentinel with Sister Marlena."

"Yes, Captain."

"And before you go, have you seen Sister Josephine?"

"I believe she's in the dining hall. Shall I fetch her?"

"No, I'll take care of that myself." Charlaine set out quickly but then slowed her pace. It would do little good to confront her in front of others; better to have her report to the captain's office.

She altered her course, climbing the stairs to the upper level. There she spied one of the knights. "You there," she said. "What's your name?"

"Sister Adriana," the woman replied.

"Find Sister Josephine, and then inform her she is to report to my office immediately."

"Yes, Captain."

Charlaine continued on her way, her mind mulling over possible solutions. She wanted to encourage initiative, but Sister Josephine's abuse of authority was not something she could overlook. She passed by Sister Leona's office, then halted suddenly and backtracked.

"Sister Leona?"

The elder sister looked up. "Yes?"

"I've asked for Sister Josephine to come here. I'd like you to be there as well."

"I shall come directly, Captain."

Charlaine soon found herself sitting at her desk, reviewing what little she knew of Sister Josephine. Temple Knights in charge of commanderies were expected to keep records of those under their command. From what she could glean, Captain Winifred had thought highly of Josephine, but what was not immediately apparent was the reason why. Her notes were sparse, to say the least, yet something had driven her to name the woman as acting captain when others were more deserving.

Sister Leona entered the office. "Am I early?"

"Not at all. Come in and close the door. Please take a seat. I wanted to talk to you about Sister Josephine before she gets here."

"What would you like to know?"

"I understand she has some seniority here, but she's far from the longest-serving knight. What I'm struggling with is why she was chosen as Captain Winifred's temporary replacement?"

"She has the respect of the other sisters."

"Respect or fear?"

"I... don't wish to talk ill of a fellow sister."

"I shall hold nothing against you for speaking the truth. After all, it's one of our most sacred vows."

"Our previous captain believed in... what's the expression?"

"Running a tight ship?"

"Yes, that's it. She relied on Josephine to keep things in order so she wouldn't need to deal with minor infractions."

"So she just let the woman have free rein?"

Leona nodded. "I tried to bring it up with her once, the captain, I mean, but she wouldn't listen."

"I've been looking over what records I can find, but with more than fifty under my command, I must admit to some difficulty remembering everything. Are you the most senior knight?"

"I believe so unless Sister Danica has more service?"

Charlaine chuckled. "No, she's only been a knight for a few years. What I'd like to do is deputize you as my second-in-command. That would mean while I'm away, you would have full authority to act in my name."

"Are you intending to go somewhere?"

"Not at present, but who can predict future events? What do you say? Interested?"

"Of course. Only, I worry my infirmity may prove burdensome."

"It's your leg that's missing, not your mind. I have a feeling your experience would serve you well."

"What of Sister Josephine?"

"I shall inform her of my decision once she arrives."

"She won't like it."

"I don't imagine she will, but if she is to progress through the ranks of the order, she must learn to follow the rules, not bend them to her will."

"I presume you don't like her."

"I neither like nor dislike her," said Charlaine, "but I shall not sit idly by and watch as someone abuses their power."

"Would that others felt as you do?"

Charlaine felt a cold hand clamp over her heart. Was the rot of the Antonine being felt up here? "Why would you say that?"

"You appointed me treasurer of this commandery. In that short time, I have come to suspect there has been some malfeasance in regard to the order's funds."

"Are you saying someone was stealing?"

"Maybe not stealing," said Leona, "but there are some questionable purchases, not to mention missing funds that can't be accounted for."

"Questionable purchases, I understand, but I'm not sure what you mean when you say funds that can't be accounted for?"

"It's quite simple, actually. Our ledgers record purchases and income, along with how much should be in our coffers. The problem is I examined what resides within our strongbox, and we seem to have less inside than we should, assuming the calculations are correct, of course."

"Who oversaw the finances previously?"

"I would assume Captain Winifred."

"And Sister Josephine?"

"Undoubtedly. She's been running the place for the last few months. She could hardly have kept us going without access to the strongbox."

"Could she simply be a poor administrator?"

"It's a possibility," said Sister Leona, "but I'd need to go over every entry. I'm afraid it will take a lot more time to know for certain."

"I understand," said Charlaine. "Keep me informed of any progress you make."

"Certainly, Captain."

A knock on the door interrupted them.

"Enter," said Charlaine.

Sister Josephine moved to stand before the desk. "You wanted to see me, Captain?"

"I did. Why you weren't at your assigned sentinel duty today."

The woman stared back, defiance in her eyes. "I felt two guards unnecessary," she replied.

"And if there were an emergency, you would expect a sentinel to leave her post to warn the rest of us?"

Sister Josephine had no response. She merely reddened, refusing to answer.

"I have no doubt you did what you thought was best," continued Charlaine, "but such an action shows a remarkable lack of judgement. Henceforth, you shall no longer act as second-in-command. That responsibility, instead, shall go to Sister Leona."

She watched the woman clench her teeth. "Is that all, Captain?"

"For now, but if I discover further infractions of discipline and good judgement, I shall not hesitate to mete out punishment. Do I make myself clear?"

"Yes, Captain."

"Good. Now go and put on your armour, and report to the front gate to relieve Sister Grazynia."

Sister Josephine bowed her head in acknowledgement, then left the room.

"That went better than I anticipated," said Sister Leona.

"I'm surprised to hear you say that," replied Charlaine. "Are not our sister knights here trained to obey orders?"

"They are, but Josephine is an angry woman. I fear if you push too much, she may take it badly."

"Is that a threat?"

"No," said Leona, "merely an observation. This is a relatively large garrison for a mere captain to command, which means a short command structure. It puts you closer to the knights, perhaps too much so and breeds familiarity."

"Let me ask you this: did you respect Sister Giselle?"

"Of course."

"So did all of us in the south," remarked Charlaine. "But there's more to being a leader than simply barking out orders. Giselle knew that and encouraged initiative."

"Isn't that the very thing that got Sister Josephine in trouble?"

"Yes, and I can see the irony in it, but we can't reward mistakes in judgement."

"Then what do we do with them?"

"We correct them; guide them to make better choices. Sister Josephine will come around in time. At least I hope she will. She has a lot to offer the Temple Knights of Saint Agnes."

"I'm surprised you didn't name Sister Danica as the second-in-command. It's the right of those in charge to pick their underlings."

"Sister Danica is far too busy to deal with all of this." Charlaine spread her arms to encompass the entire room.

Leona laughed. "Sister Danica must do as you command, surely?"

"Of course, but I assigned her other duties that will occupy her for some time."

"Anything you'd like to share?"

"Not yet, but all will be revealed eventually. In the meantime, it's best not to ask too many questions."

"I shall keep that in mind. Any other pearls of wisdom you'd care to share?"

"As it turns out, there is," admitted Charlaine. "Tomorrow, I shall be taking a trip to visit the Mathewite mission. During my absence, you'll be in charge, including keeping an eye on the training. Do you think you can handle that?"

"I do. You know you had me worried there for a moment. I thought you were going to ask me to do something challenging!"

20

THE MISSION

Autumn 1097 SR

T he mission of Saint Mathew was a modest wooden building with but a single floor, its layout a long, rectangular shape. The back half consisted of kitchen space and sleeping chambers, while the front was nothing more than a great hall in which they served meals for the poor. Even at this early hour, the dining hall was so full that a line waited outside.

"Is this normal?" asked Charlaine.

Commander Salvatore looked at the crowd. "Not at all. Sometimes it's even longer."

"I thought the city prospers."

"It does, but few of those coins make their way into the hands of those who need it most."

"How many Temple Knights do you employ here?"

"Officially, our complement numbers thirty, but at any given point, half of those are on duty. Not all of them are here, mind you. The temple itself needs guarding, while some patrol the streets in the less-wealthy parts of town, along with a few who watch the docks."

"The docks? Don't the duke's men bear that responsibility?"

"They do, but they can't be everywhere, so we augment their meagre numbers with a few Temple Knights."

"And the lay brothers?"

"Korvoran boasts a mission that can hold almost two hundred, although it has seldom seen that many. Father Rayden runs it with the help of twenty-five lay brothers. The rest work at the temple itself, the greatest part seeing to administrative matters. The city is our regional headquarters, you see, responsible for overseeing our order not only in Reinwick but also in Andover and Eidolon. Mind you, their complement is much smaller than ours."

"I expect," said Charlaine, "those other regions fall under the purview of Temple Captains, much like us?"

Commander Salvatore smiled. "They do indeed. Assignments such as that offer an opportunity for individuals to distinguish themselves. I myself was in charge of such a place when I was a captain."

"Might I ask where?"

"In Braymoor. It lies to the east of here, along the Northern Shore of the Continent."

"Was that your last posting before coming here?"

"Yes, then I served two years as an aide to my predecessor here in Korvoran. So, as you might expect, I'm pretty familiar with the area. Now, much as I enjoy the opportunity to reminisce, you're here to see the mission."

He led Charlaine inside, pausing a moment as he passed through the door. "Tell me, are you acquainted with the work of our missions?"

"I am, although I must admit to having little first-hand knowledge. I understand you provide food to the needy."

"Indeed, we do, but we do so much more." He moved farther into the room. "Feeding the poor is what we're primarily known for, but equally important to us, at least, is seeing to those in need of healing."

"Have you a Life Mage?"

"Alas, no," replied the commander. "Such things are beyond our meagre purse. We do, however, have several lay brothers skilled in traditional medicine and herbal remedies."

"And do you help the homeless?"

"Where we can, but I'm afraid the demand far outstrips our capacity to house them all. If you follow me, I'll show you the rooms we make available."

Salvatore led Charlaine past the kitchens and down a hall, where they emerged into a small common area, open to the sky.

"We call this the courtyard," explained Commander Salvatore. "There are a dozen one-room chambers in total, most designed for a single occupant. Unfortunately, the bulk of those in need are women with small children."

"Why is that, do you suppose?"

"It is a sad fact that many are abandoned by their menfolk. I'm led to believe it's a problem in most cities of the Petty Kingdoms. However, here in Korvoran, the problem is particularly distressing, considering the climate."

"I'm not sure I follow," said Charlaine.

"The weather here can be brutal, especially in wintertime, making homelessness particularly deadly. This last winter alone saw at least a dozen women freeze to death. We do what we can to keep our charges safe, but once again, we are limited by the funds at our disposal."

"Do I detect some animosity?"

"How perceptive of you. As a Temple Commander, I've had my fill of the nobles wasting their fortunes on lavish parties and gratuitous feasts. Why, if each gave even a ten percent tithe of their wealth, we would be able to feed and clothe everyone who needed our help." He lowered his head, his voice suddenly sounding old and worn out. "I'm sorry, this is not your burden to bear."

"But it is," said Charlaine. "My order is sworn to protect women. To learn they are suffering so tells me there's much work to be done." She looked around the courtyard where several women sat in the sun, some sewing meagre clothing while others watched children playing. "I wonder if I might have a word with some of them?"

"By all means, although it might be better if I were not present. I find authority figures tend to have a dampening effect when trying to get people to open up. I'll go and check in on my Temple Knights. Seek me in the dining hall when you're done."

"I shall."

Commander Salvatore turned, leaving her alone with her thoughts as she wandered around the courtyard. The children at play seemed happy enough, but their threadbare clothes and spindly appendages spoke of their abject poverty.

"Cruel, isn't it?"

Charlaine turned to see a seamstress. "Cruel?"

"Yes," the woman replied. "To give the children hope when all is lost."

"There is always hope where life exists."

"You sound just like the rest of your order." The woman's eyes came up to stare directly into Charlaine's. "If your fellow sisters truly believed their vows, they'd find our men."

Charlaine felt an icy hand clutch at her heart. "Find your men? Why? What's happened?"

"They're missing; that's what happened," the woman spat out. "Not that any of you lot seem bothered."

"You spoke of this to other sister knights?"

"Of course, but none of them seem to care. They all say the same thing, that he's run off with another woman, but I tell you that's not the case! And what about the others? Have their men also abandoned them?"

"How many other women?"

"Dozens."

"Does the duke know?"

"The duke couldn't care less, and why should he? It's not as if any of his nobles are missing."

Charlaine crouched, bringing her eyes to the same level as the woman's. "My name is Charlaine deShandria. I'm the Captain of the Temple Knights of Saint Agnes."

"Is that supposed to impress me?"

"No, but I want you to know I will do all I can to get to the bottom of this."

"That's what they all said, then they went back to their homes and forgot all about us."

"Do you know the names of any of these knights?"

She laughed. "Saints, no. And why should I? All you knights look the same to me."

"I can assure you I'm different."

The woman stared into her eyes without blinking. "You do have a different look to you. I'll grant you that."

"Tell me about your husband. When did you last see him?"

"Going on three weeks ago now. He left before sunrise, heading towards the docks."

"Is that something he regularly did?" asked Charlaine.

"Oh, aye. You see, the ships use manual labour to load up, and those who get there early get first crack at such work. It doesn't pay much, mind, but then again, beggars can't be choosers."

"Was there anything different about that day?"

"Can't say as there was."

"And what did you do when he didn't come home?"

"I was used to him coming back late, and sometimes he would nip round the Anchor for a quick drink before he came to bed. When the tower struck midnight, I got worried, so I went to the Anchor myself, but he hadn't been there."

"Did you report this to the local garrison?"

"And tell them what? That my man is missing? I don't think you understand their contempt for us folk."

"But you did inform a sister knight?"

The woman scowled. "I said so, didn't I? What do you take me for, a liar?"

"Not at all," said Charlaine, "but if I am to look further into this, I must know all the details."

"Details? I'll tell you the details. Your so-called sister knights couldn't give a rat's arse about what's going on in the dregs of the city."

"That ends today. I promise you." Charlaine glanced around the court-yard once more. "Are any of these other women in the same situation as you?"

The woman nodded, then pointed towards one of them watching the children. "Aye. That there's Miranda. Her husband disappeared five days before my Len. And over there"—she indicated a tall, rail-thin woman who gazed absently at the sky, muttering a prayer—"that's Elena. Her husband's been missing nigh on a month now, and her with child. I tell you, it's almost too much to bear."

"How long has this been going on for?"

"Who knows? Maybe a year or more?"

"And no one has looked into this?"

"Not as far as I know."

Now it was Charlaine's turn to frown, for the sworn duty of members of her order was to help women in need. Yet, despite being made aware of the situation, nothing had been done. "Might I ask your name?" she asked.

"Jean," the woman responded.

"Well, Jean, I'll tell you what I'm going to do. I'll have a word with Miranda and Elena, and then I'll do some investigating of my own."

The woman spat again. "Don't make promises you can't keep."

"I don't," said Charlaine. "And to prove it, I'll come see you next week and the week after that, if need be. I won't give up until I solve this matter, and I will hold myself accountable to you for it."

Jean began to tear up. She reached out and clasped Charlaine's hand. "Thank you," she said, her voice cracking. "Thank you ever so much."

The trip back to the Agnes commandery gave Charlaine plenty of time to think. The two other women told much the same story—of a husband who failed to return home after seeking work at the docks. She could only wonder how many other men were missing.

The gates of the commandery soon came into view, and she passed by the guards, briefly acknowledging their challenge. As she approached the dining hall, she glanced inside to spot three sister knights enjoying some afternoon drinks. The sight made her pause, and instead of continuing on down the hall, she elected to enter the room. The knights made to rise in her presence.

"Remain where you are," she said. "I merely wish to chat."

"About what?" asked Sister Marlena.

"Missing men."

"Is this about the old woman?" Damora asked, turning to her companions. "What was her name again?"

"Jean," replied Grazynia.

Charlaine was intrigued. "You've heard her story, then?"

"Of course," said Damora, "but you know how men are. It's not as if a woman has never been abandoned."

"I guess from your reply, no one's looked into it?"

"Why would we? Even if he were missing, it would be the duke's responsibility to find the fellow, not ours."

"No," said Charlaine. "That's where you're wrong. Our charge is to protect women, and that, by extension, means their families as well. The loss of Jean's husband has left her in abject poverty. We must do what we can to alleviate the problem."

Damora frowned. "What would you have us do? Question everyone who works at the docks? That would take days, maybe even weeks."

"Have you something better to do?"

They all stared back at her. She recognized the look of loathing on their faces, all except for the group's youngest member, Marlena. She alone seemed to grasp the nature of the problem, leading Charlaine to wonder why. Was there something in her past that still troubled her?

Grazynia was the first to set down her drink. "With your permission, Captain, I'll organize teams of three, then have them start asking questions. Is there a physical description of this fellow we're looking for, or maybe a name?"

"I believe his name is Len, but your first stop should be the Mathewite mission. Find Jean, and have her supply what other information she can. While you're there, seek out Miranda and Elena, for they, too, have lost their men."

"And you consider them connected?"

"I understand some men abandon their families, but for three do so within such a short period seems to defy the odds. I also believe there may be others out there in a similar predicament. Thus, I would like a group to go house to house, making enquiries."

"I volunteer," said Marlena.

"Good. Take two other knights with you, but confine your efforts to the poorer sections of town."

"You believe someone's killing them?" asked Damora.

"Possibly, but more likely they're being taken against their will."

"Slavery?"

Charlaine nodded. "The three who we know of used to work as common labourers, prime candidates for those who deal in such a vile trade."

"But slavery is outlawed," said Marlena. "Surely no Petty Kingdom would allow such a thing?"

"There is much that occurs in a given realm of which the rulers are unaware, and distant lands often seek cheap labour."

Sister Grazynia's eyes shot up. "You mean Halvaria? I'd heard rumours they used slaves, but I took them as nothing more than idle gossip."

"It's not beyond the realm of possibility. Of course, it may be that these men simply signed on aboard a lengthy sea voyage and failed to tell their wives."

"And if it turns out they have?"

"Then we notify their families of the fact, but let's proceed under the assumption something a little more nefarious is involved."

"Why?" asked Damora. "Isn't a ship's crew a far more likely explanation?"

"These were common labourers," replied Charlaine, "not skilled sailors. Unlikely candidates for such a task, considering how many idle ships' crews are in port."

"When would you like us to start?"

"Immediately. Grazynia, find two other knights to accompany Marlena, then start organizing your teams. I'd like them down at the docks before everyone turns in for the night. Marlena, I'd like a word with you before you start, so once you've dressed in your armour, come and see me."

"Yes, Captain."

"And Grazynia, I'll need a duty roster from you before you set out so we can keep track of everybody. I'll be in my office if there's anything else." She turned, making her way from the room.

She was sitting at her desk when Sister Marlena arrived.

"Come, sit down," said Charlaine.

The young knight sat, looking decidedly uncomfortable. "You wanted to see me?" she said.

"Yes. You're relatively new to the order, so I want to make sure you're comfortable leading two of your fellow sister knights before I send you out. Have you led before?"

"No," replied Marlena. "I only just arrived here a couple of months before you did."

"Even so, you seem to have settled in quickly. That's a good sign. Are you from these parts?"

"No, I'm from Abelard. Does it matter?"

"Not in the least. I was just hoping for someone with some local knowledge." Charlaine gazed down at some papers laid out on her desk. "It says here you progressed quickly during training, especially considering your relatively young age. I mean that as no insult, of course, but younger recruits tend to be less dedicated to the more serious side of knighthood."

"You mean the religious theory?"

"I do."

Marlena smiled. "I was a devotee of Saint Agnes long before I joined the order." Her face darkened as she cast her eyes down. "It's the only thing that let me survive the abuse."

"You needn't talk of it if you would prefer to remain silent."

"No, it's all right. I've come to accept what happened wasn't my fault. And in any case, my father is no longer alive to hurt me." She lifted her gaze to meet Charlaine's. "He was murdered."

"Was he a man of some means? Your records indicate a good education."

"He was a duke, though self-made."

"And you say he was murdered? Did they catch the culprit?"

"Yes. It was one of his closest advisers. Funny, when you think of it."

"I see no reason for humour at someone's demise," said Charlaine.

"He died on Midwinter night. Truth be told, if Brother Cyric hadn't been there, the murderer might have gotten away with it."

"Did you say Brother Cyric? The Mathewite?"

"Yes. Why? Do you know him?"

"I know of him. He was instrumental in saving the life of my mentor, Temple Captain Giselle."

"Giselle?" said Marlena. "She's the one who escorted me to the Temple Academy in Carlingen!"

"That must have been right before she became my captain. Strange how our lives seem so intertwined."

"Saint Agnes would say that Holy folk are drawn to each other."

Now it was Charlaine's turn to smile. "I shall take that as a compliment."

"Might I ask a question?"

"Of course."

"How long were you a member of the order before being promoted to the rank of Temple Captain?"

"Why?" asked Charlaine. "Are you looking for a promotion already?"

Marlena chuckled. "No, I was merely curious. Ever since your arrival, there've been rumours."

"Such as?"

"They say this is only your second assignment."

"That's true, but I can assure you I'm up to the task. Giselle did a wonderful job of preparing me to assume the mantle of leadership, something I intend to pass on to any who fall under my command. Now, do you know what's expected of you when you start going door to door?"

"I believe so," said Marlena. "We are to make enquiries about any missing husbands."

"Not just husbands, there may be older sons who are missing as well. Bear in mind your enquiries may raise even more questions, and some might not like us poking into their business."

"And if that happens?"

"Then you must excuse yourself from the situation. You are not there to accuse or intimidate, merely to gather information, and the best way to do that is by making friends."

"Then why the armour?"

"If you should run across those who take a dislike to your interference, it will serve to dissuade them from attempting any intimidation of their own."

"And if it doesn't?" asked Marlena.

"Then you are authorized to take whatever action you deem necessary, but I doubt it will come to that, not when there's three of you."

"And are we all to enter these houses?"

"That will be for you to judge, but if you choose to enter alone, make sure the others are within earshot. The last thing I want to deal with is one of our knights being injured."

"Understood."

21

PLANS

Autumn 1097 SR

"You're starting to look a bit weathered," noted Charlaine.

Danica glanced down at the salt stains on her clothes. "It can't be helped. It's the sea water."

"In that case, we may need to come up with something else for you to wear. A cassock is hardly the best thing for a seafarer."

"I suppose not."

"How did it go out on the *Lydia*? This was what, the third time you sailed on her?"

"Fourth," noted Danica. "She's a fine ship, and I'm beginning to understand her strengths and weaknesses. I also identified some areas of improvement."

"Improvement? It's not your ship, Danica, at least not yet."

"Yes, well, about that…"

"Don't tell me you bought it?"

"Not so much bought as borrowed. Captain Handley will permit us to make some modifications to the design provided we pay him a monthly stipend and his crew remains to man the ship."

"Generous of him," said Charlaine, "but aren't we supposed to be the ones to make up the crew?"

"Eventually, but this will allow us the chance to learn what we need to know."

"And these modifications? How extensive are they? You mentioned changing the sails—is that still in the plans?"

"It is," said Danica. "Along with a few other things."

"Such as?"

"We'll raise the sides to provide cover from archery fire, as well as the aft deck to give us an edge in battle. Of course, we can't make too many changes, or it will upset the trim of the ship."

"Trim? That's not an expression I'm familiar with."

"A ship needs to sit level from bow to stern. Suppose we put too much additional weight on the aft. In that case, the stern will be lower in the water than the nose, affecting its manoeuvrability."

"And how difficult is all this work?"

"Enough that the *Lydia* won't be sailing for a few months. The objective would be to make these changes over the winter, freeing us up for a spring relaunch."

"And I suppose," said Charlaine, "that we must pay for all these modifications along with the ship's expenses for that time as well?"

"Of course, but it's still much cheaper than building a brand new ship."

"My concern is we are making a heavy investment in a ship that still doesn't belong to us."

"I thought of that," said Danica, "but the captain assures me his ultimate goal would be to sell us the ship when we're done."

"Why would he do that?"

"He's spent a lifetime at sea and is looking forward to settling down in his old age. The proceeds from the sale will ensure him comfort in his declining years."

"Anything else I should know about?"

"You wouldn't happen to know where I could lay my hands on a small ballista, would you?"

Charlaine laughed. "No, but I'll keep my eyes out for any I might stumble across. How about your fighting complement? Any idea as to what numbers you'd be looking at?"

"I should think a half dozen would be aboard for most trips, but we'll need extras trained to take their places, if need be."

"Very well. We'll aim for ten to undergo training."

"There is one other thing," said Danica.

"Only one? You surprise me."

"Our plate armour will be more than suitable for battle, but we may end up spending weeks at sea. I should very much like to equip them with something lighter. I'd hate to see them swept overboard only to have them sink to the bottom of the sea."

"Agreed," said Charlaine. "We'll also need to acquire some crossbows, not to mention provide training in their use."

"I made some enquiries in that regard. There's a company of cross-bowmen in the duke's army. I was hoping we might use some influence to borrow a few to help prepare us."

"I'll see what I can do, but such a move would doubtless reveal our plans. That will bring greater scrutiny, especially from the Temple Knights of Saint Cunar."

"They'll find out anyway once we begin altering the *Lydia*. Not to mention I'll need to confer with our brothers, the Mathewites. In case you forgot, they're holding our funds."

"I haven't forgotten," assured Charlaine, "but I'm sure Commander Salvatore can be counted on to keep our secret for now. Still, you do raise a valid concern. I'll have to give some consideration as to how to handle the Cunars. They won't like the fact we're building a fleet, and they're not."

"Will it cause problems?"

"Undoubtedly, but hopefully not enough to interfere with our plans. You concentrate on the *Lydia*, and let me worry about our brother Temple Knights. Oh, that reminds me, weren't you going to name it the *Valiant*?"

"I will, eventually," said Danica, "but not until the ship is in our name."

"Anything else?"

"Yes, I'd like authorization to fly the order's pennant."

"I don't see a problem with that. There are plenty in storage."

"Ah, but I'd need a larger one as it would be flying from the mast, not the end of a spear. We'll want people to be able to see it from afar."

"The order used to crew the ships in Corassus years ago. What did we use back then?"

"Funny you should ask. Back in the Antonine, I found reference to something called a Battle Flag, but it was short on details."

"Then maybe it's time we designed a new one."

"Why not use our own?" asked Danica.

"Our order's flag is scarlet, with three white waves. From a distance, it might be mistaken as that of a pirate's."

"You make a good point."

"In any case, there's several months' worth of downtime ahead of you. That's plenty of time to come up with an alternative."

"By the way," said Danica, "I couldn't help but notice quite a few of the sister knights down at the docks today. What are they up to?"

Charlaine sat back. "It has come to my attention several men from the poorer section of town have gone missing. In each case, they sought employment as manual labourers down by the docks. I sent our people down there to ask around and see if anyone has noticed anything unusual."

"Anything I should be made aware of?"

"Not at present. Whoever's behind the disappearances seems to be targeting the poor. I doubt a ship's crew would be in their sights. They would be too easily missed." Charlaine leaned forward, resting her elbows on the table. "Something just occurred to me. Let's go ahead and purchase some crossbows. We'll introduce the weapon to all our knights, then choose your crew from those who prove most proficient."

"Won't that alert the Cunars?" asked Danica.

"If they ask, I'll inform them we're toying with the idea of using crossbows in battle. That ought to shock them."

Danica mimicked a low, husky voice. "How unchivalrous!"

Charlaine laughed. "Careful, now, or they might try to recruit you."

"How many crossbows do we want?"

"I think thirty would do, don't you? That allows us to train more at one time. Make sure you get plenty of quarrels. We'll need a lot if we're to train everyone."

"You know we can reuse them?"

"Of course," said Charlaine, "but once you put out to sea, the chance of recovering them will be slim. In the meantime, I'll make arrangements to go and visit the duke to see if he'd be willing to lend us some of his crossbowmen."

A knock at the door interrupted them.

"Who's there?" called out Charlaine.

"Sister Grazynia."

"Ah, the first patrols must have returned. Come in!" She turned her attention to Danica. "Let me know how things work out, and don't hesitate to ask for help if you need it."

Danica stood, bowing her head formally at her captain as her fellow sister knight entered the room. "Yes, Captain."

Charlaine waited until only she and Sister Grazynia remained. "What have you to report?"

"Four out of five groups have returned so far, Captain, but we're no closer to figuring out what happened to them. We did, however, learn of at least two other individuals who disappeared."

"Is Sister Marlena back yet?"

"Not to my knowledge."

"Hmmm, that makes five men missing. Did we get descriptions?"

"We did, but there's nothing noteworthy in terms of their appearance. They would all easily disappear in a crowd."

"Perhaps that's why they were taken," mused Charlaine.

"We made enquires of almost half the ships in port, but so far, there's no indication that any procured employment as ship's crew."

"And you got a good description of the first three men?"

"We did. The women at the mission were most helpful in that regard."

Charlaine stood, making her way to the window. "Not a lot of light left."

"Still enough to make further enquiries," said Grazynia. "Once the sisters finish eating, I'll send them back out."

"Good. Let me know as soon as Marlena's group gets back. I'm interested to see just how big this problem is."

"You think more were taken?"

"If it's slavers, then yes," said Charlaine. "If, on the other hand, we're looking at people who abandon their spouses, I doubt we'll find any more."

"If you don't mind me saying, Captain, five men missing can't be a coincidence."

"When did these other fellows vanish?"

"Both within the last month. The real question is where they all went."

"Could they be held in the cargo hold of a ship?"

"Not one in harbour," said Grazynia. "The duke's harbour master has all the ships inspected before they sail."

"Why would he do that?"

"There's a tax based on how much cargo they're carrying. It would be hard to hide slaves from someone like that unless he's complicit."

"An interesting observation. Is there only one harbour master?"

"There is."

"And is he the one who inspects ships?"

"I doubt it," said Grazynia. "If he were, he'd be awfully busy. A ship's inspection can take a while, and dozens of ships leave the port every day."

"So the question remains, where are these men?"

"Could there be a ship down the coast somewhere?"

"I hadn't thought of that," said Charlaine, "but it would make sense. Still, how would they get them out of town without being noticed?"

"Guards can be bribed to look the other way."

"True, but if that's the case, there's little we can do about it. Looking into disappearances is one thing, but accusing the guards of taking bribes is a completely different matter."

"Where does that leave us?" asked Grazynia.

"That has yet to be determined. For your part, continue to supervise these enquiries down at the docks. Meanwhile, I'll write a letter to the duke requesting an audience."

"So you'll bring up the issue of corrupt guards?"

"I'm not sure I'm quite ready to accuse them of criminal activity, but I will bring these disappearances to His Grace's attention. Only the Saints know if he'll do anything about it."

The following morning found Charlaine waiting outside the Mathewite commandery. Grazynia's enquiries yielded no additional information, but those of Marlena added three more names to the list. There were possibly more, the knight had offered, but there'd been a growing reluctance to talk of such things the more people they spoke to.

Charlaine tried to make sense of it all, but the more she thought, the more she became convinced that abduction was the most logical explanation. The only problem was she still couldn't determine how eight or more men had been spirited away without someone seeing something.

The main doors of the commandery opened, and Commander Salvatore left the building, moving at a reasonably fast gait. Charlaine hurried across the street, selecting a course that would intercept the Mathewite.

"Commander Salvatore," she called out. "May I have a word?"

The man turned his head. "Ah, Captain Charlaine. You're up early."

"As I am every day."

"I'm on my way to the Cunar commandery, but you're welcome to accompany me."

"Thank you. I will, at least part of the way."

"What is it I can do for you?"

"Your order is holding funds for us," she replied. "I thought it best to let you know we'd be making a sizable withdrawal over the next few days."

"Oh? Looking at doing some building?"

"In a manner of speaking. We're looking to acquire a ship."

"A ship? I can't say Captain Waleed will be too pleased to hear that."

"Likely not, which is why I must ask you to keep that information to yourself, at least for the time being."

"Nothing shall pass my lips," said the commander, "but it doesn't take long for word down at the docks to make its way through the city."

"I understand," said Charlaine, "but I would not like to deal with Cunar opposition just yet. There are many arrangements still to be made."

"Tell me, is this a single purchase you're making, or does your order intend to create an entire fleet?"

Charlaine blushed.

"Ah," he said. "Your face betrays you. Does this have the blessing of the Antonine?"

"My orders came from the grand mistress herself."

Salvatore smiled. "You are a master of redirection. Very well, if your order condones it, that's enough for me. However, you should be aware an objection will likely be raised by Captain Waleed. Once that reaches the Antonine, anything can happen."

"Of that, I'm only too aware."

He halted for a moment, catching her by surprise. "Tell me, what complement do you propose for these ships you're considering?"

"Six Temple Knights per vessel," replied Charlaine.

"Might I be so bold as to recommend the presence of one of our lay brothers? Such an individual would be useful for dealing with the sick or injured. My order would, of course, recompense you the cost of boarding and feeding them."

"I shall consult with our new captain and gather her thoughts on the matter."

"You mean there's a second Agnes captain in these parts? Why wasn't I informed?"

"Her rank won't take effect until the ship is sworn into service," said Charlaine, "but I'll endeavour to introduce you to her if you wish?"

"I shall take you up on that offer. What kind of timetable are we looking at—for this ship, I mean."

"We expect it to put to sea for the first time next spring."

He nodded. "Very well. I'll give some thought as to who might make an appropriate ship's healer." He resumed walking. "That reminds me, the duke is having a get-together in two days. I expect you to be there."

"What time?"

"Early evening. Dinner will be served, so you're expected to arrive shortly before dark. Don't worry about wearing armour though; the meeting is not meant to be formal."

"Might I ask who else will be in attendance?"

"You, me, and of course, Captain Waleed. The duke, too, but I doubt his wife will put in an appearance. She seldom does. Perhaps, in her stead, you might get a chance to meet his son, Fernando."

"An unusual name in these parts," noted Charlaine.

"The duchess hails from Thalemia, one of the ancient kingdoms on the Southern Coast, astride the Shimmering Sea. I believe the young lord is named after her grandfather. Calabria is down there somewhere too, isn't it?"

"It lies on the western end, but I'm not sure I would call it the same region."

"Still, I daresay it's a much warmer clime than here." He paused while he sneezed, then looked at Charlaine in apology. "I'm afraid you'll find the winters here appalling. Ever lived in the North?"

"No, but Hadenfeld had a severe winter back in eighty-seven. There were drifts almost as high as the roof."

"You won't find much in the way of snow here, but the cold?" He shivered. "Best keep indoors with a fire lit if you don't want to freeze."

Charlaine chuckled. "Any other advice you'd care to impart?"

"Yes. If Lord Wilfhelm asks you to play cards, refuse."

"Won't he take offence?"

"Not if you do so with grace and humility. The problem, you see, is the man is a notorious gambler. Not only that, but he's become an expert in separating individuals from their funds."

"You remember that gambling is frowned upon in my order?"

"As it is in mine," noted Commander Salvatore, "but that's not an outright ban."

"Do you gamble yourself?" asked Charlaine.

"No, of course not, although I've played a few friendly games of cards. Are you familiar with the custom?"

"I can't say that I am."

"The cards are broken into four families, referred to as cups, coins, swords, and sticks. You draw five of them, and then..." His voice trailed off, hastened, no doubt, by the look of disinterest from Charlaine. "Never mind," he said. "It's not for everyone, although I must admit it's a good excuse for fellowship."

"Do you play back at the commandery?"

"No, but over the years, I've found it becoming more common amongst nobles, soldiers as well. It is an excellent way to pass the time."

"I wish I had time to waste," said Charlaine. "The truth is I've been busy since my arrival here."

"That's to be expected. You only just took over as leader of your commandery. I'm sure you'll be all settled in soon enough. Why, I imagine by the time the Midwinter Feast arrives, there'll be little left to do!"

22

POLITICS

Autumn 1097 SR

C harlaine drew her cloak tighter. While officially still autumn, a stiff wind blew in from the north, bringing with it a light drizzle. Rain was nothing new to the Temple Knight, but the drops here were like icicles, causing her to catch her breath. She hurried up the pathway to where the duke's estate beckoned. A servant took her cloak, shaking out the rain as best he could while a young woman stood watching.

"If you'll come this way, Sister," she said. "I'll take you to the duke."

"Are the others here yet?" asked Charlaine.

"Captain Waleed is, but the commander sent word indicating he would be late." She started making her way down the hallway. "It's an honour to have you here," the woman continued. "Word of your accomplishments in Ilea have proven quite popular amongst the educated."

"And by educated, I assume you mean the nobility?"

"Naturally, although I must confess the servants are equally as impressed."

"I was merely doing what I thought best."

They paused at a door, and the servant looked Charlaine directly in the eyes. "I need to warn you," she said in a soft voice. "Lord Winfyre is not pleased that you were sent here."

"Lord Winfyre?"

"The Halvarian emissary. Be careful what you say. He has ears everywhere."

"Thank you," said Charlaine. "I'll bear that in mind. What's your name?"

The woman blushed. "Enid, Your Grace."

"I am a Temple Captain, not a noble. The correct form of address is Sister."

"Still, you are a woman to be reckoned with, if your reputation is anything to go on."

"What else does my reputation say?"

"That you are honourable and honest to a fault."

Charlaine chuckled. "I have never looked on honesty as being a weakness, and I would hope others felt the same way."

"Many do," the woman replied, "but the price of serving at the duke's pleasure carries a heavy burden."

"I trust your warning won't put you in peril?"

"It's a risk I'm willing to take in the name of our Saint." She took three fingers and made a wave pattern across her chest. Her action complete, she stepped towards the door and grasped the handle. "Ready?"

Charlaine unconsciously straightened her cassock. "Ready."

Enid opened the door, revealing a well-appointed room. The wooden floor was polished to a shine, while several exquisite tapestries hung from the wall in a vain effort to ward off the cold. At one end, a group of chairs was gathered around a blazing fireplace. Everything looked slightly hazy, and it took a moment for her to realize the cause. Nearby, on a table, a small brazier burned incense, the smell permeating everything.

"There she is," said Captain Waleed. "The hero of the Church!"

"I am but a humble servant," replied Charlaine.

"Nonsense," said Lord Wilfhelm. "You should bathe in the glory while you can."

"She can't," added a woman's voice drifting out from a high-backed chair. Larissa Stormwind stood, her eyes locking on the new arrival before turning to the Cunar knight. "She's taken a vow of humility, something your own order frowns upon."

"Bit silly, if you ask me," said Waleed. "One should always be proud of one's accomplishments, don't you think, Your Grace?" This last remark was directed towards the duke.

"I do," he replied. "Although I understand the good captain's reticence. It's not every day we see a knight promoted so quickly." He looked at Charlaine. "The Church must think very highly of you."

"I don't understand this sudden interest in my past," she replied. "This is not the first time we've met."

"True," continued Duke Brondecker, "but word of your escapades has become public knowledge. It seems a bard of some repute has learned of your adventures in the South and decided to immortalize them. It's the talk of the town!"

"A bard?"

"Yes, a fellow named Rascalian. Surely you've heard?"

Charlaine felt the blood rush to her cheeks. "I am not one to frequent locations where such a fellow might be found."

"But this is good, surely?" added Larissa Stormwind. "Your fame can only grow, and with it, influence within the Church, not to mention the Petty Kingdoms. You are the Victor of Alantra."

"I am no victor, merely one of many who fought to keep the land safe. I shall not take credit away from those who gave their lives for ours."

Captain Waleed smiled. "Well said, Sister. You are a credit to all of us who serve."

"Come," bade Lord Wilfhelm. "Sit by the fire and warm yourself." He waited while she took a seat, then shot a look at Larissa Stormwind. "It's unseasonably cold, don't you agree?"

"On the contrary," she replied. "Compared to my home, this is positively balmy."

"And where might that be?" asked Charlaine.

"I hail from Ruzhina. This would be a nice, warm day by our measure."

"Where's that?" asked Waleed.

"It lies on the easternmost shore of the Great Northern Sea. The kingdom itself is of little consequence, but the great city of Karslev is known throughout the Petty Kingdoms."

"Karslev," said Charlaine. "Isn't that where the Stormwind Academy lies?"

"Yes," continued Larissa. "Although the family refers to it as the Volstrum."

"An ominous-sounding name," noted the duke.

Larissa chuckled. "I can assure you it's nothing of the sort. Those at the Volstrum are more like an extended family."

"What kind of magic do they teach there?" asked Charlaine.

"We specialize in Water Magic."

"Is that all?" asked Wilfhelm. "I thought the family also produced Fire Mages?"

"We do, but not in Karslev. Pyromancers are trained in the fortress of Korascajan."

"I don't believe I've ever heard of a Stormwind who uses fire."

"No," said Larissa, "and you wouldn't, at least not from us. Any student capable of wielding the power of flame is named Sartellian."

"So you change their names?" said Waleed. "How barbaric!"

"Is it any less so than your own Church? Correct me if I'm wrong, but don't many of your initiates choose a new name when they join your orders?"

The Cunar reddened. "Yes, I suppose they do. Hmmm, I see you're far cleverer than I."

Duke Brondecker barked out a laugh. "That's what you get for trying to out-argue a court mage."

Charlaine turned her attention to Larissa. "How long have you been here, if you don't mind me asking?"

"A little over three years. My last assignment was Grislagen. Do you know it?"

"I do, though only by reputation. It borders Hadenfeld, the land of my birth."

"I thought you were Calabrian?"

"Only by lineage. My parents fled Alantra after the invasion."

"Might I ask why you joined the Church?"

Captain Waleed coughed. "The Church frowns on that sort of thing. An individual's reason for joining the order is considered personal."

"Come now," said Larissa. "Can't we make an exception, here amongst friends?"

"I must agree with the good captain," said Charlaine. "I would prefer to talk of my time amongst the order rather than the years preceding it."

"You say you are from Hadenfeld," continued the Water Mage, "yet they first posted you to the Southern Coast. That's a little unusual, isn't it?"

"I wouldn't know. I go where I'm needed."

"Yes," agreed Waleed, "and a good thing too, or we might have lost Ilea. I can't even begin to imagine the problems we'd be facing if the Halvarians had managed to gain control of the place." He raised his glass. "The Church needs more knights like you, Sister. To your health."

They all raised their drinks in a toast, and a servant appeared from somewhere to hand Charlaine a glass of wine. She drank sparingly, though Captain Waleed downed his in one gulp.

"Tell me," said Lord Wilfhelm, "are you settling in?"

"I am," she replied. "The transition to captain is much smoother than I anticipated."

Waleed smiled, perhaps a little worse for the drink; clearly he had been imbibing for some time. "The only problem with being a captain in this town is the endless paperwork."

The door opened, admitting Commander Salvatore. "I hope I'm not too late?"

"Not at all, Father," decried the Cunar. "We were just celebrating Sister Charlaine's achievements." He turned his attention to the servant. "Get the good father a drink, man, and be quick about it. He's got some catching up to do!" Waleed was a little too exuberant, and as he set down his glass, he missed the table, sending shards of glass everywhere as it shattered on the floor. He turned towards the duke, his face reddening. "My apologies, Your Grace."

"I think it's time you left us," said Father Salvatore, "before you do any further damage." His voice was kind, but the meaning behind his intense stare was clear. Captain Waleed stood, swaying a bit as he did so.

"Once again, my apologies, everyone." The room remained silent until his departure.

"I thought Temple Knights practiced moderation," said Larissa.

"We do," replied the commander, "but even the most pious of individual has been known to slip from time to time. Let us not be too hasty to judge the poor fellow. What of you, Captain Charlaine? Are you enjoying Korvoran?"

"I must admit to not seeing much of it," she replied. "Other than here and the mission your order maintains, I spend the rest of my time at the commandery."

"You must get out more," suggested Lord Wilfhelm. "See the sights, as it were. We have much to offer."

"I shall do my best."

"I hear your sister knights have been fairly busy these last few days. What's that all about?"

Charlaine steeled herself. She'd intended to raise the issue eventually, but the sudden mention of her knights unsettled her.

"It has recently come to our attention that several people have gone missing," she finally said.

"Missing? What do you mean, missing?"

"They vanished, with no warning or any evidence of misdeed. It's as if something made them disappear."

The statement piqued the duke's interest. "Who, exactly?"

"Common labourers," replied Charlaine. "No one you would know."

Lord Wilfhelm sat back, waving his hand as if to shoo away a fly. "Oh, well. I suppose we should expect that."

"We should?"

"Yes, labourers are lazy. They probably hid to avoid work. It's all the same with the poor; they want to earn a wage without doing the work."

"I believe you misjudge them, Your Grace."

Duke Brondecker looked as if he'd just been slapped. "I beg your pardon?"

"They work as labourers to put food on the table. They're not lazy, quite the reverse, actually—they're hard workers. They need to be, or else no one would hire them."

"I would agree," added Father Salvatore. "We work with them at the mission from time to time. All they really seek is a fair wage for their labours."

Larissa, likely sensing the tension in the room, changed the subject. "I hear raiders are causing trouble up at Herenstadt."

"You mean the *Sea Wolf*?" asked Lord Wilfhelm, his previous discussion all but forgotten. "The scoundrel! Why, I'd have his head if my men could catch him."

"Have you taken precautions?" asked Charlaine.

He stared at her. "Precautions? What would you have us do? It's not as if we could drop a chain across the mouth of the bay. There are too many ships coming and going to do that."

"An interesting conundrum," said Larissa Stormwind. "Tell me, Sister, what would you do if you were the duke?"

"Yes," Lord Wilfhelm added. "Do tell."

"I would anchor a pair of warships right outside the harbour entrance."

"What good would that do? The Saints' forsaken *Sea Wolf* would just sail right past them."

"Yes, but once he's in the harbour, your ships could block him in. At least then he wouldn't be able to escape."

"By the Saints, that's a marvellous idea," said the duke. "What do you think, Larissa?"

"The idea has some merit," the mage replied, "but I should think the last thing we want would be a desperate Fire Mage who's trapped surrounded by wooden ships."

"Ah, she has a good point. We're better off simply accepting the losses."

"Have you thought of tracking them down?" asked Charlaine.

"Yes, but no one can seem to find the rogue. It's as if he just vanishes."

"That's the second time such a term has been used tonight," noted Larissa. "First, the labourers disappear, and now the raider. Is there no end to it?"

Charlaine was suddenly struck by the idea there might be a correlation between the raids of this ship, the *Sea Wolf*, and the missing labourers. "How often does it attack?"

"Six times in the last four months, although this is the first time they have ventured inside the bay," replied Duke Brondecker. "So far the attacks have been staggered enough to make them unpredictable."

"And are they always at the same time of day?"

"No, but they always strike during the daylight."

"How serious are they?" asked Charlaine.

"Very. Since they started, we've lost at least ten ships, with another seven damaged so severely they were put out of commission for months. What's even more pronounced is the effect it's having on our seaborne trade. Word is some merchants are now avoiding Korvoran altogether, rather than risk taking damage to their vessels."

"He attacks out at sea too," added Father Salvatore.

"Yes," said Lord Wilfhelm. "We confirmed at least six attacks, with three more in the list of likely targets."

"Likely targets?" said Charlaine.

"Yes, ships lost at sea without any word as to how. Of course, they might have just floundered in a storm, but these were all experienced crews. It's hard to believe they would be lost to anything other than piracy."

"Even pirates need a home somewhere."

"They do," said the duke, "but you tell me where."

"Have other kingdoms suffered similar attacks?"

"Piracy is an ever-present danger in the Northern Sea, but the *Sea Wolf* seems to target us, or ships bound for our port."

"Excuse me," said Charlaine, "but are you saying they were all coming here?"

"Yes," replied Lord Wilfhelm. "Although I'm not sure what you're getting at."

"So none of the ships had just left Korvoran?"

"No," added Father Salvatore. "Not as far as we know. You consider that significant?"

"It seems to me," said Charlaine, "the loss of incoming ships is a greater burden to you, Your Grace, than those leaving. I assume these are not your personal vessels?"

"No, they're merchants," the duke said. "What makes you believe these attacks are aimed at me?"

"Incoming ships are expected to pay taxes to the duchy, but those leaving have already undertaken that burden."

"I hadn't thought of that. You don't suppose someone inside my own court is working with them, do you?"

"I doubt it," said Charlaine. "My understanding is that ships don't usually follow a strict schedule. It would be difficult to know the arrival of a particular ship and nearly impossible to arrange to intercept them."

"That's right," added Larissa Stormwind. "They'd need to know the exact route each ship took, and there are far too many to keep track of. In any case, most captains only have a vague idea of their specific route when they sail, making adjustments based on weather, the current, demand for their goods, and market prices. I'd hazard a guess most ships never take the exact same trip more than once a year."

"That being the case," said Father Salvatore, "who would most like to see Reinwick suffer financially?"

"Andover," declared Duke Brondecker. "They've hated us for years."

"Might I ask why?" said Charlaine.

"There is some bad blood between us ever since the Duke of Erlingen chose a woman of Reinwick over the King of Andover's niece. It's what led him to invade Erlingen two years ago, although I should say attempted invasion."

"I heard something to that effect on the way here. They say he was captured in battle."

"He was," the duke confirmed. "And held for a ransom that almost bankrupted his kingdom, forcing him to drastically reduce the size of his army as a result." He sat back, a smug look on his face.

"Unfortunately," added Father Salvatore, "not all the news is good. In the absence of a sizable army in Andover, the other realms in this part of the Petty Kingdoms are growing restless. I hate to say it, but I fear war will soon be upon us."

"From who?" asked Charlaine.

"Take your pick," said Lord Wilfhelm. "We're safe enough here in Reinwick, but Eidolon and Abelard have never seen eye to eye. That was largely mitigated by Eidolon keeping a substantial army near Andover. However, with them weakened so much, Eidolon can now concentrate on their eastern neighbour."

"Sorry," said Charlaine, "but I'm not sure where those kingdoms are."

"Andover, Eidolon, and Abelard form a string of countries in order from west to east, sitting on the Northern Shore of the Petty Kingdoms. Each of them has a substantial fleet."

"Of merchant vessels," added Larissa, "not warships, at least not in any significant numbers."

"That's true," confirmed the duke. "Like us, they can field no more than half a dozen warships, and those are little more than cogs carrying soldiers. Hardly the type of thing that can track down pirates, not to mention face off against a Fire Mage." He glanced at the court mage. "What about you, Larissa? Care to take on a Pyromancer?"

She smiled. "While it's true Water Mages like me can be quite useful aboard a ship, our spells pale in comparison to the destructive capabilities of a trained Fire Mage. I'm afraid I must refuse your request for assistance, at least for the moment."

Lord Wilfhelm sighed. "Ah well, it was worth a try." He turned to face the Temple Knight of Saint Agnes. "What about you, Captain Charlaine? Care to take out some of my ships and hunt down this raider? After all, you beat the Halvarian fleet!"

"Admiral Marius commanded the Holy Fleet," said Charlaine. "The victory belongs to him and his men."

"Well said," noted Father Salvatore, "but regardless of her thoughts on the matter, Sister Charlaine has responsibilities here that prevent her from accepting your offer."

"A pity," said Duke Brondecker. He was about to say more, but at that precise moment, the door opened, revealing another servant. "Her Ladyship requires your attention, Your Grace."

"Very well. Inform her I will be along shortly." The duke rose, setting down his drink. "I hate to admit it, but it appears the evening's festivities have come to an end. Feel free to finish your drinks. My servants will see you out."

He left abruptly, the door slamming behind him.

"And that," said Father Salvatore, "is our signal to leave."

23

RAID

Winter 1097 SR

D anica rubbed her hands. The winter winds had brought ice and snow, blanketing the land with white. For all its majesty, the sea remained unfrozen, but the waves grew in intensity as the season wore on. With the ship traffic dwindling, the activity at the docks ground to a halt.

Aboard the *Lydia*, however, signs of activity remained. The mainmast had been rigged fore and aft, the guard rails raised, but the work on elevating the aft deck was progressing slowly, hampered by the frigid temperatures. Around them floated all sorts of ships, battened down against the weather in an effort to wait out the cold, their crews crowding the taverns of Korvoran. Sister Grazynia strolled across the deck, her face barely visible beneath her thick hooded cloak.

"By the Saints, it's cold," she said.

"So it is," replied Danica, her breath frosting before her, "but the work must still be done."

"That, I understand, but I fail to see why we're needed. It's not as if any of us possess skill with carpentry." She looked aft, where five other sisters watched a solitary woodworker taking measurements.

"We're here to protect Church property. It would hardly do to invest all these funds only for the ship to be stolen out from beneath us."

"You believe someone could steal a ship in this weather?"

Danica laughed. "No, perhaps not."

"It wouldn't be so bad if we had something to keep us busy, but this standing around seems pointless."

"Gather the knights," said Danica, "and we'll practice with crossbows."

"My hands are frozen," Grazynia complained.

"As are mine, but the enemy can strike at any time. We must therefore be prepared. Besides, what else is there to do?"

"You make a good point." The knight strolled back to her fellow sisters.

Danica gazed across the bay. There was no denying the port had fewer ships than when they first arrived. She wondered if they were simply choosing to winter in warmer climes, but something told her otherwise. The talk all over town was of the *Sea Wolf*. Her captain had become the stuff of legend, growing in boldness with each retelling of the tale. Some said he'd made a pact with the God of the Underworld, but she knew better. It was not gods that drove him but one man's ambition.

Charlaine speculated he was in service to someone higher up the chain of command, and the idea had merit. The big question, however, was who that someone was. Danica spent time with the locals, trying to get the lay of the land from a political perspective. All she discovered were lots of opinions and very little in the way of hard facts. It appeared the average sailor cared little for such things.

She glanced towards the stern, where Grazynia pulled crossbows from the weapon storage chest while the others belted quivers around their waists. It was a strange sight, for they all wore thick, hooded jackets with mittens—the belts making them look a little like hourglasses.

They had, at least, planned for the cold weather by widening the stirrup on the end of the crossbows, enabling a heavily booted foot to secure the weapon while loading. It added some weight to the front, necessitating a firmer grip, but the sister knights, used to training with swords, soon learned to compensate.

Danica went below, returning shortly with a bale of hay. This she placed on the foredeck before moving to join her fellow knights. She drew a crossbow and loaded a quarrel, talking as she worked.

"We'll take turns trying to hit the target," she said. "There'll be an extra ration of ale to the first one to strike true."

She took aim, pulled up on the tickler, and the bolt flew through the air to sink into the target. "There," she said, looking quite pleased with herself. "Let's see who can get the closest to mine."

The sisters began loosing off their shots, all hitting the hay bale, but only one coming close to Danica's bolt.

"Good job, Anya. I don't remember you being so accurate."

"I've been practicing," replied the blonde-haired knight, grabbing another quarrel. As she placed it on the crossbow, her eyes wandered out to the harbour. A ship was nearing, its red flag easy to spot.

"The *Sea Wolf*!" she cried out. "And it's coming directly towards us."

"To the side," ordered Danica. "Don't loose until you can see your target."

They each loaded, then moved to the newly completed railing, now higher than it had originally been. Additionally, instead of simple rails, a solid wall provided a modicum of protection.

The *Sea Wolf* closed the range, then turned sharply, bringing the vessel side-on to the *Lydia*. Grazynia was the first to loose her bolt, and it sailed across the gap, sinking into the mainmast of their enemy.

Danica spotted the mage, a tall fellow with short-cropped, black hair and a well-trimmed beard. He snarled as he thrust his hands out, a streak of flame erupting from his fingertips. She focused on his head and let fly. As soon as the quarrel left the crossbow, she ducked, feeling the heat as flames shot overhead.

More quarrels flew forth to clatter against the side of the *Sea Wolf*. The enemy ship moved farther along, but Danica could still make out the Fire Mage as he ran towards the stern, the better to fire off one more spell against the *Lydia*. She reloaded and, taking careful aim, waited until he halted to begin his spell before pulling back up on the tickler.

The bolt sailed true, giving her the satisfaction of seeing it dig into his left shoulder. The mage let out a bellow, clutching the wound with his right hand, his magic forgotten for the moment.

"A solid shot," said Grazynia. "Too bad you didn't hit his head."

The *Sea Wolf* continued down the line of ships, but there was little more they could do with their mage now injured. A few arrows flew forth, striking hulls, but they did no significant damage. The ship turned once more, heading back to the bay's entrance, and a cheer went up from a nearby cog.

"It appears there are some people who appreciate your accomplishments," noted Grazynia.

"It was just a lucky shot," said Danica.

"Lucky or not, it'll be some time before that mage casts another spell. You've bought the good people of Korvoran a temporary respite."

"Perhaps, but I doubt he'll take that lying down. They'll be back, and when they do come, they'll be thirsting for vengeance. I only hope the *Lydia* is ready for their return."

"You mean the *Valiant*," said Anya. "If we're to go after that rogue, we need a name befitting our task."

"It's not our ship yet," said Danica, "and renaming a ship is not a task to be taken lightly. There are traditions to be observed."

"Such as?"

Danica smiled. "I'd go into them, but I'm afraid you'd just shrug them off as superstitious nonsense."

"You're talking of the old Gods?"

"Naturally."

"But we worship the Saints."

"One does not preclude the honouring of the other, or have you forgotten the words of Saint Agnes?"

"Fear not the ancient ways, for in them lies the seeds of true worship."

"Very good," said Danica. "But do you truly understand them?"

"Of course. According to the *Book of Agnes*, worship of the old Gods led the heathens to organized religion. Thus, when the Saints came along, they were already disposed to attend services."

"I suppose that's one way of looking at it. I would, however, propose an alternative."

"Which is?"

"The worship of the old Gods is more similar to our Church than you might think."

"But we worship people, not some mystical beings," said Anya. "Surely you're not suggesting otherwise?"

"What I'm saying is if you look past that, you'll find both religions have much in common, for they stress the importance of ritual, the veneration of life, and the need to stand together to resist temptation or fear."

"I had no idea."

"Nor would I expect you to. I grew up near here, and in all honesty, I can tell you many folks in these parts still pay homage to the ancient Gods."

"That's blasphemous!"

"Not at all. The Church does not demand unquestioning obedience, at least not outside of the Temple Knights. A person's religious beliefs are private, providing it harms no others."

"Who said that?" asked Anya.

"Saint Mathew."

"But we follow Saint Agnes."

"You need to expand your reading, Sister," said Danica. "We venerate all the Saints, not just Agnes."

The blonde knight shook her head. "The last thing I was expecting today was a discussion of theology."

"Nor did we expect a visit from the *Sea Wolf,* but we must accept things as they are presented to us."

"More words of wisdom from Mathew?"

"No," said Danica. "That one's from my father."

"Was he a philosopher?"

She laughed. "No, only a fisherman, but a more plain-spoken man you'd be hard-pressed to find."

Charlaine finished reading, then looked up. "This is quite an interesting report," she said.

"Thank you," said Danica. "I tried to be as accurate as possible."

"Sister Giselle would be proud. You did an excellent job. It says here you hit the Fire Mage. Have you any idea how seriously?"

"I'm afraid not. It interrupted his casting, but whether it will lead to long-term damage is anyone's guess."

"Still, it blunted the effectiveness of their attack. Without their Fire Mage, they possess little to damage us with."

"It's too bad we don't employ one of our own," said Danica. "You mentioned seeing a Water Mage at court. Any chance of her sailing with us?"

"I doubt it. She's too dedicated to court life. Not that I've seen much of her lately."

"You haven't been to court?"

"Not since the snow came."

"And what about those missing men?"

"It seems we ran into a dead end. The last victim disappeared more than a month ago. It's almost as if someone knows we're watching for them."

"That's obvious, isn't it?" said Danica. "Our sister knights are all over the docks, and there are regular patrols through the poorer sections of the city. A person would need to be crazy to try to abduct someone under those circumstances."

"I wonder..."

"I know that look; you're thinking."

"You make a good point," said Charlaine, "but what if they're targeting people in one of the other cities, say Herendstadt, for example? There's nothing to say they're not targeting other realms as well."

"But if that were true, they'd have an army of slaves by now, surely?"

"Could that be their intent?"

"I'm not sure I follow."

"We know slavers exist, but only on a very small scale."

"What about Halvaria? They used slaves in their galleys, if you recall."

"That's right, they did, but Reinwick is quite some distance from the Empire, and galleys aren't terribly useful up here on the Great Northern Sea. The waters are too rough."

"Then why take them?"

"I think you hit it on the head earlier," said Charlaine. "An army."

"To what end?"

"That, I have yet to determine."

"You don't believe it's another seaborne invasion, do you?"

"No. It would take a massive fleet to do that, and Reinwick has a decent-sized army."

"An uprising, then?"

"Possibly," said Charlaine, "but I saw no evidence of raids or heard of any troubles in the countryside."

"Just because you haven't heard anything, doesn't mean it's not there."

"Yes, but a slave army? They'd need thousands to take on Reinwick. And where would they attack from?"

"There are lots of places Halvaria could land warriors," said Danica. "Especially if they come ashore in the West. Still, you have a point about numbers."

"I'm not convinced that's their end game," said Charlaine. "We know Halvaria is more than willing to use slaves in their army. We saw that in Calabria, but to transport such a force would be difficult if not impossible in the waters hereabouts."

"Oh, I don't know. There are plenty of places you could hide an army."

"Such as?"

"The Five Sisters, for one. Then again, it might not be Halvaria who's behind all this."

"Then who?"

"Almost anyone," said Danica. "All the kingdoms around here hate each other. It's been that way ever since I was a little girl. Don't get me wrong; it's not the common folk behind those sentiments, but the nobility. The funny thing is, one way or another, they're all related."

"So you're saying they're all feuding relatives?"

"I suppose that's a good way of looking at it."

"Well," said Charlaine, "we can ponder the possibilities all we like, but without any proof, there's little we can do." She carefully folded the report. "I shall forward a copy of this on to the Antonine. At least if we don't have answers, we can be thorough. Anything else you'd care to discuss?"

"There is, in fact. I talked to Captain Handley, and he agrees it's time to hand the *Lydia* over to us."

"I thought you wanted to test out your modifications first."

"The truth is the *Lydia* is much more of a warship now rather than a merchant. He and his crew are still willing to hire on, but he feels his days of trading are over. He's also eager to get his payout before we end up losing the *Lydia* in some sort of battle."

"I can't say I blame him," said Charlaine.

"Which brings me to the second point."

"Which is?"

"If we're taking possession, I'd like to rename the ship."

"What's stopping you?"

"Tradition, or perhaps you might call it superstition."

"I'm not sure I follow."

"It's simple," said Danica. "When a ship is first named, the belief is, or rather was, that Akosia took note of it."

"Akosia? The Goddess of the Sea?"

"Not just the sea, all water."

"And how is that a problem?"

"It's considered bad luck to rename a ship without notifying her."

Charlaine leaned forward. "And this would involve...?"

"A ceremony in her honour."

"I think you might have a hard time convincing our fellow sisters of participating in such a ceremony."

Danica waved it off. "That's the least of our problems."

"If that's the least, what's the worst?"

"We have to find a priestess of Akosia."

"A priestess?"

"Well, they might call her a Holy Mother, like we do, but the result is essentially the same. We need someone familiar with the customs of the old religion."

"I see. And I suppose you know a way of finding such an individual?"

"I do, although I wonder what the order might make of such a request?"

Charlaine sat back. "I believe it best we leave this part out of official reports, don't you? I can just imagine those clerks back at the Antonine reading about how we used a pagan ritual to rename a ship."

"So you'll approve it?"

"It's not my place to approve or disprove."

"What's that mean?"

"It's your choice to make. You're the one in charge of acquiring ships."

"So you don't object?"

"I will support whatever decision you make, Danica, but we must make certain we do not violate any tenets of our order. What's involved in this ceremony?"

"I don't know the details, but I believe it's some form of ritual offering."

"Not an animal sacrifice, I hope?"

Danica laughed. "Saints no, nothing of the sort. We probably toss some food overboard or something. These people are worshippers of the old Gods, not bloodthirsty savages."

"Very well, let me know when everything's arranged. Oh, and I expect an invitation to this… whatever you want to call it."

"Done."

"Good. Now that's out of the way, get out of here. I have work to do."

"Yes, Captain." Danica made an exaggerated bow before she turned to leave.

"Just a moment," said Charlaine.

The raven-haired knight turned once more. "Yes?"

"Did you choose your final group of knights yet?"

"I did, as it happens." She smiled. "My first choice would be Grazynia. She's proven herself calm under pressure and is more than capable of leading others, if need be."

"Who else?"

"Anya is the best marksman I've ever seen."

"Weren't you the one who hit the Fire Mage?"

Danica blushed. "Well, maybe the second-best marksman."

"And the rest?"

"Sisters Laurel, Nadia, Vivian, and Zivka."

"Zivka? I thought you said she was useless with a crossbow."

"She is, but she has the sharpest eyes amongst the group. I could really use her as a lookout."

"Very well, I shall amend my records showing their reassignment. Since Korvoran will be your home port, they shall draw their allowance from this commandery. Once you establish your operating costs, I'll inform the grand mistress, and our funds will be amended as appropriate. In the meantime, you'll need to draw what extra coins you need from the reserve they granted you."

"Understood."

"Is everything on schedule?"

"Well," said Danica, "the modifications to the aft deck are proving troublesome, but I expect they'll be finished long before spring."

"You mentioned reconfiguring the mast. Are the new sails ready?"

"Not as yet, but they're being sewn up as we speak. We'll test fit them later this week, then make any adjustments to the rigging we deem necessary."

"Good," said Charlaine. "You're making excellent progress. Hopefully, by spring, the *Lydia* will be out there hunting down the raider that's been plaguing us."

"You mean the *Valiant*."

"You know what I mean. Now, get out of here before I change my mind and scuttle the whole thing."

"Look at you," said Danica. "Using all the nautical talk. We'll make a sailor out of you yet."

"I'll leave that to you. I'm quite content staying ashore."

24

THE VISITOR

Winter 1097 SR

Captain Waleed ascended the stairs, taking them two at a time. The Temple Knights simply watched as he made his way through the Agnes commandery, unable or unwilling to challenge the scowling Cunar. He finally halted before Charlaine's door, staring daggers at the guard.

"Tell your captain I'm here," he said, his tone leaving no room for refusal.

Sister Marlena opened the door and poked in her head. "Captain Waleed is here to see you, Captain."

"Send him in," replied Charlaine.

Waleed pushed past the guard. "How dare you!" he shouted.

Charlaine stood but remained calm. "If you are here to discuss something, then I suggest you keep a civil tongue. I will not listen to the ravings of a madman or be bullied by someone throwing his weight around. If you wish to talk, then sit, and we shall speak of things in a respectful manner. Refuse the offer, and you'll be removed by force, if necessary."

"You wouldn't dare!"

"Sister Marlena," she called out. "Fetch the guard." She swivelled her gaze to her visitor. "Your choice, Captain. Which will it be?"

Waleed threw himself into the chair. As a Temple Knight of Saint Cunar, he was used to being treated with dignity and respect and, yes, even a little fear if he were to admit it. Now, however, he found himself out of his element. He expected to face down a dragon but instead was met with a firm yet composed response.

"That's better," said Charlaine. "Now, what is it that irks you so?"

"It has come to my attention you authorized the outfitting and manning of a ship."

"That is far beyond my meagre powers."

"So you deny it?"

She paused for a moment. "No. The order came from on high."

"It is a direct violation of Church doctrine."

"What makes you say that?"

"Everyone knows my order was given domain over all ships of the Holy Fleet."

"I believe you'll find you are in error," said Charlaine. "While it's true the Temple Knights of Saint Cunar were granted control of the ships in Corassus, the actual orders related to A Holy Fleet, as in a single Holy Fleet. Last I heard, that was the opinion of Admiral Marius as well. Do you now seek to challenge that decision?"

"Don't try to twist my words. You know full well we are the order that has been given control of the fleet."

"Only in the South. And in any event, even if I did agree with you, I'm powerless to do anything about it. The orders came from the grand mistress herself."

"Then I ask that you at least put a halt to all this nonsense while we let the Antonine sort out the details."

"I can't do that."

"It's your coins that are funding this ship. Do you deny it?"

"I can assure you I made no funds available for this enterprise. The ship has been financed through a special grant from my order, a grant, I might add, that I have no control over. Nor would I intervene, even if I could."

"I am the senior order," insisted Waleed. "Cunar Temple Knights were given command over all military operations."

"No, they are given command over armies—this is a ship. My order, unless you've forgotten, used to command the Holy Fleet."

"Yes, and the Council of Peers agreed a Cunar should command the Holy Fleet in their stead."

"Only because the fleet grew substantially over the years, and we lacked sufficient numbers to crew all the ships. Here, it is a different matter."

"I fail to see the difference."

"It's true," said Charlaine, "you command the fleet in the South, but we're not talking a fleet here, merely a single ship. We're not building a ship of war capable of fighting the fleets of Halvaria, but rather a small patrol ship, to be used for neutralizing pirates and rendering assistance to vessels in distress."

"But a Cunar should command, surely? We have all the training!"

"Training? Now you've intrigued me. Tell me, what training do you possess that makes you qualified to command a ship?"

"We study tactics and strategy."

"Both of which are based on battles fought on land. Our new captain is an experienced sailor and has fought at sea. Can you say the same?"

"Captain? I was under the impression you sisters only had one captain in Korvoran."

"And so we do, but upon completion of our ship, there will be two."

He sat back, clearly thrown off by the unexpected revelation. "Who is this new captain?"

"I'm surprised you don't know. The fact that you're here tells me you've been informed of the *Lydia*'s overhaul. Did you not consider making enquiries as to her crew?"

"I thought it would be you who took up that mantle."

"Me? I was born in the middle of the Petty Kingdoms. What would I know of ships?"

"Then who is to command her?"

"That, my friend, is for me to know and for you to find out."

"I might remind you that you took a vow of honesty."

"You seem to confuse my lack of an answer for a lie. I shall reveal the identity of the *Lydia's* new captain in due time, but until I do, I must insist you keep your nose out of the affairs of my order."

"You don't have the authority to ask that of me."

"No, I don't, but Commander Salvatore does. Shall we take the matter to him?"

He stared back, considering a way to argue the point, but she had the upper hand. Salvatore was a weak-willed commander, and everyone knew the Mathewites would do anything for their sister order. He felt trapped, and the anger rose within him. There was no seeing reason with this woman, so he closed his eyes, forcing himself to take a breath, then let it out slowly.

"Evidently, we do not see eye to eye on this," he said, his voice now calm, "but I cannot sit back and permit you to continue without raising my concerns with our superiors."

"As is your right," replied Charlaine. "By all means, do as your conscience demands, but until such time as we hear back from the Antonine, I'll continue to carry out my orders."

Captain Waleed stood, bowing slightly. "My apologies if I over-reacted. I shall endeavour to keep my emotions in check in future."

"Thank you. I look forward to our next meeting."

"Then I will see you tonight," he replied.

"Tonight?"

"Yes. There's an elaborate ceremony to mark the birthday of the duchess. Were you not informed?"

"I was," said Charlaine, "but somewhere along the line, I lost track of the date. I was under the impression that was next week."

Captain Waleed smiled at her discomfort. "Make sure you look your best," he added. "Everyone will be there."

"And by everyone, you mean…?"

"Why, all the nobles of Reinwick, of course, not to mention the Halvarian Ambassador."

"And aside from him, will there be any other foreign emissaries?"

"One or two, I would expect, although I don't know who they might be. Oh, and don't forget to bring an aide."

"Why?"

"It projects a sense of importance. Besides, you might need their assistance from time to time, if only to keep track of your commitments."

"I have enough of those already."

"Trust me," said Waleed, "you'll get more. You're the talk of the town, Captain. Every noble there will want to meet with you. Use the opportunity to enhance the status of your order."

"I would rather not."

"You're a captain now, not just a sister knight. That means it's your responsibility to ensure the order has the funds necessary to operate. Talk with these people, and you'll see donations increase. That's what you want, isn't it?"

"Yes, I suppose it is."

"Good, then I'll see you there." He turned, leaving abruptly, a smile playing upon his lips.

"I'm not sure why I'm here," said Marlena. "Wouldn't Sister Danica be more appropriate? After all, she's your adjutant." They were walking up the street, the duke's estate just coming into view.

"The truth is she's far too busy with arranging things with the *Lydia*," replied Charlaine.

"You mean the *Valiant*."

"Not yet, I don't. The renaming ceremony isn't till next week, assuming I'm not wrong about that as well."

"You mustn't blame yourself, Captain. Your position requires a lot. I am curious why you chose me though."

"You told me your father was a duke. I assume that means you're familiar with the ways of nobles?"

"I am, although I can't say I agree with them."

"I've only met a few in my life," said Charlaine. "So tell me what I can expect."

"Ordinarily, I would say plenty of drinking. Were I back home, I would expect a bit of leering as well. My father was always trying to marry me off."

"I imagine we're safe on that score. Few men would entertain thoughts of being intimate with a Temple Knight."

"You might be surprised," said Marlena. "In any event, my father wasn't a real duke."

"What do you mean by that?"

"Our line wasn't noble. He was elevated to his position only after his success at the Battle of Krosnicht."

"I'm afraid that's one I'm not familiar with."

"I'm not surprised. It was a failed rebellion. Kings don't like to bring those things up in public."

"I'm sorry," said Charlaine. "I should have asked if you are comfortable doing this? If not, you can return to the commandery."

"No, I'm fine, and it'll be nice to get out for a change."

"You get out all the time."

"Only to carry out my duties."

"That's exactly what we're doing here," replied Charlaine.

"Yes, but this is different. This is people putting on their best faces, not asking families about their plights."

"I don't know. Somehow I think I'd prefer that to dealing with all these… nobles."

"They're just people," said Marlena.

"People with literally hordes of coins. The world would be a better place if they would only share them."

"You don't have a very high opinion of them, do you?"

"I guess they're not all bad. Lady Francesca was certainly generous."

"Lady Francesca?"

"Yes, the Baroness of Rizela. She helped us organize the campaign against Halvaria." Charlaine halted for a moment. "Don't mention that to anyone, especially tonight."

The street grew busier as they drew closer to their destination.

Carriages crowded the road, while servants in various liveries ran back and forth doing who knew what.

"Well," said Marlena. "It appears we have arrived."

Charlaine gazed at the duke's estate. "How does this compare to the King of Abelard?"

"About the same. King Rordan may be a monarch, but Abelard is not a prosperous country."

"You don't consider this impressive?"

"I've seen better."

"Where?"

"In Eidolon. My father took me there once to try to find me a husband. It failed miserably, of course." She looked down at the floor, and her voice lowered. "He blamed it all on me, said I wasn't good enough for the nobles there."

"Typical," said Charlaine. "I was forced from my home for much the same reason."

"You were?"

"Yes, I had the misfortune to fall in love with a noble's son."

"And he refused you?"

"No, he wanted to run away with me. His father was the one who objected—said I wasn't good enough for his son. So you see, we have something in common."

"Well," said Marlena, "that and the fact that we're both Temple Knights."

Charlaine smiled. "Yes, and that we could best any of these so-called nobles in a fight!" She paused for a moment. "I'm only joking, of course. Violence seldom makes things better."

"I find that strange coming from you. Especially as you helped win the Battle of Alantra."

"The truth is we only fought because we had to. Don't ever go seeking battle, Marlena. But if it is forced upon you, do whatever it takes to win."

They arrived at the door, and a servant guided them through the labyrinth of halls. Eventually, they emerged to stand before a double door where another servant took their names before announcing them. They stepped through to find themselves on a balcony, a wide set of stairs leading down into a great hall. As they descended, a mandolin began playing, and then a soft voice sang out.

The decks were awash with blood that day
 As soldiers battled on
 Their sword arms weak, their armour pierced

They fought with all hope gone

Yet through the smoke and bounding waves
  A sister knight appeared
  Her Saint's protection in her heart
  Her sword much to be feared.

Unto the enemy she strode
  To bring her wrath to bear
  And in the ranks of empire's ships
  A king could only stare.

Champions slain and warriors killed
  Till only king remained
  Then knight took Holy vengeance on
  The enemy that reigned.

Now you may talk of battles fought
  Of wounds and loss and pain
  But none shall stand as tall and proud
  As Temple Knight Charlaine.

She was thoroughly blushing as she reached the bottom of the stairs. Her eyes sought out the bard responsible, but the throng of admirers who rushed forward to greet her blocked her view.

Names were flung at her in a whirl, and she struggled to keep track of who was who. The next thing she knew, Commander Salvatore was there, guiding her through the crowd.

"Her Grace would like to see you," he said.

Charlaine breathed a sigh of relief as he led her across the room to where the duchess waited amongst a group of women talking in low tones, who turned as they approached.

"Sister Charlaine, so good of you to join us this evening."

"Greetings, Your Grace, and may the Saints look kindly upon you on the anniversary of your birth."

The duchess turned her attention to Commander Salvatore. "You'd better watch this one, Father. She has both wit and charm."

"Traits which we should all try to emulate," he replied.

"Come, Charlaine," said the duchess, taking her arm. "There's someone I'd like you to meet."

Marlena followed along behind, unsure of whether or not she was needed. They approached a tall individual, who turned to reveal a clean-shaven, youthful face topped off with a neatly styled head of auburn hair.

"This is Lord Draclin Winfyre, the Halvarian Ambassador."

He bowed deeply, keeping his eyes on Charlaine. In response, she merely nodded, watching him like a hawk.

"Sister Charlaine," he said, his voice higher than she expected. "Your reputation precedes you."

"As does yours," she replied. "Tell me, Lord Winfyre, what brings you to the court of Reinwick?"

The barest hint of a smile creased his lips. "I am here at the bidding of my emperor."

"I find it fascinating such an exalted individual should take an interest in Reinwick."

"He has issued a proclamation that we send delegates to all the Petty Kingdoms to promote peace and harmony between our peoples."

"Such a peace would be easier to establish were he to avoid invading our lands."

"Come now," said the ambassador. "Let us put the past behind us. Why, your Petty Kingdoms themselves have a dark and bloody past, yet do they let that dictate their future?"

"The Petty Kingdoms didn't subjugate other realms!"

Lord Winfyre wore an exaggerated look of shock. "Surely you misspeak? What of Therengia? Did they not dismantle that once-great kingdom?"

"That was a long time ago," said Charlaine.

"Yet the people of the Continent still fear its return. We are not so different, you and I. We are both capable individuals doing the work of our respective leaders. Come, let us find common ground and work towards a better future."

"I am a mere captain. Such things are beyond my power."

"Are you not a renowned hero of your order? Surely you wield influence? Now, how did that bard put it? Ah yes, 'But none shall stand as tall and proud as Temple Knight Charlaine'. That's quite the image to live up to."

Charlaine felt her anger building. "I had no part in that song, and it's far from the truth."

In answer, Lord Winfyre smiled, something she found exceedingly irritating. "The truth is whatever we decide," he said.

"What does that mean?"

"Simply that words are powerful. If you wish to maintain this affectation that you are humble, then by all means, continue to do so, but it fools no one." He leaned closer, lowering his voice. "Halvaria knows who its enemies are."

"As do I," she replied. "And don't think for a moment I'll ever forget what you did to Calabria."

Again, the look of affected outrage. "I would never make that mistake."

"Come now," said the duchess. "This is a time for celebration. Can you two not put your differences aside for at least one night?"

Lord Winfyre turned to their host. "Of course, Your Grace. You must pardon us our dispute. It comes of us both being such dedicated servants."

"His Lordship has come bearing gifts," said the duchess, holding out her arm. "This bracelet is from Halvaria."

Charlaine noted the design, unequivocally Calabrian in form. Could this have been planned? She thought back to the Antonine. The rift in the Church caused all sorts of trouble, and now she began to suspect the Halvarians had a hand in it. How else could they know she was coming here? Could word have simply reached them of her coming before the ambassador arriving? She quickly dismissed the idea, for she'd been warned of his presence months ago by the maid, Enid.

"Very nice," she finally replied. "The detail is spectacular. It's Calabrian, isn't it?" This last question was posed to the Halvarian.

"You know your jewellery," he replied. "It is, in truth, just as you imagined. The people of that fair province do marvellous work, wouldn't you say, Your Grace?"

"Yes, very nice indeed," said the duchess. "This shall take a place of honour within my collection."

He bowed deeply. "I am proud you would think so fondly of the Halvarian people."

"Calabria isn't Halvaria!" insisted Charlaine.

His smile vanished, a look of determination quickly replacing it. "It is now."

25

VALIANT

Winter 1097 SR

D anica stood on the quay, her knights in line right behind her, their
swords held point down, hands resting on the pommels.

Elsbeth Fel approached, accompanied by a half-dozen others. She had
been a difficult individual to find, for worshippers of the old religion were
loathe to reveal their true beliefs these days. It had taken weeks to learn of
her existence and even longer to finally arrange a meeting. She was not
much to look at compared to the Holy Mothers of Danica's own order, for
she wore simple clothes. The only mark of her status was an ornately
carved staff, twisted at the top, clutching a pale-blue crystal still in its
natural form.

"Greetings, Mother," said Danica. "We welcome you in peace and look
forward to receiving your blessings."

The woman's face broke out into a broad smile, revealing some missing
teeth. "I must admit to some trepidation on hearing of your request. Never
before has a Temple Knight asked for our help."

"Might I ask what made you agree?"

"I had my people find out all they could about you, Sister, and I was suitably impressed. You not only preach the teachings of your Saint, but you
live by them, and that is a rare thing in these trying times." She turned to
look at the ship, noticing Charlaine standing at the end of the boarding
plank. "Is that your captain?"

"It is," said Danica. "May I present Captain Charlaine deShandria?"

Mother Fel made her way up the ramp. "Greetings, Captain. I trust you have no reservations about this ceremony?"

"None at all," said Charlaine. "Welcome aboard, Mother, and may Akosia watch over you."

The old woman cackled. "Impressive. You even learned the proper greeting." Elsbeth walked onto the deck, then halted, looking back at the quay. "Well, don't just stand there. We've got a ceremony to complete."

At Danica's command, the honour guard boarded the ship, followed by the rest of Mother Fel's retinue. One of them, a large man, carried a wooden chest, which he soon placed on the deck. He withdrew a key from around his neck and unlocked the lid, pulling it back to reveal a virtual treasure trove of relics. From this, he removed a small blue mat and placed it down before his superior.

The old woman knelt, using her staff to help her get into position while her assistant stood nearby, holding a clay jug.

"Gather round," she said, "and hear the words of Akosia, sacred goddess of the sea." Everyone moved closer until they formed a rough circle around the woman.

"I beseech thee, oh great Akosia," she intoned. "Cast your eyes upon us this day and give us your blessing that this ship may sail upon your waters unhindered, free to wander the seas of this world and explore the majesty of your domain." She reached out, taking the jug and holding it high. "Come, Akosia, and see the *Valiant*." She emptied the jug onto the deck, allowing the liquid within to go where it may. "As the water flows into this ship, so, too, flows your presence."

Everyone remained silent. Danica didn't know what to expect next and, like many others, held her breath. Mother Fel placed the empty jug on the deck, then stood, arching her back to get the kinks out. She raised her staff high in both hands, bringing it down with enough force to shatter the jug.

"I now pronounce this ship the *Valiant*. May all who sail on her find what they seek." Her group clapped, leading the sister knights to do the same.

Charlaine moved forward, extending her hand. "Thank you, Mother Fel. Your assistance in this matter is much appreciated."

"The ship has fine bones. I've got a feeling it won't be long before they're put to the test. I wish you and yours well, Captain, even though I fear much blood will be spilt. I only hope my people will not be the ones to suffer."

"This ship is meant to protect people, not to oppress them. You have my word on that, and I know Captain Danica feels the same. Now, will you and your followers join us in a celebration of our own?"

"That depends," replied Mother Fel. "What does it entail?"

"Merely food and drink, and possibly a little singing, if people are so inclined. Everything is below deck, where it's warm."

"And will the ceremony include a sermon from a Holy Mother?"

"It will not," said Charlaine.

"Then lead on, Sister, and let the celebrations commence!"

The *Valiant* pushed off from the quay, its nose drifting out a bit before the ship began to move forward as its sail unfurled.

"Rudder hard to port," called out Danica. "And stand by on those ropes. I don't want the sail flapping around like a seagull."

Captain Handley stood at her side, observing her command of the ship. "Careful," he warned. "With that rig, she'll turn quickly."

The ship's bow angled towards the entrance of the bay, and then the wind picked up, causing the sail to billow. In response, the *Valiant* lurched forward.

"Straighten the rudder," Danica called out, then lowered her voice. "She's aching to be out at sea."

"Can you blame her? She's been dock bound for months." He gazed up at the mast. "Had I known how efficient that sail was, I might have adopted it sooner."

Danica smiled. "Too late now, she's ours. Speaking of which..." She turned her head to find one of her knights. "Sister Anya, get that flag unfurled."

"Yes, Captain!"

The blonde-haired knight began the laborious process of climbing the mast. Rope was lashed around it every couple of feet to act as handholds, but the process was still time-consuming. Anya, however, proved equal to the task. Soon, she was straddling the yardarm as best one could considering its angle, tying off a pennant to the top of the mast. Her task complete, she looked down, waiting for the command to release it.

"Let fly," ordered Danica, and the sister knight did so, allowing the wind to take hold. The pennant of Saint Agnes bore the colours of the order but reversed to avoid being mistaken for that of a pirate; hence, a white flag with three scarlet waves.

It was a stirring sight, at least amongst the Temple Knights. They all made the symbol of Saint Agnes, three fingers drawn across the chest in a wave pattern. Even Danica got caught up in the emotion of the moment before looking over to see a tear in Captain Handley's eyes. The old captain coughed to cover his discomfort.

"She's a fine ship, the *Valiant*," he said. "Now, let's see what you can do with her."

The waves picked up as they moved towards the open water. The Great Northern Sea could be difficult at the best of times, and the winter winds were known to be particularly brutal. The *Valiant* bobbed up and down as it rode the waves, then pitched to port, the sail fluttering back and forth.

"Tighten that rope," ordered Danica, pointing. The crew rushed to obey, and then the sail billowed out once more. The Temple Knights were only there to act as warriors, yet they had all expressed interest in learning how to handle their new ship.

The *Valiant* crested a wave, and then the nose dropped precipitously, smashing into the sea and sending water sluicing across the deck. Even from the stern, Danica could hear Sister Grazynia swearing at the cold as it washed across her boots.

"Zivka," said Danica. "Take the rudder."

She watched as the knight took control of the tiller. Unlike most ships, which used a steering oar mounted on one side, the *Valiant* was blessed with a centrally mounted one attached to a bar running horizontal to the deck by which its position could be controlled. Adjusting the tiller when the aft deck was raised had proved somewhat problematic, but Danica had to admit she was pleased with the results. The raised deck gave a far better view of the ship, and the steersman now stood in a more advantageous position to guide the vessel.

"Your knights are eager to take possession of the ship," noted Captain Handley. "I can't say I blame them. She sails well."

"It'll be some time before Temple Knights crew this ship. We don't have the numbers. Instead, we'll rely on outsiders to crew her, freeing us up to be the fighting complement."

"Then why have them learn how to handle the ship?"

"A battle at sea seldom distinguishes between crew and warrior. We must be prepared to take over for the injured if necessary, else we might find ourselves stranded."

Handley nodded his head. "I hadn't thought of that. Then again, I'm only a humble merchant." He chuckled. "At least I was before I sold you my ship."

"And now you're a retired captain—and a well-to-do one at that. Tell me, what will you do with your newfound wealth?"

"If truth be told, I always liked the idea of opening a tavern. Perhaps I'll call it the Lydia?"

"I would very much like to see that. Of course, you shall always have an invitation to sail aboard the *Valiant*, should you wish."

"Thank you," he replied. "That means a lot to me." He looked skyward.

"The clouds are darkening. It might be time to head back to port now that you've tested out the changes on the *Valiant*. I reckon it's more than ready for its maiden voyage, don't you?"

"I thought this was it?" said Danica.

"This? This is just assessing the construction. You should take her out on an extended voyage, something that takes days, not simply an afternoon."

"I'll need to bring stores aboard for that."

"Any idea where you'll take her the first time out?"

"When I was back in the Antonine," Danica said, "I wondered if I'd ever actually make it here, standing on the deck of my own order's ship. Now that we're ready to sail, I feel a little overwhelmed."

"That's nothing new. I felt the same when I became captain of the *Lydia*. Do yourself a favour—take it slow."

"Slow?"

"Yes. Confine your trips to local waters, at least until you get to know them. In time, you'll feel more comfortable, then you can sail farther abroad."

"Is that what you did?"

"Saints, no," said Handley. "I had cargo to deliver, but you're a Church ship, with no set itinerary and no goods to worry about. Do you have specific instructions from your order concerning your role in all of this?"

"No, it was all pretty vague. I was to command, of course, but other than that, I believe they wanted to emulate the Holy Fleet in the south."

"And what do they do?"

"Sit in port, mostly, but I'd like to see us play a more active role in keeping the trade routes open."

"So you'll go out looking for pirates?"

"At least one," said Danica.

"You're talking of the *Sea Wolf*."

"I am, but there's more to it than just finding the ship. I want to discover where they hide when they're not raiding. I don't suppose you have any ideas on that subject?"

"That's a tough one," said Captain Handley. "I suppose the most logical explanation is another country is harbouring them, maybe even employing them to do their dirty work. On the other hand, they might be hiding out on an island somewhere."

"Like the Five Sisters?"

"That would be my guess, but you'd best master your craft before you go sailing there. I hear the waters can be perilous and definitely not a place you should sail in the winter, especially when you're not familiar with the region."

"Are there charts of the islands?"

"There are, but to my understanding, they're wildly inaccurate."

"Then I'll need to make new ones," said Danica.

"Easier said than done. Have you any skill at cartography?"

"I was taught the rudiments."

He looked at her in surprise. "By whom?"

"Brother Leamund, a naval architect. He spent his lifetime studying all things nautical."

"Can't say I've heard of him, but then again, what would I know of such things?"

"Enough to know how difficult it is," said Danica. "But surely, someone must have charts of the region?"

"Only of the most rudimentary nature, and they're yours now. You'll find them in the captain's cabin, in that green chest."

"I didn't expect that."

"What else would I do with them?" admitted Captain Handley. "It's not like I'm going sailing anytime soon."

"Still, I appreciate the thought."

Charlaine set the plate down. Sister Josephine was on kitchen duty, and the food looked suspiciously undercooked. She sniffed the plate again, then pushed it aside, determined to get back to work.

The commandery housed just over sixty souls, which required a good deal of food to feed them, not to mention the demands of their mounts. Add to that the expenditures for such things as replacing broken furniture, weapons, and the need for clean bedding, and the numbers quickly climbed.

She picked up a letter and skimmed its contents. Apparently, the local saddle maker had not received a past due payment, so he sent back a saddle without any repairs being carried out. And, to add insult to injury, had charged for the service. Charlaine made a note to talk to Sister Leona about resolving the issue, then pushed it aside. A cough caught her attention, and she looked up.

"Yes, Marlena?"

"There's a new sister to see you, Captain."

"A new sister?"

"Yes, a Temple Knight. She says she's been assigned to this commandery."

"I wasn't informed of any new arrivals?"

"Tell that to her."

"All right. Send her in."

Marlena ushered in the new sister, and Charlaine was shocked to recognize her.

"Sister Lara?"

The sister knight bowed respectfully. "Yes, Captain." She handed over a sealed note. "I have my orders here."

Marlena took the note, handing it to Charlaine.

"I was sent here at my request," the woman added.

"Why would you do that?" asked Charlaine.

"After my testimony against Commander Hjordis, no one would take me. Either they blamed me for working for her in the first place, or they felt they couldn't trust me because I betrayed my previous commander."

"I see."

"Please, Captain, give me a chance. I know you associate me with the corruption of the commander, but you must believe me when I say I only did what I thought was right. How was I to know her true intentions?"

Charlaine rested her hands on the table and intertwined her fingers. She saw a woman before her who had stood guard over Danica. Not only that, but she was one of the knights who attacked and killed Brother Mateo. Was she telling the truth, or was this some trick to embed her within the commandery? Charlaine opened the letter, reading it through carefully.

"It says here," continued Charlaine, "that you were instrumental in the case against Commander Hjordis."

"Yes. She was convicted largely because of my testimony."

"What became of her?"

"She was dismissed from the order," said Lara, "and then stood trial for murder."

"And you? If memory serves, you were complicit in Brother Mateo's death as well."

"I was, but in recognition of my testimony, I was spared additional charges."

"There's a note here saying you agreed to serve out the remainder of your days at the rank of Temple Knight. I assume you know the ramifications of this?"

"I do," said Lara. "I will never be promoted, nor command any detachment or patrols."

"You could always leave the order?"

"Never. The order is my home. To leave is simply unthinkable."

"Even so, you would now burden me with the task of looking after you."

"I will earn my keep. I promise you."

Something in the woman's eyes struck Charlaine as genuine. "All right, I shall accept you into this command. I doubt Captain Danica will be so forgiving, but lucky for you, she doesn't spend much time here these days."

"Captain Danica?"

"Oh yes, she's a captain now. She commands the *Valiant*."

"I'm guessing that's a ship?"

"It is. Does that upset you?"

"No, not in the least. She's more than deserving of it."

Charlaine's eyes wandered to the plate of food, and a smile graced her lips. "Tell me, Lara, can you cook?"

"Yes, of course. Why?"

"How would you feel about being in charge of our food preparations?"

"I thought I wasn't allowed to hold any position of authority?"

"I would hardly consider the kitchen to be a command position. I believe everyone should have a chance at redemption. While you carried out the orders of a tyrant, you had the fortitude to speak out about it when it mattered most, and that was brave. I shall keep my eye on you, Lara; make no mistake. But do your job well, and you will be rewarded."

"Understood," the woman replied.

"Now," continued Charlaine, "as to your actual duties, you will organize the menu and oversee the preparation of all meals for your fellow sisters. As you know, the knights here all take turns working in the kitchen. It will be your responsibility to ensure the food is consistent in both quality and quantity. You must also arrange the purchase of supplies to that end, coordinating with Sister Leona—she's our treasurer. Naturally, you're still considered a Temple Knight, so you'll be expected to fight, if that should prove necessary. That also means you'll attend all weapons and riding practice unless otherwise ordered."

"Anything else, Captain?"

"No, that's sufficient for now. We'll revisit your position in three months." Charlaine turned her attention to her aide. "Marlena, would you be so kind as to take Lara and introduce her to Leona?"

"Of course, Captain. It would be my pleasure." She guided the new knight from the office, leaving Charlaine to ponder Lara's change in circumstances. Was this truly a repentant knight or a wolf in sheep's clothing? Only time would tell.

26

RUMOURS

Spring 1098 SR

Sister Felicity sat.

"Tell me what you discovered," said Charlaine.

"We were down at the market," the woman replied, "when we happened to overhear a conversation."

"And by we, you mean...?"

"Myself and Sister Damora."

"And what was the nature of this conversation?"

"A man was haggling over the price of some meat, not an overly unusual argument. The vendor's response, however, was surprising."

"Go on," urged Charlaine.

"He said there's a shortage of farm workers on account of those who are missing."

"Missing?"

"That's what he said," replied Felicity. "It seems that women are being forced to do more of the chores on the outlying farms as a result. Considering last autumn's missing men, I thought it best to bring this to your attention."

"You've done well. We must look into this."

"Shall I take out a patrol?"

"I'll lead it myself," said Charlaine. "If men are still going missing, we need to confirm it, else we're simply reacting to rumours and gossip."

"How many knights do you want?"

"We'll take a dozen and split them up once we're beyond the city walls. That allows us to cover a much wider area."

"You think the slavers have returned?"

"It might not be slavers, but whoever they are, they've been quiet for some time."

"Doubtless because of our vigilance," noted Felicity.

"Not necessarily. It might just have been the winter. Snow makes it much harder for people to disappear without a trace. In any event, there are no reports of further problems within the city itself, which likely means they turned their attention to the countryside. We sent word to Herenstadt and Blunden, but they've had no indication of similar troubles."

"Would they admit it if they did?"

Charlaine frowned. "People missing on this scale would have an economic impact on a city, and we're offering to get to the bottom of it. Why would they lie?"

"Perhaps they just don't care?"

"Always a possibility," said Charlaine, "but I've met some of the duke's nobles, and they seem like honest folk. I can't believe they would be so callous as to ignore the plight of their people."

"The duke does."

"True, but the duke lives an isolated life. Were it not for a few select individuals, no one would even know what he looked like."

"But you're one of those individuals, aren't you?"

"Yes, but then again, so is the Halvarian Ambassador."

"I'm not sure what you're getting at."

"Only that His Grace may have a somewhat distorted view of his kingdom."

"Interesting," said Felicity. "I shall assemble a dozen knights. Any idea of where we'll start?"

"Yes, to the south."

"Why south?"

"The border with Andover lies in that direction."

"And you think them responsible?"

"It's certainly a possibility," replied Charlaine, "and it would be easy enough to smuggle prisoners across the border, especially considering the terrain."

"You mean the hills? Yes, I remember passing through them when I first came here."

"You've been here longer than me. How would you characterize the relationship between Andover and Reinwick?"

"I'm not sure what you mean?" replied Felicity.

"Would you say they're enemies or merely business rivals?"

"I'd say there's animosity on both sides. They trade well enough, but there's always a sense Andover is out to cheat us. Not that I can blame them. I'm sure the other side feels exactly the same. As to the terrain, Northern Andover is a pretty barren place. Mind you, someone else could be using ships to carry out these abductions."

"I was thinking along those lines too," said Charlaine. "But I'm not clear on who would benefit from these disappearances, nor can I fathom where these people would be taken even if it were Andover who was responsible. Are there slave markets in Andover?"

"No," said Felicity. "At least none that I ever heard of. And as to the relationship between Andover and Reinwick, that's largely limited to the respective leaders."

"Yes, I heard something to that effect, but let's not get embroiled in politics. Assemble the knights, and we'll ride out when the bell tolls noon."

They waited until they were in the countryside before splitting into smaller groups as the road forked. The surroundings here were pleasant enough, but the melting snow had left the roads muddy, and the passage of wagons and horses had done little to remedy the situation. Rather than get bogged down in the muck, Charlaine chose to take them over fields, a decision that allowed them to observe the farmers at work.

The first worker they spotted was a woman in the middle of a field, taking seeds from a wicker basket and scattering them around. She ceased her endeavours upon spotting the knights, waiting until they drew near.

"Good day, madam," said Charlaine. "I am Captain Charlaine of the Temple Knights of Saint Agnes."

"Greetings, Sister. My name is Eloise Rundak. What can I do for you today?"

"Are you aware of any disappearances of late?"

"If you mean missing menfolk, then most certainly. My own husband went missing only last week."

Charlaine dismounted, stepping closer. "My condolences," she said. "Might I ask about the circumstances of his disappearance?"

"He went out late at night to check on the livestock. We have some cows, you see, and they were making no end of a racket. When he didn't come back, we set out looking for him, but there was no sign of where he'd gone."

"You had help?"

"Aye, I have two children, and the neighbour helped, but we failed to find anything. We thought some kind of animal took him, but there weren't any tracks that we could find."

"And have you heard of others suffering a similar loss?"

"Not at first, no, but after losing my husband, I discovered others were gone too. We tried to take it to the duke, but our pleas for help fell on deaf ears."

Charlaine swept her gaze around the field, noting the trees bordering it to the west and south. "Where is your house, relative to our present position?"

The woman pointed east. "It's over there, right by the road."

"And the field where you keep the cows?"

"Just south of us. I can take you there if you like?"

"While I appreciate the offer, I shouldn't like to keep you from your work. Directions should suffice."

The woman looked at the line of trees. "As you hit those trees, you'll see an old, worn-out gate. Behind is a short path leading to the cow pasture."

"Isn't that strange," said Sister Damora, "having a field so far from your home?"

"It can't be helped. The field behind the house is flooded from all the spring runoff."

Charlaine climbed back into the saddle. "Thank you for your assistance," she said. "We shall do what we can to determine your husband's fate."

"May the Saints bless you."

They rode on, past the line of trees. Beyond lay a green pasture where three cows grazed. Farther afield, a flock of sheep meandered around, caring little for the intruders.

"This is a peaceful place," noted Damora. "Hardly the spot for someone to come in and start abducting folk."

"Actually," said Charlaine, "it's precisely the place for such things. There's no war here, no fear of strangers. Those responsible would be able to wander around free from notice."

"I suppose that's true, but country folk are generally friendly. Wouldn't they notice strangers?"

"You raise an interesting point." Charlaine swept her gaze over the area. "This treeline could easily conceal a few men."

"Do slavers truly go to all that effort just to abduct one man? Wouldn't it be more profitable to swoop in and take a dozen? Especially when you consider they then need to be transported. If they were taken aboard a ship, it would mean exposing themselves to discovery while they're at anchor, wouldn't it? That hardly seems a worthwhile risk if you're only taking one person."

"Maybe it's not so much how many are taken as where they're taken from?"

"What are you getting at?" asked Damora.

"Everyone who has gone missing was in reasonably good health and able-bodied, correct?"

"Yes, the same qualities that would make them valuable as slaves."

"Or soldiers," said Charlaine.

"The duke has plenty of soldiers."

"I doubt His Grace would go to the extent of abducting his own people. Why would he when he can just order them into his ranks?"

"But then," continued Damora, "why would someone else abduct his people? Even if we take into account every single person who's missing, it's still far too few to form an army."

"Yes, and not enough to raise the alarm amongst the nobles."

"You don't believe them complicit in this, do you?"

"I don't know what to think," said Charlaine, "and I doubt we'll find out anything more here."

"Then what's next, Captain?"

"For a start, we'll return to the road."

"And then?" asked Damora.

"We'll ride back to the crossroads, and see if the others learned anything new."

"This is our fault. Our patrols drove these fiends out into the countryside."

"We can't blame ourselves," insisted Charlaine. "Had we not been there, then undoubtedly, more would have been taken from the city."

"What should we do about this? Send out more patrols?"

"No, we haven't the numbers. I can talk to the other orders, but I doubt they'll do anything."

"Surely, they wish to protect people?"

"Of course, but the Mathewites are already stretched to the limit, and the Cunars will consider the effort beneath them."

Damora grinned. "Not if we tell them that raiders are on the prowl."

"I like the way you think," said Charlaine, "but Captain Waleed and I aren't on the best of terms at the moment. Even so, I'll bring it up at our next meeting. Let's hope he's willing to put aside our differences for the good of the people."

"This is about the *Valiant*, isn't it?"

"Yes, but it's not something you need to concern yourself with. Now, enough of this chatter. It's time to get moving."

· · ·

Sister Felicity's group waited by the crossroads. They had ridden west, deeper into the heart of Reinwick, but found no word of anyone gone missing.

It wasn't until Sister Adriana's group returned later that they could see the whole picture.

"We met more than a dozen people," she reported, "and they all told a similar tale. By our reckoning, over twenty men are missing, and the vast majority of them live close to the coast."

"And they all just disappeared?" asked Charlaine.

"One or two of them might have fallen from the cliffs, but the rest all went missing under much the same circumstances."

"Which were?"

"Each went outside to investigate noises of one kind or another."

"Were any of them in groups?"

"Not as far as we know," replied Adriana, "but we got most of this information second-hand. We can return for a more thorough investigation, if you like, but that could take days. There are also reports of ships out at sea, but that isn't unusual in these parts."

"It sounds more and more like a ship is involved," said Charlaine.

"What do we do now?"

"It's time to return to the commandery."

"That's it?" said Damora. "These people are missing loved ones. We must do something!"

"What would you have us do? We don't have the numbers to patrol the area, and if a ship took them, as we suspect, they're long gone by now. Once we're back, I'll send the *Valiant* to investigate the coast. If we're lucky, they'll find the ship responsible."

"You say they're along the coast here?" asked Danica as she sat in the captain's cabin, staring down at a sea chart.

"Yes, that's right," said Charlaine. "The farms closer to the coast seem to be of particular interest. Those farther inland were more or less left alone."

"That's a fairly long stretch, but at least we don't need to worry about all those coves they had back in Ilea. Any ship anchored along here should be easy to spot. How long ago was the last abduction?"

"Just under a week."

"Hmmm, unfortunately, they could be anywhere by now. I'll search the area, but I doubt I'll find much." She traced her finger along the chart. "There are a couple of islands here, just north of Eidolon. I'll give them a look. There might be a sheltered anchorage that they lurk in."

"You believe that likely?"

"From what you told me, they strike at random times. A ship sitting at anchor that long would easily draw attention. If you remember the Halvarian raids in Ilea, they sat out at sea and sent in smaller boats. I suspect the same is happening here."

"Yes, but with the *Valiant*, you'll be able to see them, won't you?"

"If they remain there. The big difference is the Shimmering Sea was usually calm. Here, the situation is quite the reverse."

"I'm not sure I follow," said Charlaine.

"Currents and winds make it difficult to remain in position so far out to sea, but an island would make the perfect place to wait for your accomplices."

"So they sail back at a pre-arranged time to pick up their cargo?"

"Precisely. The real question will be what we do once we find them. One of the downsides to being a Church ship is that we don't have any authority to do much of anything."

"On the contrary," said Charlaine. "The Church is sworn to eradicate slavery. That alone gives you justification to challenge any ship you might encounter."

"If I start demanding ships let us aboard to inspect their cargo, you won't hear the end of it."

"Let me deal with the political ramifications."

"And if it's a foreign ship?"

"I don't think there can be any doubt it will be. It's not as if a Reinwick ship would abduct its own people."

"This could lead to war," warned Danica.

"You forget, you fly the flag of Saint Agnes, not Reinwick. If there's any anger from other kingdoms because of this, it'll be directed towards the Church."

"I suppose I can live with that."

"Be careful," cautioned Charlaine. "There are a lot of honest merchants out there just trying to make a living. We don't want to cause them any hardship."

"Not a problem. After all, I'll only be boarding suspicious-looking ships."

"And what constitutes 'suspicious'?"

"Anchoring in the middle of nowhere, sailing where no merchant ship belongs, that sort of thing." Danica leaned on the table, getting close to her precious chart. "This map only shows the coastline, but if it's anything like Andover, there'll be small fishing villages along the coast."

"What of it?"

"Fishermen see all kinds of things. It might be worth our while to speak with them."

"Shall I send a patrol?"

"No, I'll take the *Valiant*. At the very least, it'll show them we're here to keep them safe."

"I'll authorize some additional funds," said Charlaine. "You might find that spreading around some coins will loosen a few tongues."

"You forget, my father was a fisherman. I know how to talk to these people. Giving them coins will only make them more suspicious."

"You know what's best. Now, I should warn you Father Waleed has been causing me no end of grief. It wouldn't surprise me if he tried to use his seniority to assume command of the *Valiant*."

"Can he do that?"

"No," said Charlaine. "But if he does try, remind him that even though you're both captains, aboard ship, you outrank him. That's taken directly from the Holy Fleet, so he can't argue the point."

"What about you? Care to join us on this, if you'll pardon the expression, fishing expedition?"

"I wish I could, but you'll likely be out to sea for days, and I have far too many things requiring my attention here." She met her comrade's gaze. "This is a great responsibility, Danica. Once out there, there'll be no one to rely on other than your ship and crew."

"I'm ready for this."

"I know you are," said Charlaine. "I just don't know if I am."

"Don't go getting all sentimental on me now. You're making me tear up."

"I can't help it. You're the closest thing I have to family. Please be careful and avoid any unnecessary risks. You're out there to gather information, not take them down single-handedly."

"I couldn't even if I wanted to," said Danica. "We haven't been able to fit a ballista yet."

"Have you considered an arbalest? I believe the Dwarves are particularly good at constructing those."

"Yes, I heard that too, but they're notoriously shy about sharing them with us Humans."

"I'd still look into it if I were you. After all, we're not just any Humans—we're the Church."

"I doubt that will hold much sway," said Danica. "They're a secretive people and not overly religious."

"Yes, but as far as I know, they venerate their women, which fits in nicely with our beliefs."

"I'll consider it, but I believe the likelihood of running across Dwarves on the open sea is quite remote. They're not exactly known as sea-going folk."

"Speaking of ships," said Charlaine. "How busy are the trade routes around here?"

"This time of year, not so much, but by the time summer rolls around, there'll be ships as far as the eye can see."

"Truly?"

"Well, maybe I'm exaggerating just a bit, but trade picks up in the summer months."

"Why is that?"

"Traders come from farther abroad, secure in the assumption the weather will allow their safe return."

"Couldn't they do that in the spring and autumn?"

"The sea is a little more fickle at those times, and a sudden squall could sink an otherwise seaworthy vessel. That's considered far too great a risk for a merchant ship."

"You're well-suited to your position of captain, my friend," said Charlaine. "I wish you well."

"And I, you, Commander."

"You mean captain."

Danica smiled. "You can only have one captain aboard a ship, Sister. That means we refer to you as commander whenever you're aboard."

Charlaine smiled. "You're enjoying this far too much."

27

MAIDEN VOYAGE

Spring 1098 SR

D anica stood at the bow of the ship, letting the spray wash over her on this glorious day, the sun warming everyone as they made their way south.

She glanced at the stern to see Sister Grazynia taking her turn at the tiller. The rest of the knights were scattered around the deck while the men who made up the ship's crew kept a close eye on the sail.

Captain Handley had remained ashore, his time at sea at an end. He'd purchased an old tavern, but the place needed some work, so he now spent his time over a woodworking bench instead of charts.

Danica made her way aft to where Laurel and Nadia were fully armoured and ready for battle while the rest dressed in more mundane garb. For practical reasons, she had forsaken the traditional cassocks of her order and instead insisted on short-sleeved tunics worn over a light shirt. This was augmented by trousers and shoes, far more practical when running around a ship.

They still had the symbol of Saint Agnes emblazoned across their chests with their swords belted around their waist, but little else to distinguish them from the sailors.

Danica headed into the captain's cabin, taking a seat near the stern. The rear wall held a wooden cabinet, and she grasped a handle and turned it, lowering a flap that became a desk, with a small journal tucked into the back. This she withdrew, along with a quill and ink to begin the task of journaling.

We are south of Korvoran, but have encountered little so far. What few ships we have sighted all flew the flag of Reinwick, so we let them continue their voyages, unhindered by our enquiries. The coast here is devoid of any distinctive landmarks, the land mostly wild, but according to my charts, there are a few fishing villages just south of us. Once we locate them, I have high hopes they might provide further information about the ships sailing along this coastline.

She set down the quill and reconsidered her entry. Although Charlaine had fully explained the purpose of this voyage to Danica, those orders were not detailed in the log. Thus, her entry must include details she might not otherwise consider. Brother Leamund had stressed the importance of keeping accurate records, for once complete, they would be archived. Should someone peruse them, months or even years later, they might otherwise lack information to understand what was written.

Danica picked up the quill once more and continued to write.

People have gone missing along the coast, and it is our belief a ship is responsible. Our task on this voyage is to gain information on the vessels frequenting the coast, then identify and catalogue their names and nationalities. I have been provided with six Temple Knights to assist me in this endeavour, each trained in using cross-bows. Should I be injured or otherwise incapacitated, I left instructions that Sister Grazynia assumes command, with her first order being to return to the port of Korvoran.

A gentle knock on her cabin door alerted her to a visitor right before it opened to reveal Sister Zivka.

"We've sighted a ship," she said, "and Grazynia is altering course accordingly."

"Good," said Danica. "I shall be on deck shortly. Have Nadia take the tiller while the rest of you get into your armour."

"You suspect trouble?"

"No, but I believe it best we put on a professional face, don't you?"

"Yes, Captain." The knight left, closing the door behind her.

Danica's eyes wandered to her own armour stand, and she pondered donning it, but that might give the impression she was trying to intimidate people. Instead, she resolved to greet this vessel in her current attire. To that end, she exited her cabin, taking only a moment to strap on her sword.

The ship was anchored not far off their starboard, with its bow pointing north. A small boat had been lowered, and she watched as a group of men manhandled a large barrel into its bottom.

"Likely going ashore to get fresh water," Danica mused.

"Do we board them?" asked Sister Laurel.

"If they'll let us. Bring us up alongside, then drop the anchor."

The knight relayed the message to the crewmen, and then the *Valiant* turned slightly to port, now running parallel to the target vessel. This course would bring her to a halt within a dozen or so yards. The sails were furled, and the ship slowed.

"Ahoy there," Danica called out. "Identify yourself!"

A man moved to the railing. "The *Barlowe*," he shouted back. "Out of Wintervale. I'm her captain, Ansel Dulworth."

"We are the Temple ship *Valiant*," said Danica. "We request permission to come aboard."

"A Temple ship? In these waters?"

"Yes. We are patrolling the coast with an aim to helping those in distress."

"We're not in distress," said Dulworth.

"I understand that, but we'd like to come over and have a chat, find out if you've seen anything out of the ordinary."

"Very well. Bring your skiff alongside, and I'll let you board."

"Do we trust them?" asked Laurel.

"Until we have a reason not to," replied Danica.

They lowered the ship's boat and climbed aboard. Danica took two knights and six crewmen to work the oars. In short order, they were welcomed aboard the *Barlowe*.

"Greetings," said Captain Dulworth. "You'll pardon my astonishment, but I had no idea there even was a Holy Fleet in these parts, let alone one manned by sisters."

Danica noted the empty barrels. "I see you're replenishing your water."

"Yes, there's a natural spring nearby. Are you familiar with it?"

"I'm not, as a matter of fact. I'll need to make a note of it."

The *Barlowe's* captain moved to the port-side railing. "You can see where the stream empties into the sea over there, by those rocks. If you follow it upstream, you'll find where it bubbles up."

"Do you come here often?"

"Whenever we're in the area," said Dulworth. "I'm led to believe it's a common stopover point for quite a few merchants. It surely beats paying labourers to bring barrels of water into port."

"Might I ask how long you've been here?"

"We dropped anchor mid-morning, but it'll likely be late this afternoon by the time we're done. Why?"

"Have you seen any other ships hereabouts?" asked Danica.

"Several, but none close to shore. Are you looking for one in particular?"

"No, only trying to get an idea of how busy these waters are. This is now part of our regular patrol route."

"Good," said Dulworth. "It's about time someone took this whole thing seriously."

"What thing is that?"

"More than one ship has gone missing in this area. The general opinion is that it's pirates, but there are no survivors to actually confirm that."

"Well, we'll do our best to keep the area free of such vermin. Have you sailed here much in the past?"

"All the time," said Dulworth. "Why do you ask?"

"Have you ever seen anything suspicious?"

"We sighted what we thought was a pirate some three days back, but we had the advantage of the wind, so we made haste to leave."

"Did they pursue?"

"No, luckily for us, they ignored the *Barlowe*. Mind you, they could have just been another merchant ship. These days, it's so hard to tell the difference."

"You said you were from Andover?"

"I did. Why, do you know it?"

"I was born there," said Danica.

"Oh yes? Which town?"

"A little fishing village named Littlecliff. Do you know it?"

"Know it?" asked Dulworth. "I'll say we do. We sailed past it just yesterday. Even stopped there to pick up some moonfish. Ever seen those?"

"Many times. They're delicious when cooked in oil." Danica looked around the deck. "Might I ask what you're shipping?"

"Mostly cloth from Braymoor. There's a high demand for it in Korvoran. We also have some Abelard wine, although I wouldn't call it the best of the bunch. Would you like to take a look?"

"No, it's fine. I'll take your word for it."

"Does this mean we'll be seeing more of you in the future?"

"We'll do our best," said Danica, "but at the moment, we only have the *Valiant*."

"You ought to keep an eye out for one of those fat cogs that sails out of Eidolon."

"Why? You think they might be pirating?"

"No, but they'd make a tempting target. They have large holds and wallow like nobody's business. Easy pickings for a pirate."

"You haven't seen any cogs hereabouts, have you?"

"Can't say as I have, but they tend to hug the coast. Keep sailing south, and you're bound to locate one eventually."

"Thank you. I'll give it a try. My best regards to you and your ship, Captain. We'll let you continue with taking on water. If you ever find yourself in Korvoran with information that might help us, please send it to the Temple Knights of Saint Agnes."

"I will," he promised.

Danica and her crew boarded their skiff and made their way back to the *Valiant*. Once aboard, they continued their trip south, towing the small ship's boat behind them.

Once they were off the coast of Andover, the *Valiant* moved closer to shore and dropped anchor. Evening found Danica standing beside the railing, staring out at the shoreline. Sister Anya soon joined her.

"What's so interesting?" Anya asked.

"Home."

"That's Andover out there, not Reinwick."

"No, I mean my original home. I was born along this very shore, not too far from here in a village known as Littlecliff."

"Do you have folks there?"

"No," said Danica, "not anymore. My parents both perished at sea."

"And here you are, following in their footsteps."

"Hardly. I have no intention of drowning, and the *Valiant* is a far more seaworthy vessel than my parents' tiny fishing boat."

"Have you any uncles or cousins?"

"Not in Littlecliff, and I have no love for those who live inland. Still, I do wonder how many of my parents' friends are still alive."

"How long have you been gone?" asked Anya.

"Six years, give or take a month or two."

"And you've been in the order ever since?"

"Saints, no," said Danica. "I was sent to live with my cousins on a farm, but that holds unpleasant memories for me."

"Then I shan't press you further on the matter," said Anya, her eyes lingering on her captain.

"What?" said Danica.

"How old are you, if you don't mind me asking?"

"I'm nineteen. Why?"

"Nineteen, and you're already a captain? That's unheard of, surely?"

"I'm captain of a ship, not a commandery. My rank is due solely to my position aboard. As soon as I step ashore, I rank as a mere Temple Knight." She blushed. "No offence intended, of course."

"None taken," said Anya, "but still, only nineteen, and you've already seen battle. How extraordinary. Tell me, what was it like?"

"You mean battle?"

"Yes. We all train for it, but very few have actually seen it up close and personal."

"It's both exhilarating and terrifying at the same time. When you're in the thick of it, you can't wait for it to be over. Yet once it's done, you almost miss it."

"A contradiction in terms, if ever I heard one."

"It's hard to explain," said Danica. "The blood starts pumping with fear, and you feel... alive? I don't know how else to put it."

"You're saying you enjoyed it?"

"Not the killing, no, but the feeling of euphoria that stays with you. I suppose that must have something to do with the struggle for survival. It makes you more alert."

"Is it difficult?" asked Anya.

"Not difficult so much as physically demanding. Once the battle commences, your training pretty much takes over. You don't even think about it. Not that you should forget about your enemy, of course, but the individual weapon swings happen naturally, at least if your training is sufficient."

"Are we ready?" Anya glanced at her fellow sister knights.

"As ready as we can make you, but we'll never really know until that first fight."

"Can I let you in on a secret?"

"I'm your captain. You can tell me anything."

"I'm worried I won't do well in battle."

Danica looked at her. "That's a normal reaction. I thought the same thing before I actually fought. All the training on the Continent won't prevent you from feeling that way. It's not until you taste your first blood that you realize how effective our training is." She saw the woman pale. "When I say taste blood, I don't mean literally."

Relief flooded Anya's face. "Good, that puts my mind at ease." She looked off at the shore. "Will we go to Littlecliff?"

"I hadn't planned on it, but now you mention it, it might not be a bad idea. There's more than likely still a friendly face or two I could count on, and the fishing boats go quite far out to sea. If anyone's seen anything, it's likely those fishermen."

The following day they sailed farther south. Here, they discovered a flotilla of tiny boats casting their nets over a wide area.

"We'll keep the *Valiant* at this distance," said Danica, "and go in using the skiff. I don't want to disturb their fishing."

"Are you suggesting the ship would scare off fish?" asked Sister Grazynia.

"No, but it might interfere with the casting of nets. I want to be on good terms with these people."

She climbed down, settling into the ship's boat. Grazynia joined her, although without armour. Rounding out the group were the six men who took up the oars.

As they drew closer, Danica surveyed the tiny fleet. "Over there," she said, pointing. "Take us to that boat with the dark-brown hull."

The oars dug in while Grazynia shifted the tiller. The boat turned, heading for their target, the fisherfolk aboard staring at the unexpected visitor.

"Rupert!" called out Danica. "Is that you?"

The startled face of a weather-beaten old man stared back. "How do you know my name?"

"It's me, Danica Meer."

He squinted, but as the boat drew alongside, he broke into a grin. "Little Dani Meer, is that truly you?"

"Not so little now," she said.

"Come aboard," said Rupert. "Let me have a proper look at you."

She waited until the boats bumped sides before deftly stepping across. "The rest of you wait there," she ordered, then gave the old man a hug.

Rupert turned to his meagre crew. "Dedrick, Luther, you remember little Dani? She used to tease you because you were so skinny." He held her at arm's length, noted her garb. "What's this, now? Are you a member of the Church?"

"Yes, a Temple Knight of Saint Agnes."

"A Temple Knight? Surely not?"

"It's true. I swear it."

"How long's it been? Seems like only yesterday you were running around the beach, chasing seagulls."

"Six years," said Danica. "Although I must admit it feels like more." Danica's eyes looked shoreward. "The old village hasn't changed much."

"Why would it? The boats go out, and the boats come in. What else is there to do?" His eyes came to rest on the *Valiant*. "Do you serve on a ship now?"

"That's my ship, the *Valiant*," she replied. "I'm her captain."

"What brings you to Littlecliff? You didn't sail all the way here just to talk to me, did you?"

"Not you specifically, no, but we're on the hunt for raiders."

"Raiders?"

"Well, pirates, if you want me to be more precise. Have you seen any strange ships in these parts?"

"Plenty," said Rupert, "but they seldom pay heed to our tiny boats."

"And do any of these ships make landfall?"

"Not here, they don't, and why would they? It's not as if there's anything of value along this part of the coast. Now, out by Drumhollow, that's another matter entirely."

"Drumhollow?"

"Yes, it's an island that lies to the east. The place is home to a thick wood, but the fish seem to like it. We were up there two nights ago looking for moonfish when we spied some activity on the island."

"Does anyone live there?" asked Danica.

"Not to my knowledge, no, but we all saw it." He looked at one of his companions. "Dedrick, don't you remember?"

"I do," the younger man replied as he wiped the sweat from his brow. "We saw a group of maybe a dozen men."

"What were they doing?" asked Danica.

"That's the funny thing. They weren't doing anything other than walking along the beach, but they were all armed."

"So they wore swords?"

"Not just wore them, had them in their hands."

"Yes," added Luther. "Like they were looking for something."

"Or someone," said Rupert. "I do remember they seemed to be in a bit of a hurry."

Luther snapped his fingers. "That's right, and when they spotted us, they fled into the trees. Do you suppose they're hiding something?"

"Undoubtedly," said Danica, "and whatever it is, I intend to find out. Thank you, all of you. You have no idea how helpful you've been."

"Does that mean you're leaving us again?" asked Rupert.

"I am, but I'll be back. I promise you. In the meantime, save me one of those moonfish, will you? I have a friend back in Korvoran that's never had one."

"I will, but don't think for a moment you're going to get it for free. I have a living to make you know, and I expect a fair price."

Danica laughed. "Some things never change. Very well, Rupert, I guarantee a fair price. Now I must hurry. Be well." She climbed back aboard the skiff and began the journey back to the *Valiant*.

Rupert watched her go, shaking his head. "Well, I never. Who would ever have thought little Dani Meer would become a knight?"

"Not just any knight," corrected Luther, "a Temple Knight."

"Yes," added Dedrick, determined to have the last word, "and a ship captain to boot."

28

COURT

Spring 1098 SR

"I hear," said Lord Kurlan, "that there are problems in the countryside. The people are said to be close to rebellion."

"Where did you hear that?" said Charlaine.

"I can't say precisely, but rumours have been circulating for some weeks."

A servant walked past, and the baron snagged another goblet of wine. "You know how it is. These country folk have no respect for the nobility, and I wouldn't put it past Andover to be goading them on."

"I've been to the countryside," said Charlaine, "and learned nothing of the sort."

"Nor would you," the man insisted. "You represent the very authority they disdain."

"Might I ask when these rumours first came to your notice, Lord Kurlan?"

"Months ago, now. At the time, I assumed it was the usual grumblings of the peasant class, but as time passed, I began to realize this was something more serious."

"Are you referring to the area around your own Barony of Blunden?"

"Saints, no. My people are as content as newborn lambs. The rumours of which I speak concern the lands near Korvoran." He leaned closer, lowering his voice to provide further meaning to his revelations. "Mark my words, Captain. There will be rebellion in this land if we're not careful."

"I'm still at a loss as to how you learned of this," pressed Charlaine. "After all, you spend most of your time up north. How did you hear rumours concerning Korvoran?"

"You and I both know how quickly such news can travel, and I assure you I'm not the only noble to learn of them."

"Are you insinuating the duke knows of this problem?"

"The duke? No, but most assuredly, those beneath him are fully aware."

"If that's true," said Charlaine, "then you must see it as your duty to report the facts to His Grace as you know them."

"Report what? That I heard some rumours? Don't be silly, woman. I couldn't possibly do such a thing. I'd become the laughingstock of the court!"

"And so you choose to let this discontent fester and grow?"

"Were it within my domain," said Lord Kurlan, "I shouldn't hesitate to send in my soldiers, but I can hardly intervene when it concerns those peasants who swore fealty to His Grace."

"But they didn't."

The baron looked as if he'd been slapped. "What do you mean, they didn't? They belong to the duke, surely?"

"Yes, but most of the people out in the countryside are freeholders. They have sworn no fealty to the duke."

"Are you suggesting they are free to plot an uprising?" His voice grew louder, garnering attention from those around, particularly the Halvarian Ambassador, Lord Draclin. No, she corrected herself—he was Lord Winfyre. The Halvarian custom was to use the family name when addressed.

"Good day to you, Captain," said the ambassador. "And to you, Lord Kurlan. I trust all is well?"

"As well as can be expected, under the circumstances," the baron replied.

"Do I detect uncertainty in your voice?"

"Not so much uncertainty as indecision."

"Oh? Is it anything I can help you with?"

"I fear," said Charlaine, "that it is something he must deal with on his own."

"Not so fast," said Lord Kurlan. "I would be most interested in hearing His Lordship's advice."

"Well, in that case," said Lord Winfyre, "I would be happy to assist. Tell me what perplexes you so?"

"There are rumours of unrest, my lord. Sister Charlaine here thinks I ought to inform His Grace, the duke, but I have no proof."

A smile spread across the Halvarian's mouth. "I see."

"What would you have me do?"

"I believe the answer is clear, don't you? I know if it were my subjects, I would want to know. How about you? Were the roles reversed, and the duke discovered rumours of unrest in your territory, would you want him to inform you?"

"Of course."

"Then there's your answer."

"Ah, yes," said the baron. "When you put it that way, it's obvious, isn't it?"

Lord Winfyre bowed his head. "It is my pleasure to give you clarity, my lord. And what is Sister Charlaine's advice?"

"She agrees with you."

"Does she, now? How interesting." Lord Winfyre turned his attention to Charlaine, but the smile disappeared. "It seems our beliefs are not so different in the end."

"I do wonder where such rumours started," replied the Temple Knight.

Winfyre simply shrugged. "Who can say? The important thing is it is crushed before things get carried too far."

"Is that what you would do?"

"That is the nature of power. Without sufficient force to enforce the will of the ruler, the masses would rise up, and then chaos would ensue. Is that what you want for this land?"

"I'm not convinced an uprising is in the works. People have gone missing. What they truly want is help from the duke to find them."

"Missing, you say? How curious. I thought we were talking about talk of treason. Isn't that what you said, Baron?"

"It was," replied Lord Kurlan. "I don't know where this 'people have gone missing' idea came from. Nor, quite frankly, do I care. As our Halvarian colleague so succinctly articulated, we must use might to enforce our will, or the peasants will rise up against us."

"There's no rebellious talk," insisted Charlaine.

"So you say," said the baron, "but we only have your word for that."

"Do you doubt the word of a Temple Knight?"

The Halvarian Ambassador intervened before the baron could answer. "I'm sure Lord Kurlan meant no disrespect, but you must admit talk of rebellion is far more important to the ruling class than a few missing men."

"Who said anything about men?"

"You did," argued the ambassador.

"No, I said people."

Lord Winfyre quickly recovered. "Merely a misunderstanding. We Halvarians often use the term men to refer to any group of people. Why, you yourself must use the term to refer to your command? For example, have you never been asked how many men you command?"

"No," replied Charlaine. "We are either referred to as Temple Knights or Sisters. To do otherwise would be inaccurate."

"Then I apologize for my assumption. I must admit it's sometimes difficult getting used to local customs."

"Understandable," added the baron, eager to please. "Now, you must excuse me. I need to seek out the duke."

"I can come with you if you like?" offered Lord Winfyre.

"Would you? I would deem it a great favour."

"By all means." He turned to Charlaine. "What of you, Captain? Care to accompany us?"

"I fear my words might put you in an unfavourable light, my lord."

"Mere words do not frighten the men of Halvaria."

"In that case, I shall accompany you."

As a trio, they moved across the great hall, stopping from time to time to offer greetings to this individual or that. By the time they found the duke, Charlaine's head felt as if it were going to explode. Greeting people was not the problem, but their incessant requests to regale them with stories of her heroics were growing intolerable. She made a mental note to find the bard and put an end to such tales.

The duke looked bored standing beside his wife while she and Larissa Stormwind talked of the weather. The approach of the group gave him a chance to escape the mundane chatter.

"Ah, Lord Kurlan, so glad you could make it. I trust all is well in Blunden?"

"It is, Your Grace." The baron faltered, perhaps trying to reason out how to approach the subject. Lord Winfyre, however, dove right in. "Lord Kurlan tells me there are rumours of unrest in the region."

"There are?" said the duke. "That's the first I heard of it." He turned his attention to the baron. "Is this true?"

"I'm afraid so, Your Grace. For months now, there's been persistent rumours that malcontents are plotting against you."

"And where might we find these troublemakers?"

"I believe they are mainly confined to the south of the city. Alas, I have no specifics, but I thought best to bring it to your attention."

"You've done well," said the duke. "Now that we have warning, we can take pre-emptive action. These malcontents, I assume they're peasants?"

"Naturally, Your Grace."

"How will you deal with this news?" asked Lord Winfyre.

"With soldiers, of course." The duke saw the look of disapproval on Charlaine's face. "Peasants are very much like children, Captain," he explained. "If you give them too much freedom, they get spoiled, then you must administer a firm hand."

"A firm hand, Your Grace?" she replied.

"Yes, the application of force. I'll send in the army, and they can deal with the problem before it gets out of hand."

"There is no proof of these accusations, Your Grace."

"Then they have nothing to fear."

"Do you truly believe that?"

His demeanour turned frosty. "I am the Duke of Reinwick, ruler of the realm, given the divine right to govern this land and its people. I will not be intimidated!"

"I apologize if I've given offence," said Charlaine, "but there's still the question of proof."

"By the Saints, if we waited for proof, they'd be at our gates! We must strike before they can organize themselves."

She struggled to find an argument that might persuade him otherwise. "The Church will not condone this action," she finally said.

"This is no concern of the Church. Stick to your duty of providing for women, Captain, and let those in charge deal with threats of insurrection."

The duke turned abruptly and stormed off, calling for his general. Lord Kurlan, looking pleased with the outcome, wandered after him.

"I know you're behind this," warned Charlaine, her eyes boring into Lord Winfyre.

In response, he simply smiled. "You know nothing of the sort. I'm watching you, however, Captain. I am aware of what you did in Ilea, and if you think you're going to do something similar up here, you're sadly mistaken."

"The Church will not sit idly by and allow you to have your way."

"Your precious Church is nothing but a decrepit group of old men and women. The whole place smells of rot. Why, I would even go so far as to suggest that within ten years, it will fall apart, a victim of its own corruption."

"Don't speak of things you don't understand."

"Oh," said Lord Winfyre, "I understand it all too well. In fact, I made it my life's work to study your misspent religion and its laughable dedication to such outdated ideals. Enjoy it while you can, Captain. It won't last." With that, he turned, wandering back onto the crowded dance floor.

Charlaine fumed. The Halvarian had made reference to the Church rotting from within, the same warning she had received in the Antonine. Was it merely wishful thinking on the ambassador's part, or was he privy to some other piece of information? Maybe even a plot to overthrow the Church? She shook her head. Now was not the time to engage in idle speculation. Lord Winfyre had gotten into her thoughts, and if she let it grow, it would only consume her.

Her eyes sought out Sister Marlena only to find her deep in conversation with a lay brother of Saint Mathew. Unwilling to interrupt, Charlaine decided to get some fresh air. To that end, she made her way outside to take in the cool evening breeze.

"Troubled?"

She turned to see Larissa Stormwind.

"I couldn't help but overhear your discussion with Lord Winfyre," said the mage. "Don't let him get into your head."

"Too late for that, I'm afraid."

"He's a diplomat and an experienced one at that. I would expect no less, but you must try to push such thoughts from your mind."

"How well do you know him?" asked Charlaine.

"Personally? Not very well, but I know his type. They warned us about people like him at the Volstrum."

"That's where you learned to harness your magic?"

"It is, although it's far more than just a simple magical academy."

"In what way?"

"We were taught the ways of the court, not to mention the history of the Continent."

"And all this to wield magic?"

"Magic is but one of our weapons. Yes, it gets us in the door, so to speak, but our minds are the most potent tools in our arsenal. Our job is to advise rulers, the better to ensure that peace reigns over the Petty Kingdoms."

"Then I'd say your Volstrum isn't doing very well. War is constantly erupting somewhere or other."

"Unfortunately, you can't change hundreds of years of aggression overnight. The Petty Kingdoms were born in war; one might even say it's their natural state, but it doesn't need to remain that way."

"And you believe you can bring about a universal peace?"

"It is our ultimate goal," said Larissa. "In fact, I might even go so far as to say we are both striving for the same thing."

"Perhaps," said Charlaine, "but each takes a different route to get there."

"In the end, does it really matter? The destination is what's important, not the journey."

"Some would say the opposite. If we compromise our principles in the name of peace, are we any better than those we seek to change?"

"This is something you've obviously given a great deal of thought to. Much as I'd like to debate this further, I fear my duties as court mage must be observed. I do, however, look forward to continuing this discussion in future."

"As do I," replied Charlaine.

With the evening wearing on and her headache growing, Charlaine sought out Marlena.

"I'm done here," she said. "I think I'll return to the commandery and call it a night."

"I shall accompany you," her aide replied.

"No, that's not necessary. Stay, enjoy yourself. You can tell me all about it in the morning." Charlaine lowered her voice. "And keep an eye on the Halvarian Ambassador, will you? I wouldn't put it past him to try something with the duke."

"Is His Grace in danger?"

"Only from an overindulgence of fawning. I'm more concerned that he's too easily influenced. If we're not careful, Lord Winfyre will have soldiers riding all over the countryside, looking for imaginary revolts."

"In that case," said Marlena, "I promise to keep my eye on him."

"Excellent. Now, good night, and may the Saints be with you."

Charlaine located a servant who retrieved her cloak, for although it was spring, the evenings could still bring a stiff breeze from the sea.

Leaving the estate, she walked down the street, her mind mulling over the evening's developments. These get-togethers had become more frequent with the coming of warmer weather, but she had to wonder if all the time and effort was truly worth it. Very little work was actually done. The nobles of the land seemed to spend more time in gossip than they did dealing with the realm's affairs.

Halfway back to the commandery, a small stone became lodged in her shoe, making for a most unpleasant experience. She leaned against the wall of a building and removed it, shaking out the offending bit of debris. Now free of her obstruction, she replaced the shoe, but a nearby scuffling sound caught her attention as she tied it up.

Coming from behind her and slightly to the right, the noise was likely that of someone trying to cling to the shadows. Her senses were instantly alert as she scanned ahead, picking out any possible ambush points before her eyes settled on a distant tavern. She resumed her journey, keeping her right hand near the hilt of her sword.

So intent was she on what was behind her that the attack, when it came, took her completely by surprise. Someone had managed to get ahead and struck from an alleyway, even as she looked to her rear. The impact knocked her to the ground, her arms instinctively going out wide to break her fall. Moments later, she felt a blade scrape across her arm, ripping her cassock and leaving her with a shallow cut. She kicked out with her legs and had the satisfaction of striking a knee, and then her assailant fell to the side, his knife clattering as it hit stone.

Charlaine rolled and came up in a crouch but struggled to get her bearings in the dark. Down the street, a blur moved closer, and then a light glinted off a naked sword.

She rose, drawing her own blade and moving to intercept. Had she her armour, it would have been a simple matter to overpower this second assailant. Without it, she was forced to take care, else she would find herself impaled on the end of a sword.

Her attacker lunged, but she parried with ease, then counterattacked, striking low, and had the satisfaction of feeling her sword penetrate flesh. Her target let out a bellow before he attacked, a wild swing that sailed over her head. She pulled back, ready to strike again, but her first assailant had come to his senses and kicked out, knocking her legs from beneath her. As her knee smashed onto the cobblestones, pain lanced up her thigh. Moments later, the same man leaped onto her, driving her down onto the roadway. Knowing a dagger was only a moment from killing her, she did the only thing she could think of—rolled over, forcing him beneath her. Her head whipped back, and she felt his teeth and nose as her skull smashed into his face.

The second attacker drew closer, ready to administer the finishing blow, and he would have, had not fate intervened. A group of revellers exited the tavern, chatting away in a friendly manner. However, upon entering the street, one of them spied the commotion and called out to his companions.

The assailant to Charlaine's front turned and ran, eager to be away before he could be identified. The other fellow, his face covered in blood, heaved Charlaine to the side and quickly rose. Moments later, he tore down the alleyway, desperate to lose any chance of pursuit.

She tried to stand, but her knee would not take the weight. The revellers, seeing her distress, helped support her and half carried her back to the tavern.

29

THE HUNT

Spring 1098 SR

"I do not see any permanent damage," said the Mathewite. "You're lucky. A couple of days' rest should be all that's needed. Would you like something for the pain?"

"No," said Charlaine. "I'm fine."

"Liar," said Marlena. "I can see it in your eyes."

"When did you become my keeper?"

"Since you made me your aide. By the way, I never got the chance to properly introduce Brother Aleksy."

"I thought you brought him here?"

"I'm afraid not."

"Then why is he here?"

"I can answer that," said the lay brother. "Commander Salvatore sent me."

"To see to my wounds?"

"No, no. He had no idea you were wounded. None of us did. No, I was sent to offer my services to the *Valiant*."

"I don't know how to tell you this," said Charlaine, "but I'm not the person you need to speak to. It's Captain Danica's decision whether or not to take you on."

"A fact of which I'm well aware, but the *Valiant* has yet to return from its first voyage."

"And so you sought out me?"

"Precisely," said Brother Aleksy. "After all, you are her friend, are you not?"

"I am."

"And therefore a recommendation from you might help convince her of the necessity, don't you think?"

Charlaine looked at her knee. It was badly discoloured, but the lay brother had moved it around without any excruciating pain. Now, as he wrapped it in bandages, she was forced to admit the man knew his business.

"Very well," she said. "You've convinced me that you're competent."

"Thank you." He concentrated on his work, occasionally looking at Marlena. "When you redress this bandage, make sure it's not too tight. You want it to provide some support but not cut off the circulation."

"The what?" said Marlena.

"Circulation." He noted her confusion. "Never mind. Just don't make it too tight. Can you do that?"

"Certainly."

"Good." He turned his attention to Charlaine. "How's the head? You had a few cuts on the back."

"I head-butted someone," said Charlaine, her voice harsh. "How do you think it feels?" Silence filled the room, and then she realized her mistake. "My pardon, Brother, it has been a most trying night."

He smiled. "That's understandable, given the events that led to these wounds. Have you any idea who's responsible for this?"

"The actual assailants? No, but I'm pretty sure Lord Winfyre arranged the whole thing."

"Why would you say that?"

"Let's just say we had words at the duke's estate."

"It's all my fault," said Marlena. "If I had been there, they probably wouldn't have attacked you."

"You don't know that. They might have sent more assassins, then both of us would be dead."

"Are you sure that was their intention?" asked Brother Aleksy. "Perhaps they were trying to rob you?"

"There was no demand for coins," said Charlaine, "and who in their right mind would attack a Temple Knight? No, I'm positive their intention was murder."

"You have a point there, but why would they seek your death?"

"You must be getting close to discovering something," offered Marlena.

"Agreed," said Charlaine, "but what? All we learned over the last week is that more people have gone missing?"

"Not quite. What about the rumours of rebellion?"

"But that's all they were, rumours. Why kill me for that?"

"This reminds me of my father's death," said Marlena. "The whole family was gathered for the Midwinter Feast, along with a few guests."

"How is that anything like this?" asked Charlaine.

"The murderer was one of his most trusted advisors."

"How does that help us here?"

"Well, we all had our motives for wanting my father dead. It just ended up being someone we didn't expect."

"So you're suggesting Lord Winfyre wasn't involved?"

"All I'm suggesting is that we get the facts before we make a conclusion. That's what Brother Cyric did. He talked to all the people involved, then figured out who murdered my father."

"I'd love to do that, but we don't even know who else could be a suspect."

"What if you simplify the problem?" offered Brother Aleksy. "Who hates you enough to order an attack?"

"To kill me?"

"Not necessarily. They might have been delivering a message, a violent one for sure, but a warning nonetheless."

"He makes a good point," said Marlena.

Charlaine thought things over. "Undoubtedly, Lord Winfyre has reason to dislike me, but then again, so does Captain Waleed. You're not suggesting a member of the Church is responsible for my current condition, are you?"

"Not directly, but he may know people who could carry out such things."

"By that logic, it could be Lord Kurlan. He seemed most upset that I disagreed with him. Or how about the duke himself?"

"You believe the duke would do such a thing?" asked Brother Aleksy.

"No, of course not. I was only trying to make a point. We could speculate all day, but it's not going to get us anywhere."

"Someone attacked a captain of the Temple Knights," said Marlena. "We can't let that go unpunished."

"What choice have we?"

"Allow me to carry out some enquiries," offered Brother Aleksy.

"You know criminals?" asked Charlaine.

"I do a lot of work down at the mission. Once word gets around that a sister knight was attacked, it won't take long to find out who's responsible."

"So you're going to let your parishioners do the work for you?"

"Precisely. In the meantime, you need to rest that knee. You're lucky you weren't permanently disabled."

"Trust me," said Charlaine, "I know."

"Well, I can see that my work here is done. I shall drop by later in the week to check on you... and you"—he wheeled on Marlena—"make sure you keep her off that knee."

"Yes, Brother."

"Good. Now, I must bid you good morning, Sisters."

He packed away the excess bandages and took his leave.

"How's your head?" asked Marlena.

"Pounding."

"Shall I fetch something from the kitchen?"

"It's pain I'm suffering from, not hunger."

"Sister Lara may have an herbal remedy."

"Sister Lara," said Charlaine. "Another person who might bear a grudge. What if she was sent here to silence me after all? I did expose Commander Hjordis's disloyalty to the Antonine."

"Such speculation will do little to quell your headache. Brother Aleksy did offer you something for the pain. Shall I go and find him?"

"No, I'll be fine. Just give me some peace and quiet."

"Good enough, Captain," said Marlena. "Call me if you need anything. I'll be just outside."

Charlaine waited until the door closed before making her way to the window, hopping on one leg. A breeze blew in from the west, and she felt its cold caress wash away the pain. Looking below, she watched the city folk going about their business, and it reminded her of home. There, she would spend most of the day at the forge, perfecting a blade or fastening a pommel. It was a life she had given up until necessity had forced it back upon her. In Ilea, she'd needed to work on the armour of the sister knights, but here there was no such requirement.

She had never met the local smith, but the news he was a Dwarf was more than enough to convince her of his skill. It suddenly dawned on her that he could probably build an arbalest. She was about to call out to Marlena but remembered she was not seated. Rather than be lectured about resting, she hopped back to her chair.

"Marlena?" she called out. "Get in here. I need you."

Moments later, the younger knight opened the door. "Is something wrong, Captain?" Her eyes drifted to Charlaine's face. "My goodness, you're sweating buckets. Are you feeling all right?"

"Never mind that. Go and find Sister Leona. I want to know more about our smith."

"I didn't know we had a smith?"

"He doesn't belong to us," corrected Charlaine, "but he's under contract to keep our weapons and armour in good shape. I want to get in touch with him."

"For what? Besides, isn't that Sister Leona's responsibility?"

"Never mind what for, I need to talk to him; that should be enough. Now, fetch Sister Leona."

"As you wish, Captain. I shall find her." Marlena ran off, her footsteps receding as she rushed down the hall.

Charlaine dug out some paper and cut the nib off of a fresh quill. She sat for a moment, collecting her thoughts before she dipped it in ink and began sketching.

Barbek Stoutarm stepped into the office, doffing his hat at the last moment. "You wanted to see me, Captain?"

Charlaine looked at him. He was short by Dwarven standards, a little under five feet, if she had to guess, but his shoulders were far broader than any Human she had ever seen. He kept the top of his head closely shaven, no doubt to help keep the heat of the forge at bay, yet he had a ratty-looking beard that he had tucked into his belt.

"Am I in trouble?" he asked.

She rose, leaning against the desk for support. "I've heard only good things about your work, and I wanted to meet you," she said, holding out her hand.

He stepped forward, taking it in a firm grip. When she pressed her thumb into the space between his finger and thumb, he looked at her in surprise.

"You're a member of the guild?" he said.

"I am. Please, have a seat."

"I'm a bit dirty. I don't want to make a mess."

"Nonsense. You're no worse than my knights after weapons practice. Please, sit. We have things to discuss."

"I'm not sure I like the sounds of that. You're not cancelling my contract, are you?"

"Saints, no," said Charlaine. "I merely wish to further employ your services. Providing you're not too busy, of course."

"Ah, well," said Barbek. "In that case, please continue."

"From what I saw of your work, you're a fine craftsman."

"Thank you. I've always prided myself on not rushing things."

"Now, I know you do more than melee weapons because you also repair our armour. What I'm wondering is what other skills you might possess?"

"I'm not sure I follow?"

"Could you, for example, craft crossbows?"

"My understanding," said Barbek, "is you already employ a bowyer for that."

"We do, but we're looking for something a little heavier to mount on our ship, the *Valiant*."

His eyes narrowed. "You want me to make an arbalest, don't you?"

"And what would be your response if I did?"

He stroked his beard, his eyes looking off in the distance. Clearly, his conscience struggled with something.

"I can assure you it would only be used aboard ship," she said.

"Be that as it may, it can deal out a good amount of damage. How do I know it won't be used for ill?"

"The *Valiant* and her crew are dedicated to keeping the merchant ships safe, not plundering cities."

"And can you guarantee it won't be removed from this ship?"

"I can. In fact, we were rather hoping it would be attached to the deck using a heavy mount."

"You mean so you can swivel it?" he asked.

"Precisely. Of course, we'd need bolts for it too."

"What type of bolts?"

"The intention would be to use it against other ships, not people, so we'd need something that could puncture wood."

"No doubt you'd want a grappling hook as well."

"You can do that?"

"Of course," said Barbek. "Otherwise, I wouldn't offer. Mind you, it would be expensive, and I'd need to see the ship to be able to work out how to mount it."

"That can be arranged, although it's not in port at this precise moment."

"I would likely need to rip up part of the deck to provide enough support."

"To mount an arbalest?"

"There's more to this than simply mounting an arbalest. Once you grapple the enemy, you must have a winch mechanism to bring it close unless you have dozens of men standing by to do all the work?"

"What would this winch look like?"

The Dwarf rubbed his hands together, excited by the prospect. "I was thinking it would be mounted vertically. That is to say, a cylinder on end. Spokes would be attached, and then men could rotate it by pushing it around in circles."

"And if the grappled ship veers off?"

"An interesting point. I suppose I could set up a ratcheting mechanism."

"I'm afraid you must pardon my ignorance. What, precisely, is that?"

"The cylinder, or drum, to explain it better, would have protrusions at one end, what I like to call teeth. Into this, we drop an iron bar to stop it from spinning."

"Then how would they operate it?"

"Ah, the teeth would be slanted on one side, allowing the lock to slip. From the other direction, however, it would come up against a flat tooth and be held fast. It's rather hard to explain without it in front of you."

"And you invented this?"

"Gods, no," said Barbek. "We Dwarves have used things like that for centuries."

"How is it we never heard of such things?"

"Well, that's just it, you have, but the average Human distrusts the engineering of the mountain folk. Silly, really, when you think of it. I remember when I was in Harlingen, must be fifty years ago. No, wait, I tell a lie. It was more like a hundred. In any case, I was called in to examine a windmill that had suffered some severe damage. There'd been a fire, you see, and the inside was gutted. I took the opportunity to improve the entire thing, using a series of gears to make it more efficient."

"What happened?" asked Charlaine.

"Everything worked just fine, but when it went into operation, the other windmill operators complained their flour mills were being out-produced. In the end, they stormed the place in protest and burned it to the ground. That was the signal it was time to leave."

"I don't believe I ever heard that story," said Charlaine.

"No reason why you should. Harlingen is the capital of Hadenfeld, and that's a long way from here."

"It's not as far as you might think. I was born there."

"In Harlingen?"

"No, in Malburg, but it's in the same kingdom. I never visited the capital myself, but word would often drift out to the remoter parts of the realm."

"Well, it was a hundred years ago. They likely forgot all about it by now."

She laughed. "Probably. In any case, I can assure you no one will be burning the *Valiant*."

"That's good to hear. You know, I was a little hesitant to work with you at first, but now I've gotten to know you, I feel like we'll get along famously."

"Because I was a smith?"

"That's part of it," said Barbek, "but there's more. You're interested in making the Continent a better place." He held up his hand. "I know what you're going to say, and yes, I know that's what your order does, but there's something about you... an earnestness, I suppose: makes me want to do my part."

"I appreciate that," replied Charlaine. "Now, as to scheduling this..."

"Leave that to me," said the Dwarf. "I'll need to source some things. I was thinking of using shadowbark for the mount."

"Shadowbark? That sounds expensive."

"Yes, it will be, but this weapon has to operate around salt water. Even so, the bow will be made of Dwarven steel, so I must devise some type of covering to keep it dry, something along the lines of a canvas soaked in oil or fat."

"How many people would it take to operate this arbalest?"

"In theory, only one, but I would recommend two. One would be responsible for reloading it while the other kept the weapon trained on the target. That will allow you to fire off quarrels at a much faster pace."

"You've put a lot of thought into this already, haven't you?"

He nodded. "And now that I started, I shall think of little else. This is why I became an artificer in the first place."

"Artificer? I thought you were a smith?"

"It's a term my people use to indicate those craftsmen who are constantly devising new and improved ways of doing things. About the closest Human term would be inventor."

"I'm glad we have you on our side, then," said Charlaine. "I shouldn't like to think what would happen if our enemies had people like you."

"Ah, but they do," noted the Dwarf, "or at least we believe they do."

"Are you suggesting Dwarves work for Halvaria?"

"Not willingly, but there are rumours of how the great Dwarven strong-hold of Dun Galdrim fell to them about fifty years ago. There's been no word of them ever since."

"My condolences."

"You don't imagine you'll run across any Halvarian ships up here, do you?"

"It's certainly possible."

"And if you do?"

"That's a difficult question to answer," admitted Charlaine. "We are not at war with Halvaria, yet we recently destroyed their fleet to the south. Should they prove antagonistic towards the *Valiant*, she would be forced to fight back."

"Couldn't that lead to war?"

"The *Valiant* is a Church ship, and as such, flies the flag of no kingdom. If the Halvarians were to attack it, they would essentially be declaring war on the Church of the Saints. I doubt that's something they want to encourage."

The Dwarf leaned back in his chair. "They say war is inevitable."

"Who are 'they'?"

"Everyone. The Empire of Halvaria is like a hungry dragon, swallowing up anything in its path. Sooner or later, even Reinwick will become dragon fodder."

"Not if I can help it," declared Charlaine.

30

DRUMHOLLOW

Spring 1098 SR

T he *Valiant's* anchor made a loud noise as it splashed into the sea. Off to port, Danica gazed at the treelined beach of the southern shore of Drumhollow. The sister knights checked over their armour on the deck while the ship's crew prepared the skiff to take them ashore.

Danica had once again decided to forgo the use of her armour, electing to rely instead on the Temple Knights to keep her safe. To her mind, she wanted nothing that might negatively affect her ability to spot any clues, and she knew the constricting armour would only make such searching more difficult.

A yell announced the skiff was ready. Danica waited until all the knights were aboard before lowering herself into the stern of the tiny boat. The oarsmen dug in at her command, sending the vessel towards the narrow beach.

The water here was dark, as was typical of the Great Northern Sea. It may have been seen as an ill-omen to many, but to Danica, it was just the way it was. She had spent her early years on this sea, and its brooding nature held little sway over her, at least while the weather remained calm, for a part of her always dreaded an unexpected storm. Her parents had both drowned in a similar deluge, but they'd been in a flimsy fishing boat. It took only a moment for her to realize the skiff was even smaller, but by that time, the boat bumped up against the beach, and the knights hopped out.

"Stay here," she said to the crewmen. "We're going to need to look around. If you sense any danger, return to the *Valiant*."

Grazynia examined the shoreline. "There's no sign of any recent activity."

"Spread out," said Danica. "We'll follow the coast for a few hundred yards in either direction. If we don't find anything noteworthy, we'll head inland."

Grazynia took two of the knights east, while Anya and the rest proceeded westward. Danica looked out to sea. The sight of the *Valiant* filled her with pride. She was a fine ship, but still, part of her worried how it would fare against the *Sea Wolf*.

"We found something!" called out Anya. "There's a stream that empties into the sea, and it looks like someone has been here recently."

Danica made her way towards them. Hardly an obstacle at all, but it promised freshwater farther inland. The greenery around it had been trampled, although some had already begun to grow back.

"Someone likely stopped here to gather water," she said.

"Could it be the *Sea Wolf*?" suggested Anya.

"There are dozens of ships that sail these waters. Let's not get ahead of ourselves. Nadia, go and fetch Grazynia and the others. Once you return, follow us upstream."

"Yes, Captain," she replied before heading off.

Anya knelt. "Heavy boot prints," she mused. "These could be soldiers."

"What makes you say that?" asked Zivka.

"Sailors tend to wear shoes if they wear anything on their feet at all."

"I don't imagine that would help them in a fight."

"Fighting isn't their primary responsibility," said Danica. "Running the ship is. I agree with Anya. These are likely soldiers' boots. That tells us whatever was here was a warship."

"Not necessarily," said Zivka. "They could have been prison guards."

"That's an excellent point. In any case, they're likely armed, so stay on the alert. How old would you say these tracks are?"

"A week, at least," said Anya. "I doubt you'll find any of them left on the island."

"We can't dismiss the idea that they might have a more permanent base here, so be careful. Lead on, Anya."

Progress was slow, for they had to cut their way through the foliage from time to time. Not only that, but Anya had to stop and search several times to pick up the trail of their quarry.

Eventually, they entered a clearing to find a smattering of crude huts made of rough-cut timber, with just enough walls to support the overhanging roofs.

Grazynia poked her head inside one. "Not much in the way of shelter."

"Enough to hold off the rain," said Danica. "I suspect they only use these in the warmer weather."

Anya, who had entered another structure, knelt and looked at a centre post. "Look at this," she called out.

Danica came closer. The post was worn at its base, and the reason wasn't too hard to discern. "They used this to shackle prisoners," she said. "You can see where the chains dug into the wood."

"So this is a slaver camp?"

"Slavers or prisoners, not that there's much of a difference. Someone undoubtedly brought them here against their will. The real question is, why?"

"The water source is around here," offered Grazynia. "Could that explain it?"

"No," said Anya. "I have to assume this was a temporary gathering point. Prisoners were likely brought here so they wouldn't need to keep them on deck."

"I'm not sure what you're implying."

The blonde knight straightened her back. "Imagine you're the *Sea Wolf*, or any other ship, for that matter. You conduct a raid and capture... I don't know, maybe half a dozen people? You want to continue plundering, but you can't have prisoners crowding your deck, so what do you do? You dispatch some men to make a temporary camp, and then hold your prisoners there."

"Thus, freeing up your ship for more raids," said Grazynia. "Clever. And they built it here because it's near freshwater."

"Not only that," said Danica, "it's easy to find, thanks to that stream, yet not visible from the coast, making discovery unlikely. We wouldn't have come here ourselves if we hadn't been tipped off."

"But these buildings look older," noted Grazynia.

"Likely built last year. The winter storms in these parts would play havoc with them."

"So, where are they now?"

"This is a fairly large island," said Danica. "They likely moved on to another location."

"Why?" said Grazynia. "Especially after all the work to set this up?"

"Who knows? Perhaps they thought it too much work to repair, or maybe they feared discovery? I doubt we'll ever know the true reason."

"So what do we do now, Captain?"

"We return to the *Valiant* and map out the island. That will tell us the most likely anchoring spots. Maybe, if we're lucky, we'll find another base like this."

"Well," said Grazynia, "at least we now know what we're looking for."

"Agreed," said Danica, "but we also know they're using this island as a base. That, at least, confirms people were abducted instead of killed outright."

"Where do you think they went?" asked Anya.

"That's something we have yet to discover."

They returned to the *Valiant*, then made their way eastward, skirting the edge of the island. The vegetation here was even thicker, with tree trunks reaching out into the water. Danica thought this odd, but then the ship scraped along the bottom of the sea. They all held their breath until it cleared the shallow water, leaving a trail of mud in its wake.

"That was close," said Anya.

"Yes," agreed Danica. "Let's put some distance between us and the shore. I shouldn't like to get stranded here."

The *Valiant* turned south until it was roughly half a mile offshore. At this point, they altered course again, returning to their eastward passage. The end of the island soon came into view. At first, they took it for a small bay, but the land ran north as they advanced, so they made another course correction.

The wind shifted, now coming from the west, but the *Valiant's* new sail configuration kept them on course. Throughout the afternoon, they sailed on, with little to occupy their interest.

It was late afternoon when they again needed to adjust their direction as the land now curved off to the west, directly into the wind. The Valiant began the laborious process of tacking, sailing port and starboard in a zigzag pattern to compensate.

The island crawled past, their progress now slowed considerably. They were just about to give up when Anya's keen eyes spotted a ship anchored close to shore, with a longboat tied up alongside. Danica ordered the knights to arm themselves and stow any unnecessary gear. Crossbows were handed out, and extra quarrels distributed amongst her warriors.

Aboard the other vessel, men were spotted climbing the mast. Moments later, the anchor started rising, and then a red flag was hoisted from the mainmast.

"It's the *Sea Wolf*," called out Anya.

"Yes," said Danica, "and they have the advantage of the wind."

"Will they evade?"

"I doubt it. I'm sure they'd prefer to come in close and let their mage do all the work."

"Assuming he's healed," added Grazynia.

"Let us hope he's not," said Danica, "or this may yet prove to be a fruitless endeavour."

The *Sea Wolf* lowered its sails and began moving. At first, it appeared to be on an intercept course, but as the enemy gained speed, they turned, heading northeast.

"Bring us round four points to starboard," yelled Danica. The *Valiant* began the forty-five-degree turn, picking up speed, but it looked like the *Sea Wolf* would outpace them with the wind at its back.

Zivka raised her bow, but Danica quickly put a stop to it. "Don't bother. You'll only waste your bolt."

Grazynia came up beside her. "What I wouldn't give for a decent mage right about now."

"What kind of mage?"

"Any?"

"I'd settle for a ballista," said Danica, "but it doesn't look like we'll be so lucky."

"So they're going to get away?"

"Keep faith. The wind may yet change, and if it does, we'll find ourselves in a superior position."

The *Sea Wolf* crossed their path, though still some distance off. They all recognized the Fire Mage at its stern, standing there with a single finger raised in defiance.

The Temple Knights were furious, but Danica let it go. There were hours yet until dusk, and much could happen in that time. As if to emphasize that very point, the wind suddenly shifted. The *Valiant* picked up speed, while the *Sea Wolf* was forced to alter its course to keep at its current pace.

"Now, we'll see if we're fast enough," said Danica, more to herself than to anyone else.

A sea chase is not the most exciting of things to witness. Change comes slowly, and although the range was decreasing, it took hours before there was even the remotest possibility of hitting it with a bow.

Closer and closer, they drew. Danica ordered the archers up to the bow, and Anya let loose with a bolt in an effort to judge the distance. To their amazement, it struck the water just astern of the *Sea Wolf*. Buoyed by this example, the knights all gave a cheer. It would not be long now!

The enemy mage appeared once more, standing beside the aft rail, extending his arms out and then waving them around. Moments later, a streak of flame leaped across the water, striking the *Valiant* low on the bow.

There was the briefest smell of burning wood before the waves extinguished it.

"You have my permission to retaliate," said Danica, "but take your time. We want to make every bolt count."

Three crossbow bolts were loosed, with two falling into the sea, while the third hit the *Sea Wolf's* aft railing and stuck, giving it an almost ludicrous look.

The Fire Mage started gesticulating once more as Anya let a bolt fly. A clean miss, but near enough to cause the mage to duck, throwing off his aim, his streak of fire flying from his hand to strike the water.

"Keep up the volleys," said Danica. "You're keeping him busy."

The mage cast again, and suddenly thick, black smoke billowed out of the *Sea Wolf*.

"By the Saints," said Anya. "What happened?"

"A smoke spell," replied Grazynia. "I've seen one before."

"Keep your crossbows loaded," urged Danica as she scanned the *Valiant's* deck to where the crew stood ready. "Stand by to make a turn."

"To what side?" came back a call.

"I don't know yet. It largely depends on what the *Sea Wolf* does."

The smoke didn't so much blow around as simply float in space. The *Valiant* drew closer, then entered the area, leading many to shield their eyes.

Danica peered through the gloom, desperately looking for a sail. The *Sea Wolf* suddenly loomed up beside them, mere yards off their port bow.

"Hard to port," she yelled.

The *Valiant* slewed to the side, closing the gap.

"Loose bolts!" ordered Danica.

The crossbows let loose, and moments later, she heard them strike wood, and at least one must have hit a crewman aboard the *Sea Wolf*, for someone gave a cry of pain.

A streak of flame blew past Danica, narrowly missing her head to strike the mainmast, leaving a scorched smell lingering in the air.

"Reload," she ordered, "and loose in your own time. And for Saint's sake, keep your heads low."

The *Valiant* was only a few feet from its nemesis. The helmsman straightened the tiller, and the sides of the two ships scraped against each other, knocking several souls from their feet.

Danica was tempted to leap across, but it was too late by the time she got her footing. The ships had separated, the cold sea between them offering a sure death should someone fall. More bolts flew across the gap.

"Douse that fire!" yelled Danica, pointing at the mainmast.

She heard mumbling and ducked. Somewhere to the rear of the *Valiant*, there was a whooshing sound as if someone had blown onto a flame. Looking aft, she saw the tillerman fall to the deck, his clothes aflame.

Sister Laurel rushed to his aid, but the damage was done. With no one at the helm, the *Valiant* lost control of its rudder, slewing to starboard. The sails went limp, and the ship slowed, the *Sea Wolf* disappearing once more into the smoke.

Zivka grabbed the rudder, but it was too late. The *Sea Wolf*, now clear of the smoke, turned eastward, the wind directly behind them.

Danica smashed her fist onto the railing. "We almost had them!" she shouted.

"We'll get them next time," said Grazynia.

"If there is a next time. This sea is enormous, with wide-open sailing. Who knows where they'll get to?"

"We can still catch them."

Danica stared skyward. "No, we're running out of daylight. Without the sun, we have no way of tracking them. I fear this chase is over."

She saw their looks of disappointment. It had been a hectic chase. They had come so close, and to fail now was seen as a devastating defeat.

Finally, they drifted clear of the smoke. Sister Laurel stood over the body of the tillerman, her eyes meeting those of her captain. "I'm afraid he didn't make it," she said.

Danica felt the loss deeply. It was her decision to engage the enemy, her choice that led this man to his death. The burden of command fell like a great weight across her shoulders, and now she understood what it meant to be a leader. Part of her could look at this dispassionately, understanding their losses were light, but staring down at his lifeless body, she saw only death and loss.

"It's not your fault," said Sister Grazynia, picking up on her mood.

"Yet I must accept it as such. I am the captain of the *Valiant*, and that means I'm responsible for each and every one of you." She looked around the deck. Everybody had paused in their work and now stood, staring back at her. Were they looks of condemnation, or did they expect her to give some words of inspiration? She fought to remember the tillerman's name.

Danica moved closer to the body, kneeling before it. She bowed her head and searched her soul for words of comfort.

"Blessed Saint Agnes," she began. "Watch over this man, Gilford, and guide him to the Afterlife. He has ever been a loyal servant and showed compassion and perseverance in the face of the enemy. He served you well, oh Blessed Saint, and did his duty. Let him now stand by your side as you guide him to the great beyond." She paused, letting the silence dwell for a moment. "Saints, be with us."

"Saints be with us all," echoed the rest of the crew.

"Prepare him," said Danica, then turned to one of the crewmen, a man named Brendan. "What is the custom in these parts? Shall we take the body back to Korvoran or bury him at sea?"

"He died at sea," said Brendan. "Let him feel the cold embrace of Akosia."

"What will you need from us?"

"We'll stitch him a shroud from spare sailcloth and use some ballast to weigh down the body."

"Carry on," said Danica. "I shall be in my cabin if needed."

"What route, Captain?" asked Zivka.

"North by northwest. Inform me the moment we sight land."

"Yes, Captain."

They prepared the body of Gilford, then the *Valiant* slowed, furling its sail and finally coming to rest as the light of the day fled. The deck heaved with the waves but steadied as the ceremony commenced. The body was committed to the sea, and then the sails were once more unfurled, the journey continuing in the dark.

Danica adjusted their course several times throughout the night using the stars, only to be rewarded by the lights of Korvoran staring back at them as the coast came into view—a pale glow against the cold dark of the sea.

31

FATE

Summer 1098 SR

Danica walked around the strange contraption. "Are you sure this is going to work?" she asked.

Charlaine laughed. "So Barbek assures me. I'll admit it's a little unusual, but he seems to know what he's doing."

"Did I hear my name mentioned?" The Dwarf stomped down the deck. It wasn't as if he were angry, so much as heavy of foot. He came to a halt, looking at Danica. "What did you need explaining?"

"I'm familiar enough with crossbows to understand how this arbalest works. What I can't seem to wrap my head around are these strange handles?"

"Those are used to control the position of the weapon. This one here"— he pointed to a small circular handle with a protrusion pointing out of its edge—"is used to rotate the weapon through the horizontal plane."

"The what?" said Danica.

"It moves it around the mounting point." He rotated the wheel to demonstrate its use, causing the arbalest to swivel quite swiftly. "I used a set of gears to make it easier to move. Don't worry, I greased them well and hid them in a casing to protect them from the weather."

"Then what's this, the thing that's mounted upright?"

"That controls the elevation. Try it for yourself."

The raven-haired knight turned the wheel, causing the nose of the weapon to pitch upward.

"The combination of the two wheels gives you greater control over the weapon," he explained.

"We arranged a little demonstration," said Charlaine. "Over on the dock, there's a large bale of straw." She turned to the Dwarf. "Barbek? If you would be so kind?"

"We made this for your height"—he moved to the rear of the weapon —"so it's a bit awkward for a Dwarf of my stature." He turned the crannequin, pulling the metal bow back into the ready position. "With the weapon fully cocked, we can now load the quarrel." He reached into a box attached to the base, extracting a quarrel, then held it out to Charlaine. "Captain, would you do the honours?"

She placed the metal arrow onto the arbalest, ensuring it was up against the bowstring.

Barbek rotated both the wheels, manoeuvring the weapon into position. "Now," he said. "Watch the target."

He pulled back on the release mechanism, sending the bolt flying towards the shore, where it struck the bale low, almost hitting the dock planking.

"As you can see, I'm not the best at this type of thing. I failed to compensate for drop."

"That's all right," said Danica. "I get the idea. What kind of range can we expect on this?"

"Several hundred yards in calm waters, but I doubt you would use it at such range."

"Why's that?"

"Most of the energy produced by the bow would be expended, and my understanding is this is primarily to be used against ships. Ideally, you'd want to be close at hand."

"And you created a grapnel bolt?"

"I did, although it's not stored nearby." He snapped his fingers, then called out, "Gernik, fetch me those other bolts!" He waited as his apprentice went below. Soon, the younger Dwarf emerged from the hold, his arms loaded with strange-looking bolts.

"Ah, here he is," said Barbek.

"What have we got here?" said Charlaine. "You only told me about the grapnel, not these others?"

"I need to keep some things secret! How else would I maintain my reputation as a genius?" He selected one of the quarrels. "This one is a boarding grapnel, as you can see. It has a limited range, and before you let loose with it, you must attach a line to the end here."

Danica picked up another bolt, this one with a strange multi-flared end. "What's this for?"

"I call that the ripper. It's designed to tear through canvas."

"How does it work?"

"Aim high, into the sails. As the thing leaves the arbalest, it'll begin to tumble—that's what does the damage when it hits."

"So it shreds sails. I can see how that could be very useful."

"Not only sails," said the Dwarf. "It'll cut through ropes too. Let loose with a few of these, and with any luck, you could bring an enemy to a standstill."

Charlaine picked up a quarrel with a metal ball on the end. "What's this for?"

"I'm afraid that's a bit of a failed experiment. I tried to create something that could be used to subdue people, but it rips right through flesh. It's quite a grisly sight to behold."

"Then why bring them?"

The Dwarf shrugged. "What else could I do with them? Throw them out and waste all the effort it took to make the things?" He glanced at his apprentice, who was trying to get his attention. "Oh yes, of course, there's the bodkin quarrels as well. Those are for armoured opponents."

"You seem to have given this a great deal of thought."

"And why wouldn't I? It's not every day I get to play with things like this."

"Despite the difficulty?"

"It's precisely that difficulty that makes it so rewarding to design. My people have a saying: 'Give a Dwarf a challenge, and then stand back and watch them complete it'."

"Well, I, for one, thank you," said Danica. "This arbalest will give the *Valiant* just the advantage it needs against larger ships."

Barbek made an exaggerated bow. "In that case, I shall leave it in your more than capable hands. Now, if you'll excuse me, I have work awaiting my return to my smithy." And with that, he and his apprentice left.

Charlaine turned to Danica. "Well, what do you think?"

"That this gives us exactly what we need."

"Is it enough to take down the *Sea Wolf*?"

"I believe it is."

"Good, then it's time you went back out to sea. Any idea where you might find the villain?"

"He's been quiet of late," said Danica, "but he might be hiding out some-where in the Five Sisters. I'll start my search there."

"When can you sail?"

"Tomorrow morning. That gives us time to finish taking on stores."

"Anything else you need?" asked Charlaine.

"Only prayers," noted Danica. "The chance of actually finding the *Sea Wolf* is next to none."

"I wouldn't say that. You already found her down by Drumhollow. Who's to say you can't find them again? And in any case, the Saints are on your side. Have faith, my friend. You'll find her. I know you will."

No one living knew how the Five Sisters came to get their name, but these five islands made up a cluster that lay on the northeastern tip of Reinwick. While nominally under their control, the harsh reality was that much of the waters surrounding them were uncharted. That didn't stop rumours from growing over the years. Everything from pirate havens to sea monsters was said to exist in those waters. Some even said Akosia herself rested beneath its waves.

Danica was a lot more pragmatic. While it was possible some strange kind of wildlife called the islands home, the thought of a goddess lying beneath the waves was just a little too much to accept. As for pirates, well, that was not only possible but, to her mind, probable.

The Five Sisters were named Amity, Constance, Patience, Providence, and Verity. Amity and Verity were said to be the smallest and, therefore, unlikely candidates to hold a pirate base. The others, though, were signifi-cantly bigger, with Patience said to be the largest, although once again, there were no maps of the area to either confirm or deny this theory.

The *Valiant* started by sailing up the eastern coast of Reinwick. This spit of land reached out into the sea like a large stick, the tip of it containing a tower called the Beacon, which had been built with a fire atop to aid in navigation.

Once they reached that, they turned eastward, sighting Providence, thickly populated with trees and rough hills towards its centre. They explored its coast in a counter-clockwise direction, keeping an eye not only on the land but on the sea, lest the raider make its presence known.

For days they sailed, spotting nothing save for a few deer. With a circumnavigation complete, they continued on to Amity. This tiny island left little to the imagination and took less than a day to make a complete circuit of its waters. Daybreak saw them off the coast of Constance, and it was here the work finally began.

Danica took her time, occasionally sending the skiff inshore to confirm landmarks and springs. It started to pay off as her maps became populated with a more accurate representation of the islands.

The most likely anchorage around Constance proved to be its northern shore. Here, at its approximate centre, lay a slight inlet. The *Valiant* halted its exploration, and a small group went ashore to gather fresh water. It was during this time that the *Sea Wolf* decided to make its presence known.

The first sign of it was as it rounded the western end of the inlet, its sails billowing in the strong afternoon breeze. Danica ordered everyone to their stations and was forced to abandon the landing party, at least for now.

The *Valiant* weighed anchor, unfurled the sail, and slowly began moving. The *Sea Wolf*, coming from the west, had the advantage of the wind while the Temple ship had to turn around.

"Load the arbalest," ordered Danica.

"What type of bolt?" asked Zivka.

"Let's go with a shredder, but remember to aim high. And whatever you do, don't loose until you can guarantee a hit."

The *Valiant* turned, the wind finally filling the sail. The yardarm swung around as a great gust of wind came up, and she picked up speed.

They were heading north, perpendicular to the *Sea Wolf*'s trajectory. On the bow of the enemy ship, they could just make out the Fire Mage, waiting patiently, his arms clasped behind his back, likely judging the distance.

"Bolt away!" yelled Danica.

Zivka released the quarrel, aiming high. It tumbled through the air like a drunken seagull, and then a tear appeared in the *Sea Wolf*'s sail.

On the enemy ship, the damage went unnoticed by those aboard. The mage thrust out his hands, and a streak of fire shot across the sea. Danica instinctively ducked, but it appeared the enemy caster had misjudged the distance.

"Reload complete," called out Zivka.

"Loose in your own time," came the captain's reply.

The Temple Knight took her time, adjusting the arbalest carefully. Sure of her settings, she released the bolt, and it tumbled through the air just as before, but this time no rip appeared.

Danica was about to curse when the *Sea Wolf*'s yardarm suddenly slewed to port, for the bolt had cut through some of the ropes holding it in place. At the same time, the Fire Mage thrust out his hands again, but then something smashed into his back, and he sprawled to the deck.

Danica ran forward, peering over the bow. She had noted a sand bar on the way in, and now she ordered the ship to steer for it, luring the *Sea Wolf* to what was hopefully its doom.

The enemy was close now, arrows flying across the water. Most struck the *Valiant's* hull or the mast, but one lucky archer managed to hit one of the crew manning the ropes, and the sail rippled.

"Secure that line!" yelled Danica, her head swivelling back and forth quickly from her crew to the *Valiant's* bow. The shallow water was now beneath them. She heard the keel scraping along the sand and held her breath, for if they ran aground, it would be the end of them.

The ship shuddered but kept moving, clearing the sandbank before it turned, bringing the port side to face the oncoming vessel.

The Fire Mage climbed to his feet, then cast anew, sparks leaping from his hands right as the *Sea Wolf* struck the sandbank. Thrown forward, he hit the rail, the sparks flying high into the air, although what they were designed to do was unclear.

Temple Knights lined up against the railing, their crossbows ready. Zivka let another quarrel fly from the arbalest, the bolt ripping into the sail once more. The great sheet split down the middle, releasing the trapped wind. The *Sea Wolf*, now robbed of its forward momentum, stuck fast, its crew rushing around in a vain effort to dislodge themselves from the trap.

"Take out that mage," ordered Danica.

The knights let loose with their barrage. The first volley scored two hits, and the spellcaster, who had just regained his feet, collapsed to the deck once more, a bolt lodged in his head.

Everyone on the *Valiant* gave a cheer, but then it was the enemy archers' turn. Zivka, who had not taken time to don her armour, took an arrow to the shoulder and fell back with a curse. Danica ran to the arbalest and commenced loading.

The *Sea Wolf*, now an easy target, remained unmoving but still dangerous, thanks to its bowmen. Enemy sailors hauled out a new sail from below decks, struggling with the weight.

A volley from the Temple Knights took two more men down, and the rest ran for cover, abandoning their attempt to get their vessel underway.

"Surrender!" called out Danica.

In answer, a hail of arrows came her way. She ducked behind the arbalest as they sailed overhead, then stood once more, lining up the weapon with great care. She released the quarrel, and it tore through the enemy's rigging, sending ropes falling everywhere. Grazynia appeared at her side.

"What now, Captain?" she asked.

"Take Zivka below, then you and the rest get into your armour. We'll take that ship at the tip of a sword."

"What of yourself?"

Danica was about to refuse, but then the crew member, Brendan, moved to take control of the arbalest. "Orders, Captain?"

"Pepper them with regular bolts," she ordered, "but if they try to make any repairs to their sail, use a shredder." Her eyes met those of the sailor. "Are you sure you're comfortable using this?"

In response, he simply nodded.

"Excellent. I'll go and don my armour."

Not long later, they assembled on deck. Brother Aleksy, who had remained below to tend Zivka's injury, came up to report she would survive. He gazed across at the stricken ship and shook his head.

"Why don't they surrender?" he asked. "They must realize how hopeless their situation is?"

"I don't think they can surrender," said Danica.

"What do you mean by that?"

"I believe they work for the Halvarians."

"Why would you say that?"

"Who else has so much to gain with all this raiding?"

"Pirates?" suggested the lay brother.

"Would a pirate knowingly attack a Temple ship?"

"What you said makes a lot of sense. But if it's Halvaria, why fight on now?"

"They're fanatics," said Danica. "Willing to give their life in the service to their master."

"Isn't that exactly what Temple Knights do?"

His question startled her. "That's different," she insisted.

"Why?" said Brother Aleksy. "Because they're the enemy?"

"They've conquered many lands and enslaved their people, all in the name of their god-emperor."

"How many so-called barbarians died at the hands of the Church? Or have you forgotten the Crusades in the east?"

"You're right, of course," said Danica. She turned to her knights. "The objective here is to take prisoners, not kill outright. Defend yourselves if necessary, but our mere presence aboard their ship should be enough to compel them to surrender."

They climbed down the side of the ship to the skiff. Danica sat at the rear as the crewmen rowed, guiding the tiny ship towards the *Sea Wolf*.

The water was calm as they went, but the Great Northern Sea could be a cruel host. She knew the winds could pick up at any moment, and the cold water in these parts would soon draw the life out of anyone should they be unlucky enough to fall overboard. The thought made her laugh when she realized that, dressed as she was, she was far more likely to drown than freeze.

Overhead, the arbalest fired off another bolt. The enemy appeared quiet, although it was unknown whether it was due to losses or preparing to defend their ship in melee.

The skiff bumped up against the *Sea Wolf*. The knights gripped their swords, put their visors down, then climbed up to the deck of the enemy ship.

Danica felt something strike her gauntlet as soon as she placed her hand on the railing. Moments later, she pulled herself onto the deck, her blade slashing out viciously. Her foe backed up, his small sword badly outmatched.

"Surrender!" she shouted, but the fellow wasn't having it. He stepped forward to lend weight to his attack, but Danica brought the pommel of her weapon down onto his face, causing blood to explode all over her fist. He screamed, then backed up, trying to put as much space between them as he could.

A quick glance over her shoulder spotted the dead mage, his blood liberally splattered all over the deck. Her inattentiveness almost spelled her demise when an axe chopped down, bouncing off of her shoulder pauldron. She struck out with her sword, taking her lightly armoured opponent in the stomach, her sword sinking in. He staggered back, collapsing to the deck, clutching the wound.

She spotted another man in armour. Taking him to be their leader, she rushed for him. In her haste, her foot slipped on the mage's blood, causing her to lose her footing and slide, landing heavily on her knees.

The enemy loomed over her, his axe narrowly missing her leg as it sank into the deck. He heaved it, trying to free it, and that's when Danica thrust out her Dwarven sword. It had been crafted by a master smith, and although it had been a castoff, it still cut with an edge only a Dwarf could forge.

The tip sank into an elbow joint, sliding beneath the vambrace to penetrate the quilted under-sleeve. The warrior cried out in pain as the weapon fell from his grasp.

"I yield!" he cried out, his eyes taking in the action on his ship. "Cease fighting!" he yelled. "Surrender."

32

THE PRIZE

Summer 1098 SR

C harlaine made her way to the docks. Word of the *Valiant's* return with the *Sea Wolf* as a prize raced through the city long before they anchored. In response, the duke sent soldiers to greet them, presumably to take the pirates into custody. As she neared, one of the duke's men spotted her.

"You must be Captain Charlaine," he called out in greeting. "I'm Captain Marwen."

"Good day, Captain. What brings you here this day?"

"We are here to assume responsibility for the prisoners, but the captain of the *Valiant* is refusing to hand them over."

"I'm sure she has her reasons."

"You must talk some sense into her, else I'll have no choice but to take them by force."

"I might remind you the *Valiant* is Church property and, as such, is beyond the reach of His Grace, the duke."

Marwen clenched his jaw. Charlaine couldn't blame him, caught as he was between his sworn duty to his lord and the law of the Church.

"She has till noon to release them to our custody," he said at last.

"Or what?" said Charlaine. "Temple Knights protect that ship. Are you so eager to fulfill your master's orders that you're willing to throw away the lives of your men?"

She saw the look of indecision. The fellow was clearly at a loss as to how to proceed.

"I shall talk with Captain Danica," she said, trying to keep her tone friendly. "I'm sure this situation can be resolved to everyone's satisfaction."

"Very well," the man replied. Doubtless, he wanted to say more, but Charlaine chose to continue on her way, elbowing past the guards at the boarding ramp to where Sister Zivka waited, her arm a mass of bandages.

"Permission to come aboard," said Charlaine.

"Permission granted, Commander."

Charlaine shook her head. It was difficult getting used to being addressed so. "Where is Captain Danica?" she asked.

"In the aft cabin. She's expecting you. Shall I take you there?"

"I can find my way. Your job is to remain here, making sure no one else gets aboard."

Charlaine crossed the deck to spot a familiar face wearing the brown cassock of his order.

"Brother Aleksy, I'm glad to see you made it back unscathed. How was the trip?"

"Eventful," the lay brother replied. "As I'm sure the captain will attest."

"Were there many wounded?"

"On our side, no, although the same cannot be said for the enemy. I did all I could for them, but I'm afraid some of them won't have long before they make the final trip to the Afterlife."

"And the enemy captain?"

"He's in custody, if you can believe it. The Fire Mage, on the other hand, took a bolt to the head. He was dead long before we boarded. I shall, of course, submit a full report to my own order and will be sure to inform you of its contents."

"Thank you," said Charlaine. "I look forward to reading it."

"Might I ask what we are to do with the prisoners? I was under the impression we'd be handing them over to the duke's men, but that doesn't seem to be the case."

"I'm sure that's our ultimate goal here, but I must speak with Captain Danica first."

"Very well," said Brother Aleksy. "I shall interrupt you no further."

Charlaine knocked on the door.

"Enter," came the reply. Danica sat at a small table, a man sitting across from her, with Sister Anya standing guard behind him.

"What do we have here?" asked Charlaine.

"This is Captain Taggert, former commander of the *Sea Wolf*." Danica turned her attention to her prisoner. "This is my superior, Commander Charlaine."

"Good day to you, Commander."

"The captain here has been most forthcoming with me," said Danica.

"Would you care to summarize?" asked Charlaine.

"He claims to be under the employ of an individual, although he knows not the fellow's name."

"Can he describe him?"

"Indeed I can," the man replied. "A tall fellow, clean-shaven, with neatly styled red hair."

"Are you sure?" asked Charlaine.

"We met on multiple occasions."

"Despite that, you don't know his name?"

"I never asked," said Captain Taggert, "nor was it offered."

"And he gave you your orders?"

"Not exactly. He would meet with Master Exius in private."

"Master Exius?" said Charlaine. "I assume that was your Fire Mage?"

"Indeed, and a more ruthless man you've never met."

"How do I know you're telling the truth?"

"I am to be hanged for piracy. I would clear my conscience before travelling to the Afterlife."

"You attacked innocent merchant ships."

"I am at war," the man replied, "or at least I was."

"With whom?"

The man clamped his mouth shut, but he clearly struggled with his thoughts. Unlike Captain Marwen, however, this was not duty but the face of fear.

"What are you afraid of, Captain?"

"I didn't start out as a pirate," he admitted.

"Care to explain how you ended up here?"

"I was a merchant by trade, and the *Sea Wolf* was primarily a coastal vessel. We sailed up and down the northern coast, buying and selling goods. It wasn't a rich life, but it was a busy one. All that changed when I chanced across another merchant in a tavern. He told me Halvaria paid top coin for certain goods."

"What kind of goods?"

"Things the wealthy might purchase, mostly expensive furniture and rare fabrics. I sank everything I had into filling the cargo hold and sailed west, hoping to make my fortune."

"I'm guessing things didn't go as planned."

"They most certainly did not," admitted Taggert. "They confiscated the ship as soon as we dropped anchor and then put my crew in irons. We languished in a dungeon for months before this woman came to us with an offer."

"A woman?" said Charlaine. "Can you be more specific?"

"She was a bit taller than you, with jet-black hair and a pale complexion. She was well-dressed too, although not quite what you would expect from a noble, if you get my meaning."

"I'm not sure I do."

"Well, the cut of her clothing was expensive, but she wore little in the way of jewellery other than a ring. Strange it was, too, glowing like it had a fire within it."

"Did she have a name?"

"Not that she gave me," Taggert said. "She did, however, give us a chance to redeem ourselves. All we had to do was travel to Reinwick and carry out some raids. At first, I balked. After all, the *Sea Wolf* wasn't exactly a ship of war."

"What did she say to that?"

"I still remember her words: 'It is now,' she said. Apparently, they'd made changes to her while we rotted away in the cells."

"Tell me more about these raids. They must have given you more detailed instructions at some point?"

"They did, eventually, but that came later."

"Go on," urged Charlaine. "Continue your story."

"We had little choice but to accept our new circumstances, for the only alternative was death. They took us back aboard the *Sea Wolf*, and that's when we met Master Exius. He was to be our new commander and would issue general orders, letting me and my crew carry out the details."

"And so you sailed back to Reinwick?"

"Not at first, no," he said. "We landed on one of the Five Sisters."

"Which one?"

"Patience."

"And what did you do there?"

"We began the construction of several huts. Exius wouldn't tell us what for, but they were clearly meant to hold many soldiers."

"Why would you say that?"

"The interiors were sparsely populated, much as you would expect with warriors."

"Did you transport soldiers on the *Sea Wolf*?"

"No, but other ships arrived some months later. Of course, by then, we'd built half a dozen of the huts. From that point on, we sailed around the region, picking on whatever stray ships we found. Exius said we were trying to establish the reputation of the *Sea Wolf*."

"Did you ever land and abduct people?"

Captain Taggert shifted uncomfortably. "That was not my doing."

"Meaning you participated or not?"

"We rendezvoused with a merchant ship, although how they knew our whereabouts is a mystery to me. Two dozen soldiers came across, but I use the term 'soldiers' loosely."

"Why is that?"

"They looked more like ruffians or vagabonds. I asked Exius if they were mercenaries, but he refused to answer. In any event, we dropped them off on the coast of Reinwick. When they came back closer to morning, they had prisoners."

Charlaine stared down at the man, trying to gauge the truth of his words. "I'm assuming you took them to Drumhollow."

He looked up in surprise. "You know about that?"

"We know a great deal more than that. I'm guessing that was a temporary staging area?"

"It was. We would carry out these raids and drop off prisoners. I'm assuming other ships would then pick them up from time to time and transport them up to Patience."

"To what end?"

"I don't know. I swear."

"What do you know?" demanded Charlaine. "You must have heard something?"

"Only rumours, but I wouldn't put much faith in them."

"Let me be the judge of that. Tell me what you heard."

"They built a training camp."

"Training for what?"

"Warriors, from what I heard," he said, "but it doesn't make sense, does it? You can't abduct people and expect them to fight for you."

"Were you the only ship carrying out these raids?"

"I have no proof, but I suspect not."

"Why would you say that?"

"On at least two occasions, we dropped off prisoners at Drumhollow, only to find more prisoners there than we expected."

"And did you only target Reinwick?"

"Not exclusively, but that was our assigned area."

"Just after we arrived here, your ship raided Korvoran Bay."

"Yes, Exius ordered that."

"To what end?"

"I suspect it was his own idea. The man thought very highly of himself, even had the notion he was invincible. He likely wanted to demonstrate his superiority."

"I hear that's a common trait amongst Fire Mages," offered Danica. "They say it comes from mastering the most dangerous element, or maybe it's simply because they have tremendous egos."

"I would agree," said Charlaine. "Although whether ego is the cause or effect is hard to determine."

"So?" said Danica. "You heard Taggert's story. What do we do now?"

"I think that's best discussed in private, don't you?"

"Take the prisoner below," ordered Danica.

They waited as Anya escorted the man from the room. Charlaine took the fellow's seat, her mind elsewhere.

"Well?" said Danica.

"I can see why you kept him aboard."

"What is it you're not telling me?"

"The description he gave," said Charlaine. "The one who seemed to be pulling the strings? I'm almost certain that's the Halvarian Ambassador, Lord Winfyre."

"What do we do about it?"

"I shall definitely bring it to the duke's attention, but there's little else to be done. We can't outright accuse him, especially when the only testimony we have is from a notorious pirate."

"In spite of that, you still believe him?"

"I do," said Charlaine. "Maybe it's my distrust of Halvarians, but I can't shake the feeling they're up to something, especially after what we went through in Calabria."

"You mean at Cunara?"

"Yes. They trained locals to fight for their empire there, and it sounds like they're doing the same thing here."

"But wouldn't the armies of the Petty Kingdoms outnumber them?"

"I'm sure there's more to this. While you were out sailing around the coast, I was told of rumours of insurrection."

"Here?" said Danica. "In Reinwick?"

"Indeed, yet we saw no sign of it when we investigated those who were abducted. It's likely the Halvarians are planning on stirring up trouble in the region."

"That would certainly fit their methods," said Danica, "but how would they accomplish that?"

"Last year, as you well know, Andover suffered a disastrous loss at the hands of Erlingen. Ever since, the balance of power has been upset.

Old issues are simmering, and it wouldn't take much for them to boil over."

"I'm still not following."

"Imagine you have a significant group of fanatical followers."

Danica laughed. "Careful, you just described the Temple Knights."

"I suppose I have, but the theory is the same. Let's imagine the Church wanted to start a war. They could take some of our knights, dress them in the clothing of, let's say, Erlingen, and send them raiding across the border into Andover."

"That could easily lead to war."

"Exactly!" said Charlaine. "Halvaria wants to destabilize the region. They'd like nothing better than to have the Petty Kingdoms at each other's throats."

"Do you believe they're preparing to invade like they did down South?"

"No. At least not here. Were they to sail an entire fleet to Reinwick, they'd simply unite all the surrounding kingdoms against them. That's in direct opposition to their plans."

"Does that mean they intend to invade from the west?"

"The Halvarian Empire expands by consuming more and more of its neighbours. Invasion from the west is inevitable."

"But not yet?" said Danica.

"No. I believe their intent here is to simply weaken the region. Once they do attack, these realms will be so worn down by strife, they'll lack the warriors to send against Halvaria."

"Many of the Petty Kingdoms are already at war with each other. Why not strike now?"

"I have a theory about that too, but I'm not convinced I have the whole thing figured out."

"Go on," urged Danica.

"What is the greatest threat to Halvaria?"

"I have no idea. They're the largest empire the Continent has ever known."

"Think along military lines."

"Temple Knights?"

"Precisely," said Charlaine. "The Cunars are seen as the premier fighting force in all the Petty Kingdoms. Our own order, and the Mathewites, for that matter, are highly trained and well-disciplined warriors as well. I'm sure they'd like nothing better than to be rid of us."

"You think they were behind Commander Hjordis?"

"I doubt even she would work with the Halvarians, at least not willingly, but you must admit her actions endangered the entire order."

"So she might have been influenced by others?"

"Potentially, and that means there's a strong possibility the Halvarians have people of their own inside the Church."

"If that's true," said Danica, "what can we do about it?"

"That's just it. I don't believe there's anything we can do except stay vigilant."

"Perhaps there IS more," said Danica. "We can pass on our suspicions to those we trust and let them spread the word. Our vigilance might very well make a difference somewhere down the road."

"I like it," said Charlaine. "I'll write to Giselle as soon as I get back to my office."

"You should also send word to Cordelia and the others. They may have moved on from Ilea."

"Yes, but I must be careful how I word things. You never know who might have access to our correspondence."

"I hadn't thought of that. I suppose all our letters get stored in the Antonine's archives, and then they'd be available to anyone who cares to look."

"You make a good point," said Charlaine. "It might be wiser to ship letters by private courier."

"That would be enormously expensive, wouldn't it?"

"Yes, with little guarantee of it ever reaching its destination. Ilea lies far to the South, but we might find a river merchant willing to take the message for a reasonable fee."

"It would need to be someone trustworthy."

Charlaine smiled. "Like a Dwarf?"

"You know a Dwarven merchant?"

"No, but now I think of it, our trusty smith is a member of the guild, and they have their own ways of getting messages delivered."

"Can we trust him?"

"Did you seriously just ask me if we could trust a member of the guild?"

"I'm the daughter of a fisherman. What do I know?"

Charlaine chuckled. "Yes, I'm sure we can trust them. And just to be clear, let's list everyone we can think of who needs to be informed, then we'll split up the names and write letters."

"When do you want them by?"

"There's no hurry. I doubt messages travel quickly at the best of times. The Halvarians haven't seen fit to provide us with a timetable, but we can assume the Church is safe for now."

"Why would you say that?"

"Well, for one thing, we uncovered a plot in the Antonine. The entire Church hierarchy will be looking closely at its members. Besides, we have little choice other than to think so, for all our actions depend on being able to alert our friends of the danger."

"And in the meantime, what do we do with Captain Taggert? You know if we hand him over, he'll be tortured and executed."

Charlaine thought things through. The *Sea Wolf*'s captain had confessed to committing acts of piracy, actions that carried a death sentence in any of the Petty Kingdoms. His story was compelling but didn't excuse his crimes. Did that, however, warrant his torture? The prospect revolted her, yet she knew to give him to the duke's men would accomplish precisely that.

"I have an idea," she said.

"Which is?"

"I assume the *Sea Wolf* attacked the *Valiant*?"

"It did."

"Then that means he attacked Church property. By all rights, he's our prisoner."

"We have no place to keep him."

Charlaine waved her hand. "Let me sort out the details. Keep him aboard for now. I'll go and pay a visit to Commander Salvatore."

"Will that save him?"

"No, but at least he'll get a trial."

"They'll still likely find him guilty."

"Agreed," said Charlaine, "but a sentence of death is not guaranteed, and even if it is, it'll be clean and quick, not lingering and painful as I'm sure it would be at the hands of the duke."

"His Grace won't like it," warned Danica.

"At this point, I couldn't care less."

33

THE DUKE

Summer 1098 SR

E nid led Charlaine through the estate. "His Grace is expecting you," the servant said.

"I assume he heard about the *Sea Wolf?*"

"There's been talk of little else. People have been coming and going all morning." Enid slowed her steps, looking left and right to confirm no one else was present. "Even Lord Winfyre is here."

"To do what?" asked Charlaine.

"I don't know for sure, but rumour is, he's pressuring the duke to execute the pirates."

"And if you don't mind me asking, how did His Grace take that?"

"The discussion was quite heated. The duke agrees with the ambassador but is hesitant to take action against the Church for fear of repercussions."

"I can well imagine."

"There's something else you should know," offered Enid. Just as she was about to say more, a door opened, and a startled Captain Marwen entered the hallway.

"Captain Charlaine?" he said. "This is a surprise. I didn't expect to see you here."

"Why ever not?" the knight replied. "Is it not my order's actions that have been the talk of the court this day?"

The good captain was not pleased. "You were supposed to order your captain to hand over the prisoners."

"I promised no such thing. I said I would talk to her, nothing more."

"And did you? Talk to her, I mean?"

"You know I did," said Charlaine. "You saw me enter her cabin."

"But the prisoners are still aboard!"

"Clearly, there's nothing wrong with your eyes, Captain. It must be your memory that's faulty."

"What's that supposed to mean?"

"The *Valiant* is Church property. Set foot on her deck without permission, and there will be severe repercussions."

"You don't frighten me."

"My intention is not to frighten but to inform. Had I wished otherwise, you would well know it. Now, unless you have specific information to impart, I shall take my leave of you. His Grace, the duke, is waiting."

The mention of the duke was more than enough to end any hope of discussing the matter further. Captain Marwen stomped off down the hallway.

Charlaine watched him go. "You'd think he was a Dwarf with all the noise he's making."

"Pardon?" said Enid.

"Never mind. You were about to say something else?"

"Yes." The woman glanced around again. "I saw Larissa Stormwind this morning."

"What of it? She's a court mage, is she not?"

"Yes, but she was in a deep discussion with Lord Winfyre."

"Could you hear what they spoke about?"

"No, but they were quite animated."

"Where was this?" asked Charlaine.

"Out in the gardens. I was taking the duchess some wine and happened to pass by them. They quieted as soon as I came in sight, and then the mage hurried off."

"I shall bear that in mind. Where is the ambassador right now?"

"Still out back, as far as I know. Shall I fetch him?"

"No, I'd prefer to meet with His Grace one-on-one."

They arrived at the door to the duke's study. Enid knocked, announcing Charlaine before letting her in.

The Temple Knight walked into the room, trying to judge the duke's mood as he sat in an oversized chair, his feet up on a stool while nursing a goblet of wine.

"Ah, there she is," said the duke. "The cause of all our problems."

"Hardly the cause," noted Charlaine. "It was not I who led a pirate ship."

"True, but it is the knights under your command who are refusing to hand over the criminals."

"Those criminals committed crimes against the Church, and as such, are required to face a tribunal."

"That is MY responsibility!" shouted Lord Wilfhelm. "Nay, my right!"

"It might interest you to know that under interrogation, we made some additional discoveries."

Duke Brondecker looked surprised. "Oh? What types of discoveries?"

"We managed to verify the presence of a Halvarian outpost on Reinwick land."

"What? Are you positive?"

"As sure as we can be. We have only to send a ship to confirm the details. On that note, I hoped you might fund an expedition. After all, it is your land they're occupying."

"So you say. Who told you all this?"

"The captain of the *Sea Wolf*."

"He's lying. He'd say anything to save his neck from the hangman's noose."

"It's a lie easily dispelled, Your Grace, would you but order ships to investigate."

"I shall not send a single ship off on the word of a confessed criminal."

"And if we confirm the existence of these Halvarians?"

She witnessed panic spreading across the duke's face. "What would you have me do? Go to war with Halvaria? That would be tantamount to suicide!"

"And so you'll just let them have your land?"

"What we don't know can't hurt us."

"Except, in this case, we DO know, and it CAN hurt us. You are putting your entire duchy in peril, Your Grace. You must at least see that?"

"I'm sure the Halvarian's presence can be explained easily enough, or maybe they didn't realize we claim those islands as our own? In any case, it matters little. We've had the Five Sisters for decades and done nothing with them. In fact, I'm told the entire region is nothing but unnavigable waters with a rough coastline. If they're so inclined to occupy the place, I say let them have it. Better them than us."

Charlaine couldn't believe it. She came here expecting the duke to be concerned about the infringement of his border, but for him to show utter contempt for even investigating made the situation far worse than her wildest imaginings.

"Will you at least talk to the ambassador?" she asked.

"I shall," said His Grace. "Although I'm not sure what his response will be." He took an absent sip of his wine, then stared at it as he swirled the remains around his cup. "I imagine he will make an apology of sorts and insist this is merely a misunderstanding."

"And you will accept that?"

"Of course. The Halvarians are a cultured race, Captain Charlaine, not a bunch of savages. Now, if you told me Orcs were on those islands... well, that would be far different."

"So you would send ships to fight off Orcs, but none to see off a foreign invader?"

"Come now, let's not blow this whole thing out of proportion."

For perhaps the first time in her life, Charlaine could think of nothing to say. If the ruler of a Petty Kingdom wasn't willing to defend his own land, what could they expect when Halvaria came crashing over the borders? She knew, purely from a strategic point of view, the only thing holding back invasion was the idea that the Petty Kingdoms would unite to fight off the empire. To now see otherwise was a blow to the very foundation that had formed foreign policy for centuries.

The duke, mistaking Charlaine's silence for acquiescence, smiled. "Now, enough of this nonsense. Hand over the prisoners, and we shall put this whole matter behind us."

This was getting her nowhere. Rather than argue the point, Charlaine decided on another approach. "To fulfill your wishes, Your Grace, I must consult with Father Salvatore. He is, after all, the ranking Temple Knight in these parts."

The duke appeared mollified. "Then get on with it before matters get worse."

"May I beg my leave of you?" she asked.

"Yes, yes. Now, shoo, and sort things out with your superior."

She bowed deeply, pleased with herself. Although she had failed to get him to intervene, she at least bought some time. She turned and left, her mind in a whirlwind of thoughts.

"You want to do what?" Father Salvatore looked ready to burst. With his red face, Charlaine feared his heart couldn't take the strain.

"I'm proposing a Church expedition," she repeated, "to investigate these rumours."

"You're asking a lot, with so little to go on."

"Of that, I'm fully aware, but someone has to take action, and the duke is too scared of the Halvarians to raise a finger."

The commander sat, taking a sip of wine to try to calm his nerves. Even so, his hand shook, a clear sign of his distress.

"I do not make this suggestion lightly," she continued, "but the presence of a Halvarian force so close to the Continent, even a small one, is not something to ignore."

Father Salvatore nodded his head. "Yes, you're right, of course. Tell me, Captain, how many Temple Knights are you proposing we send?"

"As many as we can muster. The *Valiant* and *Vigilant* will escort any cogs we can hire to transport the rest of the expedition."

"The *Vigilant?*"

"Yes," said Charlaine. "The captured *Sea Wolf*. We intend to take it into service, but the name has been tarnished, so we thought it best to go with *Vigilant.*"

"I suppose it's as good a name as any. Who will command this vessel?"

"Captain Danica has suggested Sister Grazynia. She's showed great promise."

"And you will approve of this assignment?"

"I completely support Captain Danica's decision."

"This ship," said Salvatore, "the *Vigilant*. How large is it?"

"Similar in size to the *Valiant.*"

"I assume it will hold a comparable complement?"

"It will," said Charlaine. "Why? What are you thinking?"

"Brother Alexy has written, telling me of his experiences, and it's clear his presence was received warmly. I would like to see my order supply each and every ship with a lay brother capable of tending to the wounded."

"I'm sure Captain Danica would agree."

"Good," said the Mathewite. "Now, as to details, who would command this endeavour?"

"You are the most senior Temple Knight in these parts, Father."

"Yes, well, that may be, but I'm smart enough to know this is well beyond my capabilities. In any case, I'll be needed here to smooth out problems with His Grace, the duke. I should think, under the circumstances, that you yourself are best qualified for the task at hand."

"And Captain Waleed?"

"You'll need to take him along if you intend to use the Cunars, but I'll be sure to impress upon him you are in overall command. How many Temple Knights will you take?"

"For the Agneses, I'll leave behind only a skeleton staff. As I said, I hoped to supplement my forces with Cunars and Mathewites, providing any can be spared."

"I shall do what I can with my own order, though I doubt that would exceed twenty. I expect Waleed will provide a similar number. I don't suppose that many knights will fit aboard the two ships we have?"

"No, and in any case, we might need the *Valiant* and *Vigilant* to keep enemy warships at bay. We could hardly do that with that many knights embarked."

"Are they to take horses?"

"I hadn't considered that. It would push up the cost of transportation."

"What if we only mounted some of them," suggested Father Salvatore, "and left the rest on foot?"

"I fear the terrain won't be friendly to mounted troops."

"Still, even a handful could prove useful, and I doubt the enemy would have them, particularly if they sailed all the way from Halvaria."

"You make a good point. How about a dozen horses?"

"Fair enough. So we have a dozen horses and nearly seventy Temple Knights."

"Closer to one hundred," corrected Charlaine, "assuming your numbers are accurate. How many ships do you think we would need?"

"That largely depends on what's available. There are some large cogs in the harbour, but I'm afraid those belong to the duke. We will need to rely on hiring merchant vessels."

"Are you sure we can afford that?"

"Let me worry about that," said Father Salvatore. "You confer with Sister Danica, and see if you can find suitable vessels for this enterprise."

"But the cost?"

"My order has access to all manner of funds. If you recall, we held some for the purchase of your fleet."

"Yes, but that wasn't yours to spend."

"Ah, but that's where you're wrong. Those who engage in such transactions with the Temple Knights of Saint Mathew are informed that in emergencies, the order is permitted to draw upon those funds."

"So you can keep it all?"

"No, it's more of a loan but will suit our purposes. Once we defeat this menace, the Church will, no doubt, release funds to replenish our supply."

"I don't want to land you in trouble," said Charlaine.

"And you're not. I assure you. Now, there is a final matter or two that requires some thought."

"Oh? Have I missed something?"

He smiled. "Humble to a fault. I shall, as senior commander in this region, brevet you the rank of commander. It's only temporary, good for the duration of the expedition, but will ensure there's no arguing over who's in charge. I assume you would like Sister Danica to command the fleet?"

"That's the purpose behind her assignment here."

"She's terribly young. Why, she can't be more than seventeen? Do you think she's up to it?"

"She's nineteen," said Charlaine, "and as for her ability, I have no doubt she's the best person for the job."

"Well then, you best get going. We both have lots of work to do."

"When would you suggest we sail?"

"That depends entirely on what ships you hire. Which reminds me, we'll also need ships to bring supplies, especially food. Temple Knights can be ready to march on a moment's notice, but sending an expedition to a remote island is a far cry from marching out of the city."

Barbek Stoutarm leaned back and crossed his arms. "Can't be done," he declared. "There's not enough time. And to be honest, I don't even know if the *Vigilant* has the deck space to mount an arbalest."

"That's unfortunate," said Danica. "I hoped we'd have it to use against the enemy ships."

"I might be able to rig up something temporarily, say a rudimentary ballista, but it wouldn't have anywhere near the versatility of an arbalest and would have a fixed mount."

"Why didn't you say so?"

The Dwarf grimaced. "I don't enjoy doing shoddy work, and a ballista is just so... crude."

"I would be happy to let you replace it with something better at a later date," said Danica.

"Hmmm. You'd only be able to loose off regular bolts, mind you, nothing like the shredders you found so useful against the *Sea Wolf*."

"I can accept that."

"In that case," said Barbek, "I'll come out to the *Vigilant* this very afternoon and see what I can do."

"How much time would it take, do you think?"

"A day, maybe two. I have most of what I need back at my workshop, but it means I must put aside my current work."

"I shall inform Captain Charlaine of that. I'm sure she'll understand."

"The bigger issue is training your knights to operate the thing. It's a bit more complex than a crossbow."

"How long would that take?"

"A day? But we couldn't even begin the training until I finished building it. I'm afraid it will impact the timing of your expedition as well."

"I doubt that will be an issue. As of this morning, we've hired the ships we need, but it's going to take at least a week to prepare them."

"What's there to get ready?" asked the Dwarf.

"We're taking nearly a hundred knights on a naval expedition, not to mention horses. That requires a lot of food as well as somewhere to sleep. Then once we land, we must set up a camp from which to operate."

"But you have what you need for that, don't you? You're all fighting orders."

"Yes," said Danica, "but the knights hereabouts haven't been on campaign for some time. If the other orders are anything like the Agneses, they'll need to replace old, worn-out tents with something a little newer."

"Well, at least their weapons are in good order. How are you going to transport the horses?"

"We hired on the *Barlowe*, the ship we met on our first outing as the *Valiant*."

"Is it a large ship?"

"Not particularly, but it has a spacious hold. Most of the others we examined wouldn't let a person stand up straight, let alone allow room for a dozen horses."

"Just how many ships are you planning to take?"

"Aside from *Valiant* and *Vigilant*, five. Why?"

"That's an awful lot to organize. You'll need help."

"What are you suggesting?" asked Danica.

"It's only that it seems to me, with most of your Temple Knights off with this fleet of yours, you'll need someone to look after their weapons and armour."

"Are you asking permission to accompany us?"

"Well, naturally, I only ask over concern for your equipment."

"You're avoiding the question. Do you want to come with us or not?"

"I do," said the Dwarf. "Very much so!"

"I didn't expect such fervour."

"I love my work, I really do, but it's nice to get out every now and again. And my presence would also solve another problem."

"Which is?"

"I could operate the ballista for you."

"I thought you said it would only take a day to train a crew."

"Yes, but there's a big difference between training someone and making them experts. And by taking me, the *Vigilant* will get an arbalest."

"It will?"

"Yes, I never go adventuring without it. Mind you, it's not as large as the one mounted on the *Valiant*."

"Adventuring," said Danica, mulling over the word. "An interesting turn of phrase."

"What would you call it?"

"A military expedition."

THE EXPEDITION

Summer 1098 SR

C harlaine stepped over to the railing, staring out. "A stirring sight," she said. Spread out to starboard was their modest fleet. The ships were a motley bunch, usually sailing under a variety of flags, but today they flew under a different pennant, that of the Holy Fleet.

Beyond the merchant ships, and slightly to the rear, sat the *Vigilant*, keeping an ever-watchful eye, lest any of the ships find themselves in trouble.

Charlaine looked skyward. "The weather is clear. I assume that means we'll make good time?"

"Looks can be deceiving," replied Danica. "Up here, the wind can shift unexpectedly, and once we're amongst the Five Sisters, we'll need to watch for strange currents."

"I hope we find what we're looking for, or else we just wasted a lot of the Church's funds."

"Don't worry, we will."

"How can you be so sure?"

Danica met her gaze. "I trust your instincts."

Charlaine looked back out at the ships. "You belong here," she said. "You'll make a great admiral one day."

"Admiral? Let's not get too carried away. I only just made captain."

"Yes, but you're already a commander."

"For now, but I wouldn't put it past the Church to send someone more qualified to take over the fleet now we proved the need for it."

"The fleet belongs to Saint Agnes. Besides, there IS no one more qualified." She swept her hand out to sea. "All of this is your doing, Danica. None of it would be possible without you." Charlaine laughed as her eyes took in the *Vigilant* off in the distance. "You've only been in command for a few months, and you already doubled the fleet. Keep this up, and you'll soon outnumber the Holy Fleet in Corassus."

"I very much doubt that." Danica's eyes wandered to a large cog struggling in the wind.

"Problem?" said Charlaine.

"It's the *Rose*. She isn't a good sailer even at the best of times, but I fear this wind will be the death of her."

"Why is that?"

"She's a poor design," explained Danica. "Note how the mainmast is set farther back than the others."

"And that makes her a poor design?"

"That and a few other things. Her captain says she was built in Ruzhina."

"It's definitely an unusual design."

"Yes, it is, isn't it? It's almost as if it's missing another mast. The hull certainly looks long enough for it."

"You should become a ship architect," said Charlaine. "You seem to have a knack for it."

"I'm much happier at sea."

A warning shout from the bow caught their attention, and they both turned to spot a distant sail off to the northwest.

"Trouble?" said Charlaine. "We only just left Korvoran. It can't possibly be Halvarians, can it?"

"I doubt it. It's most likely a merchant, but we better investigate." Danica turned once more, seeking out Zivka. "Hoist the blue flag," she ordered.

"What does that do?" asked Charlaine.

"It tells everyone we're temporarily leaving the fleet."

"Will the merchant captains understand that?"

"Not likely, but the *Vigilant* will. The rest will keep heading straight for the Five Sisters."

Orders were given, and then the *Valiant* turned to port. The distant sail grew closer until they could make out the ship itself, hugging the coast, the typical sign of a trader. Yet when the Temple ship drew nearer, the vessel suddenly began making a wide turn to the north.

"He looks like he's trying to evade us," noted Danica.

"Might he think us pirates?"

"Flying a Temple flag? I doubt it."

"What if she's a pirate herself?"

"It's possible, I suppose, although I'm not sure why she's so close to shore. In any event, she seems to be turning around, so there's little chance of catching her now." Danica called out to the tillerman, and the *Valiant* adjusted its course. "We'll parallel the fleet for a while, just to make sure."

By late afternoon, the unidentified ship had vanished, disappearing over the horizon. Danica ordered the *Valiant* back to the fleet, taking up a position in the lead. The rest of the vessels reduced sail to keep pace with the *Rose*. Their fleet commander understood the need for such a move but didn't like it.

"It makes us vulnerable," Danica said. "If the Halvarians decide to attack us now, we'll be unable to manoeuvre."

"Can't you just increase sail?" said Charlaine.

"We could, but the fleet would scatter, making things even worse. It's hard to protect ships that move at different speeds."

Charlaine watched as one of the ships turned directly towards them, a merchant named the *Monarch*. "Something's wrong," she warned.

When the *Monarch* kept coming, Danica's crew exploded into action. The *Valiant* veered off to port as the merchant's bow scraped past. Aboard the little trader, the crew quickly reduced sail.

"Trouble with their rudder by the look of it," said Danica. "We'll circle back, and see if we can be of any help."

The *Monarch* ground to a halt. Without a full sail, the vessel was tossed around, with some of the waves occasionally washing across its deck.

The *Valiant* made a turn, then fought against the wind to make its way back to the stricken vessel. On the merchant's deck, they saw some men clustered together at the stern.

"I suspect they have a broken tiller," said Danica. "They'll need to fashion a new one."

"How long will that take?"

In answer, Danica looked skyward. "Some time yet, but darkness will soon fall, and that will slow things down even more."

"And the rest of the fleet?"

"They'll sail on and wait for us at the Beacon."

"Will they keep going in the dark?"

"That depends on the weather. So long as the sea is calm, yes, but if the waves pick up, they'll likely move in closer to shore and drop anchor."

"I didn't think the shore was that close," said Charlaine.

"It lies just over the horizon there." Danica pointed to the west. "Assuming our course is correct, that is."

"And what will we do in the meantime?"

"Try to maintain our position here. Were we in shallower waters, I'd drop anchor, but the water this far off the coast is likely too deep for such things."

They both stared at the *Monarch*, silently willing the crew to speed repairs and let them get on their way. Between the two ships, a shadow in the water caught Charlaine's attention. At first, she thought it a trick of her eyes, a discolouration of the water caused by the sun, but then it moved.

"I see something," she called out. "There, just behind the *Monarch*, a dark shape, and it's moving."

The shadow drew closer to the merchant ship, then changed course, heading for the *Valiant*. Danica watched with intense interest, yet outwardly she appeared calm.

"Aren't you going to do anything?" asked Charlaine

"Like what? Anything that size is likely to be impervious to our crossbows."

"What about the arbalest?"

"It can't target something that low in the water. The *Valiant*'s sides would get in the way."

"So we just wait?"

"That's all we can do."

The shadow got uncomfortably close before a great grey creature emerged from the sea, almost as if the tide was washing off a sandbank. Then an explosion of water thrust into the air, giving off a strange noise.

"It's a whale," said Danica, a smile upon her face. "This is a good sign."

"What's a whale?"

"An immense creature that lives deep in the water, coming to the surface to breathe, much like us."

"That thing is larger than any ship I've ever seen," said Charlaine.

"Only serpents are bigger. Legends say Akosia created the whales to keep her deep waters safe."

"And the shallow waters?"

"For those, she created the seals. You remember—we saw one down in Ilea."

"Oh yes, it scared Aurelia, if I recall." Charlaine grew sombre. "Poor Aurelia. She was so frightened of the water, and in the end, it claimed her."

"The old religion says she lives on in the underwater halls of Akosia. It's the fate of all who perish at sea. Of course, we choose to believe she's gone to the Afterlife, but I sometimes wonder if the two are not one and the same."

"You think the Afterlife is underwater?"

"I believe once a person dies, air and water make no difference. A dead person doesn't breathe after all."

"It is comforting," said Charlaine. "The very thought that we live on after our time here is done makes us feel everything in life is worthwhile."

"You mean we earn our place in the Afterlife?"

The whale rolled over, exposing a gigantic flipper that smacked the water before the behemoth dove, its flukes coming to the surface as it disappeared into the inky depths.

"I wonder," said Danica. "Do whales go to the Afterlife? I should like to think they do."

"I suppose that depends on whether or not they have souls. Then again, I'm no theologian."

Danica laughed. "We do seem to have the strangest conversations."

"That's what friends do. Who else can we talk to about such things?"

"You make a valid point. I'm sure Commander Salvatore would have a fit if he heard us talking about whales having souls."

Charlaine looked at the bubbles created by the whale's dive. "You were saying a whale is a good sign?"

"Yes. As I said, they're Akosia's guardians, but more to the point, they're said to be the serpent's deadliest enemy."

"Are you telling me sea serpents actually exist? You don't believe that old fisherman's tale, do you?"

"Can you honestly tell me, after seeing a whale, that other large creatures can't exist in the sea?"

"Yes, but a serpent?"

"Let me ask you this," said Danica. "Are dragons real?"

"Of course, we have proof of that. It's a well-documented fact that the Kurathian princes have them."

"But you've never seen one, have you?"

"No, but that doesn't mean they're not real."

"Precisely," said Danica, a smug look upon her face.

"I'll give you that one. Are you sure you're only nineteen because you seemed to have turned into the village elder somewhere along the way. I, on the other hand, am completely out of my element."

"That's because your expertise lies on land. I was born for this, remember? You said so yourself."

The *Valiant* came to rest some hundred yards from the *Monarch*. Danica boarded a skiff with several of her crew and rowed over to the stricken vessel. Charlaine could only watch as the sun sank slowly in the west, the horizon glowing red as it disappeared, plunging the area into darkness. Small lights flickered to life aboard the *Monarch* while the skiff rowed around to the stern, presumably to look at the rudder. Time seemed to drag on interminably, and Charlaine worried something had gone terribly wrong.

She needn't have worried, for not long later, the skiff reappeared, heading directly for the *Valiant*. Then noises erupted from the *Monarch*, and Charlaine saw additional lights flickering on deck. She suspected they were raising sail, although she could see nothing in the darkness. Sure enough, the ship began inching forward as the wind filled canvas.

Danica climbed back onto the *Valiant's* deck. "Did you miss me?" she asked.

Charlaine laughed. "We'd best get moving if you don't want to lose sight of the *Monarch*."

The early morning sun revealed an open sea, for the two ships had become separated at some point in the night. Danica now struggled with her conscience. Should she return to the rest of the fleet and keep it safe or search for the *Monarch*?

Zivka appeared at her side. "We spotted a sail, Captain."

"The *Monarch*?"

"No, someone else. I suspect it may be the ship we saw yesterday."

"What direction?"

"West, towards land."

"Set an intercept course. They may have word of our missing ship."

"Aye, Captain."

The wind shifted and now came from the southwest, while the unknown ship headed north, running roughly parallel to the coast of Reinwick.

"She's a fast one," said Zivka.

"Not nearly as fast as us with this wind."

They watched as the *Valiant* closed the distance. A chase at sea is a long, drawn-out affair, so it was almost noon by the time they were close enough to make out the ship's name.

"The *Water Drake*," said Danica. "Can't say I recognize the name."

"Nor I," said Zivka. "Should we alert Commander Charlaine?"

"Yes, and tell the other knights to don their armour, just in case."

"You're expecting a fight?"

"Expecting? No, but I'd prefer to have them dress for nothing rather than be surprised."

"Another sail!" called out Sister Vivian. "It must be the *Monarch*."

The new sighting was to the north and farther inshore. The *Water Drake*, seeing the *Monarch*, altered course, heading straight for the hapless ship.

"Perhaps they're going to assist?"

"I somehow doubt that," said Danica. She looked up at the *Valiant's* sail. "Can't we get any more speed out of that?" She knew the answer even before the words were done. "Never mind," she snapped as a sense of hopelessness began to sink in. The *Water Drake* would make contact with the *Monarch* long before Danica's ship could intervene.

Charlaine appeared on deck, dressed for battle. "What have we got?" she asked.

"See for yourself," replied Danica.

"Who is that?"

"We're not entirely sure. The ship is the *Water Drake*, but we don't know who commands it, or who's aboard."

"What flag does she fly?"

"That's just it; she doesn't. I wouldn't mind so much if she flew a pirate's flag, but this is something else entirely."

They watched, helpless, as the two ships neared each other, then the *Monarch* made a sudden turn to starboard, cutting across the *Water Drake's* bow.

"What are they doing?" said Charlaine.

"Captain Edgerton is trying to bring his ship closer to us."

The water around the *Monarch's* bow looked like it was foaming, and then the vessel lurched to a halt.

"What in the name of the Saints?" shouted Danica.

"The water froze," said Charlaine. "That ship, the *Water Drake*—it has a mage!"

"Load the arbalest and ready crossbows. Let's see if we can get within range, shall we?"

Charlaine noted a flash of light as the sun reflected off the shards of ice flying towards the immobile merchant. The spell was aimed high, tearing holes into the *Monarch's* sails. Meanwhile, the *Water Drake* turned, allowing the sides of the two ships to bump into each other.

"Why aren't they boarding?" said Danica. "They've got them exactly where they want them."

"That's not their objective. They're trying to cripple the ship, not capture it."

"Why would they do that?"

"Simple," said Charlaine. "To sabotage our expedition."

"By damaging a single ship?"

"Capturing it would require boarding, and let's face it, it isn't exactly a secret there are Temple Knights aboard."

"But that would mean they know all about the expedition. Who is it?"

"I'll give you one guess," said Charlaine. "How many people do you know who can use Water Magic?"

"Are you suggesting that it's Larissa Stormwind?"

"I doubt we'll get close enough to find out for sure. Look, they're pulling away."

The *Water Drake* sails filled, but something else was happening, for the water along the vessel's side circled itself, creating a vortex that pushed the ship forward.

"Unless I miss my guess, that's another spell," said Charlaine.

"Let's chase this thing down and finish them off."

"We can't. We must save the *Monarch*."

"And let our enemy get away?"

"Don't worry," said Charlaine. "I'm sure it's not the last we'll see of them. In the meantime, we need to get aboard the *Monarch* and make sure every-thing is all right. I hate to leave and then find out later their hull has been breached."

Grazynia stood at the railing as the *Vigilant* bobbed up and down on the waves. Off to the north, a bright light identified the Beacon, shining out like the sun cresting the horizon even in the early morning light.

They'd arrived two days ago, expecting to find the *Valiant*. Instead, only an empty sea awaited. Fortunately, Captain Danica's written instructions were clear. The flotilla was to remain at the Beacon for a maximum of two days before taking action to continue. The letter mollified the Cunar captain, who had tried taking command of the expedition in the absence of Commander Charlaine, but she knew it wouldn't last. If Captain Danica didn't find her way here today, events would quickly spiral out of her control.

"Do you think they're all right?"

Grazynia, startled out of her thoughts, turned to see the Dwarven smith. "Ah, Master Barbek. I didn't expect you up on deck."

"Why's that?"

"Up till now, you spent most of your time below."

"I can't help it if my stomach doesn't like the sea."

"And now?"

"It seems to have settled somewhat," he said. "Did I hear you arguing with that Cunar captain earlier?"

"It wasn't so much arguing as him berating me for my lack of leadership."

"I've seen his type before," noted the Dwarf. "Always seeking to denigrate others." He looked south, squinting. "Tell me, are my eyes deceiving me, or is that a pair of ships I see?"

Grazynia followed his gaze, a smile breaking out. "It is. By the Saints, they found us!"

35

PURSUIT

Summer 1098 SR

After a brief holdover to make repairs to the *Monarch*, the fleet sailed eastward, where the island of Providence was soon spotted. The ships turned north, skirting around the tip to proceed along its northern coast. According to Captain Taggert, Patience should lie directly north, but with no accurate charts, sailing in that direction was out of the question.

Instead, Danica hugged the shore as she had charted this area in her search for the *Sea Wolf*, so she knew what to expect. Here, with relatively shallow waters to anchor in, the fleet could rest in safety. They also took the time to send a small group inland to fetch fresh water.

They continued on the next day, Danica paying particular attention to her charts. When the coast of Constance appeared on the horizon, they turned north. Around the shores of this island they'd captured the *Sea Wolf*, so the fleet stayed on the alert, not wanting to tempt an enemy raider.

Continuing north, they skirted the western end of Constance, then headed straight into the open sea, hoping to soon sight Patience. The hope was realized when the appearance of a rugged coast with trees growing right up to the water's edge crested the horizon. The thick forestation allowed them to see very little of the great island's interior, so they anchored while the *Valiant* and *Vigilant* made short trips in either direction, trying to get the lay of the land.

Evening saw the two ships return, along with news of what they'd found. The leaders gathered in the captain's cabin aboard the *Valiant* to discuss their options.

"Let's start with what do we know," said Charlaine. "The coast here runs to the northeast and southwest. That would seem to indicate we are on the east side of Patience."

"In that case," offered Captain Waleed, "the most logical course of action would be to follow the shoreline northward until we discover the Halvarians."

Grazynia shook her head. "But they're on the north shore. That could be days of sailing, and without accurate knowledge of their whereabouts, we could easily stumble into them."

"Have you a better option?"

"I say we leave the fleet here, at least for the time being. Then, we send the *Valiant* and *Vigilant* north to map out the area. With any luck, they'll find the approach to the north shore and locate our target."

"I don't like it," said Danica. "It leaves the fleet exposed."

"How?" asked the Cunar.

"If I were the Halvarian commander, I'd have warships patrolling the coast. I know we haven't seen them as yet, but that doesn't mean they're not out there. We can't afford to leave our fleet undefended."

"What about landing our troops? They'd be safe from attack on shore."

"But the ships wouldn't. Lose those transports, and you'd be marooned. There's also the matter of our location. We quite literally have no idea where this enemy encampment is. For all we know, it could be fifty miles away. Saints alive, even if we did know, we'd still need to slog our way through this thick forest. Our best option is to leave everyone aboard ship. We'll send the *Valiant* north following the coast until we discover their whereabouts."

"When will you sail?" asked Charlaine.

"At first light. I don't want to chance unknown waters in the dark."

"And when you find them?"

"That largely depends on what we discover. I'm hoping to withdraw before they have time to react."

"And if they see you?"

"Then we'll lead them farther out to sea. I know it's not a perfect plan, but there's little else we can do. *Vigilant* will remain here to protect the rest of the fleet."

Morning brought a thick mist. Charlaine, standing at the bow of the *Valiant*, could barely make out the ship's mast. Not only did it diminish her line of sight, but even sound was dampened, creating an eerie feeling that put the knight's senses on high alert. A shadowy figure emerged from the mist, coalescing into the familiar form of Danica.

"It looks like we're not going anywhere quite yet," said the raven-haired knight. "I don't believe I've ever seen a fog this thick. Have you?"

"We got little fog back in Malburg." Charlaine looked over the railing, peering down at the water. "At least the sea is calm."

"Too calm," said Danica. "It makes my skin crawl."

"I would've thought you'd find it peaceful."

"The deepest waters run the quietest."

"Meaning?"

"This area is unnatural. Call it superstition, if you like, but I see this as a bad omen."

"I never took you for the superstitious type."

"Nor would I consider myself as such until now. I suppose being around the water so much has taken me back to my childhood."

"But we were around water all the time down in Ilea," said Charlaine.

"True, but that was the clear blue waters of the Shimmering Sea, not the cold, dark sea we have here."

"How long will this fog last?"

"The sun should be burning it off even as we speak."

Charlaine's eyes swivelled to the mainmast. Already she could make out details that had eluded her moments before.

"I see a ship," noted Danica. "I think it's the *Rose*." She waved, receiving a similar action in reply. "Looks like we won't need to wait too long after all."

As the mist burned off, the other ships became visible. Charlaine watched them appear, one by one, as if summoned by magic. It soon became a game, with each knight struggling to identify a ship before the other could. It all came screeching to a halt as their eyes befell an extra vessel in amongst the fleet. Judging by the people on deck, they seemed to be as surprised as everyone else.

"That's the *Water Drake*!" shouted Charlaine. "How did they find us?"

"By the Saints!" yelled Danica. The crew was called out, the knights ordered into their armour, and the deck was suddenly crowded with everyone preparing to meet the enemy.

"Take up the anchor," shouted Danica, "and get that sail unfurled."

The *Water Drake* made a wide turn, passing between the *Barlowe* and the *Peri*. Charlaine spotted a woman aboard the enemy vessel waving her arms around. There could be no doubt it was Larissa Stormwind, and her movements were the beginning of a spell. Shards of ice flew from her fingertips to strike the *Peri's* yardarm, where it joined the mainmast, the wood shattering with the impact. Had it not been for the rigging, the heavy timber would have dropped to the deck, crushing the crew, but luckily the ropes slowed the descent enough for them to get out of the way.

Charlaine was tempted to load a crossbow, but the *Water Drake* would soon be out of range. Instead, she watched, transfixed, as Larissa cast another spell. This time, a thick mist appeared, blanketing the vessel in a protective cocoon.

The *Valiant* slowly crept forward, the still air hindering their efforts. The *Water Drake*, meanwhile, continued on, unhampered by the lack of wind.

"How is she doing that?" asked Charlaine.

"Magic," said Danica.

"And here I thought Water Mages useless."

"Useless? Far from it. Did you notice the swirling water around the sides of the *Water Drake*?"

"No. I was too busy watching their mage. It's Larissa Stormwind, you know."

"Isn't she the court mage?"

"She is," said Charlaine, "but it appears she's working for the enemy."

"I'd like to know how they found us."

"Magic? Or maybe just dumb luck. Chances are, she knew of our plan and has likely been following in our wake."

"If that's the case, why didn't we see them?"

"Can Water Mages talk to fish?"

"I don't know," said Danica. "I didn't think fish talked."

"They don't." This remark came from the lips of Sister Anya, "but a porpoise does."

"A porpoise?" said Charlaine. "What's that?"

"They're like a whale, only much smaller," explained Danica. "People say they're a good omen."

"Not if they're giving away our position."

"Come now, you can't blame those poor creatures for doing that. It's not as if they meant us any harm. You might even say that's not their porpoise." She grinned.

"I can't believe you just said that."

"We might as well laugh at it. There's little else we can do at this point. With no actual wind, we're not going anywhere."

The *Water Drake* quickly withdrew, or at least the cloud of mist surrounding it did, for that was all they could see of the enemy ship.

"What do we do now?" said Charlaine.

"They know of our location. Our only option is to change our plans. They'll expect us to take the shortest route to their base."

"But we don't know where that is?"

"True," said Danica, "but they don't know that. They're likely assuming we know the exact location of their camp."

"Then we're close?"

"Possibly, perhaps even dangerously so, but now that the *Water Drake* knows our position, they'll likely send ships after us."

"Then we need to do the unexpected," said Charlaine. "We sail in the other direction and hope to come upon them from the rear."

"Good idea."

Anya wore a look of confusion. "But won't they come after us?"

"Let's pray not," said Danica. "I'm hoping they'll assume we fled after being discovered. It might even lead them south, back to the rest of the Five Sisters. Let them waste time there."

"When do we sail?" asked Charlaine.

"As soon as this wind picks up. Until then, we'll send the skiff out to pass the word to the others."

The sun was close to its zenith by the time the ships resumed their journey. The *Vigilant* led the way, following the coast in a southerly direction. The Valiant brought up the rear, ready to deal with any pursuit should the need arise.

In the end, their caution proved unnecessary, for there were no further sightings of the *Water Drake*. The enemy vessel was likely making all speed for the Halvarian camp, their intent to warn them of the expedition, but even that was mere speculation. In truth, they could only guess at the empire's plan.

It didn't take long to find the southern shore of Patience, and the fleet soon turned in a northerly direction once more. The shoreline remained rocky, leading to much speculation regarding the ease of landing knights.

Two days later, they passed what would turn out to be the island's westernmost portion. From now on, the land sloped to the northeast, this time on their starboard side. The vegetation thinned here, the coastline showing signs of small beaches rather than outcroppings of trees. Danica suggested this was due to the wind and prevailing currents in the region, but Charlaine had her doubts.

Eventually, the trees began to change. Instead of the thick pine forests, they'd thus far sighted, oak trees made an appearance.

"There," said Charlaine, pointing. "Beyond those trees, do you see it?"

"Yes," said Danica. "It looks like a mountain."

"More like a big hill. If we can get some people up there, we might have a better idea of the surrounding countryside."

"We'll drop anchor and send a small group ashore. Do you want to go with them?"

"Yes. I'm eager to see the area first-hand."

They lowered the skiff and rowed ashore, where Sister Marlena waited along with two Mathewites.

"This is Brother Klavel," said the aide. "While this"—she indicated a rather short, plump individual—"is Brother Leonov. He has some experience with traversing this type of terrain."

"A woodsman?" asked Charlaine.

"No, a hunter," the man replied, "but the skill set is not too dissimilar." He gazed off at the nearby trees. "There's a path over there that seems to take us in the right direction. Would you care to lead?"

"I shall leave that in your capable hands, Brother Leonov."

They left the beach, following a route taking them almost directly east. Not so much a path as bare spaces between trees, resulting in an uneven stroll, and several times Charlaine tripped on roots that poked through the surface. Marlena, for her part, took things in stride, walking quietly while scanning the surrounding area. Leonov kept up a decent pace, only slowing occasionally to get his bearings.

"Is this much like your home?" asked Charlaine.

"I grew up in Ruzhina," the Mathewite explained. "The forest there is thick, but there are hills to the east, much like those found here."

"Ruzhina? Isn't that where the Volstrum is found?"

"Yes, in the great city of Karslev, but that's some distance from my home."

"Have you ever been there?"

"Once, when I was young, but I didn't enjoy it."

"Why not?"

"The city is awash with foreigners seeking training as mages."

"I didn't realize they trained foreigners," said Charlaine.

"They'll train anyone they deem worthy."

"And what makes one worthy?"

"You're asking the wrong person," said Leonov.

"I know," piped up Marlena. "Magic is hereditary. If you don't have it in the blood, you can't learn to cast spells."

"Ahhh," said Charlaine. "Now I understand. One of our order, Sister Teresa, had the ability of healing; at least that's what Gwalinor said."

"Gwalinor?"

"Yes. He's a Sea Elf and an accomplished Life Mage."

"Never heard of a Sea Elf before," grumbled Brother Klavel. "Do they have gills, like fish?"

"No, they're related to regular Elves but spend a lot of time at sea instead of living in the woods."

"I've never heard of a sister who could heal," said Marlena.

"She's the first, as far as I know," said Charlaine. "But I haven't heard from her since I left Ilea."

"Likely still training," noted Brother Leonov. "They say students at the Volstrum spend years before they're ready to cast their first spell."

"And that's considered normal?"

"For the Volstrum it is, and who's to argue? They produce the most powerful mages in all the Petty Kingdoms."

"Something we'll need to keep in mind if we face off against Larissa Stormwind again."

"That woman is a pest," spat out Klavel. "She's already damaged two of our ships. They were easy to repair, but next time we might not be so lucky."

"I'm fully in agreement with you there," noted Charlaine.

The trees grew sparser as the land developed a noticeable incline. When they cleared the line of trees, a large hill came into view.

"Doesn't look so bad," said Leonov. "Come, we'll see how quickly we can get to the top."

The climb was steep in places, so much so that they were forced to continue on hands and knees at one point. They reached the top at noon, and the sight before them took their breath away. The island was immense, stretching out to the east as far as the eye could see, while to the north, the sunlight glinted off the water, tiny black specks occasionally interfering with the light.

"Ships," said Charlaine.

"Yes," agreed Marlena, "and at least a dozen by my reckoning. They appear to be in a natural harbour."

"There are buildings," said Brother Klavel. "Along with what looks like a courtyard."

Charlaine tried to estimate the size of the place, but with only trees to compare, it was difficult.

"It's a small village, wouldn't you say?" stated Marlena.

Charlaine, busy looking to the west, spotted her own fleet, sitting upon the waters of the Great Northern Sea.

"What do you make of it, Brother Leonov?" she asked. "Do you believe an army could march that distance in a day?"

"Easily," the Mathewite replied. "And with the hills as a reference point, it would be difficult to get lost. I would say we landed at an opportune spot, wouldn't you?"

"Most definitely. Now, all that remains is to return to the fleet and finalize our arrangements for the assault."

That evening, a meeting was arranged aboard the *Valiant as it* lay at anchor. Grazynia came, bringing Barbek with her if only for him to leave the *Vigilant* and stretch his legs. Even Captain Waleed put in an appearance, and Danica's cabin felt small with the five of them gathered around the charts.

"Welcome, everyone," said Danica. "I know you've all been waiting for the chance to take action, so without any further delay, I'll let Commander Charlaine take over."

Charlaine moved up to the table. Upon their return, they'd roughed out a sketch of the island, which now served as a convenient aid.

"Captain Taggert indicated the camp is on the North Coast," offered Charlaine. "From our vantage point up in the hills, we saw the bay, not to mention the huts they built. We also spotted at least a dozen ships, although we don't know if there are others out at sea."

"Any warships?" asked Captain Waleed.

"Well, if they're planning to make raids, as we suspect, they'd need principally cargo ships, not ships of war, but I doubt they'd leave them unprotected. The real question is, how many?" Charlaine paused a moment, considering her next words carefully. "In the South, they mainly used provincial troops, which were lightly armoured compared to Temple Knights. The bigger problem here will be their numbers. There's a very real chance they have more warriors than us and possibly even more warships."

"And your plan for dealing with that...?" asked Captain Waleed

"Close with the enemy as quickly as possible and board them."

"Where do my Cunars fit in?"

"Ideally, they would land on the beach while the *Valiant* and *Vigilant* keep the enemy ships busy. We'll try to coordinate this as best as possible with the attack from the landward side."

"I wish I'd rigged that other arbalest," said the Dwarf. "It would be of tremendous help against enemy ships."

"So it would," said Charlaine, "but we cannot undo the past. Let us, therefore, concentrate on our battle plans. The Cunars and Mathewites will carry out the bulk of the attack, while the Agneses are needed for ship-boarding and capture. If they should prove victorious, then by all means, they will land and assist in the attack."

"It's a good plan," noted Waleed. "Although, doubtless, it will require some adjustment once we arrive. You are a credit to your order, Commander. My compliments."

Charlaine looked around the small cabin. Collectively, they represented years of experience, yet she still wondered if it would be enough.

"I must warn you," she said, "there is a tendency, here in the Petty Kingdoms, to make light of the Halvarians. I can assure you they are fierce warriors and a match for any army on the Continent."

"Aye, it's true," said Barbek. "They conquered the Western lands easily enough."

"Let us hope the same cannot be said here."

36

STORM

Summer 1098 SR

The knights who made up the overland contingent disembarked and stockpiled supplies while the *Valiant* prepared to get underway. The assault would come soon enough, but before it did, Danica's ship had the unenviable task of mapping out the coastline. The last thing they wanted to do was run aground on a shoal, so they decided the *Valiant* would proceed up the coast, noting any obstacles to navigation. Once they drew closer to their target, they would send out a shore party, the better to estimate their enemy's true strength.

The skiff finally drew alongside, and Zivka reported the crew was back aboard. With the sails unfurled and the anchor raised, the Holy Fleet's flagship set sail. A strong wind drove them north, but even more forbidding were the dark clouds threatening rain. Despite the warning signs, or maybe because of them, the small ship made rapid progress.

Late in the day, they came upon the spit of land that marked the transition from the western coast to the north. The *Valiant* reduced sail, making ready for a wide turn to starboard. They were halfway through when they spotted the sail of a small vessel, smaller even than their own. It represented a far greater threat by its presence than by its size, for now the element of surprise was lost. If word was carried to the Halvarians, it could well end in disaster.

Zivka loaded the arbalest, then raised the tip of it for maximum elevation. In theory, the weapon should be good up to a range of one hundred yards, but a heaving deck and uncertain wind could throw off even the best of calculations.

Danica gave the command, and the bolt flew forth, falling short. Aboard the enemy ship, men ran around the deck, eager to take up the lines and alter the sail, anything to put more distance between them.

The *Valiant* made a slight adjustment to its course, and the wind suddenly filled the sails. The change was so quick that Danica feared the canvas might rip, but it held. Zivka reloaded the arbalest, this time selecting a shredder. The press of canvas gave them the advantage, and the tiny vessel grew closer.

Round the tip of the spit they went, then all thoughts of pursuit died, for beyond were three warships, each flying the flag of Halvaria and sailing right for them.

The *Valiant* had one advantage, and one only—the wind blowing up from the south allowing them to turn hard to port and proceed out to sea. Her crew adapted quickly, turning the tiller and making adjustments to the yardarm. The mainmast creaked under the strain while the deck angled to port as the steep turn commenced. Danica held on for dear life, watching as water splashed over the guard rail.

A bolt shot out of somewhere, and her eyes tracked back to see a ballista mounted on the lead Halvarian's foredeck. The enemy ships were like nothing she had ever seen before. They were similar to cogs, but with two masts and a lot more canvas to catch the wind.

"Can we outrun them?" asked Nadia.

"No," replied Danica as she looked skyward, noting the darkening clouds. "We need to buy time," she said. "There's a storm brewing, and once it hits, we'll make our escape."

"Buy time? How do we do that?"

"Bring us around. We'll make a quick pass and try to take out some sails."

The ship turned against the wind, its forward momentum slowing considerably. The Halvarian ships, the wind at their backs, surged forward, closing the distance quickly.

Zivka let off another bolt, but the *Valiant* tossed about on the waves, throwing off her aim. A hail of arrows flew towards them, several striking the deck. The enemy warship loomed up to port, and then Zivka let loose with another shredder.

Danica heard lines snap as the bolt tore through them, and then the enemy's forward sail flapped out into the wind, the rope securing it cut.

The *Valiant* laboured to turn once again, its nose moving ever so slowly. They were in real peril of coming to a complete stop, then they caught a rogue gust of wind that carried them past the point of danger, picking up speed just as the rain began.

With one of the Halvarians out of control, the other two moved in for the kill, their decks swarming with archers. Arrows flew like hail, some bouncing off the knights' armour, but luckily, none hit the crew. Danica watched as a well-dressed man appeared on the deck of a vessel, his hands moving in the beginnings of a spell. She snatched up a crossbow, quickly loading it before taking aim.

As the rogue's fingers glowed with green fire, she let loose, the bolt catching the fellow in the bicep, causing him to lose his concentration. He fell, now out of sight, but a flame shot skyward, unleashed but no longer under control.

The *Valiant* pitched back as it rose on a wave, then there was the sickening feeling as it plunged into the trough. Danica fell to her knees as sea water washed across the deck, threatening to take her to the deep. She clutched the railing with all the strength she could muster, remaining aboard, but the crossbow was gone, lost to the sea.

She looked up when lightning lit the sky, swiftly followed by the booming crack of thunder. The rain came down in torrents, pushing all thoughts of battle aside. It was still a battle of survival, not from the fight, but the raging storm.

Above her, on the yardarm, a trio of crewmen struggled to reduce sail. One of them slipped from his perch and disappeared into the storm, carried away by a great wave.

Another wave loomed menacingly before them, and Danica feared it would smash them to pieces. She held her breath, but the warship was borne aloft, giving the Temple Knight an unprecedented view of the enemy.

The damaged Halvarian ship, unable to make repairs to its mast, was dangerously close to shore. The other two, desperate to avert a catastrophe, spread out to avoid colliding. One had a huge rip in the mainsail, but the other still chased the *Valiant*.

The boat fell suddenly, and Danica lost her footing again. She had a sensation of weightlessness, then the deck lurched towards her with unprecedented speed. Her ankle twisted painfully before she dropped to her knees with a resounding thud.

The ship pitched violently to starboard—it felt like riding a wild horse trying to throw her from its back. Sister Laurel slid by, smashing into the railing before lying still. Moments later, a great wave shot across the deck, threatening to wash her overboard.

Danica lunged out, half crawling, half diving towards the stricken knight. She grabbed Laurel's arm just as they heaved to port, her other hand grasping the rail in desperation.

The *Valiant* now pitched at almost thirty degrees, and for a moment, Danica feared the ship might keel over. She held her breath, praying to Saint Agnes to spare them, and then the vessel righted itself. With her arm hooked over the railing, she pulled Laurel closer, then spotted Zivka rushing by, her precious arbalest all but forgotten.

The crew member, Brendan, meanwhile, fought the storm to keep the tiller under control. Zivka was soon there, and together, they lashed it into place. The ship continued northward at an unworldly speed, tossed about like a leaf on the wind.

From the shores of Patience, Charlaine looked out upon the fleet. The wind had risen substantially, whipping the sea into turmoil, and she feared for their safety. The *Vigilant* was doing well, easily riding out the worst of it, but the *Rose* was in trouble. Never a good sailer at the best of times, it tore away from its anchor and started moving towards the shore. With sails full of wind, there was no hope of controlling it. Sure enough, the mighty ship shuddered as it ran aground, letting out a large grating sound loud enough to be heard even above the storm.

She saw men struggling on deck, trying to get their ship's boat in the water. Just as it was over the railing, a great wave struck, shattering the skiff against the hull. She looked around, seeing the drenched forms of Temple Knights, each one bearing witness to the great tragedy unfolding before them.

"To the boats," she ordered. "We must save those we can."

They rushed to man the boats with all haste, then pushed out into the storm. In front of her, one skiff flooded with water even as it entered the sea, its occupants dumped overboard. They took the defeat in stride, dragging the small boat back to shore. Charlaine felt her own vessel pitch up, and then the nose suddenly fell, threatening to knock her loose. They managed to crest the next wave, holding their breath as another broke against their bow. The knights dug in with oars, moving towards the *Rose*.

The merchant's crew abandoned ship, some climbing down the side using ropes, others diving into the water to escape almost certain death.

Charlaine brought her boat alongside, reaching out and plucking a man from the water. The *Rose*, lifted by another great wave, shot forward, the hull rupturing as it hit some rocks. The waves tossed the ship about mercilessly. Men swam, determined to reach the shore, but the cold, green waters of the Great Northern Sea claimed them one by one.

The ship's boat maintained its position for as long as it could, but it became clear it was a fool's errand, and Charlaine ordered them ashore before things only got worse.

The storm brutally battered them about, the ship's boat striking rocks as it drew closer to shore. The only saving grace was the shallow water, allowing both rescuers and rescuees to wade ashore. Charlaine fell to her knees, sucking in great gasps of air. Behind her, all was chaos as the storm ravaged the ships of the fleet.

It wasn't until the wee hours of the morning that the winds finally died down. With the first light of dawn came relief. The survivors climbed out of their makeshift shelters to gaze upon the destruction.

Now, little more than a shell of its former self, the *Rose* lay still, its ribs protruding from the water like a colossal skeleton. Out in the bay, the fleet had taken a beating, their sails in tatters but otherwise intact. Only when Charlaine counted them did she realize one was missing, although she couldn't for the life of her remember which one.

The answer was soon supplied by Grazynia, who had rowed ashore aboard the *Vigilant's* skiff, her dour expression leaving no doubt as to her opinion of events.

"We lost the *Millicent*," noted the blonde captain. "She likely shed her anchor sometime during the storm." Her gaze fell across the great wreck. "I assume that's the *Rose*?"

"It is. Run aground during the storm. We saved a few, but I'm afraid most perished."

"And your knights?"

"All accounted for, as are the horses."

"Thank the Saints we set them ashore."

"The *Millicent* carried sister knights," said Charlaine. "Almost half our complement."

"With your permission, I'll go out and look for them. I don't like leaving you unprotected like this, but I doubt she got very far."

"Let's hope not. We need those knights." She spotted the hesitation on the part of Grazynia. "What aren't you telling me?"

"The *Peri* is taking on water. Repairs are underway, but it doesn't look good."

"Anything else?"

"My own ship has suffered some damage to the mast. We made temporary repairs for now, but eventually, we'll need to replace it."

"Any word from *Valiant?*"

"No, but she's a tough ship. I expect she found a nice inlet somewhere to wait out the storm."

Charlaine looked out on the bay, surveying the damage. "This storm has cost us dearly. We were relying on the knights aboard the *Millicent* to capture those enemy ships. Without them, we lack the numbers we need."

"My men are ready to fight," said Captain Waleed. "We should ignore the ships and carry out a landward attack."

"And how would you have us return home?"

"We can simply march everyone back here."

"With prisoners and wounded?" said Charlaine. "I believe you underestimate the difficulty. No, we must engage their fleet."

"To capture it?" asked Grazynia.

"Capture or destroy. In either case, we can't allow the presence of Halvarian warships in these waters."

"That puts us in a rather precarious position."

"Go and find the *Millicent*," ordered Charlaine, "and let us pray the enemy does not come looking for us."

"And if they do?" asked Captain Waleed.

"Then we must hope they will be merciful."

"You think that likely?"

"No," replied Charlaine, her mood souring. "At the Battle of Alantra, they tied captured Temple Knights to their masts, high up where everyone could see them."

"By the Saints, that's barbaric, even by their standards."

"This is not just a fight between two armies, but a battle for the very soul of the Petty Kingdoms and those who live here."

"We shall triumph," insisted Waleed. "Our faith will see us through."

"It's not our faith that leads us to victory," said Charlaine, "though that, of course, plays a part. We win because we choose our battles carefully."

"I've yet to see an enemy who could withstand our mastery of arms. I say have at them, and let our swords slay all who oppose us."

"You would have us take this fight to the enemy before we have all the information we need? No, we shall wait for the *Valiant's* return. Only then will we know the enemy's true strength."

"The *Valiant?* For all we know, she may be lost. We can't wait here for a ship that may never return. We must march now and catch the enemy unawares."

Charlaine turned on Captain Waleed. "I command this expedition," she said, "and I alone decide when and if we continue."

"If? You can't be serious? After we came all this way? I'll not be branded a coward for failing my duty."

"Your duty is to follow orders," she barked out. Her statement brought her up short. Was this what she was reduced to? Merely shouting out orders? "I'm sorry for that outburst," she said. "I do not doubt your dedication, Captain Waleed. I assure you we will not abandon this attack, but we cannot simply walk into battle without careful preparation. Such a move would only serve our enemy's interests. Your knights are crucial to this, but they cannot do it alone. Without the sea under our control, we would be marooned here."

The Cunar captain stared back for a moment before nodding. "Wise words. I regret my outburst and ask your forgiveness."

"There's nothing to forgive," said Charlaine. "You displayed a passion for your order. That is understandable."

"No, I overstepped. You are the commander here, not me, yet I must confess I did harbour doubts about your ability to lead."

"Because I'm a woman?"

"No, because you're not a Cunar. Ever since I joined the order, it was made clear to me that only the Temple Knights of Saint Cunar were trained to command in battle. Yet here I find myself under the command of an Agnesite." Charlaine was about to speak, but he held up his hand. "Please, let me finish. It was wrong of me to question your abilities, just as I am wrong in seeking to undermine your authority. You may rest assured I shall not do so again."

"Thank you, Captain. It's comforting to know I'll have your guidance and wisdom in the coming days. Now, we have much to do, you and I, for we must send out small parties."

"To what end?"

"First," said Charlaine, "we need to find a navigable route to this Halvarian base."

"And then?"

"Then we will watch and learn as much about the place as we can. We are in uncharted waters here. Although I saw a Halvarian training camp back in Calabria, it is by no means certain the same rules apply here."

"Meaning?" asked Waleed.

"The training of the abductees could well be complete, in which case we could be facing a much larger enemy."

"What do you know of their training methods?"

"Not much, I'm afraid. In Cunara, we found the warriors turned against their masters once the attack commenced."

"Do you believe the same could happen here?"

"That's difficult to say. One thing we did learn, though, is that mages were present."

"Mages?" said Waleed. "A pox on them all. Magic should be banned outright."

"Magic itself is not inherently evil. Rather, it is the practitioners who often cause problems."

"You're thinking of that Stormwind woman?"

"I am," said Charlaine. "We saw her quite clearly aboard the *Water Drake*. That, of course, does not render all mages our enemy."

"I have yet to see one who was of any use. How about you?"

"A Life Mage healed me back in Ilea. A Sea Elf named Gwalinor."

"An Elf? They are as bad as these Halvarians."

"Why would you say that?"

Waleed shifted uncomfortably. "It is not generally known outside of my order, but we have battled the woodland folk before."

"This is news to me," said Charlaine. "Can you be more specific?"

"Not without breaking my vows. Suffice it to say it was many years ago."

"I didn't know there were that many left on the Continent."

"And if it were up to us, that would certainly be true. However, our campaign was cut short by the mountain folk."

"Are you trying to tell me the Temple Knights of Saint Cunar fought Dwarves?"

"No, although it came close. It is not, by all accounts, something the order wishes to repeat. Thankfully, the campaign was brought to a halt through diplomacy."

"I had no idea."

"Nor is there any reason you should have. Amongst us, it's known as the Hidden Crusade."

"Why are you telling me all this?"

Captain Waleed shrugged. "As a mark of respect. I have borne this burden for far too long, as have my brethren. It is time those outside my order become aware of our missteps."

"I shall bear that in mind going forward."

37

INLAND

Summer 1098 SR

In the *Vigilant's* absence, the remaining Temple Knights began constructing a series of huts to establish a more permanent base as protection from the fickle weather of the Great Northern Sea. Charlaine thought a dock of some sort might be helpful, but lacking the expertise for such an enterprise, she put the idea to the side for the time being.

The *Vigilant* sailed back into their makeshift port, the *Millicent* following in its wake. The merchant ship had been blown about in the storm, and its captain felt it had a better chance of survival by weathering the worst of it out at sea.

Charlaine was thankful for its return and immediately ordered all sister knights ashore, the better to protect them from further storms. Small groups were sent out with orders to explore the immediate area, while a permanent watch was placed on the hill to the east, the better to keep an eye on developments up north.

Two days had passed since the storm, yet still no word came of the *Valiant*. Charlaine feared the ship lost, but then even worse news came from Captain Waleed. Charlaine first spotted him at the treeline, making his way towards her at a pace that said he was in a hurry yet slow enough to maintain his dignity.

"You have something to report, Captain?"

"I do," he replied. "Although I fear it will not be to your liking."

"Go on," she urged.

"Our scouts report some of the Halvarian ships are missing."

"Which ones?"

"Three, and I fear, by their formation, they may be warships."

"When was this?"

"Early this morning. They headed westward, following the coast. Should they continue in that direction, they'll soon find us."

"There is some time yet," said Charlaine. "Any word from our other scouts?"

"I'm afraid not. Then again, they have quite some distance to traverse. I wouldn't expect them to return till later this evening." The captain's eyes drifted out to the fleet. "How do you suppose the *Vigilant* would fare against a Halvarian warship?"

"Difficult to say. Grazynia's a good captain, but the Northern Fleet is nothing like those down south. I have no idea what a battle would even look like up here."

"Had we sailed out of Corassus," noted Waleed, "it would be a simple matter of ramming and boarding, but up here, the Northern Sea makes such tactics impossible. More likely, they'll keep their distance and use those mages of theirs to set fire to our ships."

"Then we must close with the enemy."

"What are you thinking?"

"We put Temple Knights aboard each ship to defend."

"That only works if they get close enough to board."

"Then we'll need to ensure they do," said Charlaine.

"But then they'll just burn the ships!"

"Ships are valuable, and undefended ones will be a temptation they can't resist."

Captain Waleed shook his head. "Make up your mind. Are we going to send knights across or not?"

Charlaine smiled. "Oh, we'll send them across all right, but they'll remain below decks until such time as the enemy boards. What ship's captain could resist the idea of capturing an enemy vessel?"

"These are Halvarians we're talking of—they're fanatical."

"True, but they know as little of us as we know of them. They'll be eager to capture prisoners if only to find out what we know."

"Those merchant vessels are not the most manoeuvrable of ships."

"Then we'll anchor them close together."

"How close together?" asked the Cunar.

"Ideally, bumping up against each other, but I'm no ship expert."

"That could lead to damage, couldn't it?"

"I'm inclined to agree. However, the closer we have them, the less likely for a warship to sail between them."

"And the *Vigilant?*"

"It should be farther out," said Charlaine, "where it can use its superior handling to advantage."

"And you think that will be enough?"

"What choice have we? It would be a different matter if the *Valiant* were here, but we must deal with the cards fate has given us."

"Might I make a suggestion?"

"By all means," said Charlaine. "I would welcome it."

"If we were to pool all the ship's boats, we could use them to counterattack."

"Like pirates?"

Captain Waleed grinned. "It's an old Kurathian tactic. Centuries ago, a great admiral named Sarin faced off against the fleet of the Sea Elves. This was, you must understand, a period of significant expansion when Kurathian ships set forth to explore the unknown sea."

"What happened?"

"The princes kept sending more and more ships to the east. The Elves finally sent a fleet to put an end to our maritime enterprises once and for all. They met off the coast of the great Southern Continent, near a place known as the Grey Cliffs. They had the advantage of numbers and their ships were much faster than ours, yet ultimately, we were the victors."

"So you defeated the Elves?"

"Only their fleet. Unfortunately, our losses were too high to continue the campaign."

"So, in reality," said Charlaine, "neither side won."

"We prevented them from attacking our home."

"Yes, but they also stopped you from sailing east, didn't they?"

"I suppose they did. In any event, it was the use of these small boats that turned the tide. Sarin waited until the enemy was engaged in boarding actions, then sent boats loaded with warriors to board from the opposite side."

"A clever tactic. I like it. So much so, I'm putting you in charge of it."

"I am honoured," said Captain Waleed. "I promise I won't disappoint you."

"I assume you'll use your own men?"

"I will. What of the shipboard contingents?"

"I'll use sister knights. We'll need the Mathewites to protect our new base. I'd hate to defeat their ships only to have everything ashore burned to the ground."

"When do we start preparations?"

"Immediately. The first order of business will be to determine how close we can get those ships. That alone could take the best part of the day. To accomplish that, I must meet with all the captains. I'd like you to take a full inventory of the fleet and see how many boats you'll have at your disposal."

"They'll still need their boats to come and meet with you, won't they?"

"That they will. My intention is for all the boats to go ashore at the first sign of the enemy, but you'll need to know in advance how to distribute your men."

"Understood," said Waleed. "Anything else?"

"Yes. You might consider praying. We need all the help we can get."

That evening, as they gathered on the cold, windless night, the beach looked pristine in the moonlight. All the captains were present, save for the *Valiant's*.

"I brought you here," said Charlaine, "to discuss strategy."

"Strategy for what?" asked Captain Longrit. "And how does the *Millicent* fit in?"

"Rest assured, I'll get to individual ship assignments shortly. To start off, I'd like to talk about the enemy fleet. We estimate their number of ships to be about a dozen, of which we think five are warships." She took a breath before continuing. It was difficult to speak of such things without alarming anyone, so she resolved to take her time, explaining as she went. In this way, she hoped to reassure them everything was under control. The alternative was they might panic, fleeing in their ships at the first sign of trouble, stranding the Temple Knights ashore.

"You all saw the hill that lies to the east. We've had people up there watching things to the north."

"And?" prompted Ansel Dulworth, captain of the *Barlowe*.

"We've word some of the ships left the enemy harbour and are heading westward. By our reckoning, they could be here as early as tomorrow morning."

"You truly believe that likely?"

"Had I believed otherwise, we wouldn't be here this evening. You know your ships better than me, so I'd like your opinion on what I'm proposing."

"Which is?"

"At this moment, three enemy ships are approaching, possibly more. The

Vigilant can fight, but against those odds, she'd have little chance of success. I'm hoping to even out those odds by offering them a tempting target."

She saw the captains pale at the mere thought.

"Let me finish before everyone panics," she urged. "We would place Temple Knights aboard each and every vessel, keeping them out of sight until the enemy comes close enough to board."

Captain Edgerton looked like he was ready to lose his dinner. "Are you actually suggesting we let those Halvarians aboard our ships?"

"I am, or at least come close enough that we can drop a boarding ramp."

"Just how many knights would be aboard?"

"That will vary by size of ship, but I would think upwards of a dozen, and they would each be in their plate armour."

Edgerton relaxed, nodding his head. "You had me worried there for a moment, but a dozen Temple Knights is much more reassuring. When would they come aboard?"

"Not until the enemy is sighted. We sent scouts up the coast, along with horses, so we should have ample warning."

"And if they come in from the sea instead of following the coast?"

"The *Vigilant* will lie offshore to our west, on the watch for just such a development. I can assure you, gentlemen, I gave this much thought. In addition to taking aboard knights, we shall also deploy another force manning the ships' boats."

"I assume," said Captain Edgerton, "that means you want us to hand over all our skiffs?"

"Yes. We're hoping once the Halvarians close, their focus will be on their targets rather than the smaller craft."

Captain Longrit shook his head. "It'll never work. The Halvarians are experienced mariners."

"So were the Elves," added Captain Waleed, "but it didn't help them against the Kurathians."

"What in the name of the Saints," said Edgerton, "does that have to do with our present circumstances?"

"He talks of the element of surprise," said Charlaine. "If the Halvarian Fleet is anything like what we fought in Alantra, their tactics will be quite blunt."

"Meaning what, exactly?"

"They will close quickly, and if they see any indication of resistance before they board, they'll use magic to soften up the target. I'm told it's the way seaborne warfare has been conducted for centuries."

"That's hardly reassuring," replied Captain Longrit. "We'd be far better off to sail back out to sea and return when they leave."

There it was, the first sign of running. She must put an end to it quickly before the sentiment spread.

"And how would you know when that was?" asked Charlaine.

"We could watch the coast from afar."

"You mean from a ship that the enemy could see? Unless you have an invisible one that we could use?"

"No," said Longrit, "of course not, but running is a far better solution than waiting to be captured."

"Ah, but you won't be," said Captain Dulworth. "As soon as they board, the knights will emerge from the holds and defeat them. Isn't that right, Captain?"

"That's the plan," noted Charlaine. "We keep them busy while Captain Waleed and his men attack from behind."

"But how do we know which ship they'll target?" asked Longrit.

"That's where you come in. What I'd like to propose is you anchor your ships as close together as possible, or at least close enough an enemy warship couldn't pass between."

The ships' captains all stared into the fire, quietly thinking things through.

"Your opinions, gentlemen?" pressed Charlaine.

"A solid enough plan," said Captain Dulworth. "Might I suggest we run chains between the ships? That would definitely dissuade them from sailing through us."

"Very well. Anything else?" She looked at each in turn.

"We'll anchor bow and stern," added Captain Edgerton. "That will prevent drift."

"The water is quite shallow," offered Longrit. "Maybe we can put some stakes in there?"

"Don't be foolish," said Edgerton. "That could damage our own ships just as easily as the enemy. One bad gust of wind, and someone would puncture their hull."

"Point taken," said Charlaine, turning to Captain Dulworth. "Now, these chains you mentioned, could they be shortened in an emergency?"

"I suppose they could. Why? What is it you're thinking?"

"If a ship is boarded, the next vessel beside it could pull closer, allowing more knights to transfer ships."

"That could prove dangerous. The water might be relatively shallow here, but it would still be enough to drown a man... or a woman, for that matter."

"That's a risk we'll have to take."

"In that case," said Longrit, "I'm in. What about the rest of you?"

They all nodded.

"There you have it, Commander. We are in agreement. All that remains is for you to give us the details."

"Good," said Charlaine. Her eyes wandered towards the bay. "The *Barlowe* will form the end of the line. I'd like *Millicent* to her port, followed by the *Monarch* and finally, the *Peri*. That keeps our two largest ships on the outside of the formation."

"How do you want us, relative to shore?" asked Longrit.

"Keep the beach to your port side, if you can."

"Good idea," noted Captain Dulworth. "That'll make them think twice about attacking the other end of the line, but I'd feel safer if your knights were aboard ship now instead of waiting till the enemy is sighted."

"I understand. Once the ships are in position, send us your boats, and we'll load you up with Temple Knights."

"We'll get right on it at first light," said Dulworth. "No sense in doing it in the dark. Now, unless there's anything else to discuss, we should get back aboard our ships."

"By all means," said Charlaine.

She watched as they left the fire, the captains discussing the strategy amongst themselves.

"They sound confident."

Charlaine turned to see Barbek Stoutarm. "Where have you been?" she asked.

"Lurking in the background. I've found, over the years, Humans are not so talkative in my presence."

"What did you think?"

"It's a solid plan."

"Anything you'd care to add?"

"As a matter of fact, there is. We have an abundance of rope aboard the *Vigilant*, as I'm sure there is amongst the other ships of the fleet."

"And?"

"I'm proposing we remove the ballista from the *Vigilant* and mount it ashore."

"I'm not sure I like that. It leaves the ship unarmed."

"Nonsense. It still has its knights. If we had enough time, I'd simply build a new one, but I doubt the Halvarians will give us that luxury."

"What makes you think it would be any more effective than mounting it aboard the *Vigilant*?"

"It probably wouldn't, but the *Vigilant* can't be everywhere at once. At least with a shore-mounted weapon, there would be a good reason for the enemy to remain farther out."

"Excellent idea. You'll need to coordinate your efforts with Captain Grazynia."

"Might I also ask for the loan of a dozen knights? The Mathewites would be more than sufficient, along with some of their mounts."

"Their mounts?"

"I don't have the time to get into details, but from one guild member to another, I'm asking you to trust me."

"I can do that," said Charlaine. "You take what Mathewites you require. If you need more rope, send word to the other ships."

"I'll get onto it right away."

Sister Marlena appeared to her left.

"Something wrong?" asked Charlaine.

"Not at all," replied her aide. "I'm here to remind you to eat. We can't have you passing out from hunger in the middle of a battle."

Charlaine laughed. "What have you got?"

"Little more than a vegetable stew, I'm afraid. The meat has gone bad. Unless you prefer dried meat?"

"Let's save that for another day, shall we?"

"So the stew, then?"

"Yes, and don't forget to eat some yourself. It's going to be a busy day tomorrow, assuming the enemy shows up."

"And if they don't?"

"Then it'll likely be the next day."

"If we're lucky," said Marlena, "maybe they won't show up at all."

"I'd like to believe that, but my gut tells me otherwise."

Marlena stared off at the fire.

"Worried?" asked Charlaine.

"I've never been in battle before."

"Nor I, until I went to Ilea."

"Were you scared?"

"Nervous, but not scared. People will tell you battle is terrifying, but it's precisely what you trained for. When the fighting starts, your body will know what to do."

"Any advice?"

"Concentrate on the here and now instead of worrying about what the future might bring. Some warriors sharpen their weapons to prepare for battle, while others study the Words of Agnes, but the result is the same: keeping your mind occupied."

"Wise words," said Marlena. "Is that what you did before Alantra?"

"No," said Charlaine, chuckling. "You might say I ignored my own advice, but the truth is I had little time to prepare. Then again, we did pray just as the battle commenced."

"Agnes must have watched over you."

"It's a nice thought, but I wouldn't go counting on the Saints alone to save you. Content yourself on relying on your fellow knights and to your mastery of arms."

38

CONFLICT

Summer 1098 SR

Danica was cold, so cold she was shivering. Opening her eyes, she noticed the wooden timbers beneath her covered with frost. She was relieved that the weather had cleared when she looked skyward, yet there was a bite to the air. She exhaled only to watch as her breath hung before her face. Her eyes instinctively went to the sail to find it hanging limply. Sister Anya stood by the stern, a deathlike grip on the tiller.

"Good to see you awake, Captain," she called out, her teeth chattering.

"Where are we?"

"Far to the north if that's any indication." She nodded towards the bow, causing Danica to follow her gaze. Off in the distance was a frozen landscape like none she'd ever seen before. Large chunks of ice floated around the place, while behind, mountains of white stared back at her.

"It's the edge of Eiddenwerthe," said Anya. "Either that, or we've reached the Underworld."

"You can't just sail to the Underworld," replied Danica. She moved across the deck to the prone form of Sister Laurel. Turning her over, she checked for a pulse. "Come and help me, Anya. We must get Laurel inside."

She grabbed the unconscious knight by the armpits, dragging her towards the captain's cabin. Anya was soon there, endeavouring to make her numb fingers work.

"Where is everyone?" asked the captain.

"Some made it below, but many of the crew perished."

They hauled the injured knight to the door and pulled her inside.

"Help me remove her armour," said Danica.

"What about the ship?"

"There's no wind. It's not going anywhere."

They struggled to remove Laurel's armour but had her down to her padded undercoat soon enough. Their task complete, they lifted her into the captain's bed, covering her in blankets. Danica rubbed her own hands, feeling pain as the blood returned.

"We're doomed," said Anya. "The Saints saw fit to punish us by sending us to this land of ice and snow."

"Nonsense. We are merely far to the north. For centuries there's been rumours of a frozen wasteland up there."

"Then why isn't it on any maps?"

"Why would it be?" said Danica. "Who in their right mind would want to return to a place like this?"

"How far north do you reckon we are?"

"North isn't the problem."

"Why would you say that?"

"Pick any point in the north, and the Continent will lie southward. The real question is how far east or west we are from our previous position. Those winds could have pushed us as far east as Ruzhina or westward, beyond the shores of the Halvarian Empire, although admittedly, that would stretch things a bit."

"What's our next step?"

"First, let's go below and see if anyone else survived. We can't exactly sail this ship with only the three of us."

Danica braced herself, then opened the door, letting in cold air. Stepping outside, she made her way to the hatch that led below. It took several pulls to free it of ice, and then a warmth flooded up.

"Who's there?" came a voice.

"Zivka, is that you?" called out Danica.

"Yes, and Nadia is here as well."

"Any crew members?"

"A few."

"Down you go," said Danica, looking at Anya. She followed the knight down the ladder, closing the hatch behind them.

"Well, at least it's warmer down here than up there." She spotted the tillerman, Brendan.

"How many survived?" she asked.

"Half a dozen of us," the sailor replied, "not including the knights. Enough to sail her, should the wind pick up."

"Always assuming we don't get frozen in," added Anya.

"We've plenty of food," said Danica, "and water, for that matter. Our sails are also intact, and there appears to be little damage below our waterline. Start by searching through everyone's belongings and pulling out any warm clothing. Armour is to be left below decks. Your gambesons should help keep the cold at bay. The biggest issue is likely to be your hands."

"We could fashion some mittens," said Brendan. "There's more than enough sailcloth available. They won't be as warm as wool, but they'll be quick."

"Then do so, and the sooner the better. Once this wind picks up, we'll need to get the *Valiant* under control. Speaking of which, see if you can't spare some extra canvas for the tiller. I don't want anyone's hands freezing to it. In the meantime, I want one knight on deck at all times."

"I'll go," offered Zivka.

"Very well, but as soon as you get cold, call someone up to replace you. This is no place for heroics."

"Am I looking for anything in particular?"

"Yes," said Danica. "Any change of wind, even a slight one. Should we be blessed with that, we'll need everyone on deck to unfurl that sail."

Danica strode up and down the deck, using the movement to generate heat. Occasionally, she would peer over the railing, fearful ice would encase the ship, but it seemed disinclined to do so. All morning they waited for the wind, praying for delivery from the cold, forbidding landscape.

She heard a splash and looked over the starboard railing. A white shape loomed below, and her first thoughts were of a corpse, come from the Underworld to take their souls. Much to her surprise, a strange creature rose to the surface. It looked like a porpoise, but its white body had a long, spiral protrusion jutting out from its head. As she watched, it spat out water, much as a whale would.

"By the Saints," called out Sister Nadia. "What is that thing, a unicorn?"

"I'm not sure," Danica replied, "but my guess would be a porpoise of sorts. A good omen, I would say."

They both watched as the strange creature returned to the depths. Just as it did so, Danica felt a faint breeze against her cheek.

"Did you feel that?" she asked.

"I did," said Nadia. "It was slight but still, better than nothing."

"Call the crew up. We'll unfurl the sail and see if it picks up."

Everyone came on deck, eager to be free of their icy exile.

"Anya, Laurel, fetch some poles. We may need you at the bow to fend off any approaching ice." Danica scanned the ice field. "Vivian, operate the tiller while Brendan and the others take care of the sail."

The canvas dropped, with everyone watching in expectation. A tiny breeze licked at the sail and then picked up until it filled, and the *Valiant* crept forward.

"Turn slightly to port," shouted Danica.

A large chunk of ice moved closer, and then the ship turned ever so slowly, missing the ice by several yards. Danica let out a sigh of relief.

"We're free," called out Anya.

"Straighten the rudder," said Danica, "and take us due south." She moved to the stern, her eyes taking one last look at the frozen wasteland behind them. A group of the strange porpoises briefly rose to the surface, and she felt a moment of wonder. Few had journeyed to the farthest reaches of the north, and likely fewer still would have borne witness to these magnificent animals.

"You just saw more of those things, didn't you?" asked Sister Nadia.

"I did, a whole family, from the look of it. They'll never believe this back in Korvoran."

"Perhaps we'll return here someday."

"Perhaps, but if we do, it'll be with warmer clothing and a couple of ships."

"It would make a pleasant change from fighting."

"So it would," replied Danica, "but I'm afraid that's our lot in life. We are Temple Knights after all."

The wind took them south, although at an admittedly slow pace. The chill in the air stayed with them throughout the day, but by dusk, a warm wind came from the west, freshening the sails and giving them new hope. The sea got rougher, feeling more akin to what they were used to near Korvoran, yet still, the sight of land eluded them.

Early the next morning, they began to wonder where the storm had borne them, for still, there was no land in sight or ships, for that matter, giving them all the impression they were the only living creatures for hundreds of miles.

The day wore on; though, in truth, it felt like no progress was made even though the *Valiant* kept moving through the water, for the scenery remained unchanged. When they finally spotted land off to the east and adjusted their course, a large group of ships heading south along the coast was sighted. And there could be no denying who they were.

"Halvarians," said Nadia. "Do you think they found our camp?"

"I doubt it," replied Danica. "I suspect our previous encounter has got them panicking, so they sent out all their warships to hunt us down."

"Seven, just for us?"

"No, that's far too much force for one ship. The *Water Drake* has most likely informed them of our fleet. Why else send such numbers?"

"What do we do?"

Danica stared at the enemy fleet, considering their options. "We engage them," she said at last.

"All of them?"

"No, we're a faster ship, and the wind is in our favour. With any luck, we can harass the ships in the rear, maybe even draw them out into deeper waters, away from the rest of the expedition. All knights into their armour. We'll soon have a fight to deal with."

A sea battle is not quick, by any means. Ships are ponderous things compared to troops, yet slowly but surely, the *Valiant* drew closer to its enemies, heading roughly southeast, the wind coming from the north.

"Stand by with that arbalest," ordered Danica. "Standard bolts."

Zivka looked up in surprise. "Not a shredder?"

"No, the range is too great."

Time crawled as the Temple ship raced through the waves. The wind was strong, causing it to tip to starboard, forcing Zivka to increase the elevation of the arbalest. The enemy ships kept heading south, unaware of their presence.

Their surprise, however, didn't last long, for the two rear vessels turned to the east in an attempt to come about. In response, the *Valiant* turned south, now heading straight towards the enemy.

"Watch the range," ordered Danica, "and loose your bolt when you think it within range." She turned towards Nadia, who still stood beside her, eyes glued to the Halvarian vessels. "We'll close the range before making a hard turn to starboard."

"Is that wise?" replied the knight.

"They're turning into the wind, and for a brief moment, they'll be almost dead in the water. That's when we make our move."

They could make out individuals aboard the closest Halvarian ship. It faced roughly northeast now, archers lining the railings. Their first volley fell short, but the *Valiant*'s arbalest struck out, smashing into a railing.

"Reload with grappling hook," ordered Danica. "Knights to the port side."

"You mean to board?" asked Nadia.

"We have little choice. They have considerably more archers than us."

"But they outnumber us."

"Yes, but we are Temple Knights. Trust to your training, Sister Nadia, and we will win through this day."

A hail of arrows rained down. Several struck the sail while others drove into the deck. One even hit Danica's shoulder but merely bounced off her pauldron.

Their nearest opponent, now turned into the wind, came to an almost complete halt. That's when the *Valiant* took advantage of their position to come up alongside before turning sharply to port, their bow crashing against the Halvarian vessel's aft end.

Zivka let loose with the grapple, and it sailed across, smashing into the railing of the enemy ship. Moments later, a couple of the Valiant's crew rushed over to man the winch.

Danica drew her sword, racing forward, calling for her knights to follow. There was a slight gap between the two vessels, for they'd separated after their collision, but the enemy drew closer as the crew worked the winch.

"Stand by to board!" she called out, steeling herself for the leap. A shudder reverberated along the hull as the ships crashed into each other again.

"Now!" she yelled.

The decks of the ships were similar in height, and the Halvarian archers waited there for them but fell back at the sight of armoured knights leaping across.

Danica swung out, taking an archer under the arm as he tried in vain to avoid her blade. She rushed forward, gaining the deck, then struck again. Beside her were Zivka and Nadia, their weapons drawing blood, while behind them followed Vivian and Laurel, ready to bring vengeance to the enemy.

The Halvarians fell back, giving up control of the stern, but then Danica noticed a line of resistance forming, with a well-armoured individual ordering the men to stand.

She lunged forward, the tip of her sword digging into someone's leg. An arrow sailed forth, ricocheting off her helmet, and thankful for the protection of her armour, she swung. Another clatter as something struck her leg, and then she was on the attack again, adrenaline coursing through her when her foot slipped on blood. Her leg flew out from under her, tumbling her to the deck. As soon as she hit, men rushed forward, pounding on her with hatchets and swords.

Her helmet blocked most of her view, and she struggled to make sense of what was happening. Moments later, she heard someone cry out above the noise of the fight, and then someone grabbed her arm and pulled her up.

A fellow knight rushed past her into the enemy line just as the deck beneath shifted, jarred as the ship slewed around, smashing once more into the side of the *Valiant*. The two ships were now parallel, and Danica feared the Halvarians might counterattack, swarming onto the Temple ship unopposed, but the fight on the deck kept them busy.

The melee moved past her, and she took a moment to flip up her visor, trying to better understand how the battle progressed. She looked aft to see another Halvarian ship bearing down on them. Off in the distance, two more were slowly turning, clawing their way back towards the fight.

Danica returned her attention to the melee on deck. One of her knights was down, blood dripping from a greave. She rushed forward, desperate to fill the gap.

The Halvarians appeared to have an unending number of warriors. The Temple Knights continued the fight, their swords wreaking terrible damage against their lightly armoured foes. The fight became an endless struggle between life and death, between the superior training and equipment of the sister knights and the seemingly endless Halvarians.

Danica wondered if they hadn't all died and were now fighting an endless battle in the Afterlife. Muscles ached, armour was dented, but they fought on.

A grinding noise rumbled across the deck, and Danica risked a look across to the *Valiant*. The second Halvarian ship had completed its turn and now brushed up against the other side of the Temple ship, effectively trapping it between two Halvarians.

"Back! Back!" she yelled, but the sound of battle drowned out her words. She turned, intending to sprint for the *Valiant*, but lacked the energy to do anything but stumble. A heavy weight struck her back, driving her to the deck, her sword flying from her blood-soaked gauntlets. She rolled to one side, dislodging her assailant and had the satisfaction of seeing him sprawl, much as she had. Instinctively, she reached for her belt, drawing her two daggers. They were large, as such weapons go, designed not so much for cutting as puncturing. She struck out, driving one into her attacker's chest, penetrating the quilted padding.

More of the enemy gathered around her, striking out with spears and axes, forcing her to adopt a fetal position to survive the furious onslaught. Someone grabbed her head in an attempt to force open her visor. Death was coming. Suddenly she remembered Charlaine's words at Alantra: "If we are to die this day, then let us die well. Free your mind of life's burden and let the spirit of the Saints infuse you."

Danica felt a calmness take hold of her as if Agnes herself looked down on the fight. Her foot kicked out, and then she exploded into action, driving daggers out to either side. She didn't stop to take note of whether or not they brought death to the enemy but stabbed out again and again. The sound of fighting surrounded her, the screams and yells now drowning out the sounds of swordplay itself.

Her legs were bruised; blood flowed freely, yet somehow she found the strength to get to her feet and carry on. She was the sword of Agnes, the living embodiment of a Saint, and she fought with newfound energy as if her body was no longer hers to control.

39

BATTLE OF TEMPLE BAY

Summer 1098 SR

C harlaine looked out from her position aboard the *Barlowe*. All four merchant ships sat side by side, anchored both fore and aft to prevent them from bumping into each other. Long timbers were cut and placed between them to provide a bridge of sorts that would allow Temple Knights to quickly reinforce any ship in danger of falling to the enemy.

To the north, the land jutted out, forming what she decided to call Temple Bay, although it wasn't a bay in the truest sense of the word. At the farthest outcropping of land, she placed a trio of Mathewites to keep watch. As she glanced northwest, she recognized the telltale column of smoke—the signal the enemy had arrived.

She'd prepared for this moment, sending the *Vigilant* out to sea along with a dozen sister knights. The rest were parcelled out amongst the merchants, ready to spring into action at the first sign of trouble.

Ashore, she'd gathered what boats the fleet could muster and divided them into three groups under the command of Captain Waleed. He and his Cunars were ready to attack. However, he would need to use his own judgement as to where and when, for the Halvarians' plan of attack was no more than mere speculation on Charlaine's part.

To the north, just beyond where the *Peri* lay at anchor, stood the wreck of the *Rose*. Aboard the remains, Barbek Stoutarm had reinforced what was left of the deck, installing the ballista along with a special surprise. A few Temple Knights of Saint Mathew waited with him, eager to do their part.

With the trap now set, all they could do was wait. Charlaine moved to the *Barlowe's stern* to watch how the enemy attack proceeded. With the wind coming from the northwest, it had been decided the merchant ships would be better off to face downwind, the better to attempt an escape should it prove necessary. She doubted flight would be an option, for the Halvarians had a reputation of being ruthless. She had, however, relented, allowing the merchant captains at least the belief that such was possible.

The wind picked up slightly as the first two ships rounded the cape, moving parallel, their sails partially furled, although the reason for such a decision was unclear to Charlaine's mind. Shortly thereafter, more ships came into view, following in the wake of the first ones.

"They're sailing slower to maintain their formation," said Marlena.

Charlaine smiled. "You know about ships, do you?"

"A little, although I'm not an expert by any means. My brother Sebastien had an interest in military matters. He wanted to be a knight, or so I thought, but it turned out he was only placating Father."

"And so you became one instead?"

"You might say I saw it as my calling."

"Any regrets?" asked Charlaine.

"None whatsoever. It's been difficult at times, especially the training, but I feel at home amongst my sisters. They are, in a sense, the only true family I ever had."

"Have you kept in touch with your brother?"

"I have two of them, actually," said Marlena. "Sebastien is the younger, while Ernst is... well, I suppose he's the duke now. You know, I hadn't considered that."

"Do you miss your old life?"

"Not at all. Life as a Temple Knight is far more rewarding. It feels like we're doing something to make the Continent a better place. How about you?"

"I was a smith before I joined the order," said Charlaine. "I continued the practice down in Ilea, but since coming here, I've been far too busy to spend any time working a forge."

"And do you miss it?"

"I do. Perhaps, when this is all over, I'll see if I can't help Barbek with some of his work. There's nothing quite like the satisfaction of forging a new blade."

"That's what you're doing here, isn't it? Forging new blades, only they're Temple Knights instead of steel."

Charlaine laughed. "I suppose that's one way of looking at it."

The enemy ships cleared the cape.

"Five of them," noted Charlaine. "I thought there'd be more."

"They could be farther astern."

"We'll know soon enough."

The closest ship turned towards them, along with the one following in its wake. The others, farther west, kept sailing due south.

"It looks like they're going to hit us on both sides," said Charlaine.

"They're large ships," said Marlena. "How many men do you think they carry?"

"Likely many more than us, but I doubt they'll be as well-armoured. My hope is that they're provincial troops."

"Provincial?"

"Yes," said Charlaine. "In Ilea, Halvaria used warriors from their conquered territories to man most of their ships. If they do the same here, they'll be relatively lightly armoured and of poorer quality than their elite warriors."

"Why is that?"

"Simple. They don't want to give them enough power to rise up against their masters."

"And their elites?"

"They'll be here too," said Charlaine, "likely aboard the flagship, which-ever one that is. Now, get the knights under cover. We don't want to offer them targets."

"Why hide? They'll board, no matter what, won't they?"

"Halvarians often employ mages. If we let them see Temple Knights, they'll likely stand off and use fire to destroy the fleet."

"So we must lure them in with the promise of an easy capture?"

"Precisely."

"I'll relay the order." Marlena left, issuing orders as she went.

Charlaine continued to watch the enemy. The west column began its turn, making their intentions clear. The two lines would sail up to either end of the merchant ships. Evidently, the thought of four prizes drew them in. The real question was where their mages were.

The wait was agonizing as the Halvarians drew closer, yet Charlaine knew patience was their most important advantage.

The eastern column was finally near enough to read the name embossed on the ship's bow—*Terror*. Men swarmed its decks as archers loosed off volleys. A few arrows clattered to the *Peri's* deck, but most fell short. It would only be moments now before blood was spilt.

The second column was still some distance off. Charlaine considered calling up the knights, but that was a surprise best left for a more opportune moment.

The *Terror* approached, a second ship close enough behind it to read its name. "*Warrior*," said Charlaine, although none were present to hear. She felt her heart pounding, waiting for that moment when chaos would break upon them.

The *Terror* nosed up beside the *Peri*, then threw grapnels. Men tugged on ropes until the Halvarian vessel was snuggled against the merchant ship's side.

The *Warrior* looked poised to turn to starboard to come up along the stern of the *Peri*, but just as the rudder swivelled, a bolt flew out from the wreckage of the *Rose*, digging into the nose of the *Warrior*. The Temple Knights of Saint Mathew pulled on the rope, for Barbek had created a capstan—a vertical post rotating around a central axis. Onto this, he'd mounted bars, allowing Temple Knights to haul in the line by pushing the capstan in circles.

The rope grew taut, and then the *Warrior* shifted sharply to port. With sails still unfurled, it continued moving until its bow struck the same shoals that had spelled the *Rose's* death. A great grinding noise echoed over the bay as the ship came to an abrupt halt, knocking many of its crew to the deck.

Warriors swarmed over the *Terror's* sides, flooding onto the deck of the *Peri*, obviously expecting a fight, but what they found instead was an abandoned ship. They were looking around in confusion, unsure of how to proceed, when the sister knights swarmed across the bridge from the *Monarch*.

Charlaine watched from afar as Marlena led them, slicing into the enemy soldiers, driving a wedge into their numbers. The Halvarians, caught by surprise, could do little but fall back, their leaders ineffective against the sudden onslaught.

She wanted to join them, felt the lure of battle tugging at her heart, yet knew her fight was yet to come. From her position on the *Barlowe*, Charlaine could only watch as the western column closed in. The lead ship was more ornate, with gold leaf surrounding the name on its bow—*Devastator*.

Her own contingent of knights on the *Millicent* stood ready, waiting to reinforce any boarding action against the *Barlowe*. Charlaine realized her presence had caught the attention of what was undoubtedly the Halvarian flagship. A streak of flame shot towards her from the *Devastator's* bow, and she had the presence of mind to duck in time to avoid being hit. Instead, the flames struck the stern railing, turning the air hot as it flew past, and the distinctive smell of charred wood assaulted her nose.

She kept in a crouch and shuffled down the deck, trying to evade detection. Another flame shot overhead as a rain of arrows came crashing down, rattling against her armour but doing no damage. Charlaine crept closer to the railing, trying to determine the enemy's position.

From afar, she heard a horn, the signal that Captain Waleed was leading his boats into the attack. The bulk would assault the Halvarians to the north, while at least a dozen Cunars were slated to help against the *Devastator*.

The *Barlowe* shook as the Halvarian ship thumped up against her. Grapnels were then tossed, snagging the rails, and the enemy pulled their own ship closer in preparation for boarding.

More arrows flew towards her, sporadic and ill-timed, almost as if they were a delaying tactic. Then a boarding ramp was dropped down from the *Devastator*, its metal claws digging into the *Barlowe's* deck, and a slew of Halvarians swarmed across. Not the lightly armoured provincial troops she had expected, however, but their elite warriors, wearing heavy armour, chainmail akin to the Temple Knights of Saint Mathew. Charlaine had a quick glimpse of someone at the *Devastator's* stern, directing the attack, but her line of sight was soon blocked as warriors rushed the deck of the *Barlowe*, hurtling towards her with weapons drawn.

Her sword came up to block, knocking aside a long-shafted axe even as another blade scraped along her vambrace. She backed up, giving herself some room to fight. The Halvarians pushed against her, many bypassing her entirely to spread out along the deck.

She couldn't see her fellow sister knights counterattacking, but then again, she didn't need to. The clash of weapons spelled it out for her. Her sword struck out, smashing into a foe's forearm, not breaking the chainmail links, but the weight of the blade did its job, shattering bone while driving her opponent back.

Fellow Temple Knights appeared at her side, forming a line, pushing forward, driving the mail-clad enemy back. Charlaine's opponent went down beneath the onslaught, and she found herself at the very edge of the boarding ramp. She didn't hesitate, plunging forward to charge onto the *Devastator's* deck.

Sparks flew towards her, and then she felt a hail of stones strike her, hissing as they dug into her helmet. The heat grew so intense, she had to tug the thing from her head and cast it aside, the embers still sizzling as it crashed to the deck.

Now, with a better view of the fight, she spied the Fire Mage at the stern, beside a man in plate armour embossed with gold decorations. The spellcaster's hands thrust forward, his mouth echoing words that summoned the power of nature's most destructive element. A wall of flame erupted directly ahead of Charlaine, then edged towards her, its heat distorting her view of the mage.

She rushed forward, leaping through the fire. As she landed, the leather straps on her armour sizzled. Even her hair smelled of smoke as she charged headlong, ready to cut down the enemy caster. Up the aft-deck steps she ran, only to come face to face with the armoured fighter.

"So," he said, his voice mocking. "If it isn't the heroine of Alantra."

"Surrender," she demanded, "and your life shall be spared."

He raised his eyebrows. "How generous of you to make the overture. I'm afraid I must decline the offer."

He stepped to the side as the mage let loose with another spell, flames shooting out from his fingertips, but this time, instead of striking her, they twisted around her, creating a whirlwind of sparks. Charlaine felt her arms go immobile, her entire body suffused with pain as if every muscle in her body was on fire. Her sword clattered to the deck, and then the spell lifted her upward until her feet dangled beneath her. The mage held her there, bound and unable to move as the enemy leader stepped closer, sheathing his weapon.

"We shall crush you," he said, "just as we have crushed everyone else who dared to stand against the might of the Halvarian Empire."

Charlaine struggled to understand what was happening, a sight that clearly amused the fellow.

"Do you like it?" he asked. "It's called the tomb of fire. It's a particular favourite of Rovantis here."

"Yes," said the mage, "and I can keep it up all day, if necessary."

"Who are you?" Charlaine croaked out.

"I am Lord Augustus Conwyn, Governor of Thansalay."

"Never heard of it."

"Nor would I expect you to. It lies on the northern coast of Halvaria, far removed from these waters." He leaned in closer, enjoying her grimace of pain. "I must admit, you show considerable tolerance. Most would be screaming in agony by now."

A bolt flew past, narrowly missing Rovantis, and he looked to his right to see grey-clad knights climbing over the railing. The distraction cost his master his life, for as the mage turned, he lost his concentration. Released from her torment, Charlaine fell to the deck and immediately sprang forward, knocking Lord Conwyn off his feet. She landed on top of him, grabbing his neck and squeezing with all her might. The Halvarian fought back, grasping her forearms, trying to pry them loose, but years of working a forge had honed her muscles. The lord's eyes glazed over just before he went limp.

Rovantis, alarmed by the new intruders, sent a streak of flame towards the Cunar knights, hitting one dead centre, sending him tumbling from the railing into the sea.

Captain Waleed rushed forward, axe in one hand, shield in the other, smashing into the mage. Using his shield to stun his foe, he then finished him off with an efficient strike that cleaved the man's skull in twain.

"Are you all right?" Waleed asked.

Charlaine rose. "I'm fine," she replied. "Just a little singed." She turned, looking down at the main deck before them, where the scarlet tabards of Saint Agnes mixed with the grey of Saint Cunar as Temple Knights carved their way through the Halvarian host.

Remembering the presence of the other Halvarian vessels, she moved to the aft railing expecting another ship to begin their assault, for at least one had followed in the *Devastator's* wake. Instead it fled, even as the fifth vessel attempted to defend itself from the *Vigilant*. Moments later, weapons were thrown down as the Halvarians, realizing there were no reinforcements coming, gave up the fight.

"I shall round up the prisoners," said Captain Waleed.

Charlaine looked northward, spotting the *Warrior* flying the standard of Saint Mathew. The sounds of battle quieted as Sister Marlena climbed the steps.

"The *Terror* has fallen, Commander."

It took a moment for the news to sink in. "Truly?"

"Yes. The Cunars boarded the *Terror* while we kept their warriors busy. With their retreat cut off, they threw down their weapons. What of the *Vigilant*?"

"She's fighting even as we speak," replied Charlaine, "but they had the largest contingent of knights. I doubt it will take them long to rout the enemy."

A warning cut them off. "More ships approaching," someone yelled. Charlaine looked north where a pair of ships rounded the cape, their design leaving no doubt as to their origins.

"More Halvarians," said Marlena. "What do we do now?"

In answer, Charlaine simply watched them round the spit of land followed closely by another ship, with its distinctive triangular sail for all to see. The sight gave her hope. "Unless I miss my guess, those are now Temple ships."

The *Valiant* sailed into Temple Bay, accompanying the two large warships, each flying the flag of Saint Agnes.

Charlaine watched as a familiar figure climbed down into a skiff and rowed towards them. "About time you showed up," she called out.

Even from above, Charlaine saw a smile break out on Danica's face. "I see you kept yourself busy," the younger captain replied. The boat bumped against the side of the *Devastator*, and then a rope ladder was lowered. The raven-haired knight climbed aboard to be greeted with an embrace.

"Glad to see you're all in one piece," said Charlaine. "We were worried when you didn't return."

"It couldn't be helped. We were caught in a storm and blown far to the north. It didn't help much that we didn't have any decent charts of the area. We had to find our way back by dead reckoning."

"And so you decided to capture a couple of ships along the way?"

"Well, what can I say?" said Danica. "I couldn't let you have all the fun."

"You did well, but what puzzles me is how you found the manpower to sail those things?"

"Actually, they still have their original crews, minus their officers, of course. I put Temple Knights in charge, with one crew member apiece from the *Valiant* to provide advice. These provincial Halvarians were all forced into service as an alternative to execution."

"So they're all criminals?"

"Under Halvarian law, yes, but I believe you'll find the majority of them are regular folk. I suspect many would serve us if we deigned to simply pay them."

"Wouldn't they want to return home?"

"Not unless they wish to die. And in any case, they've been aboard ship so long, they know little else."

"The question now is what do we do with them? Between all these Halvarians, we have more prisoners than crew. Certainly, some of the provincials may elect to join us, but what do we do with the rest? We're not exactly equipped to handle this many prisoners."

"I think you'll find there are plenty of chains aboard these ships," said

Danica. "The Halvarians like to lock up anyone who commits even the slightest infraction."

"Somehow, that doesn't surprise me," said Charlaine. "We'll begin by taking them ashore. Once we sort out the willing, we'll chain up the remainder to keep them out of mischief."

"And once this campaign is over?"

"That's for the Church to decide."

40

DISCOVERY

Summer 1098 SR

C harlaine inched forward, parting the branches with her hand. Beyond lay the Halvarian camp, a collection of dozens of buildings surrounded by a log palisade. She could see some of the interior courtyard from their vantage point. Within, the empire's soldiers, distinctive in their chain armour, marched around groups of unarmoured men, armed with spears and shields but little else.

"This is just like Cunara," Charlaine said. "I expect one of those buildings will be heavily fortified. That's where we'll find their leaders."

"How many of those should we expect?" asked Captain Waleed.

"Hard to say. At Cunara, there were only a few dozen, but I gather most of the warriors there were indoctrinated over a much longer period."

The Cunar captain grunted. "Is this how they train all their provincials?"

"I can't speak to all the conquered lands, but it was certainly so in Calabria."

"What should we be watching for?"

"They'll have mages amongst their number, although I can't swear to numbers."

"And these trainees, will they fight?"

"They might," said Charlaine. "They did at Cunara, at least in the beginning, but we can't assume the same is true here."

Captain Waleed shook his head. "I don't like this. We already have our hands full, keeping an eye on prisoners. Liberate this place, and we'll have even more to look after."

"What other choice do we have?"

"Simple. We execute the prisoners. That would free up all our knights for this assault."

"How can you even suggest such a thing? Have you no compassion?"

"I might remind you, Commander, that only a few days ago, they all tried their best to kill us. Death is the price we pay as warriors."

"Not under my command. We will show compassion to our enemies, not execute them all out of hand."

"It's your choice," said Waleed. "I shall respect your wishes, but that leaves us very few Temple Knights with which to carry out the assault."

"Then we must adjust our plans."

A tap on her shoulder caused Charlaine to turn.

"Down there," Marlena whispered as she pointed. "Do you see them?"

Below them, a trio of soldiers made their way through the forest, obviously looking for something, for they stopped several times, peering into the woods on either side.

"What's this, now?" said Captain Waleed. "Halvarians out for a stroll in the warmth of the afternoon?"

"I doubt that," said Charlaine. "Let's get closer and see if we can't discover what they're up to, shall we?"

They backtracked, descending the rise to the forest floor. It didn't take long to pick up the Halvarians' trail, for the path was well worn. As they drew closer, voices echoed back.

"They must be here somewhere," came a high-pitched whine. "How far could they have gotten?"

"Don't be a fool," answered a baritone. "They escaped, didn't they? Do you honestly think they'd hang around here?"

The third man chuckled, his voice older and rougher. "They won't last long in these woods. If the bears don't get them, the wolves will."

"Wolves?" came the high voice. "Nobody said anything about wolves. We should get back to camp."

"Don't be stupid," replied the baritone. "If we come back empty-handed, it'll be three days in the pit."

Charlaine gave Marlena a hand signal, sending the younger knight off to the right of the road.

"Come," whispered Charlaine. "We'll cross to the north and shadow them until Marlena's in position."

"I'm with you," said Waleed, rubbing his hands together. "Nothing like a few prisoners to get the information we need."

They moved slowly, trying to be as quiet as possible. They'd set out from Temple Bay, leaving their heavy armour behind, relying on the thick gambesons to protect them from any danger. This was, after all, merely a scouting mission rather than the assault itself. Ahead of them, a Halvarian cried out in alarm.

"Who are you?" he shouted.

"Surrender yourselves," said Marlena, "in the name of the Church."

"Not likely," replied a gruff response.

Steel struck steel, then, as running feet came towards them, Charlaine and Waleed emerged from cover. At the sight of the Temple Knights, the two Halvarians halted, dropping to their knees and supplicating themselves.

"Must be a Halvarian custom," said Waleed. He moved forward, removing their weapons.

Soon thereafter, Marlena appeared, a rip in her gambeson and blood on her blade. "I'm afraid the other fellow is dead. He refused to surrender."

"We'll take his body," said Charlaine. "We don't want to let the enemy know we're here."

"Easy enough," added Waleed. "We'll just have these two carry it."

"Won't they notice they're missing?" asked Marlena.

He chuckled. "Likely they will, but knowing what we just overheard, they'll think they deserted." He poked the prisoners with the tip of his sword. "All right, you two, get up and get moving. We haven't got all day."

They advanced up the road to find the body. Marlena had killed him with an efficient thrust in the heart, easy enough considering his lack of armour. They gathered up his axe, then the two prisoners lifted him from either end.

"Right," said the high-voiced man. "Where to now?"

"Back to Temple Bay," said Charlaine.

"Where's that?"

"Follow Sister Marlena. She'll lead the way, and don't get any ideas about escaping. Captain Waleed here was just telling me how he delights in killing prisoners."

The captain looked at her with an overdone look of exasperation. "I didn't say I delighted in it, merely that it was our duty." He glanced at the prisoners. "Consider yourself lucky Captain Charlaine captured you."

"That's commander," said Marlena. "At least until this expedition is over."

"I stand corrected."

. . .

The trip back to their base was uneventful. They'd considered searching for the escaped prisoners, but the risk of discovery was far too great, considering there could be other groups of Halvarians out looking for them.

Back at their own base, the prisoners finally dropped the body of their comrade before they fell to the ground themselves, exhausted.

"Take them over to the other prisoners," ordered Charlaine. "We'll interrogate them later."

She looked out at the bay where the captured warships were anchored in a line while men worked to re-float the *Warrior*.

"She's in fine shape," came the gruff voice of Barbek. "We just had to patch a couple of holes."

"I'm surprised she's still aground."

"Ah well, it took us some time to empty the hold. We need to lighten her, you see, to get her off the rocks."

"And now?"

"Now we're using ropes to haul her backward. You can't make it out from this angle on account of the other ships in the way, but we have a half-dozen ships' boats pulling her astern."

"I noticed the prisoner count is down."

"It is," said the Dwarf. "We convinced a few more to join our cause. I told them their other choice was that we'd hand them over to the Duke of Reinwick. They didn't seem too impressed with that option."

"Can't say I blame them. I'm sure the only result of that would be death at the end of a noose."

"They're not bad people once you get to know them."

"You have been busy."

"I can't help it. I'm a Dwarf. What else was I to do while you were off gallivanting in the woods?"

Charlaine laughed. "Gallivanting? Is that what you believe we were doing?"

"No, of course not."

"While we were out, we managed to capture a couple of guards from that base we're after."

"Captured, you say? Mind if I have a chat with them? Perhaps I can convince them to tell us what we need to know."

"By all means," said Charlaine, "but they must be treated humanely."

The Dwarf grinned. "I wouldn't have it any other way. Now, where are these fellows? I do assume they're men?"

"Yes, they are. Marlena is around here somewhere. She can take you to them."

"Then I shall see to it immediately."

"Seek me out when you're done. I'm eager to hear what you learn."

That evening, they met aboard the captured *Devastator*. They'd found a decent map of the enemy training camp on the flagship, which simplified things considerably.

"Thoughts, anyone?" asked Charlaine.

"How about a straight naval assault?" said Captain Waleed. "We have the ships now."

Charlaine considered it. "It would mean landing knights in ships' boats, making them vulnerable."

"Agreed," said Danica, "and they might flee deeper inland. I'd hate to spend months hunting them down."

"So something to cut them off, then," mused Charlaine. "Or at least to bottle them up behind that palisade until our knights are in position."

"Doesn't sound too difficult," said Barbek. "You have the manpower, or should I say the knight power?" He chuckled at his own remark.

"Getting our people ashore is one thing. Assaulting a prepared defence is quite another. We must also deal with the possibility they have mages."

"Oh," said the Dwarf. "That's no longer a possibility; it's a fact. The prisoners confirmed it."

"Can you be more specific?"

"They revealed three gifted individuals, although I suppose that might be four if Larissa Stormwind is present. Two of those are Fire Mages from the sounds of it."

"And the third?"

"That's where it gets worse, I'm afraid. From what they described, there's a Death Mage to deal with."

"A Necromancer?" said Danica. "Are you sure?"

"What else would you call someone who can rip memories from your mind?"

"How ghastly," said Sister Marlena. "How do we handle such a threat?"

"The same way we do with all our enemies," explained the Dwarf, "with steel. Of course, the real danger is what she might do with her magic."

"Which is what, exactly?"

"Well, she could animate corpses for a start or even suck the life force out of you. Armour won't give you much protection against such magic."

"Are you an expert in such things?" asked Danica.

"Me?" said Barbek. "Saints, no, but I've heard stories."

"What about that Halvarian lord?"

"You mean Lord Augustus? He's stubborn and a fanatic—he won't reveal anything. I still believe we should throw him overboard with an anchor attached."

"Now, now," said Charlaine. "We need to be charitable to our enemies."

"Should we?" said Danica. "They weren't so to Sister Cordelia."

"If we stoop to their level, we are no better than them. If we ever want to defeat them, we must do so on our own terms."

"I don't fear the Halvarians," said Captain Waleed, "or their Necromancer, but that palisade of theirs presents a problem."

"How tall is it?" asked Danica.

"Seven, maybe eight feet?"

"And is there a fighting platform on the other side?"

"No," said the Cunar. "At least not that we could see from our height advantage."

"In that case, we have two choices: go through it or over it."

"Axes would take far too long to cut through," said Barbek. "I would suggest going over."

"That means ladders," said Danica.

"Easy enough to make. It's not as if there's a shortage of wood."

"We'll do both," said Charlaine. "The ladders will lead, but once they establish a foothold, we'll get a few people working with axes to make an opening."

"Fine by me," said Captain Waleed. "How do you want to divide up our knights?"

"The Halvarians have no warships remaining, save for the *Water Drake*. We'll use the *Valiant* and *Vigilant* to take care of her should she be present."

"And if not?" asked Danica.

"Then you concentrate on capturing those merchant vessels," said Charlaine. "We'll bring the bulk of our forces aboard the *Barlowe* and *Monarch*, but we'll need our Cunar brethren to secure the perimeter around the camp to prevent any Halvarians from fleeing. I shall lead the landing force myself, but I want Captain Waleed to take charge of bottling up the enemy."

"You can count on me," said the Cunar captain.

"Where would you like me?" asked Barbek.

"You?" said Charlaine. "This is not your fight."

"But it is. These Halvarians destroyed the great Dwarf city of Dun Galdrim. No Dwarf worth his forge could sit back and let them get away with that."

"In that case, I'd like you to accompany my own group. Your skill set could prove particularly useful once we get inside the camp."

"Meaning?"

"Some trainees may be shackled."

"I'll be sure to bring some tools."

"Might I suggest," said Danica, "that we bring along another ship, perhaps the *Peri*? We can use it to set up a floating infirmary to deal with the wounded."

"Why not simply bring your people ashore?" asked Captain Waleed.

"Too dangerous. We don't know what kind of animals live in this region, not to mention stray Halvarians who might want to exact some form of revenge. There's also the matter of weather to consider. The last thing I'd like is for wounded to be left out in the rain."

"You make a good point," said Charlaine. "Though one of the captured Halvarian ships might be better suited. They're much longer; thus less inclined to move around in the waves. Have a look at them and see what you think. I'll leave the final decision up to you."

She took a breath, looking around the room. Up until now, the largest group she'd ever led into battle was half a dozen sister knights. Now, however, she was responsible for nearly a hundred. Charlaine looked down at the map.

"Captain Waleed, you'll take all of your Cunars and the Mathewites, along with what horses we have. I'll use the sisters for the seaborne assault."

"That won't give you much in the way of an army," said Danica. "Especially since we'll need some for ship-to-ship fighting."

"We don't need many to land ashore. The idea is to threaten them. If they come out of their camp to fight, so much the better, as Captain Waleed will be able to attack from behind."

"And if they hold up inside?"

"Then," said Charlaine, "the presence of a few knights in boats will make little difference. We'll commence the siege once everyone's ashore."

"What of our other ships?"

"We'll leave them here with minimal crews. Unfortunately, we'll need to leave knights to guard the prisoners. That can't be helped, but if we bring them aboard the vessels that stay behind, we can shackle them in the hold. At least that makes them easier to watch."

"Who'll remain behind?" asked Danica.

"I hoped Sister Marlena might be up to it."

"Me?" replied the young knight. "I'm barely more than a recruit."

"Yet more than capable of giving orders," said Charlaine, "as your experience as my aide has proven. Are you willing to accept this responsibility?"

"Yes, of course."

"Good," said Charlaine. "Then the matter is settled. We'll begin making preparations immediately with an eye to sailing at first light the day after tomorrow. That should give us ample time to construct ladders, sort out the prisoners, and get everyone aboard."

"I'll see to the prisoner transfer," said Captain Waleed.

"Please coordinate your efforts with Captain Danica. We don't want any arguments over the use of the ships' boats."

"And I'll oversee construction of ladders," offered Barbek. "I'll use the Mathewites. There should be enough of them to get the job done, and their axes will prove most useful for the task."

"In that case," said Charlaine, "I'll let you get to it."

They all started filing from the room.

"A moment, Danica, if you will?" said Charlaine.

The knight halted, letting the others leave before speaking. "Something wrong?" the younger knight asked.

"I wanted to speak to you about the fleet."

"What about it?"

"We left Korvoran with two warships, but we'll be returning with nine. Maintaining that many ships will prove expensive, not to mention the difficulty in crewing them. I'd like your thoughts on the matter."

"A fleet this size was definitely not what the grand mistress expected, but I believe we can make it work."

"And where would the funds come from?" asked Charlaine. "Surely you don't have enough to cover all the expenses?"

"No, but I'm hoping we'll capture some of those Halvarian merchant ships, then sell them off to raise some funds. It would be a temporary solution, but if we have enough for the short term, I'm hoping the Antonine will see the wisdom in funding us."

"And if not?"

"Then we'll burn the excess ships," said Danica. "I don't want to see them in the hands of the Halvarians."

"Might you consider selling some warships to the Petty Kingdoms in these parts?"

"I thought of that, but it would only serve to sow more discontent between them. There's already a great rivalry amongst the coastal kingdoms. Handing out warships, particularly these large Halvarian vessels, would only make things worse. The other option would be to beach them until such time as we could afford to operate them."

"And as to the crews?"

"That's the biggest issue, in truth. The Holy Fleet in Corassus consists of galleys rowed by Temple Knights. These ships, however, require those experienced in sailing ships rather than rowing. That's a different category altogether."

"How do you see us resolving the issue?" asked Charlaine.

"I think our order would consider them as auxiliaries, much as the Cunars hire on extra warriors when they go to war. Our own knights would still make up the fighting complement, of course."

"We'll bring the matter to the attention of Commander Salvatore once we return. He might have some suggestions on how we should proceed."

"An excellent idea. Anything else?"

"Yes. I wanted to tell you you've far exceeded my expectations so far, Danica. I'll be recommending they appoint you as the admiral for the Northern Fleet."

Danica blushed. "I'm humbled."

"You've earned it. Now get out of here. You've plenty of work to keep you busy."

41

THE FLEET

Summer 1098 SR

Charlaine watched the distant shore as the *Valiant* made her way northward.

"It's so peaceful here," she said.

"The calm before the storm?" quipped Danica.

"I suppose so. You know, it's strange to think, but it wasn't so long ago that I was just a simple smith."

"I doubt you were ever simple. You're here, where you belong, Charlaine, where Saint Agnes needs you."

"I like to think so, but I can't help but feel she wouldn't condone all this loss of life."

Danica shifted her feet, looking down at the deck. "I must tell you something…"

"Go on."

"When the *Valiant* fought those two warships, I thought us doomed."

"Then why did you fight?"

"We had to, in order to save the rest of the fleet. It wasn't as if the *Vigilant* could have taken on seven enemy ships all by itself. I knew, going in, we would be sacrificing ourselves for the greater good, but I was resigned to that."

"And?"

"We came up alongside the first ship, and a great melee developed. It soon became apparent we were vastly outnumbered, but we fought on, determined to do our duty. I went down, swarmed by the enemy. Blows rained down on me, yet somehow, miraculously, I survived, then I found it: some inner strength that let me carry on as if a divine presence possessed me."

"You felt the blessing of the Saints," said Charlaine. "I read it's not an uncommon phenomenon amongst those who are devout, although I must admit it's rare amongst those of our order."

"Why is that, do you suppose?"

"I don't know? Perhaps other orders inspire more devotion? Their rules of behaviour are much stricter than ours."

"Do you think the spirit of Agnes possessed me?"

"No, but maybe you released something that's always been buried deep within you. Call it divine inspiration, if you like."

"Are you suggesting I'm a zealot?"

"No, you're not a fanatic, if that's what you're worried about."

"What about you?" asked Danica. "Have you ever felt that way?"

"Not precisely. My faith gives me the strength to carry on, even when things seem hopeless. As a smith, I learned perseverance is as important as skill, but I never thought of that as divine."

"And yet you're the most devout person I've ever met. You don't just recite the teachings—you live them."

"As do you," said Charlaine.

"I don't see that. I thought Barbek's idea of tying Lord Conwyn to an anchor was reasonable."

"That was frustration speaking. Deep down, you're a decent, caring person."

"I want to be, truly I do, but sometimes I struggle."

"We all have fears and doubts. The true test of a person's courage is carrying on in the face of them. Hold to your beliefs, Danica. In the end, it's all that separates us from our enemies."

They fell silent, watching the waves roll by. The seas were relatively calm today, with a gentle breeze blowing in from the northwest. Off in the distance, a large shape rose to the surface, lingering there for a moment.

"Another whale," said Danica. "A good omen. We saw them in the north when the storm blew us far out to sea. They weren't like this one though. Instead of grey, they had white skin and a great horn protruding from their head."

"Like a unicorn?"

"Similar, but pointing forward, not up."

Charlaine laughed. "Now, you're pulling my leg."

"It's true, I swear it. Nadia saw it too."

"What was it like farther north?"

"A land of ice and snow. Well, I say land, but there was nothing but ice as far as I could tell. I'd like to return there someday and explore it further, maybe even make some maps of the area."

"Does anyone live there, do you think?"

"I'd be surprised," said Danica, "but then again, stranger things have been discovered. Brother Leamund had all sorts of stories of unusual things, all of them second-hand, mind you. They say down towards the Kurathian Isles, there are gigantic sea dragons."

"Eiddenwerthe is a mysterious place," said Charlaine, "and our race has only explored a small portion of it. Perhaps one day you'll become a great explorer and expand our knowledge of the unknown lands."

Danica smiled. "I'd like that, but I suppose we best concentrate on dealing with these Halvarians for the present." She glanced northward. "We made good time. Once we round that spit of land, we'll be close to our target."

"That soon?"

"Aye, but Captain Waleed will need more time to get into position. We'll anchor just the other side of that outcropping, then sail at first light tomorrow."

"Good," said Charlaine. "That gives me time to transfer over to the *Barlowe*. Barbek will be expecting me."

"I'll send out a ship's boat to scout out the enemy. Less chance of discovery that way."

"Send word if there's any changes I should know about."

"Anything else?"

"Yes, I'm sure a prayer wouldn't go amiss. These days, we need all the help we can get."

"Now, there's a thought," said Danica. "A Temple Knight praying. Whoever would have thought of such a thing?"

Below decks on the *Barlowe*, the sister knights readied themselves. Many sharpened swords while others saw to their armour, making minor adjustments to buckles and belts. Charlaine walked amongst them, offering words of encouragement. Battle was a bloody affair, and she knew some of her charges might not see another dusk. Tomorrow would bring the horrors of war up close and personal. Blood would permeate the air, and with it, putrid flesh from gangrenous wounds. Win or lose, it would be a battle not soon forgotten, at least by those who survived. Would future generations remember the sacrifice of these Holy Warriors? Would anyone mourn their passing?

For perhaps the twentieth time, she fretted about her plans. She went over them, again and again in her mind, trying to convince herself all was good, but truthfully, she had little experience in such things. Would she lead them all to victory, or would it turn out to be a disaster?

"Would you pray for us, Captain?"

Her maudlin thoughts interrupted, Charlaine looked down to see Sister Damora staring up at her.

"Yes, certainly," she replied.

The room fell silent, so much so that the only sound in evidence was the sloshing of water against the ship's hull.

"Blessed Saint Agnes," she began. "We call upon you today to give your blessings to this endeavour. To watch over us as we fight in your name. Give us the strength to triumph over our enemies and keep us safe that we might serve you in all your glory. And if we should fall this day, then let us pass to the Afterlife having earned your respect and admiration for our devotion." She went silent, counting to five in her head. "Saints be with us."

"Saints be with us all," echoed the sister knights.

They sat in silence a moment longer, each knight contemplating their own fate. This was a ritual most Temple Knights practiced, thinking of the coming battle before the chaos of war descended upon them. Charlaine watched as many silently mouthed prayers of their own while others simply returned to their work of sharpening swords and adjusting straps.

Sister Josephine sat on the port side, rubbing away at an invisible stain on the back of her gauntlet. The knight clearly struggled, her obsession growing more pronounced with each stroke.

Charlaine moved closer, noting her charge's pale features. "Sister Josephine," she said. "Is there anything I can help you with?"

The woman looked up, panic in her eyes. "It is merely a stain, Captain, but I can't seem to remove it. I can't go into battle like this. It's a disgrace."

Charlaine placed her hand over Josephine's, stilling the action. "You are in the Saints' hands now, Sister. They care not whether your armour shines, only that you do. Do your duty this day, and the Saints shall look upon you with favour."

She watched as the look of panic dissipated, replaced by that of determination. "Yes, of course," said Josephine.

Charlaine continued down the length of the ship, inwardly cringing at her own words. Inspiring others was a requirement of any good leader, yet to her, the words sounded hollow. She knew she'd not been a knight for long, and this, more than anything, fed her doubts. Yes, she was older than most of her charges, and yes, she'd proven herself in the south, but how much of that could simply be attributed to luck? Captain Giselle was an exceptional leader, and the credit for the great naval battle rested squarely on the admiral's shoulders. What, then, had she contributed to the matter, other than her presence?

As she reached the bow, she turned, her eyes drifting over the complement of Temple Knights. How many would die? How many more souls would burden her conscience until her final days?

Her thoughts drifted back to Alantra—so many perished that day. Amongst them, many she considered friends. Panic rose in her, that she was out of her depth, that she would lead them all to ruin, but then, just as quickly, a calm descended upon her, quieting her fears. Saint Agnes brought her here, where she was needed. This was her calling, of that she was sure, and that knowledge gave her strength.

The early morning light revealed a deck full of sister knights resplendent in their plate armour. Alongside the *Barlowe*, two longboats were tethered, ready to take them ashore once the ship was in place.

Their scouts returned with news that the *Water Drake* was nowhere to be seen. It was a disappointment, for the presence of that vessel would be undeniable proof of Larissa Stormwind's betrayal. As it stood now, it would be a matter of the mage's word against the knight's—of little use, considering the high esteem in which the Duke of Reinwick held Larissa.

The wind picked up, filling the sails as the *Barlowe* rounded the spit of land. Charlaine looked at the boats, concerned for their welfare, when the water got choppier, but she needn't have bothered, for both remained undamaged. Valiant led the fleet to her front, with *Vigilant* some distance to the north, both moving quickly as if someone let them off their leashes.

To their rear, the *Monarch* struggled to make the turn. The merchant vessel was not the most manoeuvrable of ships, but fortunately, as they turned, the sails filled, giving her the impetus she needed to continue on her way.

A yell drew Charlaine's attention to the port side, where the *Devastator* ploughed through the waves. It was a strange sight as the captured Halvarian flagship bore no troops, instead relegated to serving as a refuge for the injured. Even so, it was impressive, for the empire spared no expense in outfitting the vessel. The ship was massively expensive to begin with, yet the addition of gold decorations and scrolled woodwork easily doubled its cost, if not tripled. She wondered how many mouths that much gold could feed, and then the thought struck her that those gold fittings might pay for the upkeep on the rest of the fleet.

A crewman called out as their target hove into view. The Halvarian cargo ships floated peacefully at anchor, seemingly unaware of the impending attack.

The Holy Fleet crawled at what felt like an agonizingly slow pace. It wasn't that they were slow—the shoreline passing on their right quickly dispelled that notion—but now that the target was in sight, Charlaine was eager to begin.

The first sign of panic amongst the Halvarians was by a skiff halfway between the dock and its intended destination, one of the merchant ships. Upon sighting the invading fleet, its occupants pointed fingers and then turned their small boat around, heading towards shore.

Charlaine saw movement aboard the closest merchant ship as men moved about, unfurling sails and attempting to pull up the anchor. The *Valiant* turned slightly to starboard, steering directly for it. The *Vigilant*, farther out to sea, kept moving eastward, intent on cutting off any ship that might choose to flee.

Ashore, men raced towards the safety of the palisade, a bell ringing out an alarm. There were no signs of warriors at the moment, but the enemy was now alert to their presence. It would not take long for troops to issue forth.

"This is it," said Charlaine, turning to face her knights. They all stared at her in expectation, their visors up, revealing their fear and anticipation. "This battle," she continued, "will decide who rules the Great Northern Sea. Should we fail this day, the Halvarians will see it as a weakness. They will infest these islands with their ships and warriors, preying on those who sail these waters. Yes, we defeated their fleet, but now we need to continue our victory by wiping all signs of the empire from these shores."

The Temple Knights gave a cheer, then moved to the railing as they waited for the next command.

"Man the boats," Charlaine ordered, watching as her knights climbed down into the skiffs. Barbek stood by her side, making a deep bow, his arbalest cradled in his arms.

"After you," he said, looking right at her.

"Don't you need your tools?" she asked.

He smiled back. "Already done. I put them in the boat earlier this morning. All except for this." He held up his arbalest.

Charlaine used the rope to lower herself over the side of the *Barlowe*. The ship's boat waited, bobbing slightly in the waves, her knights holding the oars vertically while everyone else climbed aboard. In Ilea, she found boarding a boat a real challenge, the fear of drowning a constant companion, but now, after so much sailing, she spared little thought for such a fate, instead dropping the last few feet to land amongst her warriors. She sat at the bow while the Dwarf lowered himself into place.

Sister Damora took the tiller as Charlaine gave the order to push off from the *Barlowe*. They drifted away from the other boat, helped along by the judicious use of an oar or two against the merchant's hull.

"Take up the oars," Charlaine ordered, then waited as they were placed into the oarlocks. She nodded at Damora to call the time.

"Stroke!" called out the knight, and the boat slowly moved towards the shore. Used to discipline, the sisters rowed in perfect unison, moving them inexorably closer to the enemy. Charlaine kept her eye landward, watching for any signs of movement.

"They'll come out soon enough," said Barbek, clutching his arbalest. "Don't you worry."

She risked a glance aft to spot the other ship's boat following along behind, slightly to their west. Trees blocked most of her view of the enemy, but she knew that would soon be rectified. Sure enough, once they cleared the wooded shoreline, the full length of the palisade came into view.

From Charlaine's position on the water, the Cunar cavalry was easy to spot, sitting in an open area west of camp. However, the rest of the brother knights were not visible, leaving her wondering where they might be. She forced herself to concentrate on her own knights, consoled by the fact there was naught she could do about it at the moment. She must trust in Captain Waleed and the Temple Knights of Saint Cunar, the finest warriors in the Petty Kingdoms.

Even as she watched, the camp's gates opened wide to release men equipped with spears and shields, leading a large group of warriors marching in formation. Even from this range, Charlaine could identify the stylized gold dragon that decorated their dark-green tabards. These were elite Halvarians, the cream of the empire's army. They would not easily be beaten.

She wanted to scream in frustration, sitting helplessly as she was in a boat, yet all she could do was watch as more and more men poured forth until it was abundantly clear she'd seriously underestimated their numbers.

In total, seven companies emerged, each identified by their war banners. These she'd not seen before, for her encounters in the south were against ships and small raiding parties. Two of the companies had golden dragons atop their standards, while the rest had a simple crown, presumably identifying them as mere provincials. Charlaine felt a knot growing in her stomach as she beheld the enemy forces.

"Row," she shouted, desperate to help her comrades. "Row with everything you've got!" Her attention was focused solely on the battle before her, the ships no longer her concern. She wanted to leap out of the boat and run as they crept closer to shore, but a quick look over the side revealed the water was still too deep.

The sounds of conflict pulled her back to the present. Ashore, the enemy now engaged with Captain Waleed's forces. From her vantage point, all she saw were the backs of the enemy's green tabards advancing towards the Cunar knights.

Finally, the boat's keel struck sand, and then she was over the side, sprinting through knee-deep water to reach the shore.

42

BATTLE

Summer 1098 SR

She reached dry land and waited for her knights. Half a dozen of them pulled the boat farther up, lest it float away, while the rest took up positions on either side of Charlaine.

To her front, she could make out the lighter green tabards of the provincial troops surrounding the mounted Cunars. The grey-clad knights had engaged the bigger threat, the elite Halvarian warriors, but in their haste, they'd allowed themselves to be flanked. Farther east, the rest of the Cunars, those on foot, struggled to hold the line close to the palisade.

Captain Waleed had planned to send warriors east and west, but Charlaine saw no sign of the Mathewites, but then she felt a tug on her arm. Barbek pointed towards the east, farther down the beach.

"There," he said. "Do you see them? A large mass of Halvarians fighting someone in the trees. That must be the Mathews."

Charlaine was now forced to make a terrible decision. Before her, the Cunars fought a superior enemy. The presence of her own forces could easily turn the tables. On the other hand, the brother knights of Saint Mathew were in danger of being overwhelmed. She glanced at the other longboat, now disgorging its complement of sister knights.

"Josephine," she called out. "Take your knights and assault the enemy before you."

She waited only a moment as the rest of her knights formed up on the beach, then turned to her smaller company. "This way," she yelled. "We must hurry."

They cut across the front of the camp, its doors now shut. It was a risky move, for had there been archers on the walls, they'd have ample opportunity to play havoc amongst the knights. Instead, they proceeded without interference, and soon the sounds of battle grew stronger.

Charlaine caught a glimpse of brown in amongst the green of the Halvarians. It appeared the beleaguered Mathewites were holding on despite being vastly outnumbered.

She led her knights directly into the rear of one of the provincial companies, taking them by surprise. Lightly armoured as they were, they were quickly overcome by the sister knights' superior training. Resistance melted away, many throwing their weapons to the ground and prostrating themselves in the Halvarian manner.

Charlaine kept her warriors moving, intent on reaching their beleaguered brother knights. Soon the Mathewites' brown tabards mixed with the scarlet of her own order, the tide of battle changing.

Halvarian elites turned on the sisters with a new-found fury, determined to see the battle through to the end. Charlaine fought for her life as the enemy pushed forward unexpectedly, driving her own troops back.

An axe dug into her shield, the weight of it threatening to pull it from her grasp. She countered with a vicious slash, but her sword only scraped along chainmail, doing no actual damage.

A spear thrust towards her face, forcing her back, and then two more reached out, one taking her in the hip. She felt the tip scrape along her tasset, but the metal held, protecting her thigh. The axe pulled free of her shield as she retaliated, and the sudden change threw off her balance.

The axe wielder raised the two-handed weapon on high, intending to bring it down onto her head. But just then, she stepped forward, using her damaged shield to smash into the man's face, sending him stumbling back with a broken nose. She followed up with a thrust, taking him in the neck, and he collapsed, blood turning his tabard crimson.

Her sword pulled back, ringing out as a mace struck it, the shock of the impact racing up her arm, numbing her fingers. Her foe quickly struck again, the weapon smashing against the side of her head with a glancing blow. It rang in her ears as it knocked her helmet askew, impeding her vision.

Unable to see her enemy, she staggered back, raising her weapon to defend herself. Another blow struck her chestplate, forcing her back even farther, and she tripped on something, sending her sprawling.

She could see nothing, yet the sounds of fighting continued above her.

Releasing the strap from beneath her chin, she tossed the helmet aside, allowing her a view of the surrounding carnage with all of its mangled flesh and broken bones.

A scarlet-clad knight rushed past her, pushing back the Halvarian line, sword held high for an overhead strike. From Charlaine's left came the battle hymn of Saint Mathew, its choral notes an eerie counterpoint to the sounds of battle.

She got to her feet, her eyes trying to make sense of the mayhem. Somehow the fighting had twisted around, and she now looked out into the makeshift harbour where the *Valiant* snuggled up against a merchant vessel while the *Vigilant* moved in on another. The entire scene appeared quite tranquil, a stark contrast to the chaos that surrounded her.

Charlaine hefted her sword, feeling its reassuring weight. The blade was covered in blood, with nicks and scratches all along it, yet the three embossed waves on the pommel gave her the strength she needed to carry on. She was a Temple Knight, and she would continue the fight.

She rushed into battle, her sword striking a Halvarian soldier, nearly cleaving him in two, and she pushed on, forcing another back with her shield. Her faith carried her onward, slashing, thrusting, and smashing her way into the enemy warriors. In her wake came the Temple Knights of Saint Agnes, slicing their way through the Halvarian ranks like a storm of steel.

In that instant, there was only the cold fury of her Saint and an enemy waiting to be vanquished. Her body took over, her limbs repeating those movements every sister knight knew by heart.

On and on she went until none remained to face her wrath. When something hit her on the shoulder, she instinctively wheeled around, ready to cleave them in twain. Before her stood a Temple Knight of Saint Mathew bleeding from multiple wounds, his tabard soaked in the blood of his enemies.

"It is over," he said. "The rest flee into the palisade."

Charlaine wanted to pursue, but fatigue washed over her. She slumped to her knees.

"Thank the Saints," she said, struggling to catch her breath. Her muscles ached, her back was sore, and even her mind fought to overcome the exhaustion. Brother knights gathered discarded weapons and herded prisoners into small groups, the easier to control them.

"What of the Cunars?" asked Charlaine.

"See for yourself," the knight replied, pointing.

Grey-clad knights milled around the entrance to the palisade, disarming those attempting to seek safety within its walls. Charlaine forced herself to stand, willing her legs to work, then made her way towards the gate. She soon spotted Captain Waleed, who had a nasty cut to the face, but aside from that, appeared uninjured.

"We routed them," he proclaimed. "By the Saints, that was a tough fight. Much as I hate to admit it, if it hadn't been for your knights, we would've been overcome."

"And ruin your reputation for victory?" she replied. "I think not."

His eyes turned to examine the massive wooden gate. "I don't suppose they'll surrender? It would make things so much easier."

"I wouldn't count on it. There's still a Necromancer around here somewhere. I doubt she'll just throw her hands up in the air and come out."

"Yes, it's far more likely we'll need to pry her out of there kicking and screaming. In the meantime, there are prisoners to look after. Unless you want them executed?"

"No," said Charlaine. "Many of these provincial soldiers were likely forced into this without any say in the matter. Some are doubtless from Reinwick itself."

"Those missing people you were looking for?"

"Precisely."

"We never should have doubted you," said Waleed. "I'm sorry."

"The past is over and done. It is the future we must now deal with."

"How would you like to proceed?"

"Pull back from the palisade, but leave a group of horsemen ready to respond if anyone should sally forth. In the meantime, we'll get the wounded aboard the *Devastator* and bury the dead."

"What of those still inside?" asked Captain Waleed.

"Let them remain, for now. They're not going anywhere, and a spot of rest will make all the difference for everyone concerned."

The day wore on. Those who could be saved were rowed out to the *Devastator* while the others awaited death ashore. Most of the Halvarian prisoners were mere peasants from the surrounding Petty Kingdoms, forced into servitude at the end of a sword. With the death of their masters, they seemed lost, as a sheep might be without a shepherd to guide them. More than a few stared out with blank eyes as if their very soul had been excised, leaving nothing behind save for an empty vessel.

Captain Waleed posted pickets around the palisade's perimeter, lest anyone attempt to flee its confines. The gate, however, remained closed, mocking the Temple Knights, denying them the ultimate victory.

Charlaine sat on the beach, her eyes drifting out beyond the ships to the Great Northern Sea.

"How are you?" came the familiar voice of Danica as she sat beside her. "I hear you were in the thick of it?"

"I suppose I was. How were things out there?" She nodded towards the *Valiant.*

"Other than a couple of ships attempting to flee, there's little to report. You, however, look like you've gone to the Underworld and back."

"It was a tough fight. Apparently, the elite Halvarian warriors don't believe in surrender."

"Where's your helmet?"

"Lost in battle somewhere, after a mace put a great big dent in it."

"I'll lend you mine," said Danica. "You'll need one if you're thinking of entering that camp."

"I appreciate the offer, but we have yet to make a final decision on how to proceed."

"What about all the ladders we made?"

"We'll still use those," replied Charlaine, "but once our knights drop from those walls, they'll have no way of getting out until the gate falls. I also toyed with the idea of assaulting the gate itself."

"Do we know how many Halvarians are inside?"

"No, although we do know there's at least one Necromancer in there, not to mention two Fire Mages. I wish I knew more about their capabilities."

"It's a pity we don't have a Ragnarite with us," said Danica. "Then we'd have a better idea about what to expect."

Charlaine got to her feet and stretched her arms. "Well, I can't sit around here all day. Have you seen Captain Waleed?"

"He's over by that group of trees. He and his men are sifting through the prisoners, separating the fanatics from the regular folk."

"What's that third group?"

"Those are the unfortunate souls whose memories were ripped from them. I doubt even a Life Mage could help them."

"We must put an end to this now," insisted Charlaine, "before anyone else is made to suffer at the hands of this dark magic."

They walked along the beach, the Cunar captain moving to intercept them as they drew closer.

"Commander," he said in greeting. "It's good to see you hale and hearty."

"Danica tells me you separated the prisoners," said Charlaine.

"I did. Three-quarters of them want to go home, wherever that is. They seem to be from all over the Northern Kingdoms."

"Do we have any idea of Halvaria's actual plan?"

"I'm afraid not," the captain replied. "Most of them are more than willing to cooperate, but they don't know any details. One thing's for sure though; they were trained to fight in a battle formation, not as raiders."

"Likely easier to control," mused Danica, "and they lack the numbers for a full-scale invasion."

"Yes," agreed Charlaine, "and that, more than anything else, leads me to suspect they were meant to provoke a war between the kingdoms."

"Yes, but which ones? There are half a dozen that could be the target."

"I believe we can narrow it down a bit. After all, the *Sea Wolf* harassed Reinwick, and they only have one neighbour as far as land goes."

"Andover," said Danica. "But their army was reduced by its loss to Erlingen."

"It matters little to Halvaria."

"I'm not sure how that would work," said Captain Waleed.

"Imagine they land this bunch on Andover's coast, then march overland, crossing the border into Reinwick. You know how fast word of an invasion would spread. War would be declared within a fortnight. Of course, for that to work, they'd need to pass for soldiers of Andover."

"And how would they do that?"

Charlaine looked at the palisade. "I imagine the answer would be in there, somewhere, likely in the form of tabards or surcoats, maybe even a few flags of Andover."

"But this group would scarcely be considered a threat," said Waleed, "at least to the duke's army."

"Easily defeated or not, it doesn't matter. The nobles would be fuming over the attempt. They'd march the army first and ask questions later, especially since they see Andover as weak at the moment, considering their recent loss."

"But how could they possibly think Andover would attack a numerically superior Reinwick?"

"They would see their traditional enemy as trying to flex its muscles and re-establish itself as a military power. The enmity between Andover and Reinwick cannot be dismissed so easily. It's deeply ingrained in their culture, has been for years."

Waleed shook his head. "Well, thankfully, we put an end to that little escapade. The question now is, how do we get inside? What if we burned the place to the ground?"

"We can't take the chance of destroying any evidence. No, we'll need to carry out an assault. Can the prisoners give us a better idea of how many remain inside?"

"As a matter of fact, they already have. According to this lot, most of the training masters remained inside."

"Training masters?"

"Yes, I presume they're more like slavers than real warriors. Of course, the Death Mage is still there, along with their Pyromancers."

"You mean Fire Mages?" said Danica.

"Yes," said Charlaine. "The bane of my existence."

"We've killed them before. We can do it again."

Charlaine gazed skyward. "It's too late to do anything today. Send a ship back to Temple Bay, and bring everyone here as soon as you're able."

"And the palisade?" prompted Waleed.

"Keep it under close eye. If they should decide to venture out, I want a group of knights ready to stop them at a moment's notice. In the meantime, I'll go chat with Barbek, see if he has any ideas."

"He's a Dwarf, not a Temple Knight. What does he know of warfare?"

"He's not a knight, I grant you, but sometimes it takes an outsider to offer a fresh perspective. Just because he's not a member of the Church doesn't mean his opinions don't carry weight."

"It's your right to seek advice from whomever you choose. I only hope you're not wasting your time."

"Time is the one thing we have in abundance."

"For now," countered Waleed. "I might remind you this is a Halvarian camp, and we have no idea when ships might arrive carrying more supplies, or warriors, for that matter."

"That's a valid point," said Danica.

Charlaine nodded. "Agreed. Send the *Vigilant* to escort the other ships, and have *Valiant* stand out to sea, best to spot any ships before they become a problem."

"Yes, Commander."

"And Captain"—she turned to Waleed—"see if any of those prisoners are sailors. We know they abducted some from Korvoran, and frankly, we need all the crew we can get. We have more ships than sailors at the moment."

"Not quite," corrected Danica, "but you made your point."

"Then get to work, everyone, and pray we resolve this situation before Halvaria decides to send reinforcements."

Somehow, Barbek had managed to find a small stool and sat upon it as he wiped his arbalest down with an oiled rag.

"I wish we had an Earth Mage," he said. "Then we could part those logs that make up the palisade. Either that or drop a couple of trees across them."

"Would that work?" asked Charlaine.

"What? Parting logs?"

"No, dropping trees on the wall. It occurs to me the southern end of the palisade is very close to the forest. I imagine it wouldn't be too hard to locate a tree that would be high enough."

"I can't guarantee it would knock down the wall, but at the very least, you'd have a ramp to climb up. How sturdy would you say that palisade is?"

"I don't know," replied Charlaine, "but we can look if you like."

The Dwarf rose. "Then let's not waste any more time. Gather a couple of knights as an escort, and we'll go and take a look now before it gets too dark to see our own noses."

Charlaine called for three volunteers, and they headed into the forest where the trees would conceal them as they worked their way towards the southern end of the enemy camp. Captain Waleed had joined them, eager to determine where they were headed.

He thought it unlikely anyone would be able to see anything with the palisade logs in place, but even adjacent logs could have small gaps between them, more than sufficient for peering out, and so they kept to the shadows. It wasn't long before they had their answer. Now, all they needed to do was ready the final assault.

43

THE FINAL ASSAULT

Summer 1098 SR

K nights crouched in the early morning gloom, ready to spring into action when needed. A trio of burly Cunars stood ready with axes, eager to begin the process of felling a tree as Charlaine, Barbek, and Captain Waleed stood close by.

"It's important they cut the trunk just so," whispered the Dwarf, "else all of this will be for nothing."

"Fear not," said Waleed, keeping his voice low. "This is not the first tree my men have cut down. In any case, I also have people standing by with ladders and more behind us, ready to charge through should the breach prove successful."

Charlaine looked around. With everything in place, all that awaited was for her to give the command. "Very well," she said at last. "You may begin."

Waleed nodded, and then the axemen began chopping, the noise breaking the stillness of the dawn as it echoed throughout the forest.

"Well," said Barbek. "If they haven't guessed we're up to something yet, they must be deaf."

They chopped at a large pine that stretched up higher than a ship's mast, chosen precisely because of its size, for its diameter greatly exceeded those logs used in the palisade. It was hoped this extra weight would be more than sufficient to bring down a section of wall.

Charlaine found herself holding her breath and forced herself to breathe. Wood chips flew as the axes did their work, but little progress was made by the time the sun rose. The exhausted knights were replaced by three more, but the tree remained resistant to their efforts, dulling blades and causing at least one axe to lose its metal head.

Barbek leaped into action, cutting a wedge of wood and driving it into the handle from above to secure the top of the axe. With the tool temporarily repaired, the work continued.

The tree, finally ready to cooperate, creaked a little, then a tearing sound echoed through the forest as it toppled, ripping the remainder of itself free of the cut stump.

The great tree fell forward, its upper reaches seeming to move in slow motion until a tremendous crash announced it struck the palisade. The logs making up the wall shattered, sending shards everywhere.

Charlaine had hoped at least one log would be dislodged, but as it turned out, she needn't have worried, for three fell under the onslaught of the giant pine tree, with a fourth twisting aside.

"Attack!" she shouted.

Charlaine rushed forward, grey-clad Temple Knights following her through the gap, leaping over a fallen timber that rolled to the side. Inside the camp, everything was in chaos. The tree trunk, tall as it was, only took up a small amount of space. On the other hand, its branches reached out on either side, impeding attackers and defenders alike.

Charlaine moved left, paralleling the remaining wall, secure in the knowledge that one flank remained safe. She cleared the branches to see three large buildings lined up perpendicular to the front gate. The largest of these possessed an elevated porch from which a person had a commanding view of the training yard, or at least would have, were it not for the giant pine.

She led the knights towards it as a man stepped from its door. He grasped the danger immediately and gave a yell even as his hands traced strange symbols in the air. Charlaine didn't need to be told he was a mage of some sort. She instinctively moved farther left, using the corner of another building as cover.

Flames shot past, striking a Cunar Temple Knight. He fell, screaming, the smell of burning flesh tainting the air despite the fact the man's helmet remained in place.

She waved over a pair of knights. "Get around behind the building," she said. "I'll see if I can distract him."

They began moving, circling to the left while she stepped out into the open. The Fire Mage, having completed his first spell, looked around, seeking a suitable target. Upon laying eyes on her, he cast again, his voice higher this time, revealing his panic.

She ran with all the speed she could muster, not for him, but for the great pine's branches, anything that would obscure his vision of her. His spell went off, sending a streak of flame that exploded when it hit the tree. Charlaine heard the wood pop and crackle as the fire hit it, then ran out, making directly for the villain.

From nowhere appeared a Halvarian warrior, a huge beast of a man with a great club. She had only a moment to react before the fellow's weapon struck her bicep, knocking her towards the burning branches. She turned, stabbing out in a vain attempt to force him back. With the tree so close, she had little space in which to swing her weapon, so she opted instead for a more direct approach.

Gripping her sword in both hands, one on the hilt, the other at the tip, she leaped onto him, trusting in her gauntlets to avoid being cut. She felt the impact, felt the blade slice her hand, but her forward motion and the weight of her bore him to the ground. He landed with a grunt, the wind knocked out of him. Charlaine kept her wits about her enough to place the weapon across his throat.

"I yield," he squeaked out as he dropped the club.

She had no time to deal with the fellow. Instead, she rose to her feet and kicked the weapon out of his reach. A scream caught her attention, and her eyes turned back towards the Fire Mage. The two knights she'd sent around the back of the building had reached their target, cutting the mage down before he could utter another spell.

Knights now flooded the training field, searching through the buildings. She had a brief glimpse of Captain Waleed to her left, who, accompanied by a second knight, had just kicked in a door when a thick, green mist erupted from the doorway. Both staggered back, coughing, then Waleed's assistant fell to the ground. There, he twisted around, clawing at his throat before finally lying still, his limbs akimbo.

Captain Waleed, meanwhile, yanked off his helmet and tossed it aside as he stumbled around, gasping for air. Out of the door came a woman dressed in dark green, with a gold mask covering the top of her face, leaving only her mouth exposed. One of her hands shot out, sending spikes of green hurtling towards the Cunar Captain to strike him on his breastplate. The metal smoked and burned as acid ate away at it.

Charlaine rushed forward, determined to put an end to the woman's reign of terror. The Necromancer wheeled around, her fingers moving like she was gathering strands of thread from the air before she threw them forward, dark tendrils reaching out towards the Temple Knight.

Charlaine struck out, a mighty blow that severed one of the fingers of death, then two others wrapped around her sword arm, holding it tight even as a third grabbed the top of her shield, trying to pull her to her knees. She knew some ghastly force was at play here as she felt the tendrils crushing her.

Letting go of her shield, she withdrew the dagger from her belt, slashing out at the spell that bound her. A tendril snapped, dissipating into nothingness, and she tumbled to the ground, her own resistance pulling her backward. A second slash cut the remaining black finger, and then she scrambled back to her feet.

Undeniably upset by the sudden turn of events, the Death Mage looked upward, holding her hands out on either side; the sky darkened, and the wind whipped up around her.

Charlaine knew little of Death Magic, but one thing was sure, it didn't look good, so she rushed forward, not even bothering to retrieve her shield. The distance was crossed in an instant, and then she stabbed out with her sword.

The Halvarian mage never finished her spell, for the tip of the sword took her in the chest, puncturing her heart, killing her instantly.

Charlaine paused as she noticed the sounds of fighting dissipating. Captain Waleed, more or less recovered from his ordeal, ordered knights to search the buildings, one by one.

"Rock and stone," shouted Barbek, still clutching a loaded arbalest. "Do you Temple Knights always need to be so efficient? You could at least have left one for me!"

"If you feel so determined," said Charlaine, "then help me search this building."

"Now you're talking," said the Dwarf. He advanced to the door and gave it a kick. It flew open, banging against the wall.

Charlaine followed him into the building, which consisted of a single room with three beds present, along with a table littered with papers and parchments. She perused their contents while the Dwarf rummaged through a trio of small chests.

"These look like reports," noted the knight. "Accounts of how the training is progressing." She halted her search, drawing forth a letter and moving to the window so she could hold it up to the light.

"What have you there?" asked Barbek.

"It's from Larissa Stormwind, addressed to someone named Azreth."

"Another mage, perhaps? Possibly even that Necromancer."

"That would be my guess."

"What does it say?"

"It looks like an analysis of the duke's army. It's quite detailed, even going so far as to describe the garrison composition in Korvoran."

"So she was a spy? Hardly a surprise, considering her attack on us."

"I agree," said Charlaine, "but at least now we have some proof. The real question is, who does she work for?"

"The Halvarians! Why else would we find that letter here?"

Charlaine returned to the table, picking through more papers. "Did you find anything interesting in the chests?"

"It's mostly clothes, by the look of it." He paused before withdrawing a dagger. "Well, well. What have we here?" He moved to the doorway to examine the blade, then tossed it aside. "Never mind, it's not the best quality. Definitely not a Dwarven blade." He cast a glance Charlaine's way. Seeing her interest, he wandered over.

"Looks like you found something else."

"I have indeed." She paled as she read.

"What is it? Is something wrong?"

She looked at the Dwarf before passing him the paper, then allowed him time to read it.

"Well?" she asked. "Is this what I think it is, or am I reading too much into it?"

"Saints alive, do you know what this means?"

"Unfortunately, I do."

"What do we do about it? Should we tell Captain Waleed?"

"No," said Charlaine, "at least not for now. I'd like to get Danica's opinion of this before we take it any further. In the meantime, I would ask you to tell no one of what we found."

"Probably for the best," he replied. "It's difficult to predict how he might react, considering its contents."

She carefully folded the letter. "Come, let's row out to the *Valiant* and chat with Danica, shall we? After that, I'll have a better idea of how to proceed."

Danica stood at the railing, watching as the skiff approached. "What brings you all the way out here?" she asked.

"This boat, obviously," answered the Dwarf.

Charlaine chuckled. "I believe she meant the purpose of this visit."

"Then why didn't she just say so? You Humans have the strangest customs."

A rope ladder was tossed over the side, and the two visitors climbed aboard.

"Good to see you, Commander."

"That's captain, now," said Charlaine. "The expedition is over."

"Not until we return to Korvoran."

"We need to talk privately."

"And by privately, you mean...?"

"Only the three of us."

"This way," said Danica. "We can use my cabin."

They exchanged no words until safely ensconced within the captain's quarters.

"What's this all about?" asked Danica.

Charlaine withdrew the letter. "We found this while we were searching the Halvarian camp."

Danica took it, perusing its contents.

Your Supreme Holiness,

Our plans are proceeding well. The Temple Knights have proven to be even more susceptible to influence than we could ever have predicted. As such, our infiltration of the order has, so far, gone undetected.

Given a suitable time frame, I expect our agents to sow enough discord and chaos to make them useless as a fighting force when the invasion begins. They have already begun to exert control over those in positions of authority. The next step will be to cause disharmony between the Holy Army and the rest of the Church.

I trust his Imperial Majesty will be pleased with this news and send him reassurances of my undying loyalty. I shall entrust this message to Lord Augustus Conwyn for

Danica looked up.

"Yes, I know," said Charlaine. "It's unfinished."

"Can we trust this?"

"Why wouldn't we?"

"This spells out things rather clearly. You'd think the person writing this would take a little more care, lest it was intercepted."

"Likely they intended to use a phoenix ring," said Barbek.

"A what?"

"A phoenix ring, or two of them, to be exact. Are you not familiar with the concept?"

"I'm afraid not," said Charlaine.

"It's pretty straightforward. A mage commissions two identical rings. They need to be of exceptional quality, of course, else the magic won't hold. The idea is you use one ring to seal a note, and only the matching ring can break the seal."

"Couldn't someone cut around the seal?" asked Danica.

"You'd think so, wouldn't you, but that won't work. Any attempt to bypass the seal would cause the note to be set aflame, thus destroying it. Hence, the reference to a phoenix."

"How is it you know so much about this?" asked Charlaine.

In answer, he held out his hand, displaying a ring. "Mine has a bear on it, but the effect is the same. I use it for guild matters."

"Where do you get these rings?"

"Well, obviously, a jeweller has to make them, but it's a Fire Mage who imbues it with the magic. They're easy enough to commission if you can afford it."

"And do they always work in pairs?"

"That's the usual arrangement, although I've heard of sets of three on rare occasions. Our guild master has dozens of the things, each one used for a different recipient."

"He must have a lot of fingers," added Danica.

Barbek chuckled. "He only wears them when needed. He also lives in a Dwarven stronghold, so they're in safe hands."

"Is that how you sealed our letters to our fellow sisters?"

"It was, as a matter of fact."

"Wait a moment," said Danica. "Does that mean your guild master is privy to every letter? He'd need to be, wouldn't he? Especially if he has to reseal them for delivery to someone else."

"You are correct, but he would never betray that trust unless, of course, the Dwarves were threatened. Think of him and the guild as trustworthy allies."

"The question," said Charlaine, "and the reason we're here, is we need to decide what to do with this information. I'd appreciate your thoughts on the matter, Danica."

"I say we alert the Church. This might help explain some of the problems they've had of late. Do you think Commander Hjordis was one of their agents?"

"Either that or one who was influenced. My concern is who we notify. Send this to the wrong person, and we'd be putting a lot of people in danger."

"Send it to the grand mistress," said Danica. "If we can't trust her, who can we?"

"I would suggest you make yourselves a copy first," said Barbek. "That way, you'll have a constant reminder of what it says."

"I can take care of that right now. Let me get my paper and ink." Danica opened up a small drawer, folding down its door like a desk, then pulled up a stool and got to work.

"We'll need to send the original," she said. "It's not as if my handwriting is anything like whoever wrote this."

They waited as she penned a copy, then handed the original to Charlaine, who, in turn, gave it to Barbek.

"I'll write a letter later to accompany it. Can I trust the guild to see this delivered?"

"Of course," replied the Dwarf. He took the letter, staring at it a moment in thought. "You know the guild will be concerned about this. If the Cunars are now corrupt, it has far-reaching consequences for peace in the Petty Kingdoms."

"What about the other orders?" asked Danica. "What about ours?"

Charlaine thought it over carefully. "We must be careful who we entrust with this information. Hjordis showed us we're just as susceptible to this as our brother orders."

"So our entire Church is now suspect?"

"No, I would imagine their efforts were mainly focused on the Cunars. They do, after all, make up the bulk of the Holy Army. Just to be safe, however, we'll limit discussions with only those we trust most."

"That's an awfully short list," noted Danica.

"So it is," Charlaine agreed.

44

THE END

Autumn 1098 SR

D ancers twirled around the floor in graceful movements as the bard, Rascalian, played the lute, his melodic voice floating along with the music. Charlaine, never the one for such finery, stood to the side, other matters occupying her thoughts. Danica came up beside her, her eyes on the nobles and their fine clothing.

"It's a bit much, isn't it?" said the younger knight.

"It's the way of nobility, to display their wealth through their clothes and jewellery. In a sense, we're no different."

"How can you say that? We took a vow of poverty."

"And yet here we are in fine tabards and expensive armour. Are we really all that different?"

"Of course," said Danica. "We care for others. These nobles only care for themselves. At least we were here to return most of the missing men to their families, not that His Grace even noticed. That reminds me, did you get a chance to talk to the duke?"

"I did."

"And?"

"Let's just say he didn't take kindly to the news that Larissa Stormwind was in the Halvarians' employ."

"We don't know that for sure."

"True," said Charlaine, "but she definitely worked with them. Maybe they had a mutual objective in mind."

"I'm not sure I follow?"

"Larissa Stormwind was trained in Ruzhina. It's possible that particular kingdom wanted unrest in the region for its own purposes."

"It still amounts to the same thing."

"In any case," said Charlaine. "I think His Grace was more annoyed he lost a mage, even if it was one he couldn't trust."

"Well, they are an important status symbol. If you want to be a military power in the Petty Kingdoms, you need a mage or two, if only for appearance's sake. The loss of one, even one as bad as Larissa Stormwind, makes Reinwick look like a poor cousin in the eyes of others."

"That won't help the region. Andover was already humiliated, and now Reinwick has fallen in stature. How long do you suppose before one of the other kingdoms hereabouts decides to take advantage of that?"

"That's not our responsibility," said Danica.

"Isn't it? Who else will strive to keep the peace? You saw that note—an invasion is coming. Maybe not this year, or the next, but sooner or later, the Halvarians are going to flood across the border, and without the Holy Army to hold things together, the result looks bleak."

"There is hope. Look what Ludwig did in Erlingen."

The mention of Ludwig turned Charlaine's thoughts inward. Did she still harbour feelings for him? She knew she did, yet the passion of youth had faded, replaced instead by a sense of comfort at the thought of him.

"I should write to him," she said.

"To what end? You're not suggesting a reconciliation, are you?"

"No, that ship sailed years ago, but I feel I owe him a warning. If war is coming to the Petty Kingdoms, then perhaps he can help stem the tide of invasion?"

"How? He's only the son of a baron, isn't he?"

"He is," said Charlaine, "or at least he was. He might even be the baron by now. In any case, the Halvarians likely know he's the one responsible for the defeat of their plans there. He should at least be alerted to the possible danger of retaliation."

"And how would you write that, precisely? 'Hello, Ludwig, how have you been? By the way, someone is trying to kill you!' I can't imagine that would go over very well, do you?"

Charlaine laughed. "I shall try to be a little more subtle than that. Besides, I don't even know where he is at present."

"Not an insurmountable problem. You know he's the son of a baron. Send the letter to his home. He's bound to return there sooner or later. Or better yet, go and visit Erlingen. Someone down there will probably have word of him. He certainly was the talk of that tavern."

"Spoken like a true leader."

Captain Waleed approached, bowing his head slightly in greeting. "Good day, Sisters," he said, his voice raspy. "Good to see you hale and hearty."

"And you," said Charlaine. "Though I see your voice has not yet recovered."

"It has not, nor is it likely to, according to Father Salvatore. I'm afraid that vile Necromancer is to blame, but at least I'm still here to tell of my experience." He paused a moment, looking slightly embarrassed. "I wanted to congratulate you, Charlaine. You proved your mettle and did an excellent job leading the expedition. I wrote to my superiors telling them of your accomplishments."

He turned his attention to Danica. "And you, Captain, surprised us all. Perhaps the fleet in the hands of Saint Agnes is not so bad after all."

"I'm glad you think so," said Danica, "but I'm afraid our success has been tempered by the finances."

"In what way?"

"The *Valiant* and *Vigilant* remain under our control, but providing enough crew for the remaining ships has proven troublesome."

"You're not going to scrap them?"

"No, at least not the warships. They shall be kept in reserve until funding can be found."

"And the merchant ships?"

"Those of our own fleet returned to their regular trade route. Those captured will be auctioned off to the highest bidder. It's hoped we'll raise enough funds to keep the *Devastator* afloat, minus most of its gaudiness. We shall, of course, rename it. I hardly think *Devastator* is quite the image we wish to project."

Captain Waleed nodded knowingly. "I suppose that puts the idea of a large fleet to rest?"

"Not quite," said Charlaine. "There are still pirates to guard against, not to mention remaining on the lookout for Halvarians returning. To that end, I proposed we establish a permanent presence on Patience."

"How did the duke take that suggestion?"

"He rather liked the idea, even went so far as to grant us title to Temple Bay. Mind you, it'll be years before it will have a proper port."

"I wish you all the luck with it," said Waleed. "I myself am reassigned, pending the arrival of my replacement."

"I trust you're not in trouble?" said Charlaine.

"Not in the least. It's a reward for services rendered."

"Where are they sending you?"

"I don't know," he replied. "Although I hear the east is always short-handed. If I don't see you again, then farewell, and may the Saints watch over you." He left them, wandering over to join another small group.

"That was a surprise," said Danica. "We must keep an eye on his replacement."

"Indeed, but you know what I'm looking forward to the most?"

"I give up."

"Sitting in my office and dealing with the mundane day-to-day tasks of a simple captain."

EPILOGUE

The Antonine

Winter 1099 SR

Captain Nicola took her seat, staring at the mound of letters littering her desk. Year's end was always the most onerous of times, for reports from all the commanderies flooded in, each eager to put such matters behind them before the Midwinter Feast. One, in particular, caught her attention, and she picked it out, examining the seal.

"What have we here?" she murmured, although no one was there to hear. She rose, crossing to the door and knocking quietly.

"Come," came the reply.

Captain Nicola opened the door, revealing the grand mistress standing by the window, gazing westward.

"We received a letter, Your Grace."

The grand mistress turned. "You'll need to be more precise, Nicola. We receive many letters."

"This one has come by way of the smith's guild."

"Oh? We rely on many of their members to support our order. I hope there isn't some problem with payment?"

"I cannot say, Your Grace, for it remains unopened. It does, however, indicate on its outside that it comes from Captain Charlaine."

"Charlaine, you say? How curious. You'd better let me have it." The grand mistress held out her hand, and Nicola handed her the letter. It took only a moment to break the seal, and then she devoured the words.

"Bad news?" asked her aide.

"Indeed. This missive, sent over a year ago, confirms what we suspected for some time. Somehow, the Halvarians infiltrated the Church."

"Not exactly a surprise," said Nicola. "Though I am curious why she would send word by way of the guild."

"Evidently, she doesn't trust our own couriers," replied the grand mistress. "I can't say I blame her after the trouble we had with Commander Hjordis."

"A nasty business, that."

"Yes, but on top of everything else, this is particularly bad news."

"How so?"

"You wouldn't have heard," continued the grand mistress, "but there was talk of the Cunars changing their strategy regarding the empire."

"Changing it how?"

"I believe the term used was 'defence in depth'. The idea is that, instead of concentrating their forces in the border kingdoms, they would disperse them evenly amongst the remaining realms."

"Wouldn't that weaken them?"

"That was my thought, but the Council of Peers bowed to the wisdom of the Cunar Grand Master. The plan is to begin construction of new commanderies throughout the Petty Kingdoms, then move the Temple Knights to their new assignments once they're complete."

"How long will that take?" asked Nicola.

"They expect to complete their reorganization within the next five years."

"But that would leave the border with Halvaria woefully unprotected. In light of Charlaine's letter, surely we must do precisely the opposite?"

"Indeed." The grand mistress stared at the letter a moment, considering its contents. "I shall issue orders this very day, calling for the construction of new commanderies of our own."

"Could we not simply take over those vacated by our brothers?"

"No. If their order is corrupt, as this indicates, word would reach the Halvarians. This must be done with as little fanfare as possible."

"It will be hard to hide once construction begins," said Nicola.

"Then we need to find a way to keep it quiet."

"And how shall we staff them? We lack the numbers for such a task."

"Then we shall begin a recruitment drive. War is coming, Nicola, and we can no longer count on the support of the other orders."

"You believe it that serious?"

"This may very well spell the beginning of the end for the Church."

CONTINUE THE SERIES WITH WARRIOR LORD

If you enjoyed *Temple Captain,* then *Servant of the Crown,* the first book in the Internationally Best Selling *Heir to the Crown* series awaits your undivided attention.

START READING SERVANT OF THE CROWN TODAY

SHARE YOUR THOUGHTS!

If you enjoyed this book, I encourage you to take a moment and share what you liked most about the story.

These positive reviews encourage other potential readers to give my books a try when they are searching for a new fantasy series.

But the best part is, each review that you post inspires me to write more!

Thank you!

A FEW WORDS FROM PAUL

Temple Captain marks the second book in the story of Charlaine deShandria. In the first book, Temple Knight, things were told purely from Charlaine's point of view. In this tale, however, there are two captains, Charlaine and Danica, thus the action follows both. Even as their careers progress, events are developing over which they have little control. These outside incidents have far-reaching consequences for the Church in general and the Temple Knights of Saint Agnes specifically. Will Charlaine be up to the challenge?

This book also reveals more details concerning the events of Warrior Knight. The next book in the series, Warrior Lord, runs concurrent to Charlaine's adventures in the north, illustrating just how intertwined the fates of these two characters truly are.

This story, indeed this whole series, couldn't have been written without the support and encouragement of my wife, Carol. She acted as editor, public relations, number one fan and assorted other titles I won't mention for fear of sounding too sentimental. In addition, I must thank my daughters, Amanda Bennett, Stephanie Sandrock, and Christie Bennett, for their support and encouragement. I can't forget a shout out to our gaming friends, Brad Aitken, Stephen Brown, and the late Jeffrey Parker, for their steadfast support and being willing victims.. er, participants in the worlds I create.

I should also like to thank my BETA team for their continued feedback that has helped shape this series. Thank you to: Rachel Deibler, Michael Rhew, Phyllis Simpson, Don Hinckley, James McGinnis, Charles Mohapel, Lisa Hanika, Debra Reeves, Michell Schneidkraut, Susan Young, and Anna Ostberg.

Finally, a big shout out to you, the reader, without whom there would be no demand for my writing. I hope you enjoy reading Temple Captain as much as I did writing it.

ABOUT THE AUTHOR

Paul J Bennett (b. 1961) emigrated from England to Canada in 1967. His father served in the British Royal Navy, and his mother worked for the BBC in London. As a young man, Paul followed in his father's footsteps, joining the Canadian Armed Forces in 1983. He is married to Carol Bennett and has three daughters who are all creative in their own right.

Paul's interest in writing started in his teen years when he discovered the roleplaying game, Dungeons & Dragons (D & D). What attracted him to this new hobby was the creativity it required; the need to create realms, worlds and adventures that pulled the gamers into his stories.

In his 30's, Paul started to dabble in designing his own roleplaying system, using the Peninsular War in Portugal as his backdrop. His regular gaming group were willing victims, er, participants in helping to playtest this new system. A few years later, he added additional settings to his game, including Science Fiction, Post-Apocalyptic, World War II, and the all-important Fantasy Realm where his stories take place.

The beginnings of his first book 'Servant to the Crown' originated over five years ago when he began running a new fantasy campaign. For the world that the Kingdom of Merceria is in, he ran his adventures like a TV show, with seasons that each had twelve episodes, and an overarching plot. When the campaign ended, he knew all the characters, what they had to accomplish, what needed to happen to move the plot along, and it was this that inspired to sit down to write his first novel.

Paul now has four series based in his fantasy world of Eiddenwerthe, and is looking forward to sharing many more books with his readers over the coming years.

Manufactured by Amazon.ca
Bolton, ON